MATCHED
in
MERRIWEATHER

MATCHED
in
MERRIWEATHER

A Jane Austen in Wisconsin series
Book 1

Michelle Cox

 Woolton Press

Published: 2024
Printed in the United States of America

Print: 979-8-9987571-2-9
Ebook: 979-8-9987571-3-6
Library of Congress Control Number: 2025909356

For more information, address:
Woolton Press
285 N. Cambridge Ct.
Grayslake, IL 60030

Second Edition

DEDICATION (POSTHUMOUS)

To my mother, Susan Louise (Glab) Bonnet *1944–2024*
This is the first of my books you never got to read, Mom, but I hope
you'll help it along just the same. Someday I'll write the fantasy we
talked about. Promise.

OTHER BOOKS BY MICHELLE COX

The Henrietta and Inspector Howard series:
A Girl Like You
A Ring of Truth
A Promise Given
A Veil Removed
A Child Lost
A Spying Eye
A Haunting at Linley
A Christmas at Highbury

Stand-alone novels:
The Fallen Woman's Daughter

The Merriweather series:
Matched in Merriweather
Uncovered in Merriweather

CHAPTER ONE

"Harriet, they're finally here!" Melody Merriweather declared, hurrying as best she could toward the front of the shop despite the rather large box she was balancing.

Harriet paused in her diligent arranging of the candy sticks in the wall of jars behind the counter to glance over her shoulder. When she saw the box, she turned fully.

"You'll never guess!" Melody set her delivery on the far end of the counter and reached for a pair of scissors, slicing through the packing string and peeling open the flaps of the package. From a nest of cedar wood chips, she lifted out a smaller box, thin and mint green with a swirling chocolate font. Inside, wrapped in crisp tissue paper, lay a beautiful lavender silk scarf with tiny white polka dots. Melody drew in a breath. They were even more beautiful than she had hoped.

"Oh, my!" Harriet whispered. "Who's that for? Your mother?"

"No!" Melody laughed. "We're going to sell them!"

Harriet's brow furrowed. "Sell them?" She glanced at the floor-to-ceiling shelves of the Merc, neatly stocked with dry goods. "Here?"

1

"Yes! Why not?" Melody hurriedly dug out more boxes, brushing off stray wood chips, and began stacking them haphazardly on the counter. They were just what the dusty old Merriweather Mercantile needed! A certain flair of . . . well, of something more refined. And, truth be told, she was tired of selling sacks of flour and fishing poles and cans of soup. She wanted to sell something fun!

It had been barely a month since Melody had been called home from Mundelein, her lovely college in Chicago, to take over the running of her family's general store. Upon hearing the news of her father's heart attack, Melody had rushed back . . . only to find that Pops wasn't *quite* on death's door, as her mother's exaggerated letter had implied, and that, worse, they were expecting Melody to take over the dreadful Merc, at least until Pops recovered. She had protested fiercely, saying that it should be Freddy, her older brother, who should have to abandon *his* expensive school and take over, but Pops had just tut-tutted the suggestion, as if it were ludicrous. Next, she tried insisting that she knew nothing about running a shop, but this, too, had fallen on deaf ears. In the end, it was Pops, lying prostrate in his hospital bed, who had convinced her to at least try.

Melody reached for another box inside the parcel, this one bigger. Carefully, she opened it and pulled out a lovely velvet cloche hat.

"Hats, too?" Harriet's eyes grew wide.

"Yes, *and* gloves," Melody said, rifling through the wood chips in search of glove boxes. Finding one, she opened it to reveal a pair of pink leather calfskin gloves. "Here, feel these," she urged Harriet as she herself rubbed the gloves. "They're as soft as butter!"

Harriet did as she was bid and let out a little gasp. "They must cost a fortune!"

Melody laughed again. She had discovered them in the Barnum's Supply catalog, which sat forlornly on her father's desk in his makeshift office, and had promptly ordered them without a second thought. They had indeed cost a pretty penny, but Melody was sure the ladies of Merriweather would appreciate something other than the sensible, serviceable line of clothing supplied by Montague's down the street. And, she had reasoned excitedly, maybe if they sold well, she might actually make a profit, enough to spruce up the Merc a bit, as it was, to her eyes, anyway, looking a bit shabby. Her father might even *thank* her for the idea when he returned and saw how well they were selling.

"Here, try them on!" she said to Harriet.

"Oh, no! I . . . I couldn't."

"Yes, you can! Here." Melody planted the cream cloche on top of the girl's pretty chestnut curls and then took the lavender scarf and wrapped it stylishly around her neck. Harriet reluctantly pulled on the gloves.

"You look gorgeous!" Melody declared, adjusting the scarf slightly. How she missed dressing up for dates to see the latest film at the Biograph or to go dancing at the Aragon in Chicago. Merriweather, by contrast, had little to compare. Sure, they had the opera house and the Avalon, but none of the big names ever came here, and there certainly were no dance halls.

"You think so?" Harriet turned her head this way and that, a faint smile creeping across her face.

"Yes, of course you do!" Melody plopped an elbow on the counter and rested her chin in her hand as she studied the girl. Harriet, while not college material, was really very sweet. At eighteen, she was only two years and eleven months younger than Melody herself, more Bunny's age. However, Melody had already decided that Harriet was infinitely more mature than her spoiled little sister.

"Tell you what!" Melody declared. "I'll let you borrow one for your next date." She flashed one of her mischievous grins, which never failed to elicit admiration amongst her court of friends back at Mundelein.

Harriet's cheeks flushed as she pulled off the hat. "I don't have a beau. If that's what you mean."

"Don't have a beau? You must be joking! Why not?" Melody studied her again. Harriet was not what one would call a beauty, but she was lovely in an innocent sort of way. Despite the freckles that dotted her nose and cheeks, she might even be considered rather attractive. Her eyes were a very pretty shade of green, and her nose, Melody decided, was perfect. Best of all was her sweet smile, which was accented by two dimples when she laughed. Melody was *sure* she could find her a suitor; after all, hadn't that been her specialty back at Mundelein? Matchmaking? She had, in fact, developed a bit of a reputation in that department.

"I could help you, if you'd let me," Melody suggested pleasantly, picking up stray wood chips and pitching them into the box.

"Help me? With what?" Harriet looked genuinely confused.

"Help you to fall in love, of course!"

Harriet's blush deepened. "Oh, but I—"

"What in God's name is all this?" came a shrill voice from the back of the shop.

Melody's neck stiffened. "It's a batch of new products, Mrs. Haufbrau," Melody said crisply, while Harriet hurriedly removed the scarf and gloves and set them carefully on the counter.

Mrs. Haufbrau arched one eyebrow as she picked up one of the gloves, only to toss it aside, its buttery softness apparently not having the desired effect. "New products? For who? Rockefeller?"

Melody inhaled sharply. Mrs. Haufbrau was another staff member she had inherited—one who was not, unfortunately, as pleasant as young Harriet, nor as malleable. Indeed, Mrs. Haufbrau was anything but. Likewise, she was positively ancient, way older than Melody's mother, and several degrees sterner, which was saying much. Why her father had hired Mrs. Haufbrau all those years ago was a mystery to Melody, though maybe it had actually been her grandfather who had hired the old crone when he had started this behemoth back in the 1800s.

"Some people in town might like to have a change of style, Mrs. Haufbrau," Melody retorted as she began piling the boxes back into the original package.

"Is that so?" The older woman crossed her arms stiffly while Harriet mysteriously bent to look for some unnamed item on the shelves below the counter. "Which farmer's wife do you think is looking for a change of style with a Depression on? But you probably wouldn't know anything about that, would you?"

Melody bit the inside of her cheek. Of course she was aware of the Depression! Hadn't they had to let their gardener go? And the kitchen girl who used to come on Saturdays to help Helenka? What was her name? Sadie?

"These might be fine for Chicago people," Mrs. Haufbrau went on, "but not people here. This ain't high society, you know!"

"God forbid I'd suggest that Merriweather, Wisconsin, is high society, Mrs. Haufbrau. But we could all use a little color, don't you think?" She looked pointedly at Mrs. Haufbrau's boring gray dress. That was all she ever wore—gray or black, as if in eternal mourning.

"With scarves made out of silk and calfskin gloves?" Mrs. Haufbrau scoffed. "Does your father know?"

"No, he does not, Mrs. Haufbrau," Melody replied. "And I'd kindly ask that you not to go blabbing to him with your tattletales of the shop. He's very ill, you know, and he doesn't need you pestering him."

Mrs. Haufbrau looked as if she had been struck. "I have no idea what you're talking about!"

"Oh, I think you do." It was obvious from Mrs. Haufbrau's muttered comments and loud sighs whenever Melody made a mistake—which was frequently, she had to admit—that the woman thought herself infinitely more suited to the job of manager. Indeed, Melody detected more than a little resentment coming from Mrs. Haufbrau that *she* had not been asked by Louis Merriweather to take over in the current crisis, and Melody was beginning to suspect the woman of running to the hospital with the Merc's account books in hand. "And, anyway, my father isn't here right now. *I* am."

"Oh, yes. We all know *that*," Mrs. Haufbrau snipped. "Loud and clear."

Melody fumed. She wished she could simply dismiss Mrs. Haufbrau, but she knew it would be a mistake. For one thing, her father would have a fit.

The shop bell tinkled, then, which blessedly broke the tension. However, when Melody observed whom it was who had entered—Imogene Kaufmann—she half wondered if continuing to spar with Mrs. Haufbrau would be more agreeable.

"Hello, Imogene," Melody said tightly as the timorous, middle-aged woman crept toward the counter with a box of her own. Imogene Kaufmann was a spinster who lived in the small apartment above the Merc with her very old and very deaf widowed mother. There was a time, several years ago, when Imogene had worked in the shop, but she had eventually been forced to quit when old Mrs. Kaufmann began wandering the streets of Merriweather, sometimes in her nightgown. It was probably a good thing, however, that Imogene had given up the Merc, as Mums was convinced that she was a secret kleptomaniac.

"Whole boxes of Hershey bars just gone!" Mums used to complain back when she herself had routinely taken shifts at the Merc. No matter how much Pops would explain away this and other thefts, Mums wasn't having it. There seemed to be some deeper animosity between the women that Melody had never understood.

"Oh, hello, Melody!" Imogene's small ferret eyes did not initially meet Melody's but instead darted furtively between Mrs. Haufbrau and Harriet. "Don't you look nice?" she squeaked, finally peering at Melody now. Imogene was probably only forty, but the corners of her eyes were chiseled with deep wrinkles, and a thick white streak of hair ran down the middle of her head, as if she were a skunk. "But, then, you always look nice, don't you?"

She cleared her throat and looked as though she was attempting to stand up straight, but her grossly rounded shoulders would not obey. "I've often commented to Mother how well you look. How fresh. Fresh like a daisy, I always say. How fortunate for you. And for your family. How *is* your family? Are they well? How is your poor father? I hope he is well. You must be glad to be home, glad to be out of Chicago. I've often said to Mother, I don't know how poor Melody had the courage to leave home. I simply can't imagine it, and yet there *are* times when I have thought it might be nice to have a holiday. I've said as much to Mother, but she doesn't fancy it. No, she doesn't fancy it. Still, we can always hope, can't we? But we are so very glad you are home safe. We did say ever so many prayers, Mother and I. So, you see, prayer does work. Sometimes, I must admit, my faith wavers, but seeing you, standing here before me looking so well certainly does prove the power of prayer and I'm quite encouraged. Quite encouraged by you, Melody. I remember when you were just a little girl. So sweet, running around here. I would often tell Mother all about your antics. Your father doted on you. Still doted on you even when you were gone. He would tell us all about your adventures, and I would tell Mother. Why, just the other day—"

"Can I help you with something, Imogene?" Melody interrupted, her patience flagging. "Something I can get for you?"

"Get for me?" Imogene seemed puzzled. "Oh, no! No, I don't need a thing. No, see, I've made these soaps." She shuffled the box in her arms to open the lid. "Just out of lye and a bit of aromatics. But they work real good. Different scents, you see." She picked one up and sniffed it. "This one's peppermint." She held it up to Melody, who felt she had no choice but to smell it. There was a *faint* aroma of mint. Imogene reached for more. "There's rosemary, and lavender, and rose, and bergamot, and"— she sniffed one deeply—"I think this one is just plain." She dropped it back in the box and looked eagerly at Melody.

Melody smiled wanly, wondering what on earth Imogene was after. "Yes, they're nice, Imogene," she said politely, deciding that Imogene must have finally cracked under the pressure of caring for her mother, locked up all day in the upstairs apartment.

"Well, what do you think?" Imogene asked hesitantly, carefully closing the lid.

"About what?"

"Well, I was thinking you might like to . . . well, to sell them. If you'd like. If you think they'd sell. They probably won't. But they might. You never know, do you?" She chuckled nervously. "I used to tell Mother that all the time when I worked here before. 'You'd never guess what I sold today, Mother!' I used to say. 'A card of buttons! An oil can!' Remember when the Merc sold oil cans, Melody? Or maybe that was before your time . . . Or seven mousetraps! I *did* sell seven mousetraps in one day. Did you know that, Melody? Sold them all to Ned Werner. Came in with a rat problem in his barn. I told him that our traps weren't nearly big enough for rats, that he should stop in at Rhombergs's for some poison, but, no, he took the seven mousetraps instead. Don't know whatever happened. He's dead now, so I can't ask him. But maybe his son, Del, would know. I must remember to ask him next I see him. Goes to show, though, doesn't it?"

Melody bit her lip, trying to think of what to say. While they did have a somewhat pleasant aroma, the soaps were horribly misshapen, not perfect ovals like the bars of Kirk's or Lux they carried. She was sure no one would even give them a second look, much less buy them. "Well, I . . . I don't think we need any more soaps, Imogene. We already sell several different types. And I'm not sure we have the shelf space."

"*I* think you should take them." Mrs. Haufbrau sniffed, having irritatingly observed the whole exchange. "Can't hurt, can it? And people like homemade stuff. Honest, down-to-earth stuff." By the way she emphasized each word, Melody was sure she was mocking her imported new products, which made her all the more determined to reject Imogene's soaps.

"I don't think so, Imogene."

"Oh, but Melody, please!" Imogene urged in a rare form of pleading. "You can have half the sale price. Or more than half. Or whatever you think. I just need . . . we just need a little extra money, and I thought that maybe . . . maybe this might be a way."

Melody squeezed her eyes shut. As much as she wanted to thwart Mrs. Haufbrau, she couldn't bear to refuse this poor woman, who, despite her eccentricities, as well as Mums's dislike, had always been kind to Melody as a little girl. Likewise, she knew deep down what her father would do if he were here. "Oh, alright, Imogene. I'll put them out, but I can't promise they'll sell."

"Oh, Melody! Bless you! I can't wait to tell Mother! She'll be pleased as punch, she will be! Oh! I'm going to tell her now!" She hurried toward the door, the box still under her arm. "Oh!" she exclaimed, perhaps realizing she was carrying away the product. "How silly of me!" She scurried back to the counter. "Here you are. I must go now!" She practically ran out of the shop, then, as if afraid Melody might change her mind.

Melody rubbed the back of her neck and then picked up the box, making a point of *not* looking in Mrs. Haufbrau's direction. "I'll go see where I can put these," she said.

"*I* can find a place," Mrs. Haufbrau offered.

"No, *I* will, Mrs. Haufbrau," Melody declared before making her way toward the back of the shop, near the meat counter, where the cleaning products were displayed. Melody studied the shelves filled with shampoos and soaps and even whisk brushes and mops, noting that this area of the shop could definitely use tidying, but she didn't have time for that right now. She was eager to find places up front for her silk scarves and pretty hats. What was she to do with a box of ugly soaps? Finally, she bent and pushed some disinfectant on the bottom shelf to the side. It was not the most advantageous placement, she knew, but no one was going to buy them anyway.

"That's not the best place for those," Cal called from behind the meat counter.

Melody let out a sigh. She wasn't sure she had the strength to argue with Cal, too, especially since nearly every interaction with him seemed to end, if not exactly in an argument, then at least in a bit of a huff.

When she first met Cal Fraiser on the day she took the shop's helm, she had admittedly been struck by his thick dark hair—a lock of which seemed to perpetually hang over one eye— and his angled jaw, the stubble upon which grew darker as the hours ticked along, she had since keenly observed. He had abruptly called up a vision of Heathcliff, which had caused a delicious little shiver to travel down her spine, but all intriguing imaginings were immediately dashed by his apparent contempt of her. She had introduced herself, politely holding out her hand and batting her eyes just a little, but he had merely glanced at her, frowned, and gone on wrapping a beef roast.

Cal's uncle, Lyle, was the Merc's real butcher, but he had recently been laid up with first an amputated toe and now a case of dropsy. Distraught at the thought of letting the Merc down, he had persuaded his nephew Cal to come down from Dodgeville and take his place until he could get better. Cal, to his credit, had so far shown himself to be a good stand-in, as he was quite skilled with a knife, but it was clear he was only here out of duty to his uncle, as he was unhelpful in every way other than the prompt cutting and wrapping of chops and sausages for the customers. Calling him "surly" would be generous.

Well, that wasn't exactly true. He *was* somewhat conversational with the customers, and he was kind to Harriet and respectful to Mrs. Haufbrau, but with Melody he seemed not exactly critical, but certainly aloof.

"I'll find a better place later," Melody said now as she approached the meat counter. "I can't be bothered right now."

Cal shrugged and went on slicing the lamb loin laid out on the butcher's block.

Typical. "You know, between you and Mrs. Haufbrau, I'm always seem to be doing something wrong. I've a mind to stay home and eat bonbons while you two run the shop!"

Cal tilted his head slightly and raised an eyebrow. "You shouldn't let her get to you," he said after a few moments and then tossed his hair back with a quick backward nod. "That's what she wants." He stared at her with those mysterious dark eyes, and for a second, she thought he was going to smile, so she preempted it with one of her own. But he *didn't* smile; he went back to slicing.

"Why, Cal Fraiser," she said lightly, "are you offering me advice? I didn't think you cared."

He went on slicing. "Just pointing out the obvious."

"Well, she makes my blood boil!" Melody exclaimed, deciding that the moment between them, if there *had* been a moment, was gone. "How dare she tell me that the scarves and hats I bought won't sell! She hasn't even seen them all."

"She's right, though. They aren't going to sell." He wiped his hands on the blood-streaked towel hanging from his apron belt. "You've been away too long."

Melody gritted her teeth. *Away too long?* Was this to be her life now? Receiving lectures from the likes of Mrs. Haufbrau and Cal Fraiser, not to mention the occasional one from Mums? Just a few months ago she had been studying the Romantics—Shelley and Wordsworth and Byron! And now she had to worry about the price of boots or their inventory of candy bars or the . . . the disapproval of this . . . this *person*, who clearly believed himself superior to her. The unfairness of it nearly killed her.

"How's Lyle?" she asked sweetly. "Feeling better?"

"You mean, when is he coming back?" Cal put his hands on his hips. "Soon, I hope." He stared at her. "When are *you* going back to Chicago?"

Melody drew in a sharp breath. "Not soon enough," she retorted and tried to march as regally as she could back to the front of the shop.

At least she had Harriet, Melody comforted herself as she took her place behind the counter, glancing at the young girl innocently straightening shelves. Yes, Melody decided, tightening her apron, Harriet was the only decent one among them, and she resolved there and then that she would reward her new friend by making her her protégée. Harriet would be well placed, romantically, that is, Melody vowed, before she returned to Chicago—hopefully in time for Mundelein's Winter Ball in January. It would be her triumph, and she would leave the awful Cal and Mrs. Haufbrau to stew in their own Merriweather juices.

CHAPTER TWO

Unfortunately, there was no time to begin schooling Harriet in the ways of romance or to arrange the new products, so busy was the shop for the rest of the afternoon. And, truth be told, a bit of wind had gone out of Melody's sails regarding her pretty new things. She was able to dismiss Mrs. Haufbrau's disparaging comments as being that of an old crab, but Cal's were harder to ignore.

But why? *What did he know of ladies' scarves?* she grumbled as she pulled the door of the shop closed for the evening and locked it. Nothing, of course. She pulled at her Chanel duster—she had bought it at Marshall Field's last spring with Cynthia, and it had proven absolutely divine for drives up Lake Shore Drive with the gang in Charlie's Buick Century or Douglas's V8 Sport after football games!—and began walking slowly up High Street.

It was Cal's comment about her being away too long that stung, she realized, as if he thought she didn't belong here anymore. Though if she were being honest, she *was* finding life back in Merriweather just a tad bit stifling when compared to her life in Chicago, which now seemed blissfully carefree. She trudged past Ben's Bakery and Grassell's Shoes and waved limply at Mr. Rhomberg, locking up the hardware store, and tried not to think about what all of her friends were doing without her.

Her best friend, Cynthia—or at least her best friend besides Elsie, of course—had promised to write every single day, which she had dutifully done, in the beginning. But now that they were well into September, her letters had already dropped off considerably.

It's not you, dearest! Cynthia had gushed in her last letter. *It's just that I'm so terribly busy. You know how it is. Though it's really not the same without you! We are all too, too sad!! We are praying very earnestly for your father to get better so that you can finally come back to us! Even Sr. Bernard is praying.* At the mention of Sr. Bernard, Melody had paused in her reading. She couldn't believe that she actually missed Sr. Bernard, Mundelein's president, but then again, Sr. Bernard had been more friend than a disciplinarian, acting as a nurturing mother to so many of the girls, including Melody, despite the many silly scrapes she had gotten herself into.

Douglas reports that your father is in a very bad way, and none of us can imagine what you're going through. How selfish we are to want you all to ourselves, and yet we are quite lost without our queen. How are we ever to get by? But knowing you, you've probably already replaced us by now with much more interesting characters. At this juncture, Melody had lowered the letter and let out a brief snort. *And poor Douglas! I really do think he is a little in love with you. How he pines!*

Melody sighed now as she plodded along. Douglas Novak. What was she to do with him? He had obviously not revealed to the gang that he was more than just "a little in love" with her—indeed, not a month ago, here in her own backyard, he had *proposed* after rescuing her from a prank that had gone awry at a convent in Dubuque, Iowa. At first, she had thought he was joking when he had gone down on one knee and pulled a ring out of his pocket. Even after he had put it on her finger and asked her to be his wife, she still couldn't believe it. She had allowed him to kiss her, which she quite enjoyed, truth be told, but had not committed beyond telling him, "I'll think about it, Dougie." She knew her answer had crushed him, but she couldn't help it.

She kicked a pinecone from the path. She supposed she *did* love Douglas in a certain way; after all, they had had so many jolly times together. It still made her laugh to recall the look on his face when he had discovered her masquerading as a nun, or when he had toppled off a makeshift tower during his fraternity's production of *Romeo and Juliet*, or any number of hijinks they had gotten themselves into. But was this the stuff of marriage? She wasn't sure. She had used the excuse of her father being ill to put off the decision, telling him that she needed time to think, as everything had happened so fast.

This was the reason, she told herself, why she didn't wear the ring. She had only kept it on for about ten minutes after he had driven away, stuffing it back into its box before her mother's eagle eye could spot it. If Mums knew of the engagement, there would be no end to her harassment to accept him, the son of a wealthy surgeon in Chicago.

Despite Melody telling him that she needed time, however, Douglas annoyingly repeated his proposal with every letter, which Melody thought a bit unfair and also imprudent. Did he really think he could badger an answer out of her? Did he not understand the pressure she was under to keep the Merc running, not to mention her worry about her father? She was therefore purposefully vague in her letters back to him, instead telling him all about the antics at the Merc, her eccentric staff, or any old thing, really, that popped into her mind.

And, anyway, didn't people say that absence makes the heart grow fonder? Maybe their separation would prove telling, she had reasoned, though this logic seemed to be backfiring, as poor Douglas was already fading faster than she suspected a true love should in the space of a month.

She bent and picked up a stray stick. If everything had continued as it had, with her and Douglas and Cynthia and Charlie having lovely adventures at school, she supposed that their relationship would have naturally progressed toward marriage. Wasn't that the reason she had been sent to Mundelein in the first place? To find a husband from Loyola, the men's college next door?

Deep in thought, she turned down Ridge. It was by far the most prestigious street in town, with its old Victorians and Queen Annes and Gothic Revivals, all built back in the town's heyday when it was flush with money from the lead and then zinc mines. The sun was just setting, lighting up the leaves of the huge oak trees that formed a cathedral-like canopy for the length of the whole street.

At last she reached "The Willows," her family's rambling Queen Anne, set back from the street and surrounded by a low wrought-iron fence. It had been nicknamed such by Pops, probably because of the giant weeping willow in the backyard that grew beside a little creek. Melody tossed the stick and walked slowly up the stone path. Everything in Merriweather seemed to be made of stone.

The smell of roasting chicken hit her as she stepped through the front door. Chicken paprikash. It was one of Helenka's specialties, and one of Melody's favorites. At least there was that.

"I'm home!" she called, but no one responded, which didn't surprise her. She could hear Bunny playing piano in the back parlor, which had been converted into a music room, complete with a large old-fashioned upright piano, when they were children. They had all been given lessons, but it had been Bunny who had taken to it. "Like a fish to water!" Pops would announce proudly to his customers, as if they cared.

Melody rifled through the mail basket on the little Chinese entry table, but there was nothing for her. Again. Why didn't Elsie write? Elsie Von Harmon had been her shy, awkward roommate at Mundelein, and Melody had delighted in welcoming her into her inner circle, though Elsie was ever so quiet and ridiculously studious. Melody had immediately set about trying to find the perfect love for poor Elsie, but before she could, Elsie had run off with the college janitor! It had been an absolute scream, and Melody smiled, even now, at the hand she had played in helping the lovers escape—which was how she had ended up in a convent in Dubuque in the first place, having decided, without Elsie's knowledge or approval, to disguise herself as her friend until Elsie could safely get away. It had been the perfect ruse, in Melody's opinion, anyway—that is, until her father had taken ill and she had had to rush home.

Melody made her way to the kitchen, where Helenka, dressed in a light blue uniform, was putting the final touches on the meal and scurrying between the stove and the large prep table in the middle of the room.

"Where's Mums?" Melody asked, her stomach suddenly rumbling at the sight of the buttermilk biscuits piled on a platter, which oddly resembled Helenka's blonde hair, piled on top of her head.

"Hospital. She will be home in minute," Helenka answered in her thick Polish accent without looking up. Her mother and Helenka had some kind of bizarre mental connection, so if Helenka said Mums was on her way home, it was more than likely the case. "Go tell Bunny it is ready almost."

Melody slipped out of the kitchen and down the dark hallway. *Why was it always dark in here?* Annoyed, she pressed the switch at the end of the hall, illuminating a beautiful Tiffany fixture, and crossed the tiny foyer trimmed in dark walnut wainscoting.

"Bunny!" she called and was about to enter the front parlor when her mother bustled in.

"Oh, Melody! I'm glad you're back." Mums immediately switched off the light and began removing her hat. "Who turned this light on?" she asked, setting her handbag on the Chinese table.

"Oh, Mums, you're as bad as Pops. Why have all of these things if we never use them? We might as well live in a shack." Melody gripped the banister and swayed a little as she used to do when she was a little girl.

"Well, it just might come to that, the way things are going."

Melody stopped swaying. She was used to her mother's exaggerations, but something niggled. "I'm sure it's not all that bad, Mums."

"Well, I've just been to see your father, and he isn't at all hopeful. But come along. Dinner's almost ready, and we shouldn't keep Helenka waiting. Bunny!" she called toward the back parlor.

The playing stopped.

"What do you mean, he's not hopeful?" Melody followed Mums into the dining room. Helenka was busy arranging the dishes, including the large serving platter that held the chicken and cream sauce, in the middle of the table.

"Hello, Mums!" Bunny said and gave her mother a quick kiss on the cheek before plopping into her seat. "How's Pops?"

"Well, he really would have appreciated a visit from you. You haven't been there in three days!"

"I do have school, you know." Bunny's bottom lip stuck out a little. "I'll go tomorrow."

"Well, as it happens," Mums said, pulling out her chair at one end of the table and sitting down. "I have some news."

"What news?" Melody asked, reaching for a biscuit.

"Thank you, Helenka," Mums said as Helenka placed a bowl of egg noodles near her. "Won't you join us?"

It was the same question Mums asked Helenka every night, one which was really just a thinly veiled cue for Helenka to remove herself.

"No, thank you. I will eat in kitchen," Helenka responded, the same response she had given for the last twenty-five years. Indeed, Melody could not remember a time when Helenka was not a part of their household, and she suspected that Helenka was in fact her mother's best friend. And though they went through this charade of mistress and servant each night, Melody was pretty sure that the two of them sat down to lunch together each day and shared coffee and cookies in the afternoons.

"What news?" Melody repeated now that the ritual had been completed.

"Your father may be coming home!"

"Home? When?" Melody paused in the piling of chicken onto her plate. Finally, a glimmer of hope. Maybe Pops would be able to get back to the Merc faster than any of them had expected!

"Well, there's no definite time," Mums put in. "Perhaps in a few weeks or maybe next month. I'm hoping before Christmas."

Melody let out the breath she had been holding. So, nothing imminent. Probably nothing more than wishful thinking on her mother's part.

"Oh, how exciting, Mums!" Bunny took a drink of her milk. "Do you think he'll be able to come to my recital?"

Melody rolled her eyes.

"Well, I'm not sure about that, and I wouldn't call it exciting. It's going to be an awful lot of work. We'll have to convert the front room into a bedroom for him," Mums mused.

Melody dished some noodles onto her plate. "Convert the front room?"

"Well, he'll never be able to make it up the stairs, now will he? No, the doctor was very insistent on that point."

A sliver of her previous hope resurrected. If the doctor was discussing provisions, perhaps it was a reality. "Well, why did you say he's without hope?"

"When did I say that?"

"When you first came in! Something about us having to live in a shack?"

"A shack?" Bunny exclaimed.

"Oh, that. Well, he really is quite worried about our finances. Says we might have to rent out some rooms."

"What rooms?" Bunny frowned.

"Honestly, Bunny. Our extra rooms here." Mums cut into her chicken. "With Freddy gone, there are two empty rooms, if you count the guest room. And if you and Melody moved in together that would be one more." She took a bite. "Then, there's always the attic. We could convert that."

"But that's not fair!" Bunny exclaimed again. "You can't do that, Mums!"

"Well, 'fair' doesn't come into it, Elizabeth," Mums said, waving her fork vaguely. "Do you think *I* want strangers traipsing all over the house?"

"Why don't we just raise the rent on the Kaufmanns?" Bunny whined, dangerously ignoring her mother's use of her given name, a telltale sign of "a mood" coming on.

"I suggested that, but he says since they can barely pay the rent already he won't do that to them."

"Yes," Melody agreed, thinking about Imogene and her horrible little soaps. "I don't think they could manage more than they are paying now."

Mums gave her a quick, questioning glance. "Well, your father said he's not sure how long we can hold on without some extra income, not with the Merc going as it is."

"What's that supposed to mean?" Melody set down her fork.

Mums threw her a look. "I wouldn't know, Melody. I assume it means the store is losing money."

Melody's face grew warm. *Losing money?* How could that be? And even if it was, how would he know? She had yet to bring him any of the books. A bothersome image of Mrs. Haufbrau came to mind, confirming her earlier suspicions. *How dare she!*

"You can't be extravagant, you know, Melody," Mums went on. "Do you really need an extra shop girl? What's her name? Hattie?"

"It's Harriet. And, yes, I do need her, Mums," she said stiffly. "And it wasn't me who hired her in the first place." She wanted to suggest that if anyone should be dismissed, it should be Mrs. Haufbrau or even

Helenka, but she knew not to resurrect such a sore subject. Likewise, it was unwise to suggest it at this moment, as she was pretty sure Helenka was listening on the other side of the swinging door that led into the kitchen.

"What's she like, anyway? This Harriet? Her mother's nuttier than a fruitcake. Don't know what Earl Mueller ever saw in her. A bit slow in the head. Lyle said he once saw her up on Christmas Tree Hill, all dressed up in some white dress and dancing around in the night." Mums shook her head dismissively. "She's from somewhere out near Livingston, I think. Do you know, Helenka?" Mums shouted.

"Linden," Helenka called back.

Melody sighed. "Well, Harriet's a very good worker, and yes, we do need her. We could use another girl, actually. It wouldn't hurt Bunny to take a shift or two and help out." Melody glared at her sister. "Especially with the Harvest Fest coming up. We could use the help."

Much to her surprise, Mums paused in her chewing and looked like she might actually be considering the proposal. Bunny, however, quickly squashed it.

"Mums, you know I can't do it. I'm the president of the League this year!"

"Yes," Mums said, resuming her dinner, "what am I thinking? No, Melody, Bunny will be much too busy that day. You know that."

"'Busy' is not the word I would use. Don't forget that *I* was once the president of the Junior Ladies League, so you can't fool me," she said to Bunny. "You'll just be standing around behind a table of pies, batting your eyes and making small talk."

"Now you're just being mean!" Bunny said, her voice quivering, dangerously close to the tears she was seemingly able to produce at any given moment.

Melody pushed her plate away, suddenly not hungry. "Excuse me."

"Don't you want dessert?" Mums asked, concerned.

"It's cherry dumplings," Helenka called from behind the kitchen door.

"No, thank you," Melody answered moodily.

She climbed the stairs and threw herself on her French wrought-iron bed and stared up at the dormered ceiling. In high school—which seemed like a hundred years ago now—she had cut out pictures of Clark Gable and Barbara Stanwyck and other movie stars from the pages of *Vogue* and *Harper's Bazaar* and taped them up with cellophane. She hugged her chenille pillow and stared at the stylized black-and-white images, trying not to cry. Why was she the one having to make all the sacrifices, while Mums and Bunny and Fred all went on with their lives as usual? Why was Bunny still taking piano lessons, for God's sake? Didn't that cost money? It was ridiculous!

Angrily, she sat up and pulled open her top desk drawer to grasp the stack of old letters hidden there. The top one was from Douglas. She skipped the salutation and the report about the gang's recent activities and quickly jumped to the heart of it.

You really know how to cut a guy up, Mel. Don't leave me hanging. Please give me some indication to let me know if I can even hope. Why don't you come back for a visit? I'll introduce you to my parents, and everything will be swell; you'll see. Please marry me, Mel. I know you thought it was just a rash question, and I apologize for not making it more romantic, but gosh darn it, you make a guy crazy. I can't think straight when I'm around you. Please say yes, Mel. You won't regret it. Yours, hopefully forever, Douglas.

Melody tossed the letter onto the dresser. She had selected it because she thought it would make her feel better to know she had a choice, an escape from her situation, but it only left her feeling all the more confused. She hugged her chenille pillow again, wishing she had someone to talk to. If only her father were here, she mused. She could always count on him to cheer her up, and she desperately needed cheering right now. But on a more serious note, she wanted to ask him about the Merc's state of affairs. *Was* it really losing money? And were they really as bad off as Mums was suggesting? Melody rolled over on her side. They must be if Mums was considering lodgers. Melody lay there several minutes, stewing, before finally tossing the pillow and sitting up. If her father couldn't come to her, she would go to him. Yes, she decided, a walk would do her good.

CHAPTER THREE

Visting hours at Victory Memorial ended sharply at five o'clock, but Melody had quickly learned that passing the nurses packs of cigarettes from the Merc allowed her to slip in past the normal time. Thankfully, she still had an unopened pack in her handbag, which she covertly passed to Nurse Hawkins, who, as it happened, was one of Melody's favorites.

"Don't stay too long, though." Nurse Hawkins deftly slipped the cigarettes into her uniform pocket. "His other two visitors just left, and he needs to rest."

"Other two?"

"Two men. Big guys. Rough-looking," Nurse Hawkins murmured, already turning her attention back to a stack of charts. She looked up for a moment, though, and gave a quick tilt of her head in the direction of her father's room. "Like I said, don't stay too long."

Melody proceeded down the darkened hall and paused outside her father's door, listening, and then gave it a swift knock.

"I told you to get out!" her father shouted.

"Pops?" Melody said tentatively, poking her head around the door. "You okay?"

The deep frown on Louis Merriweather's face suddenly melted. "Mel! What are you doing here? Isn't this chicken paprikash night?"

"Oh, Pops!" Melody groaned, fighting the urge to cry at the sight of him lying alone and helpless in the dark room. The bedside lamp was on, but it cast large shadows and only served to accentuate the wrinkles around his sunken eyes. He looked weaker than ever. Melody hesitated. "I . . . I just had to come see you."

"That bad, eh?" He gave her a lopsided grin. "Well, come sit down. Tell me all about it." He patted the space on the bed beside him, which, truth be told, wasn't all that big considering his girth.

Melody squeezed in beside him and tried to hug him as best she could.

"Well, out with it. What is it?" he asked kindly when she finally sat up and looked at his unshaven face. For a moment, she reconsidered pouring out her woes to him. Shouldn't she be listening to his?

"Nothing, really, Pops. I just came to see you is all." She tried forcing herself to smile.

"Mel, you should know by now, I can always tell when you're fibbing. Something's up. What is it?"

"Oh, Pops!" she cried, unable to hold it in any longer. "I can't do this! I can't run the Merc all by myself."

Pops patted her hand. "Sure you can, Mel. Sure you can."

"No, I *can't*, Pops!"

"I did it when I was your age."

Melody twisted her lips. "But you had Grandpa there to help you. All I've got is Harriet and Cal—who doesn't want to be there *at all*, by the way—and old Mrs. Haufbrau, who's positively insufferable!"

Pops surprised her with a little chuckle, which slid into a wheezy cough. "Marcella? Don't mind her rough edges, Mel. She won't steer you wrong. She knows the Merc better than anyone, 'cluding me. Been there forever."

"Then, why don't you put *her* in charge? She thinks she is anyway. You don't really need me." In truth, this was a conundrum that had been circling in Melody's head for a while. Why *had* Pops insisted on handing the running of the Merc to *her*—a twenty-one-year-old girl who had spent the last three years living in a college run by nuns in Chicago? *Why not* put it in the hands of his best employee? Well, maybe not best, but obviously the oldest?

"Business is always better in the hands of family, Mel."

"Then why can't Freddy come home and do it?" Melody whined, trying, once more, to fob the burden of the Merc onto Freddy.

"He's only got one year left, Mel. That would be silly."

"Well, why can't Bunny do it?"

"Bunny's still a kid, Mel. You know that."

"She's hardly a kid! She's seventeen!"

"Well, she has to finish high school. And anyway, Mel, she's not as mature as you."

Privately, Melody agreed, but she wasn't going to admit it. "Well, as soon as she graduates, she's going to have to step in and help. That's all there is to it. Freddy worked here when he was in high school, and I'm doing my share now; it's only right that Bunny take a turn when I'm back at Mundelein!"

Melody expected him to refute this argument, as he usually did regarding anything that had to do with Bunny—couldn't everyone else see how spoiled she was?—but he did not. He didn't say anything at all, just looked at her with sad, tired eyes.

"Listen, Mel. I need to tell you something."

Melody's skin suddenly prickled.

"The truth is, you won't be going back to Mundelein," he said, his voice haggard. "Not when I'm better. Not ever."

All the air seemed to go out of the room.

"What?" she whispered.

"Now, Mel, you've got to be strong." He took her hand but then paused, as if trying to figure out how to phrase his apparent bad news. "Turns out, we're broke, basically."

"What do you mean we're broke?" Melody asked faintly.

"Lost it all. Uncle Joe invested all our money, badly it seems, and now we have nothing. 'Cept the Merc, of course."

Melody frantically tried to understand what this meant exactly. "But . . . but can't Uncle Joe help us? Seems he got us into this mess. Can't he do something?"

"Now, Mel. There's another thing I gotta tell you, but you've got to be brave."

Melody's stomach clenched. She didn't want to hear whatever her father was going to say . . .

"Uncle Joe's gone.

"What do you mean, gone?"

"He . . . he shot himself, apparently," Pop wheezed. "Out in Vegas."

"Shot himself?" Melody felt sick. She hadn't been remotely close to her father's brother, who lived somewhere near Detroit, but a suicide? It was horrible. "I . . . I'm sorry, Pops," she managed. "What was he doing all the way out in Las Vegas?"

Pops shrugged. "Gambling with whatever he had left, I'm guessing. Anyway, he shot himself. A Nevada sheriff called me."

Her poor father. To lose his only brother after so much tragedy had already happened. And in such a horrible, sinful way. "Oh, Pops," she said. "I'm so sorry. Does Mums know about Joe?"

"No, she doesn't. And she can't know. You've got to promise me, Mel. Promise you won't tell her. The shame'll kill her." Privately, Melody thought her father's grief should supersede her mother's pride, but she didn't say anything, knowing that her father practically worshipped Mums.

"So, you see, Mel. There ain't much hope of you goin' back to school. I'm sorry, girl. Can't be helped. But something tells me you'll be fine. You'll land on your feet; you always do. Didn't like you that far away, anyway." He rubbed her cheek with the back of his hand. "Aw, don't cry. I can't take it when you cry."

Despite her wish to avoid causing her father further distress, Melody could not hold back her tears any longer. As if to hide them, she buried her face in his massive stomach while she sobbed. Pops patted her back. "Hey, Mel. It's okay. Things are bound to get better. You'll see. I've still got a few tricks up my sleeve."

Melody could not imagine what those would be. Finally, she sat up, wiping her eyes with the backs of her hands. "But Mums said the Merc is losing money."

Pops raised both eyebrows. "Did she now? Your mom is smarter than she lets on. Can't get much past her." He gave her a small smile. "You're a lot like her, you know. You're the brains of the family." Melody doubted this, given the fact that Freddy was at Harvard Law School, but she obliged her father by keeping silent. "The truth," Pops went on, "is that the Merc never did make all that much money. It was the moonshine that propped it up. Shame that Prohibition ended."

"But isn't . . . isn't that a good thing? Now we can sell it legally."

"Yeah, but now everyone can, and we can't charge as much. See?"

Melody nodded absently, desperately trying to think of a way out of this mess. It *was* too bad about the moonshine. But if they couldn't sell alcohol for a huge profit anymore, perhaps they could sell something else. But what? An image of her new hats and scarves and gloves flickered into her mind, a slow spark of hope igniting. Maybe it *was* a good thing she had spent the money on them. Maybe they could make up the difference where the moonshine had left off? It seemed doubtful, but it was better than doing nothing. Anything would be better than letting her father down. And, if she were honest, she couldn't possibly accept the fact that she was stuck in Merriweather forever. She had to find a way to get back to Chicago.

She leaned forward and kissed him on the forehead. "Don't you worry, Pops. I've got a couple of tricks up my sleeve, too," she said with more confidence than she felt.

"That a girl," he said faintly. "I knew I could count on you, Mel."

She reluctantly stood. "I suppose I should go now. I've got stuff to do, and you've got to rest. I wouldn't want to overstay my welcome." She tilted her head in the direction of the nurses' station.

"You could never do that, girl." He smiled wanly. "Not in my book anyway. Not a day goes by I don't think about you. You take care of Mums, won't you? Promise?"

Melody suddenly felt a tendril of fear creep round her heart. Why was he talking this way? "Course I will, Pops. Until you get better, that is." She tried to say it nonchalantly, but her throat felt hot and tight as she swallowed the tears that were welling again. She studied his face, but his eyes were already closed in exhaustion. Where was her once-youthful father who used to swing her around in the backyard or take her fishing in the creek behind the house?

"I'll be back tomorrow if I can," she called out in her merriest voice, though in truth her heart was breaking as she turned and hurried down the hall.

CHAPTER
FOUR

Harriet Mueller hurried down Magnolia Street towards the cluster of little stone houses that used to be the original mining village of New Grimsby before it had grown into a bigger town, the whole of which, back in 1876, had been renamed Merriweather, after Melody's grandfather. Harriet's grandfather had been a miner, too, but he had unfortunately *not* struck it rich and had consequently not had anything named after him besides his son, Earl. Earl, Jr. had become a miner, too, and, like his father before him, had produced only a single child, this one a girl, Harriet, before he had met his demise in a mining accident.

Harriet flipped open the metal mailbox attached to the house and seeing nothing in it, as usual, let it drop with a bang as she opened the front door. The air was hot and thick with the smell of cooking tomatoes. Mom was canning again.

Shrugging out of her coat, she hung it on a peg near the door. The cottage's front half was really just one big room, the kitchen part off to the left, and a sitting room to the right. Her mother, an apron dangling from her thin waist, her gray hair frizzled more than usual, stood at the stove, carefully tending the big canning pot filled with mason jars. The table was covered with fresh tomatoes of varying sizes, picked that morning from the garden out back.

"Harriet. There you are," her mother said without turning around. "I got a sandwich made for you there, but then maybe you can help me."

Harriet followed her mother's gesture to where a thin egg, ketchup, and tomato sandwich sat on a plate near the sink. Next to it was a tall glass of milk.

"Did you eat?" Harriet asked, eagerly picking up the sandwich and taking a bite. Thanks to their little flock out back, eggs were a frequent dinner item. And a lunch and a breakfast one, too. In fact, Harriet and her mother rarely had meat except when they had enough left over from Harriet's wages to purchase some. Or when Cal gave her scraps or sold her the unwanted bits for cheap. Rosemary Mueller could take anything—even pig's feet or tripe or beef tongue—and create something delicious. She definitely had a gift. And she had a green thumb, too. The whole backyard and part of the front was taken up with rows of vegetables and herbs and fruit bushes. It was a blessing, really, to have been left this cottage and little patch of land after her father had died, as the ability to grow most of their own food was the only thing getting them through these rough times. Many a hobo knocked at their door, begging, and thus far no one had ever gone away empty-handed. Harriet wondered how they knew to always stop at their house. Probably the garden in front?

"I'm not hungry right now," Rosemary answered. "Not with the heat of this."

Harriet wolfed down the rest of her sandwich and brushed the crumbs off her fingers. "What are we gonna do with these, Mom? The shed's almost full."

"Well, I don't know. Put 'em under the beds maybe." Rosemary laughed.

"Maybe I could take some to Cal. You know, as a thank-you?" Harriet picked up some of the fresh tomatoes and began to rinse them.

"Now that's an idea. Think Melody or Marcella would want some, too?"

Maybe Mrs. Haufbrau would like some, though Mrs. Haufbrau was as thin as a twig, all sharp angles, as if she never ate at all. Whenever Melody offered the staff anything stale to take home, Mrs. Haufbrau never indulged. Harriet, by contrast, took everything she could.

"I could ask, I guess." Harriet set the clean tomatoes near the pot of boiling water meant for blanching and tried to decide if Melody would appreciate jars of tomatoes. Her family was obviously well-off. After all, they owned the Merc and had a lovely house on Ridge, complete with a housekeeper. A housekeeper! *Maybe* Melody would like some jars of tomatoes, but Melody was a hard one to predict.

Harriet had known Melody all her life, watching her in the schoolyard from afar, amazed by her effortless popularity even back then. Melody was one of those girls who was always bubbly and light—the kind that people, especially lonely ones, seemed to gravitate toward.

But after Melody had graduated from eighth grade, Harriet had lost sight of her when Melody and a few other lucky ones had gone on to high school. And after that, Melody had gone to college! Imagine! *College!* And in Chicago of all places. It took Harriet's breath away. She could never do that in a hundred years. Leave Mom and, well . . . everyone.

Like most of her classmates, Harriet had quit school after eighth grade. She considered herself exceptionally lucky to have been hired the day after graduation by Mr. Merriweather, seeing as how jobs were scarce—and she was even more grateful when he had kept her on during the worst years of the Depression. She, like everyone in town, had been dismayed by his recent heart attack. Everyone had expected the Merc to close, at least temporarily, until maybe Fred could get back from out East, so they had been thoroughly shocked when it was announced that it was not to be Fred, but *Melody* who would be returning to help out.

Harriet had worried that Melody would be different after living in such a big city with all those rich people, but to her delight, Melody was just as bubbly and friendly as ever. Maybe a little *too* friendly, given Melody's offer earlier today to help her fall in love. Harriet's cheeks flushed all over again, and *not* because of the heat of the kitchen. She should have explained to Melody that her help in that department probably wasn't necessary, since, more than once, she had caught John Schneider, the young farmer who delivered eggs to the Merc, staring at her. *And* that just a few days ago, he had actually asked her to walk out with him at the Harvest Fest!

Harriet quickly gathered up another armful of tomatoes and tried to redirect her thoughts to where she had left off, which was how unchanged Melody seemed to be after her stint in Chicago. You would expect someone like that, so rich and popular, to be mean and haughty. But she was not. She was kind of like the big sister Harriet had always wanted. Bunny Merriweather was lucky to have her. But then again, Bunny and Melody had never really gotten along. Bunny was different than Melody. Quieter and more reserved. Almost aloof. Almost, Harriet dared to think . . . a snob.

No, Melody was unique, that was for sure. She was a marvel to Harriet, so much so that sometimes Harriet could barely think what to say to her. She could never run something like the Merc! The thought of it made her stomach quell. Somehow, though, this made her want to work all the harder for Melody. Not only did she want her heroine to succeed, but God only knew if she could ever find another job if the Merc failed. Not now. A couple of girls from her class had gone all the way to Madison and even Chicago to find jobs as nannies or maids.

Her friend, Kate, had been one of the ones who had tried going away, but she had returned after only a week. But it wasn't because of homesickness, which would have been the case with herself, Harriet knew—it was because Kate was simply too wild and too proud to be some rich family's maid. Harriet had gently tried to suggest this before Kate had gone off, but, as usual, Kate hadn't listened.

"Why don't you take some out to Kate?" her mother asked, as if she could read Harriet's mind.

"I was just thinking that." Harriet looked out the window. It was still a little bit light, and the thought of a walk across the field in the cool evening air appealed. "But don't you need help?"

"No, go on. I'm almost finished for the night, and you should go now before it gets too dark. Take some of the beans, too. And maybe a jar of beets."

"You know what she's like." Harriet pulled back the gingham cloth that hung from the sink to hide the pipes and grabbed the old basket. "If I take too much, she'll be offended."

Rosemary sighed. "I still don't know why she insists on living in one of those badger holes. Silly, that is. Could be here with us. Ask her again, will you?"

"I'll ask, but you know what she'll say." Harriet put two jars of tomatoes in the basket and allowed her mother to add a jar of beets but waved away the beans. She grabbed her navy cardigan from the peg.

"Hurry now, though, Harriet. Don't want you to run into any fairies."

Harriet bit her lip. She had been hearing about the fairies since she was a little girl.

"You know what they're like, this time of day," her mother said warily. Though she admitted to never having actually *seen* a fairy, Rosemary Mueller attributed all sorts of unexplained happenings to them—a two-headed calf born over at the Portzen's, a broken jar in the shed, a lost handkerchief, the list was endless. Harriet, for her part, wasn't entirely sure what she believed, but she had discovered that it was easier to just go along with her mother's strange mythology.

"Yes, I'll be careful."

Harriet stepped outside and welcomed the cool air hitting her overheated face. She followed the worn path around the back and headed across the field toward Christmas Tree Hill where hundreds of badger holes had been dug out by the early miners before they built proper houses.

Kate Kerwyn, or "Indian Kate," as she was better known, had established residence in one of these. Kate had been taken in as a toddler by the Kerwyns after being found wandering out by the old Wareham farm. Gus Kerwyn had delivered the little girl to the county sheriff, who guessed, due to her long black hair and sharp cheekbones, that she might be from the Sauk tribe up near Prairie Du Chien. When he drove her up there, though, no one claimed her. The sheriff continued his investigation for months while the girl remained with the Kerwyns. It wasn't the first case, he had noted grimly, of finding abandoned children. The worst was right after the Crash—parents abandoning kids, unable to feed them.

Finally, after months of searching, which included putting out a national wire for the girl's parents, he declared her an orphan and made plans to drive her to Madison or Milwaukee to deposit her in an orphanage. By this point, however, the Kerwyns couldn't bear to part with her, so they kept her. "Like a pet," Kate would often say derisively, which Harriet thought very unfair. After all, the Kerwyns were a good, kind family.

"Not as kind as you think," Kate had once spat, and Harriet knew she was referring to Ray, one of the older boys, whom Kate had a particular aversion to. It was Ray who had supposedly come up with the nickname "Indian Kate."

"Indian Kate, Indian Kate," the school kids would chant. "Took a fish for bait and then was late. Indian Kate, Indian Kate. Ran through the gate and never found a mate."

There were endless variations to the litany over the years. Rather than fight this image, Kate had decided to embrace it and had taken to wearing her long black hair in two braids while defiantly demanding that her teachers call her "Indian Kate" as well—which, of course, they never did.

It was because of Ray that Kate had decided to leave Merriweather in the first place. It wasn't just the nickname that made Kate hate him; he had always singled her out, she had confided to Harriet, including one time when he trapped her in a closet shortly after her tenth birthday and had done . . . well, unspeakable things.

Kate had only been gone to Stoughton for a week, however, before she had unexpectedly returned and taken refuge in one of the badger holes. No one, including Harriet, could understand her behavior. Mrs. Kerwyn had even hurried over to Christmas Tree Hill and pleaded with

Kate to come back home, saying that it was dangerous for a young girl to be living out in the wild by herself. "Anything could happen!"

"Yes, anything *could* happen," Kate had responded bitterly and reminded her foster mother that, thanks to growing up as the dark pet of seven blond and blue-eyed children, she had long ago learned how to defend herself.

"Kate?" Harriet called, picking her way through the rutted ground. Old Russ Thomas often let his cows graze on this land, and their hooves, when the ground was wet, would create deep ruts that were hard to see in the weeds and the descending dark. "Kate?" Harriet called again, nearly stumbling.

"Over here," came a voice from beside the creek.

"What are you doing?" Harriet asked as she made her way over, watching her friend cut a tall stalk of grass with a little switchblade.

"Cutting this grass. I've been trying to make little baskets out of it." Kate looked up, her dark eyes bright. "Come on, I'll show you." She straightened. "What's in there?" she asked over her shoulder, as she led Harriet back toward her dwelling.

"Tomatoes. And some beets," Harriet answered gingerly.

"I told you I don't need charity." Kate roughly pulled open the hand-hewn door of the arched hole framed with rocks.

"You know Mom," Harriet tried to say lightly. "I wasn't going to get out of the house without something. Anyway," she said, looking around the one-room shelter, "you can't live on nothing."

Harriet had been in Kate's badger hole a couple of times, but she was always surprised by how warm, even cozy, it was. In the corner was an old wood-burning stove, presumably left by a previous mining family. It emanated heat, with a chimney that penetrated the earthen ceiling and burst through a pipe that had been cut into the sod above. Harriet set the basket on the hard-packed dirt floor, noticing as she did so that Kate had added a patchwork quilt to the bed in the corner and hung a few dented pots on pegs driven into the walls. There was even a small table with two chairs and braided rugs on the floor.

"Where'd you get all this?"

"Some from the dump, but mainly Edmund. He's the one who got the stove working. Here, look at this." Kate put a small woven basket, slightly misshappen, in Harriet's hands.

"You made this?" Harriet turned it over carefully. It reminded her of a small robin's nest. It wasn't the best, as far as baskets went, but it was nonetheless impressive, being made only out of weeds. She tried to hand it back.

"You can have it," Kate said.

"Oh, no! I can't take this. You should keep it!" Harriet exclaimed, not sure what she would do with it anyway.

"No, in exchange for the tomatoes," she said, nodding at the jars.

"Oh . . ."

"I'll make you a better one. Eventually. Think I could sell them?"

"Well . . . maybe," Harriet faltered. "If they were bigger."

"Yeah, that's what I'm working on." She pointed to a pile of reeds strewn across the tabletop, and the beginnings of several more baskets.

"Where would you sell them?"

"I was thinking at the Harvest Fest?"

Harriet looked at the basket in her hand again. While it was certainly impressive, Harriet wasn't convinced they would sell. "You mean like in a booth?"

"No, not in a booth!" Kate snapped. "Where would I get a booth? No, I mean, just around. I haven't gotten that far."

Harriet pursed her lips. This was typical Kate. Not thinking ahead. "Well, you could try," she offered. "Couldn't hurt." Privately, she wasn't sure how Kate would pull this off, even if she did have decent products to sell. Simply lay them out on the grass or walk around hoping someone would buy them? The image caused her to momentarily wonder if perhaps she and her mother could sell something . . . Maybe tomatoes? But who would want those? Everyone had canned tomatoes.

"You gonna be there?" Kate asked.

"Yes, I . . . I'm going with John Schneider."

"John Schneider?" Kate looked up. "From the old Schneider farm?"

Harriet nodded, unable to suppress a small smile.

"He the oldest one?"

"The oldest boy. He has an older sister."

"My, my!" Kate said with a teasing grin. "You're doing well, aren't you?"

"It's just walking through the Fest," Harriet protested, unable to keep from laughing a little. "It doesn't mean anything. He was just being kind, I'm sure."

Kate raised an eyebrow. "Harvest Fest one day, wedding bells the next."

Harriet laughed again. "Stop it, Kate," she said, giving her friend a spontaneous hug. "Oh, why don't you come stay with us? At least for the winter. You can't stay here! You'll freeze."

"And leave this charm?" Kate gestured at the earthen walls. "No, I like it here. And anyway, Edmund said he'd come and help me fix it up for the winter."

Edmund Bertram was a cousin of the Kerwyns who lived across the lower hollar from the Gartners and who had accordingly spent many a summer day swimming in Pennalt's Crick with both the Gartner and the Kerwyn kids, including Kate. Besides Harriet herself, Edmund was probably the closest Kate had to a best friend. He and Kate had always gotten along, even as little kids, and he had been extremely distressed, so Kate said, to discover her living in a badger hole on her own. But much like Harriet's previous efforts, no part of Edmund's begging for her to see reason had apparently had any effect on the stubborn young woman.

"But won't you be lonely?" Harriet urged.

"Of course not! I like being alone. And, anyway, I've got a lot to do." She nodded at the reeds.

"I know you think it's charity, me asking you to stay with us, but it's not," Harriet insisted. "You know I always wanted a sister."

Kate took Harriet's hands in hers. "I know," she said, sincerely. "But I'll be okay." She gave Harriet's hands a squeeze. "Tell you what. If it gets too bad, I'll come."

"Promise?"

"Promise."

CHAPTER FIVE

"What do you mean you already promised?" Melody asked as she handed a stack of hat boxes to Harriet, who was perched precariously in the big display window of the Merc. "When?"

Harriet placed the hat boxes on the ground and, in response to Melody's pointed finger, handed over the rakes that were prominently displayed next to bushel baskets and checkered wool blankets. "The other day when I helped him with the eggs. He just sort of asked, so I said yes."

Melody groaned internally. She wasn't sure what she was more frustrated with—her hurried attempts to create a new window display before the shop opened for the day, or her thus-far failed attempts to get Harriet to see reason, at least in matters of the heart.

In truth, she was still reeling a little from Pops's revelation that their whole livelihood now depended solely on the Merc. But while she had despaired last night as she knelt beside her bed in prayer, her fears had somewhat dissipated with the early morning sun. She was *sure* she could make the Merc profitable again, not only to help Pops and the family, but, if she made enough money, she might be able to get back to Mundelein. Not returning to her old life, to her friends and . . . well . . . to Douglas, too, was inconceivable. She had to find a way.

Melody surveyed the mess on the floor and picked up the black silk shawl she had brought from home. "Here, drape this over the crates," she instructed, handing it to Harriet. "Yes, that's it! Perfect." In the wee hours of the night, Melody had convinced herself that their ticket to financial success lay in the sales of her luxury items. But in order to do that, she decided, they needed to be displayed prominently in the front display window. It would be the perfect place for them, especially with the Harvest Fest coming up. But that meant removing the current items.

She glanced at her thin wristwatch. They would have to hurry if they wanted to finish before Mrs. Haufbrau turned up. "Here," Melody instructed, handing Harriet some soup cans from the clutter on the floor. "Stack these on the crates. No, under the shawl! That's it! Now put one of the hats on it." Melody's first thought had been to order proper hat stands, but she didn't dare risk another expense.

Harriet did as she was told, carefully stacking the cans to create an impromptu hat stand, but when she tried to balance one of the hats–– a pretty madcap–on it, it kept falling off. "It won't stay!"

Hiking up her navy-blue shop skirt, Melody climbed into the window next to Harriet. After several tries, she finally got the hat to balance, barely, on the hidden soup cans. "There we are!" She looked at it proudly. "Now get another."

Harriet obediently began fumbling with the nearest hat box while Melody continued to drape several of the silk scarves so that their patterns were accentuated. "What exactly did he say?" Melody asked, turning her attention back to the other pressing matter.

"Who?" Harriet handed her a hat, this one a fedora felt. "John?"

"Yes, of course John." Melody placed it delicately on another stack.

Harriet faltered. "He . . . he asked me if I would walk through the Fest with him. If I got off early enough, that is."

Melody bit the inside of her cheek. John Schneider *was* handsome, in a yeoman sort of way, if one liked that sort of thing. She had tried, in a moment of benevolence, to compare him to Adam in Wordsworth's "The Farmer of Tilsbury Vale," which proved to be difficult since she in truth did not completely understand Wordsworth, rather just liked the *idea* of Wordsworth. She tried again, this time attempting to imagine him as Henry Fonda in *The Farmer Takes a Wife*, but sadly, this comparison fell short, too, as, honestly, who could possibly compare to the dreamy Henry Fonda?

"But, Harriet, he's a farmer." She gave a light chuckle. "That isn't what you want, is it?"

"What's wrong with being a farmer?" Harriet seemed genuinely confused.

Melody adjusted her tone. "Harriet, dear. Have you not noticed how he sometimes smells?"

"Well, that's just the farm on him. He doesn't smell at church."

Melody closed her eyes. This was going to be harder than she thought. Elsie had been a difficult protégée in that she played her cards close to her chest, but she was intelligent. Almost too intelligent—which was not exactly what she could say about Harriet.

"All I'm saying, dear," Melody said, repeating the term of endearment, "is that you should keep your options open. After all, you don't want to become a farmer's wife, do you? Think of the endless work, the mud, the hundreds of children you're sure to have to produce . . ."

"Yes, well, think of all the fresh food, though," Harriet answered a little sullenly.

"Food! There's more to life than fresh food, Harriet." Melody twirled a pink scarf.

Harriet did not look convinced. "It's not as if he asked me to marry him; it's just meeting up at the Harvest Fest is all."

"Yes, well, we might be terribly busy that day, so I wouldn't necessarily plan on it."

"What on God's green earth is all this?" cried Mrs. Haufbrau. She must have entered through the door in the back by the meat counter. "Were we robbed?" Her face was one of genuine concern as she hurried over, removing her black hat mid-trot.

"No, Mrs. Haufbrau. I'm rearranging the window." Melody tried to keep her voice matter-of-fact.

"But why? It's all set for the Fest! We worked on that all last week!" Mrs. Haufbrau brushed past Melody and peered at the half-constructed display. She let out a snort of disgust. "Why are you putting those there? This is supposed to be the fall display!" She pointed to the hand-painted sign at the top of the window, which read "Get Ready for Winter!" The Merc had many such signs, constructed long ago, which were repeatedly pulled out and hung, like clockwork, as the year marched along.

"Well, this *is* a 'Get Ready for Winter!' display," Melody retorted. "Just a different sort than usual."

"With silk scarves and thin gloves?" Mrs. Haufbrau scoffed. "I said it once, and I'll say it again, Melody Merriweather, if you had an ounce of sense, you'd realize that those things are never going to sell." She angrily flipped the sign on the front door from closed to open. "And to take up the whole front window during the Harvest Fest is just plain foolish!"

Melody's chest heaved, and she was about to throw out a dart of her own, but Mrs. Haufbrau beat her to it.

"Fine, if you want to put this rubbish back in ladies' wear, but not the front window! All you're doing is causing bad blood with Montague's down the street. Leave ladies' clothes to them."

"Montague's doesn't have a monopoly on selling ladies wear, Mrs. Haufbrau." Melody crossed her arms tightly. "I'm sure everyone will know we're still the Merc." She untangled her arms and awkwardly waved a hand at the shelves stocked with dry goods and other sundries. "And if Montague's wants to start selling flour and saltines, then by all means, let them!" She took a breath. "Sometimes it's good to mix things up a bit."

"Not if it's costing money the shop can't afford," Mrs. Haufbrau muttered.

Melody had another retort on her lips, but she refrained when the shop bell tinkled, and Mrs. Borman and Mrs. Penrose came in.

"Hello, Mrs. Borman, Mrs. Penrose!" Melody called out cheerily, scrambling to pick up the mess still on the floor.

Mrs. Penrose gave her a polite smile and then turned to Mrs. Haufbrau. "Need some water tablets, Marcella." She nodded toward the back counter where the tonics, restoratives, opiates, and physics were kept, all the especial favorites of Mrs. Haufbrau, who obligingly hurried over.

Mrs. Borman, meanwhile, stepped closer. "Whatcha got there, Melody?"

Melody felt a little thrill. This was her chance! Mrs. Borman was not the most ideal client, living as she did in a small four-room frame house on Dodge Street, but Melody was determined to try. She pulled a blue silk scarf with a striking paisley pattern from the display and ran it through her fingers. "Just the thing!" Melody entreated. "Isn't it beautiful?" She twisted it this way and that. "It's all the latest in Chicago." She held it up to Mrs. Borman's face. "It matches your eyes perfectly!" She wished she had a mirror. She would have to get one!

Mrs. Borman smiled and blinked rapidly. "Well, how much are they?"

Melody hesitated. They had cost her a dollar each, but she desperately needed to make a profit. "Only two dollars," she tried to say convincingly.

"Two dollars!" Mrs. Borman pulled back. "Too rich for my blood!"

"Well, how about a dollar fifty?" Melody pleaded, hoping to make a sale before Mrs. Haufbrau returned.

"Nah, I'll take half a dozen eggs. And a pair of shoelaces. Black." She nodded to where they hung behind the counter.

"I'll ring you, Mrs. Borman," Mrs. Haufbrau called, hurrying now toward the front.

Melody rolled her eyes. Honestly, Mrs. Haufbrau was like a one-woman show.

"And how have you been, Regina?" Mrs. Haufbrau asked. She counted out twelve eggs and put them gently into Mrs. Borman's shopping basket before reaching for a pair of laces. "All ready for the Fest?"

"Oh, yes. Rita and her little ones is all geared up for the parade," the woman answered. "They're coming over to ours first. Gonna bake a cobbler. Got some real nice gooseberries down by the river."

"Oh, yes, I know the place you mean. Got some down there myself. Anything else I can get you, Mrs. Penrose?" she said to the other woman, who had since meandered to the front.

"No, just the water tablets. Thanks, Marcella." The two women stepped over the strewn boxes and soup cans. "How's your father?" Mrs. Penrose paused to ask, surveying the disarray.

Melody straightened up, scooping back a lock of deep brown hair that had come loose from the low bun she was trying to sport nowadays. "He's coming along. Thanks for asking."

"Well, it'll be good to have him back." Mrs. Penrose sniffed, her eyes darting once more to the scattered items before heading out.

"Two dollars is what she's charging for those scarves," Mrs. Borman said under her breath as they exited, but Melody heard it. She refused to turn around and face Mrs. Haufbrau, whom she was sure had heard it, too.

"Here, Harriet," Melody said, unwrapping another of the scarves from its thin box and tissue. "See if you can drape it, there," she said, trying her best to ignore Mrs. Haufbrau, though she could feel the woman's beady eyes on her. "Mrs. Haufbrau, if you're not going to help us here, perhaps you could find something useful to do." She faced her nemesis. "Maybe unload the apples that were delivered yesterday."

"Well!" Mrs. Haufbrau drew herself up. "You can bet I'm not helping with that." She nodded at the window and retreated to the storeroom.

Melody watched her go and then turned back to Harriet, who gave her an uneasy smile.

"Come on, Harriet, we need to finish this." But before she could hand Harriet another box, the shop bell tinkled again. This time, however, it wasn't another housewife looking to buy shoelaces or a tin of coffee, but rather a young man dressed very dapperly in a blue checked windowpane suit. It was Wesley Elton. Melody hadn't seen him in years.

"That you, Melody?" His face lit up with a big smile as he removed his hat. "Heard you were back. My, aren't you all grown up?" He looked her up and down appreciatively.

"Well, you took your time coming over to say hello," she said, batting her eyelashes just a little. Not that she was, or ever had been, remotely interested in Wesley Elton—for one thing he was too short—but she couldn't help flirting. Just a little.

"Just got back from Milwaukee." He waved his hat. "Training to be an accounts manager over at the bank. I'm a teller now, you see, but I got big plans." He gave her a wink. "Nice of you to come help out," he said. "Not really your thing though, is it?"

Melody's eyes narrowed. "Why do you say that?"

"Well, if I remember right, you never set foot in this place if you could help it." His eyes flicked to Harriet, who was still trying to get the hats to stay perched on the hidden soup cans. When his gaze lingered for an extra second, an idea—a perfectly delicious idea—occurred.

"Do you know Harriet?" she asked.

"Don't think so." He studied Harriet again, who, at the sound of her name, looked up. "You a Mueller?"

"Yes." Harriet gave a hesitant smile. "How'd you know?"

"Got the look of the Muellers. Is Dale your brother?"

"My cousin." She went back to trying to arrange the hats.

"Ah! Used to fish with him sometimes. He moved, didn't he?"

"Yes. To La Crosse. When the mine closed. Got a job at the button factory."

"You're down in New Grimsby, aren't you? One of those tiny little mining cottages?"

Harriet gave an embarrassed little nod.

"Think I've met your mom, actually. Dale brought me round once. How's she doing?"

"Okay." Harriet twisted her hands. "Canning a lot," she murmured and then looked nervously at Melody.

An awkward silence followed, after which Wesley gave Harriet a dismissive smile before turning back to Melody. "So, how long you in town for?"

"I'm not really sure. Maybe until Fred comes home," she fibbed. She had no desire to share the details of her current predicament.

"Ah, yes. Old Fred. Where's he at now? Never hear from him."

"He's studying law at Harvard," Melody said distractedly, trying to think of a way to get the conversation between Wesley and Harriet to continue.

"Law, huh?" Wesley pursed his lips. "That's funny. I was always better at English than him, but I guess you never know, do you?" He smiled as he shrugged. "Now, *I* was blessed to be good at words *and* numbers, you see, so I went the numbers route. It's quite a bit more complex."

"Yes, I'm sure it is. Can we get you something?" Melody tilted her head toward the interior of the shop.

"Oh, yeah. How about . . ." He looked around. ". . . a paper."

"Sure thing. Harriet will ring you, won't you, Harriet?"

Harriet threw her a confused look, which Melody returned with a stern nod.

"Yes, of course," the girl said, making her way through the stacks of boxes to the edge of the window display.

"Here, let me help." Wesley offered his hand. Harriet took it and jumped down. "What's all this, anyway?"

"It's a new product line," Melody chirped. "A pretty hat or a pair of gloves would make a lovely present for your sweetheart."

Wesley grinned. "Don't have me a sweetheart. At the moment."

"What about your mother, then?" she asked, ignoring his suggestive look. "You could buy it for her for Christmas, before they sell out. How about one of these velvet hats?"

Wesley shifted and gave a false little laugh. "Don't know much about ladies' hats. Maybe a scarf, though. How much are they?"

Melody hesitated. "Only a dollar and a half."

Wesley nervously rubbed his chin. "A dollar and a half, huh?"

"Shouldn't be a problem for you, not with a big job at the bank, right? And you'd be the first in town to have one!"

"Well, if I'm the first," he said, his eyes looking her over again, "seems I should get a discount."

"Why, Mr. Elton!" she countered, determined not to be undone. "As the first, you should be paying a premium."

"Tell you what." He picked up a yellow scarf. "I'll be the first to buy one of your new things, but you've got to do something for me, then."

Melody was growing tired of this tête-à-tête, but she desperately wanted a sale. "Such as?"

"Go to the Harvest Fest with me." He handed Melody the scarf. "Then I'll buy it."

Melody blinked rapidly. "Well, that's so far away, Wesley. And anyway, I wouldn't possibly be able to leave the shop. But Harriet, here," she scrambled, "would love to go."

"What?" Harriet exclaimed. "But you said—"

"Not at all, Harriet! After your afternoon shift, I'm sure I can handle the shop."

"But, what about John?" she blurted before Melody could stop her.

"Who's John?" Wesley asked.

"I'm already going with John Schneider," Harriet said with what seemed to almost be defiance.

"The Schneiders out past Christmas Tree Hill?" he asked, wearing a look of surprise.

"Yes." Harriet crossed her arms.

Melody closed her eyes, trying to think. "I have an idea!" she said suddenly. "How about the four of us go? Harriet and I should be able to leave at four—the parade will long be over by then, and I'll have Mrs. Haufbrau close up. How about that?" She looked to both of them for approval. Harriet's expression was one of bewilderment, while Wesley was smiling broadly, like the cat who had finally caught the canary.

"That's fine," Wesley said, thrusting his thumbs in his waistcoat pocket.

"But, I don't think—" Harriet began, but Melody swiftly cut her off.

"No! It's all settled. Tell John to be here at four." Before anyone could argue further, Melody moved adroitly behind the counter. "That'll be a dollar sixty-five, with the paper. If you still want it, that is."

He grinned. "Of course I still want it."

Melody quickly rang him up, pushing down the appropriate buttons on the old hulking cash register, their numbers nearly worn off with use. While she waited for him to dig the money out of his wallet, she carefully folded the scarf, tucking it into its original mint-green box, and hoped she wasn't making a mistake by suggesting they all go. She probably shouldn't leave the shop in the hands of just Mrs. Haufbrau and Cal, but it was the only way to get Wesley and Harriet in close proximity. As for John Schneider, she would take care of *him*!

Wesley handed her the exact amount, which Melody hastily deposited in the register and then slammed the drawer shut.

"You'll stay for the bonfire after, right?" he said slyly. "That's the best part. Or are you too sophisticated for that now?"

"Well, you know I'd love to, Wesley," she managed to say sweetly, as she placed the scarf and a *Merriweather Herald* in a brown bag. "But I might have to go visit my father then."

He frowned. "That time of night?"

"Well, I'll see." She handed him the bag. "You just be here at four."

Wesley looked briefly at Harriet and then back at Melody. "I guess it's all settled then." He tipped his hat. "See you ladies later."

Melody gave him a little wave and, once he was back out on the street, let out a little cry of delight. Two birds killed with one stone! She turned to share her excitement with Harriet, but Harriet's face was dark.

"Oh, Melody! Why were you trying to get me to go with him when you knew I was going with John? I don't have the slightest interest in Wesley Elton!"

Melody was surprised by Harriet's tone, which was the closest she had ever heard to being one of anger. "Why not? He's perfect! He's just your height. He's a sharp dresser. And he's handsome. And he's got a good, solid job at the bank. That's saying a lot."

Harriet crossed her arms. "I think Wesley's more interested in *you*."

"Me?" Melody scoffed. "He'd never be interested in me. I'm just Fred Merriweather's little sister. And didn't you see the way he looked at you?"

"No," she said uneasily, "not really."

"Harriet! You're such a charming innocent. Don't worry. I'll be there with you. And!" She gestured widely at the window display. "We made our first sale!"

Harriet seemed unimpressed.

Melody sighed. This was certainly going to be harder than she thought.

"But I—" Harriet muttered.

"Was that Wesley Elton?" Mrs. Haufbrau huffed, making her way to the front of the store with a large basket of red apples.

"Yes, it was. And you'll never guess!" Melody beamed. "He bought a scarf!"

CHAPTER SIX

As it turned out, Wesley's purchase of a silk scarf was not the beginning of an avalanche of sales. In fact, his turned out to be the one and only the whole week. The rest of the products sat lonely in the window, waiting for someone else to take interest. Well, that wasn't exactly true. Plenty of people took interest, especially the town's young women, who paused, tempted, on the sidewalk in front of the display, but none of them ever came in and purchased anything.

Melody tried to remain hopeful, but in truth, she was beginning to despair of her current plan succeeding in saving the Merc.

Consequently, whenever she got the chance, she pored through Barnum's Supply catalog, looking for cheaper products she might order to make up the difference, but nothing stood out. Maybe slippers and robes for Christmas? Over and over, she recounted her last conversation with her father and tried to think of a way out. The Merc, he had said, had made the most money in recent times with illegal moonshine. It *was* too bad they couldn't go back to those days, she mused. Now, unfortunately, as Pops had stated, it was too plentiful and too cheap. But what if she could somehow make it different or unique? That seemed unlikely, though, given the fact that she didn't know the first thing about the brewing of moonshine. Nor did she even know where her father's old still was, though she had a sneaking suspicion it was probably hidden in the Merc's cellar.

The cellar, with its earthen floor and walls, had always seemed a mysterious cavern to the young Merriweather children, particularly to her and her brother, who longed to explore its many nooks and crannies . . . at least until Pops had told them it was full of giant spiders and even a bogeyman, which had been enough to quell their curiosity. She realized now that it had probably just been his way of preventing them from disrupting the operations of his still.

Melody listlessly closed the Barnum catalog. It was Sunday, but she had come in hoping she might be inspired without having to wait on customers or evade Mrs. Haufbrau's spying eyes. As predicted, Mums had complained. "On a Sunday? You're just like your father! Wanting to work every day of the week. Well, look where it got him, Melody! In the hospital with a heart attack!" In the end, however, Melody had convinced her that it would only be for a few hours, though that time had already passed very quickly with little to show for it. Her thoughts returned to the still. Perhaps she should explore the cellar now while she had the chance, though the prospect filled her with unexpected dread.

As children, she and Freddy had for the most part obeyed Pops's warnings about the cellar, but one summer afternoon, when she was just six, Freddy had dared her to go down. Melody had protested fiercely, saying that she was going to tattle on him for trying to get her to disobey the rules, but he trumped her by saying he would tell Mums that it had been she who had stolen a whole tin of cookies from the pantry, thereby turning what had started as a dare into blackmail. Faced with this new threat, Melody had proceeded down the rickety stairs, only to be rewarded for her bravery with the sight of a dead cat, rotting and stinking on the dirt floor. She had screamed and run back up the wooden planks of the stairs, colliding squarely with her father, who had in turn promptly punished Freddy for his prank. Freddy, amidst relentless tears, had repeatedly claimed—and still did to this day—that he had not known about the cat. Regardless, it was enough for Melody to never go down into the cellar ever again.

Melody stood abruptly. This was silly. She was *not* still afraid of the cellar! And, anyway, it would only take a few moments to see if there was a still down there or not.

Melody roughly pulled open the bottom drawer of her father's desk and rummaged for the flashlight. She quickly found it and slid its button forward, relieved when a beam of light erupted. So far, so good. Flashlight in hand, she marched toward the meat counter. The cellar door was cut into the floor right in front of it, which was why it was almost impossible to access during store hours, as customers were always standing on it as they waited for their meat to be wrapped.

Bending down, she dug the brass ring from its circular groove in the wood and pulled, lifting the door several inches before it slipped from her fingers and fell back down with a thud. It was heavier than she'd thought! Melody tried again, this time pulling with both hands, and managed to get it open. Shakily, she held it with one hand while she unfolded the plank of wood from the inside of the door that served as a brace. Carefully, she let go and silently cheered when the brace successfully held the door, albeit at an angle.

The smell of earth and mold hit her immediately as she peered into the dark hole. It was pitch-black. She shined the flashlight down into the darkness, but she could only see a small bit of the dirt floor at the bottom of the stairs. For a quick moment, she reconsidered her plan, but then, with fresh resolve, plugged her nose and gingerly stepped onto the first step. It creaked. She paused, waiting to see if it would hold, and then took another. There were no walls or railings to hold on to, and the steps themselves had no back risers. They groaned dangerously with every step as she wobbly tried to keep her balance.

When Melody finally reached the bottom stair, she stopped there to quickly shine the flashlight at every corner of the room, half expecting to see the dead cat. When she was sure that there was nothing—at least nothing in the open—she tentatively stepped off, annoyed that her pulse was racing faster than it ought. She spotted a lone bulb hanging from a cloth cord in the middle of the room and hurried to it, still holding her nose. With her flashlight hand she reached up and pulled the chain, praying that the light still worked. Miraculously, it did, and she let go of her nose, releasing the air she had been holding in her lungs, and looked around curiously. The room was big and cavernous, certainly, but not as big as she remembered.

There were barrels all along the far wall, filled with what looked like old apples or maybe hickory nuts. Dirty wooden crates and crockery jugs littered the floor. Her eyes darted to the room's corners, looking for the still, but she didn't immediately see it. She took a few steps forward, careful not to step on anything, especially anything living, say, a spider, or worse, a rat. As she got closer to one of the corners, she noticed a heap of metal tucked behind a row of barrels. Hoping that this might be it, she shined her flashlight on the hulk and indeed saw what could only be a still!

There was another lightbulb hanging here in the corner, so she pulled the chain and further illuminated the metal contraption in front of her. A big copper kettle with tubes sticking out of it was connected to other smaller, round containers and a row of dials. She rubbed the dust from one, revealing an arc of meaningless numbers and a lifeless needle, which lay at zero. She picked her way around it, inspecting it for any obvious damage, but there was none she could see. She wondered if it still worked. *Surely it must?* She would have to find someone who knew how to operate it. *But who?*

Lyle would have been a good one to ask, she suspected, but he was obviously out of the question now, being laid up as he was. Maybe Mr. Portzen or old Mr. Wareham? She tried to remember who had always been hanging around the Merc when she was a child, but she hadn't been here enough. Or when she had been, she wasn't cognizant enough to have paid much attention to who came and went. Probably everyone from her father's generation knew how to make moonshine, she considered, but who could she ask that wouldn't report her efforts back to her father? That was the other thing. If she did decide to brew moonshine, she didn't want Pops to know about her plan until she was successful, as he was sure to try and talk her out of it for one reason or another. It would have to be someone who—

There was a noise above her.

Melody froze, listening. It was footsteps, heavy. She was sure she had locked the front door. The footsteps, she could tell, were coming closer to the cellar. Whoever it was would be able to tell from the propped door that someone was below.

"Hello?" she called weakly. "We're closed."

"Who's down there?" shouted a male voice.

Before she could respond, the intruder pounded down the stairs, and Melody saw, with aggravating relief, that it was only Cal, gripping a baseball bat in a very threatening way. At the sight of her, his face went from menacing to merely exasperated. "What the hell are you doing down here?" he asked, lowering the bat.

"Me? What are you doing down here?" Melody put a hand on her chest, trying to quiet her pounding heart.

"I thought we were being burgled." He held up the bat.

"Well, why are you here in the first place? On a Sunday?"

"Sometimes I come in and clean the counter or get things ready for Monday. We're too busy on Monday mornings to do it properly."

Melody considered this. "Well, how did you get in?"

"I have a key. Though the front door was already unlocked."

"Does everyone have a key?" she asked, piqued, refusing to acknowledge her error.

"Everyone except Harriet, I guess. That's really only three of us." His eyes narrowed as he observed her more closely. "What are you wearing?"

Melody felt her cheeks grow warm. "They're trousers, if you must know."

"I can see that."

Melody couldn't tell if he approved or not. Probably not. "All the film stars are wearing them now." She gave her head a little toss. "Katharine Hepburn . . . Marlene Dietrich . . . ," she faltered, unable to think of any others on the spot.

"Well, I wouldn't say that was *all*, but you do as you like. You will anyway." His tone was dismissive.

"I could say the same for you, you know."

Cal's brow wrinkled. "Me?" he scoffed. He ran a hand through his hair, his eyes traveling up and down her again, and let out a deep breath. "Look, why are you down here, anyway? Planning to make some hooch?" He nodded at the dusty still.

"Actually, yes," she said with another toss of her hair.

Cal's bemused face immediately twisted into one of concern. "You're not serious."

"Yes, I am. I'm hoping it will bring in some extra cash."

"Like you've done with your scarves?" he added wryly.

"Look, if all you're going to do is stand around and tease me, you can go back upstairs. I know what I'm doing."

"Melody, listen." Cal took several steps closer and put a hand on her upper arm. Melody felt a little ripple of something, which she tried to ignore. Her eyes went to his hand, and he quickly removed it. "Making moonshine isn't a good idea," he said, thrusting his hands in his pockets. "It can be dangerous. If you don't do it right, you can kill people. It happens all the time. That's why there's a law against it now."

"Well, I'm very capable of learning. I just have to find someone to teach me. You wouldn't happen to know how, would you?"

"No, I don't, and I wouldn't tell you if I did." He looked at the still again and then back at her. "Does your father know you plan to do this?"

Melody gritted her teeth. "That's odd, for a moment I thought you were Mrs. Haufbrau. You sound just like her."

Cal rolled his eyes.

"*No*, he doesn't know, as a matter of fact."

"Then why are you doing this?"

"I have my reasons." She examined her nails.

"Is it money?" Cal's voice was low.

Melody looked up. In the partial glow of the basement light, his cheeks looked all the more chiseled. Likewise, he had not shaved this morning, so his face was covered with a thicker stubble than usual (*Did he not go to church?*), which vexingly made him all the more attractive.

Melody pulled her eyes away and considered lying, but in the moment, she couldn't think of a believable excuse. Why else would someone want to make moonshine? She let out a deep sigh and nodded. "I went to see Pops last week, and it seems that . . . well, that things aren't going so well."

"What do you mean?" Cal's dark eyes widened. "Is your father worse?"

"No, not that. Well, I'm not sure, actually," she murmured, thinking about his weary eyes and exhausted state. "I meant that the Merc's losing money, apparently, and I . . . I need to find a way to make up the difference," she said, deciding not to tell him the full extent of the situation. It was too embarrassing to admit that her uncle had lost all their money and then shot himself.

"And you thought that making moonshine would solve your problem?" he asked, his tone softer than she expected. He was looking at her in a way that was either pity or . . . or something else.

She shrugged. "Well, it worked before."

"Yeah, during Prohibition. But it's easy to buy cheap whiskey now," he said, maddeningly echoing her father.

"Yes, but maybe our homemade stuff can be better quality, something people might pay extra for." She hated how desperate her voice sounded.

Cal shook his head. "I don't think so. It's nothing special. And it takes a long time and a lot of experimenting to get something different and exceptional. It's more complicated than you think. You need a corn mash and malted barley and yeast, and then it takes several weeks to ferment and bottle. And it's easy to get it wrong and actually kill people, as I've said."

"Well, I have to do something!"

Cal looked around the cellar until his eyes fell upon the barrels along the wall. He stared at them for several moments. "Why don't you sell something easier to make?" he finally said, turning his attention back to her. A rare smile hovered.

"Like what?"

Cal walked over to one of the barrels of rotting apples. "What about cider?" He picked up a wrinkled apple. "It's perfect!"

"Why cider?"

"Cider is an old drink. It's what the miners used to drink before they had beer, even back in Cornwall—at least that's what my grandpa told me. He used to prefer it to beer, but it's hard to find unless you make it yourself."

"Do you need a still?"

"No, that's the beauty of it. As far as I know, it's pretty simple. And it would be cheap to make. Uncle Lyle might know."

"But would people buy it?"

Cal shrugged. "It's worth a try. You're not out much if it doesn't work. But it might sell. Especially with Christmas coming."

Melody wasn't sure.

"Tell you what. I'll run over to Lyle's today and ask him," Cal said. "See if he'll make a batch. Then we can test it and see." For once, his eyes were bright with something other than criticism. Melody barely recognized him.

"Why are you helping me?" she asked suspiciously.

He shrugged again. "Maybe because I don't want the Merc to go under any more than you do."

"I didn't think you cared. About the Merc, I mean," she added hastily.

"I *don't* care. Not for myself, anyway. But I *do* care for Uncle Lyle. This place is all he's got. And as soon as he's back on his feet, I can get back to my old job delivering lumber and then back to school."

"School?" Melody blinked. "You go to school? Where?"

The usual animosity returned to Cal's eyes. "*Yes*, I go to school," he said almost disgustedly. "Or I did, anyway. I was taking night classes at the University of Madison before Lyle got sick."

"You were?"

"Why do you look so surprised?" His brow furrowed. "Did you think you were the only one that had to give up something they loved? Or is it that you just didn't think I was capable of anything else?"

"I . . . why didn't you tell me?"

"You never asked." His eyes searched hers. "Look, I gotta go," he muttered, pulling his gaze away. "I'll get Lyle to start a batch of cider tonight, and you can see what you think." He made a move to leave, but then stopped. "You know, if you weren't always thinking about yourself, you might have time to learn more about the people who work for you. You know nothing about any of us. Doesn't that bother you?"

He didn't wait for an answer and instead charged across the room, inadvertently knocking the bulb before he jogged up the steps.

Melody stared after him, her heart pounding. Yes, of course she was bothered! By *him* in particular! She put her hand up to still the swinging bulb, fuming over who was worse—Mrs. Haufbrau or Cal.

They were each as bad as the other, she decided as she pulled the grimy chain to extinguish the light. One thing was for certain, she needed to write a long-overdue letter to Douglas as soon as she got home. She had neglected him for far too long. She would tell him how much she missed him, how she hoped she might return very soon.

She heard Cal above her pound across the floor and bang through the front door.

Yes, Douglas was *exactly* the person she needed right now, she told herself. Someone kind and agreeable and . . . well . . . even a bit worshipful. Someone the exact *opposite* of the boorishly critical Cal Fraiser.

CHAPTER
SEVEN

For the next two weeks, Melody was on pins and needles waiting for Cal to bring in a sample of cider. She was sorely tempted to ask him how the project was coming, but she refused to give him the satisfaction. He had not said a word to her in all of this time, which, considering that they worked not more than fifty feet apart, was ridiculous in the extreme. It proved what she had always suspected—that he was churlish, rude, and pretentious, not to mention pig-headed. And since, in her view, anyway, he had started their current icy impasse, she refused to speak first.

However, she *was* getting more desperate as the days ticked along and only one pair of calfskin gloves (the boring brown ones) and one scarf (a black one) had sold. At this rate, she would never make it back to Chicago!

Harriet, too, had been more reserved than usual, and though Melody would have loved to blame this on Cal as well, she was pretty sure Harriet's sullen attitude was more due to her rearrangement of the Harvest Fest plans. But it wasn't as if she had completely eliminated John from the equation, Melody argued with herself; she had merely added *to* it. Several times, she had tried to bring up Wesley in casual conversation, but her efforts had fallen flat. Honestly, no one appreciated her at all.

As she roughly swept the front of the shop, Melody decided that if Cal did not speak to her by the end of the day, she would have to break down and address him, if only to ask about the cider. For all she knew, he had abandoned the project entirely!

She was utterly surprised, then, when she turned, dustpan in one hand, broom in the other, to see him saunter up from the back carrying an old brown jug.

"There you are," he said, setting it on the counter with a thud. His tone was one of nonchalance, and there was a self-satisfied smile about his lips, which irritated Melody, despite the fact that she was seeing what could only be the cider! "Want to sample it?" he asked pleasantly, as if nothing in the world was wrong.

"That's it?" Melody exclaimed, setting down the dustpan and putting one hand on her hip. "That's all you have to say to me?"

Cal shot her a confused look. "What else do you *want* me to say?"

Melody pressed her lips together in frustration and repressed her urge to . . . to reprimand him . . . scold him . . . something! It would get her nowhere, though, she guessed, and she had to concentrate on what was most important—the cider! She glanced at the clock above the door. It was almost five, near enough to closing, and as good a time as any to break open the jug.

"Yes, let's sample it." She leaned the broom beside the candy jars. "I'll see if I can find some glasses. Mrs. Haufbrau!" she shouted toward the back. "Do you want to sample Cal's cider?"

Melody strode to the office, still trying to make sense of Cal's temperamentality and praying that the cider would be good enough to sell. She rummaged through her father's bottom desk drawer. Many a time, she had seen him throwing back a shot or two in his office. Sure enough, she managed to unearth several mismatched shot glasses. She carried them out to the counter where Cal and Harriet were waiting. Cal had uncorked the jug.

"What's all this?" Mrs. Haufbrau asked, coming up from the back as Cal began pouring the cider into the tiny glasses.

"It's cider. Lyle made it," Melody explained.

Mrs. Haufbrau's wrinkled brow wrinkled more.

"If it's good enough, we're going to sell it." Melody chanced a glance at the older woman.

"Sell it?"

Cal handed a glass to each of them and then took his own in hand and raised it in salute. He seemed happy, almost buoyant, and Melody felt an immediate reciprocal flutter of excitement, which annoyed her. What did she care what Cal Fraiser's mood was?

She raised her glass briefly and then took a sip. Then another. Melody was not all that familiar with cider, but this, she had to admit, was good. Better than good, really.

Cal downed his, and Harriet did too.

"I like it!" Melody announced, pouring herself some more.

"Me, too," Harriet agreed and held up her little glass.

"It's definitely good enough to sell, don't you think?" Melody excitedly asked the little group as she refilled Harriet's glass.

"It *is* good," Mrs. Haufbrau said, setting her still nearly full glass down, "but you can't sell this." She pushed the glass to the middle of the counter with just one finger, as if the liquid inside were poison, and then drew herself up stiffly.

"Why not?" Melody's brow knitted.

"You don't have a liquor license. And I'm certainly not going to do anything against the law."

Melody rolled her eyes. "We don't need a liquor license! Who's going to stop us? The police?" she scoffed, knowing, as everyone did, that Chief Meyers rarely left the station, and when he did, it was usually to waddle down the block to the Miner, the corner tap.

"It's a good point, Mrs. Haufbrau," Cal said diplomatically, "but I think we can get around it because it's a homemade item. And we're not actually *serving* it here."

Melody was impressed by this impromptu response, but Mrs. Haufbrau was not. "That doesn't make an ounce of sense, Cal Fraiser, and you know it. You don't fool me. Selling homemade cider is no different than selling homemade moonshine or hootch or whatever you want to call it, which is very much illegal."

"For God's sake, Mrs. Haufbrau, my father sold moonshine from this shop for years, and you know it!" Melody exclaimed.

"What he did or didn't do under the table or behind closed doors is none of my business. I, however, did not touch it. Just as I won't touch this."

"Well, given the fact that every cop in town, including the chief, bought moonshine from him in the past, I think we're safe selling what is basically fermented apple juice. We're selling it, and that's that." Melody looked quickly at Cal, but she couldn't decipher his expression. Admiration? Disapproval? Probably disapproval. *Oh, what did she care!*

Mrs. Haufbrau moved from behind the counter with stately grace. "Well, I, for one, will not." She pulled on her coat and tightly tied the belt. "I'll quit first."

"Do it, then," Melody blurted, her blood suddenly racing. She was tired of being bullied by Mrs. Haufbrau.

"One of these days, I just might, *Miss* Merriweather." Mrs. Haufbrau walked out of the shop, the bell tinkling wildly.

"Oh, no!" Harriet exclaimed. "Do you really think she'll quit?"

"No." Melody poured the three of them another glass of cider, wondering why the old crone had emphasized *Miss*. "Which is a shame. She's ridiculously tied to this place for some reason."

She gave Cal a sideways glance. As usual, his face was impassive.

"Look, let's forget about what Mrs. Haufbrau said for right now." Melody looked from one to the other. "We need to discuss how we're going to sell this. Any ideas?"

"Well, seems to me, we first need to figure out who's going to make it. Lyle can't manage a project this big. He's not strong enough." Cal ran a hand through his hair. "He made this as a favor, but that's it. And I'm guessing none of us have the time."

Melody drummed her fingers on the counter. It was true; none of them had time during the workday to brew it, and she couldn't expect any of them to do it on their own time in the evenings or on weekends. Perhaps she could have Helenka do it? No, she would protest, Melody knew, saying she had too much work already. And even if she *could* convince Helenka to do it, Mums would obviously find out, and then she was sure the whole thing would be shut down in one fell swoop, never mind Mrs. Haufbrau.

"My . . . my mother could do it," Harriet suggested tentatively. "She already makes her own cider. It's good."

"Is it as good as this?"

Harriet's eyes darted to Cal. "It's . . . it's better, I think. But that's just my opinion," she added hurriedly.

"Knowing your mom, I don't doubt it," Cal said ruefully. "But do you think she would be interested?"

"Probably," Harriet answered slowly. "You'd need to give her all the supplies, though."

"Well, yes, of course." Melody began to pace a little. "*And* I'd pay her." She turned to Cal. "How much do you think we could sell each jug for?"

"A dollar?"

"A dollar? Is that all?" Melody cried.

"Well, you can't price it too high. Start out low and get people interested. Then, if it gets popular, we can raise the price, especially going into the holiday season."

"And where are we going to get the apples? I don't think the Schneiders would have enough. Maybe they'd sell us a few more bushels, but that won't cover it."

"We could start with them and get more up north. I know a few orchards. There's a lot of big ones near Gays Mills." Cal turned his attention to Harriet. "What about twenty cents for every jug your mother makes? Would that be fair?"

Harriet's eyes opened wide. "Oh, yes! That's more than fair, I should think."

"Could she have some ready by the Harvest Fest?" Melody asked tentatively.

"In two weeks?" Harriet scrunched up her face, thinking. "I suppose so," she murmured. "I'll go ask her, should I?" She glanced at the clock. "She'll be expecting me back soon anyway."

"Alright, then," Melody said. "Fingers crossed that she'll say yes."

Harriet reached for her coat behind the counter and plopped on a floppy knitted hat, her chestnut curls sticking out haphazardly. "Oh, I think she will! See you tomorrow!" she called and hurried from the shop, the bell tinkling gently.

Cal turned to Melody. "She's a sweet kid, isn't she?"

"Yes . . . she is," Melody faltered, a bit confused by his choice of words and by the fact that he was even continuing the conversation at all.

"She's a real asset to the shop, isn't she? The customers really seem to like her." He poured himself another shot.

"Yes, they do." She studied him. He seemed oddly happy. Perhaps it was merely the success of the first batch. She smiled at him, pleased that, whatever the reason, they were getting along again and decided to ignore their recent standoff. "As a matter of fact," she confided, deciding on the spur of the moment to press her luck, "I've resolved to help her fall in love."

"Fall in love? Harriet?" His brow wrinkled. "Isn't she a little young?"

Melody's grin—and her hope that he would share her enthusiasm—vanished. "Young? She's eighteen!"

"Well, I guess I wouldn't know." He shrugged and disappointingly set his glass down. "I should get going, too."

"I . . ." she hesitated. "I guess I didn't thank you. For the cider." She picked up the jug and came around from behind the counter. "Here," she said, holding it out.

"Keep it."

"Are you sure?" She could never bring this home; Mums would have a fit.

Cal flipped his hair out of his eye. "Sure, I'm sure. I've got more at home. Lyle's first attempts."

"I'll save it for Harriet, then," she said reluctantly, forcing the cork back in it and setting it on the counter. "Well, anyway, thank you for . . . for helping me with all this."

Cal shrugged again. "Like I said. I don't want this place to go under."

"Think it will work? The cider, that is?" she asked, trying to resurrect his previous good mood and not wanting him to go just yet . . .

"Your guess is as good as mine. But, yeah, I think it stands a chance."

He turned to leave, but then paused, longer than seemed necessary, and Melody felt her pulse falter a little. She was standing so close to him that she could see a tiny scar on his right cheek and could almost feel his body humming with some unnamed tension. His eyes flicked to her lips for half a second before he pulled his gaze away. He shifted slightly. "Hey, I'm sorry about what I said in the cellar. It wasn't fair."

"Oh." Melody wasn't sure what to say.

"I was . . . I guess I was wondering—"

"Yes?" she asked eagerly.

The shop bell tinkled, startling them both, and they turned in unison to see Mrs. Ehlers enter.

"Oh, are you closed?" the woman asked, her eyes darting around the shop. She turned and looked behind her. "The sign still says open." She jabbed a thumb at the door.

Melody cleared her throat and took a step back from Cal. "Yes, we *are* closed, Mrs. Ehlers. I just forgot to switch the sign." Mrs. Haufbrau, having stomped off, had neglected her usual nightly duty. "But do come in. I'd be happy to help you."

CHAPTER
EIGHT

Melody couldn't help being nervous as she made her way down Ridge. The morning of the Harvest Fest had finally arrived, and she was filled with last-minute doubts. Harriet's mother had indeed agreed to make the cider and had managed to somehow produce twenty jugs, which was more than Melody had hoped for, but, still, now that it was the day of, she was suddenly worried it wouldn't be enough. After all, the Harvest Fest was one of the biggest days of the year for the Merc, with people coming in from all over the region, not just Merriweather.

Bunny and Mums had left early in the Daimler, the back seat and the floor laden with the pies Helenka had spent all of yesterday baking. Mums was in a fluster as to which tent she should occupy for the day, as she was, in truth, on half a dozen committees and felt a loyalty to each. Melody was pretty sure the Daughters of the American Revolution would win out, as that was her mother's particular favorite, though the Temperance League was a close second.

Melody always found her mother's participation in the Temperance League to be a bit hypocritical, as not only did Leola Merriweather enjoy an occasional glass of wine with dinner, but Pops, before his heart attack, anyway, had been known to down two shots of whiskey before bed each night for the whole of their married life. Not to mention his moonshine production on the side. Whether or not Mums had ever been aware of the still, Melody wasn't sure. All she knew was that her mother seemed to think that temperance did not apply to them, but that it should be encouraged amongst the poor, whose consumption of alcohol was akin to sinfulness, since not only did they not have the money to spend on such things, but overconsumption inevitably led to "joblessness, homelessness, general lawlessness, and depravity." Melody had more than once tried to argue against this faulty logic, but her mother was quite resolute.

As Melody turned down High Street, she could already smell the wood burning in the hog roasters, jointly manned by the Odd Fellows and the Knights of Columbus, who for this one day called a truce and worked together despite their extreme differences in philosophies. Big white tents had been erected overnight in Fountain Park, and already people from various clubs and organizations were scrambling to set up and display their wares, which included pies, candied apples, Cornish pasties, bread, knitwear and blankets, pottery, and pamphlets encouraging membership or salvation—or sometimes both. At the far end of the park, where patches of mist still hung in the morning air, the Elks were setting up the horseshoe tournament and the tug-of-war. Melody could hear the sharp ring of their hammers driving the metal stakes into the ground. Boy Scouts, meanwhile, were unfolding wooden chairs and placing them as best they could in straight or nearly straight rows on the uneven ground in front of the gazebo. As Melody hurried along, it was impossible not to get caught up in the excitement.

When she finally reached the Merc, she didn't immediately go in, but instead took a moment to stand in front of the big front window to give the new "Get Ready for Winter!" display a quick once-over. Given the fact that sales of her luxury items were almost nonexistent, she had considered switching the window back to its normal autumn display, but in the end had decided against it. Not only would she not be able to bear what she was sure would be Mrs. Haufbrau's self-satisfied smirks, but she hoped to sell a few of the items today, especially since people from outside of Merriweather would be strolling the streets. Besides, she could hardly display their new product in the window in plain brown jugs. No one would even know what it was.

Melody stepped inside and switched on the lights, giving the interior of the Merc a quick check. The window's previous items—mittens, boots, woolen blankets—had been moved to the back shelves, except the rakes, which were now leaning precariously in a front corner. Likewise, she had instructed Cal to move the barrel of polished apples to sit just inside the door, as well as the bushel baskets full of ripe pears, walnuts, and freshly dug potatoes. Mrs. Haufbrau had immediately complained that it made the front of the shop too crowded, but Melody had chosen to ignore her and had actually added to the congestion by placing several jugs of cider on the floor in front of the counter. On the shelves nearby, she had arranged more of the scarves and gloves, which had required her to move all of the soup and some of the tins of vegetables to the back, but what did that matter? Who would want to buy a can of barley soup or garden peas on a day like today?

Everything seemed in order. The candy jars were all fully stocked, the magazines crisp and standing at attention in their rack to the right of the cash register, and the floor swept. She set her handbag on the counter and withdrew a small bunting she had forced Bunny to help her make late last night from scraps found in Mums's sewing basket. Bunny had of course protested, saying that she had to catalog the pies, but Melody had insisted, reminding Bunny that she was the better seamstress. Together, they had created a rather charming little bunting in reds and oranges and yellows, some of them plaid, some plain, and a few of them polka-dot. Melody hurried now to tack it into place across the front counter before Mrs. Haufbrau arrived, since the woman was sure to criticize it for some reason. Too silly? Too cheerful? You could never tell.

Melody stood back to admire her handiwork and jumped when she heard none other than Mrs. Haufbrau—and what sounded like Cal?— come in through the back. She took a steadying breath and glanced at her wristwatch. It was almost time. Already, people were beginning to mill outside, looking at the display while they waited for the shop to open. Melody offered up one last prayer that today would be a success.

With only one minute to eight, she decided it was time, and, smoothing her apron, moved toward the door to switch the sign, but Mrs. Haufbrau intercepted her.

"I'll get it! And where's Harriet? You need to rein that one in a little," Mrs. Haufbrau advised over her shoulder as she flipped the sign. "She never tried that when your father was here."

Melody bit back a retort and instead smiled at the customers as they began hurrying in, eager to make last-minute purchases before the festivities began. She had hoped, after seeing them take note of the items in the window, that they might browse the front shelves displaying the hats and scarves, but they did not even give them a second glance and instead marched straight back to the meat counter. Melody tried not to be discouraged. Where *was* Harriet?

A faint worry entered Melody's mind, then, that perhaps Harriet would dodge today as a way of avoiding the arranged double date, but Melody quickly quashed that as impossible. For one thing, Harriet had never once, as far as she knew, missed a day of work. And secondly, she was pretty sure that Harriet would not miss the chance to be with John Schneider, even if it meant being in the company of herself and Wesley.

Melody repressed a sigh and rang up Mr. Dixon. She supposed she really *should* have words with Harriet, she mused, if only to stop Mrs. Haufbrau's complaints, but just then Harriet bustled in, looking very red about the face, as if she had been running.

"I'm sorry, Melody!" she murmured as she shrugged out of her coat and tied on her apron. "Mr. Thomas's cows got into our garden again, and I had to help Mom get them out before they ate all the corn. Oh, hello, Mrs. Cole, can I help you?" she asked the woman who approached the counter.

For the rest of the morning, people crowded into the Merc to buy newspapers, cigarettes, apples, candy, crackers, and other small sundries. They were certainly ringing up sales, but, Melody noted wearily, they had yet to sell a single luxury scarf or hat or pair of gloves. And they had only sold two jugs of cider.

Every once in a while, Melody would suggest one of the luxury items while ringing up a customer, but they always said the same thing: "Too rich for my blood!" And she positively cringed when she heard Mrs. Koenig say to Mrs. Owens on their way out, "What's Lou Merriweather thinkin', sellin' stuff like that? Must be trying to pay his medical bills. Well, who'd buy that rubbish? For a dollar fifty? Criminal, that is."

Likewise, when she suggested the cider, most housewives turned up their noses, and most men shook their heads. "Cider is it?" Mr. Weston asked, scratching his head. "Thought it might be corn oil. Nah, don't want to carry that big jug around all day, Melody. Maybe some other time." Annoyingly, it was only Imogene, when she suddenly appeared at the counter midday, who correctly identified the contents of the jugs without being prompted. Melody had not seen her come in.

"Oh, hello, Melody. Came down for a few minutes to see the sights. Mother's dozing right now. She does nod off more and more these days. Selling moonshine?" She nodded at the jug nearest the register. "Or is it cider? Father had a jug just like that 'fore he died. Still have it somewhere, I think. I should look to see if anything is left in it. A drop of that might help Mother. Her toes do ache her so. And no wonder—all crippled up, they are. Can't bend 'em to save her life. I tried once to straighten them, but you should have heard her scream. Bloody murder, you'd a thought. And then there's her back. Permanent crick in it, she says. Can't move it too well. And usually her right shoulder. But that's just in the mornings. Yes, I just might do that. Might go look for that jug. Gotta be somewhere—couldn't have just disappeared."

Melody sighed. "Is there something I can get you, Imogene?" Melody tried to keep her voice friendly, but this was not the time for idle chit-chat. The Merc was packed with people.

"Get me? Oh, no!" She let out a little laugh that sounded more like a cough. "Heavens no. I just came down to check on the soaps. See if any sold. Might need to refresh the stock, you see. I've loads more upstairs. I've even tried a few new scents. I tried oatmeal, but that didn't work so good. It all just crumbled. I also tried coneflower, seeing as there's so many of those around, but it wasn't a pleasant scent. Smelled kind of like weeds mixed with cat urine, really. But I'm on to a new one—pinecone." She took a quick breath. "Have you sold any? Any at all?"

Melody blinked after this barrage, unprepared for the question at the end. She was almost sure they had not sold any of Imogene's soaps, but she glanced sideways at Harriet for confirmation. Harriet gave her head a quick shake.

"No, not yet, Imogene," Melody answered. "I'll let you know when—if—we ever need more." As much as she wanted to say 'I told you so,' she refrained, sadly knowing all too well what it felt like to have a failed product.

Imogene's eager face crumpled. "I see. Yes, I see." She looked about to say something more, but Melody cut her off.

"If that's all, then, Imogene, I'll take the next customer." She made a point of looking beyond Imogene to Miss Yates, who was waiting patiently.

Imogene turned and saw the line that had formed behind her and quickly stepped aside. "Oh, my! Yes, I'm holding up the line. So stupid of me. But, then, I'm always doing stupid things. That's what Mother always says. No, I'll be going." Despite this farewell, however, she still hovered near the counter, wringing her hands, as if not knowing what to say or do next. Melody looked up briefly to give Imogene a forced smile and then turned her attention back to Miss Yates. When Melody looked up again, Imogene was gone. She did feel bad for the woman, but, she told herself resolutely, there was nothing she could do.

The Merc remained crowded until around three o'clock, when people began clearing to line the streets for the parade. Exhausted, Melody took advantage of the lull and grabbed an apple from the barrel. They had been so busy that none of them had had time to eat lunch. She took a big bite as she propped open both front doors so that they might be able to at least hear some of the parade. As children, she and Freddy and Bunny had always looked forward to this part of the Harvest Fest the most.

"Why don't you both quickly eat?" Melody suggested to Mrs. Haufbrau and Harriet. "We can watch the parade while we do."

Harriet eagerly reached for her lunch pail and pulled out her thin egg sandwich, the same thing she ate every day, but Mrs. Haufbrau did not follow suit.

"We should restock while we have the chance," Mrs. Haufbrau chastised and started straightening the magazines.

"We can do that later, Mrs. Haufbrau! Can't you ever just appreciate anything?" Melody called over her shoulder. She could hear trumpets coming from the far end of High Street as well as the rat-a-tat-tat of drums. "Cal!" she shouted. "Come see the parade!"

"I've got to restock the case!" he called back. Melody gritted her teeth. Well, she and Harriet would watch it, even if the other two had no wish to. Who could help being in a cheerful mood when a marching band was passing!

The Merriweather Marching Band was playing "Stars and Stripes Forever," and they were followed by the Drum and Bugle Corp, which had traveled down from Dodgeville. At the sound of "The Battle Hymn of the Republic," Melody's spirits soared a little. She glanced over at Harriet and was pleased to see the big smile on her face. At least Harriet was enjoying it as much as she was, and for a brief second, she wished Harriet was her sister instead of the annoying Bunny.

It was a fairly long parade, with several bands, a few tractors, representatives from most of the town's churches and clubs riding in horse-drawn carts, as well as a troupe of acrobats who had come all the way from Green Bay. Melody thrilled at the sight of them doing cartwheels and flips and somersaults in their red-and-black uniforms! All too soon, however, it was over. The town firetruck rumbled by finally, bringing up the rear, its siren wailing mournfully.

With a little sigh, Melody turned back to the Merc. Now that the parade was finished, people would be crowding toward the gazebo, where the mayor would give a speech and then the Merriweather band would perform more songs. Following that would be the tug-of-war, hayrides, and then later the bonfire out by Dalsing's farm, which, once she was older and in high school, had replaced the parade as the Harvest Fest event she looked forward to the most.

At the thought of it, Melody glanced at the big black clock above the door. It was going on four already! Both Wesley and John Schneider should be here any minute, and she and Harriet needed to be ready! She instinctively looked around for Harriet, but, to her surprise, the girl was nowhere in sight.

"Do you know where Harriet went?" Melody called to Mrs. Haufbrau, who was busy ringing someone up at the back counter.

"I think she's in the storeroom," Mrs. Haufbrau replied, though she kept her eyes on her task. Melody had yet to inform the older woman that she wanted her to manage the Merc while she herself sauntered around the Fest with Harriet, Wesley, and John. She had been dreading mentioning it all week, but she was going to have to do it sooner than later. It was nearly time to go! But, she considered, perhaps she was worrying for nothing. Perhaps Mrs. Haufbrau would relish being in charge. And, anyway, it wasn't as if Melody was going to *enjoy* herself, trying to distract John Schneider while Wesley and Harriet got to know each other better. If Harriet would only give Wesley a chance, Melody mused for the hundredth time, she was convinced that Harriet would fairly quickly see the advantage of choosing him over John Schneider.

"Oh, hello, Mrs. Schaffer," Melody said distractedly to the woman who had just set her shopping basket on the counter. "Enjoying the Fest?"

"Oh, yes!" the woman exclaimed. "Such a good day for it. I think we must have set a record today. Don't ever remember this many people. Think half of 'em must be from Dodgeville."

"Probably." Melody moved behind the counter and absently rang up Mrs. Schaffer's items, all the while keeping an anxious eye on the door. *Where was Wesley? And more importantly, where was Harriet?* "You staying for the music?" Melody asked.

"That's my favorite part! Me and Bob go every Friday to the Avalon to hear the numbers."

Melody was considering whether Mrs. Schaffer might therefore be a good candidate for the purchase of a new pair of gloves or even a jug of cider when Wesley Elton strolled through the door. He was dressed smartly in a light blue serge suit, complete with a sporty new boater's hat, and he looked every part the dashing hero.

"Here you are, Mrs. Schaffer." Melody hurriedly handed her several packages. "Enjoy the rest of the day."

"Oh, I will!" the woman called out as she stepped around Wesley, who was surveying the shop, hat in hand now. "Say hello to your poor father for me."

Melody waited until the woman had exited and then shouted "Harriet!" toward the back of the store.

Wesley grinned, lazily twirling his hat. "Hello, Melody. How's the Fest going?"

"Busy." She tried to smile. "Harriet will be here in a minute. I don't know where she got herself off to."

"Where's Schneider?" he asked, peering around.

"He isn't here yet. Harriet!" she called and then turned quickly back to Wesley, who was still grinning like a Cheshire cat.

"Did you catch the parade?" he asked.

"Yes, most of it."

"You're staying for the bonfire, right?"

Melody was thankfully spared from answering by the sudden appearance of Harriet, dressed in a pretty, yellow shirtwaist dress with a tiny floral print. Melody was impressed by her effort. And, if she wasn't mistaken, she thought she saw Wesley's eyes light up a little bit, too. Harriet put her arms awkwardly behind her back.

"Don't you look nice, Harriet!" Melody exclaimed.

"Is John here?" she asked eagerly, looking past Wesley.

"Not yet, but—"

"Well, I'll be off now," Mrs. Haufbrau said, suddenly appearing beside Melody, startling her.

"Oh! Mrs. Haufbrau! I didn't see you there." Her brow creased. "But why are you wearing your coat? Are you going somewhere?"

Mrs. Haufbrau's eyes narrowed. "I'm going over to the Methodist church."

"Right now?"

"Yes. I'm in the women's choir," she said, as if this explained everything.

Melody stared at her blankly. "What does that have to do with anything?"

"I *did* tell you, you know," she said matter-of-factly, drawing herself up. "We perform every Harvest Fest. We raise money for the orphans in Mozambique."

"But . . . but you can't just leave!"

"I do every year. Your father always let me leave early on Harvest Fest day. I *did* remind you, though I did suspect—rightly, it seems—that you weren't listening, which is not my fault."

Melody racked her brain trying to remember this conversation. She was sure Mrs. Haufbrau had not mentioned it. "Well, I was just about to leave with Harriet!"

Mrs. Haufbrau raised her eyebrows. "Well, seems you're going to have to change your plans, seeing as *you're* in charge, as you like to remind us every blessed day of the week. So, here you are. Be in charge." She glanced at Harriet for confirmation, but Harriet just stared, her mouth slightly open. "Well, anyway," continued the older woman, "I have to get on, or I'll be late."

She marched stiffly out the front door, the shop bell tinkling wildly.

"I'll stay and help," Harriet insisted. "I'll explain everything to John when he turns up. You don't mind, do you, Mr. Elton? Or better yet, you two go, and I'll handle the shop," she suggested. "I'll be fine. And Cal's in the back."

Stunned by this unexpected turn of events, Melody's mind was reeling. How dare Mrs. Haufbrau! But she couldn't waste time thinking about that! She needed to fix this quickly unraveling situation . . .

"Don't be silly, Harriet," she said with forced calm. "Mrs. Haufbrau is right. It should be me that stays. You and Wesley go on, and when John shows up, I'll tell him to go find you."

"But maybe we should wait for him?" Harriet looked unconvinced, as did Wesley, truth be told.

Melody glanced at the clock. She didn't want to risk John turning up before Wesley had a chance to be alone with Harriet. "It's already almost four thirty! Perhaps he isn't coming after all. Are you sure he said he'd come?"

Harriet blinked. "Well, yes. I'm pretty sure. Can't we just wait a little longer?"

"No, he probably got tied up with something. Some farm stuff. You two go on. If he turns up, I'll send him on," Melody said in her cheeriest voice. "And I'll slip out to the bonfire if I can."

"But what about the evening rush?" Harriet pleaded.

"I'm sure I'll be fine. And, anyway, Cal's in the back, as you say. Go on!" Melody gestured eagerly at the door. "Enjoy yourselves!"

"Well . . . " Harriet looked at Wesley apprehensively. "I guess . . . "

Wesley reluctantly held out his arm to Harriet. "Shall we, Miss Mueller?"

Melody watched them go, ignoring Wesley's frown at her on the way out and allowing herself to bask in a brief moment of triumph before it was replaced by a sudden feeling of panic when she observed that a small crowd of customers had somehow accumulated at the front of the shop. How *was* she going to manage the Merc on her own?

"Could you hurry a bit, Melody?" asked a man at the counter. "The band is gonna be startin' soon, and I don't want to miss it." Several others in line grumbled as well. One woman toward the back set her basket down on the floor and walked out. Melody's stomach clenched. They could not afford to lose any customers!

"Yes! I'll hurry. It won't take but a minute." She quickly rang up the man but fumbled to get everything bagged quickly.

Another person walked out.

"Cal!" Melody shouted frantically. "Cal!" she called again when there was no answer.

"Yeah?" came a responding shout, finally.

"Could you come up front, please?" She hurriedly rang up the next person, who thankfully only had a few items.

Cal appeared, his hands on his hips. "Yeah?"

"I need you to help me here at the counter." She didn't look at him, guessing that he was probably scowling. "Now, please," she said, throwing him a quick glance.

He made no effort to hide his annoyance as he slowly removed his bloodstained apron and stepped behind the counter. "Hello, Mr. Tierney," he said politely to the man Melody was ringing up. "Enjoying the Fest?"

"Sure am! The band'll be startin' in a minute, though, and I need to get over there before the missus gets upset. I only came in for a few things. And a pack of Camels." He nodded at the packs of cigarettes displayed neatly beside the candy jars.

Cal reached behind him and pulled out a pack. "Who won horseshoes?" he asked, plopping them in a bag along with a bottle of aspirin, a *Saturday Evening Post*, and three Hershey bars.

"For the kids," Mr. Tierney said sheepishly, nodding at the candy. "Merle Koenig won again this year."

"That'll be $2.47," Melody announced.

Mr. Tierney laid the exact amount on the counter, stuffed the bag under his arm, and hurried out. "Be seein' ya!" he shouted over his shoulder.

Melody quickly turned her attention to the next customer, and the next and the next, Cal faithfully attending her, until finally the shop was empty, at least for the moment. Melody took a step back and let out a deep breath.

"Thanks." She shot Cal a brief smile. "I guess we're lucky no one wanted any meat."

"Where's Mrs. Haufbrau and Harriet?" he asked, perplexed.

"Mrs. Haufbrau's off singing in the choir." Melody gave a little shrug. "Apparently she does this every year, but she neglected to tell me."

"Well, where's Harriet, then?" He crossed his arms. Melody did not fail to notice that his shirt sleeves were rolled up, the hair on his muscled forearms exposed. She pulled her eyes away.

"I . . . I let her leave early."

"You let her leave early? On one of our busiest days? Why?"

"Well, I didn't think it would matter so much, not with Mrs. Haufbrau here. She's more than efficient." Melody was saved from having to elaborate further, however, when the bell tinkled, and none other than John Schneider entered.

For a moment, Melody didn't recognize him. Gone was his usual old brown coat, and his dirty overalls had been replaced by nice trousers, along with an argyle wool vest and a dark green jacket. With his broad shoulders and blond curls, he looked rather handsome. More than handsome.

"Hello, Miss Merriweather, Cal. Is . . . is Harriet here?" His eyes darted nervously around the shop, and he shifted awkwardly.

"As a matter of fact, John, you just missed her," Melody said pertly.

"She already left? I know I'm a little late. We had a breech birth, you see, but—" He removed his cap and began twisting it.

"Yes, well, there was a bit of a mix-up, really. Truth is, I was hoping to join the two of you at the Fest with Wesley Elton. Do you know him?" she asked. "From the bank?"

John shook his head slightly, clearly still confused.

"Well, anyway, Harriet and I thought it would be terrifically fun to double up, but it seems I'm stuck here now. And since you didn't show up, we saw no other option but for the two of them to go. Together, that is." She tried to keep the delicious delight out of her voice, but it was hard. This was just the sort of thing that would have been an absolute scream back at Mundelein with the gang! But the look on John's face now was not one of silly, faux disappointment—such as Charlie or even Douglas would have sported in this situation—but one of true hurt. His cheeks were bright red, and he swallowed hard.

Suddenly, Melody felt a twinge of regret. But, she quickly argued with herself, it wasn't *her* fault that Mrs. Haufbrau had left, nor was it her fault that John had been late. And besides, it really was for his own good that he not labor under any delusions. Harriet wasn't right for him, and the sooner he realized this, the less hurt he would be in the long run. It was hard to be the voice of reason, but someone had to do it.

"Well, I'm sure you can find them if you go look," she offered.

John did not answer, just gave a slight nod and pulled his cap on as he moved toward the door.

"Hey, John!" Cal called.

John paused, his hand on the doorknob, and looked over his shoulder.

"The cheese you brought in last week is good. We've already almost sold it all. Thought I'd tell you."

John gave a nod, accompanied by a weak smile, and then stepped out. He seemed to hesitate once outside before finally meandering to the right.

"What's this about you and Wesley tagging along?" Cal asked. "Whose idea was that?"

Melody twisted a lock of her hair. "Well, it was just an idea. I thought . . . Look, it was the only way that I could think of to get the two of them together."

"John and Harriet? They were already going together. Harriet told me."

"No! I mean *Wesley* and Harriet." She blinked several times. "You must see how perfect they'd be."

"No, I don't." He raised an eyebrow. "Is this what you meant by helping Harriet to fall in love?"

"Yes." Melody tossed the lock of hair she had been twirling. "If you must know, I'm doing Harriet a favor. It's obvious John Schneider isn't for her, but she's too young and innocent to see it. She'll only get her heart broken."

"What would you know about it?"

"More than *you*."

"Do you know anything about John Schneider? He's solid."

Melody wasn't sure what that had to do with anything. "Well, Harriet doesn't want to marry a farmer."

"Why not?"

"You wouldn't understand."

Cal continued to stare at her for several uncomfortable moments. "I hope you know what you're doing," he said finally. "Seems to me Harriet and John were fine on their own." He grabbed his apron from under the counter where he had shoved it earlier. "I don't think you need me up here anymore; I'm going back to the meat counter where I belong."

"You can't just abandon me up here!" Melody called. New customers had started filing in.

"Well, I am."

"How . . . how dare you!"

"Go ahead and dare me," he shouted. "See where that gets you."

CHAPTER NINE

"Go on and dare me!" Wesley held up his half-empty beer glass. "Dare me to drink the rest of this in one go."

"I don't know if I should, Mr. Elton. I think you've already had enough," Harriet said uneasily. After quickly perusing all the booths, they had ended up in the very crowded beer tent, located at the far northern end of the park. The makeshift bar, sagging slightly in the middle, consisted of two-by-twelve planks of lumber laid on top of barrels.

"*Wesley!* How many times do I have to tell you?" Wesley rolled his eyes. "Call me Wesley. Please. I hate being called Mr. Elton. It reminds me of my father," he slurred. "Or the bank."

Harriet rubbed her arm and wondered, not for the first time today, if this was all a big mistake. "I'm sorry. Wesley."

Wesley downed the last of his beer and held the empty glass up. "Told ya."

Harriet wasn't sure what to say. Should she congratulate him? "Perhaps we should get a seat before they're all gone?" she urged. He was already trying to flag down a bartender for another. "Or maybe I should go and save you a seat?" Harriet suggested, a faint hope rising that he might become so inebriated by the time the band started that he would simply remain in the tent. Then she would be free to look for John . . .

Wesley squinted at her, and for a moment, he looked as if he was considering her suggestion, but then he pulled at his lapels and held out his arm. "No, I wouldn't think of deserting you," he slurred with a slight hiccup. "Where are my manners? And of course I want to hear the music. Let's go."

He smiled at her in such an attractive way that it confused her. He seemed bent on entertaining her, impressing her, but she couldn't figure out why, especially since Wesley had seemed more interested in taking Melody than her. Which made sense. Why *would* someone like Wesley Elton be interested in her—plain ole Harriet? But Melody had been insistent. And, Harriet had to admit, Melody knew more about such things than she did.

She glanced at Wesley, trying to assess him anew. She supposed he might be considered handsome with his ginger hair and trim mustache. His suit, likewise, was very fine indeed. It must have cost a fortune, not to mention the gold wristwatch he wore.

She looked around again for John, but he was nowhere in sight. It was so unlike him to be late. *Had something happened to him? Or had he simply changed his mind?* Worried, Harriet gripped Wesley's arm tighter, and he, possibly mistaking her meaning, smiled down at her.

Wesley led her back down the row of booths and stopped at the one at the end, where a big kettle was sitting atop a fire. A man stood beside it, mixing popcorn and a thick syrupy substance with a big wooden paddle.

"Would you like some caramel corn?" Wesley asked.

Harriet smiled and nodded. He had already bought her an ice cream earlier. *And* a hot dog. She felt positively spoiled in that regard. Her mother had often told her that the way to a man's heart was through his stomach, but Harriet was rather of the opinion that this should apply to the fairer sex as well.

"One, please." Wesley held up his finger at the woman manning the booth, and she handed him a white paper bag full of popped sugary corn. Wesley fished in his pocket for some change and laid it on the red-checked tablecloth.

"Here you are." Wesley held the bag out, and Harriet took a couple of kernels. Caramel corn was one of her favorites, truth be told. Her mother often made it on cold winter nights.

"Thank you, Wesley," she said with genuine gratefulness. He was beginning to grow on her a bit. "You've been very kind."

"You're welcome. Any friend of Melody's is certainly a friend of mine."

Unsure as to how to interpret this comment, Harriet was trying to think of something to say when she spotted Kate, of all people, standing not far from the gazebo.

"Kate!" she called, waving. "I'll just go say hello," she said to Wesley, squeezing through the crowd.

Kate had set up her own version of a booth by taking two chairs—which looked suspiciously like the ones in front of the gazebo—and placing a rough-hewn board atop them. Upon the board was draped a braided rug, and on top of that were several interesting-looking baskets.

"You made it!" Harriet surveyed the wares before her. "Have you sold any?

"Only two. But better than nothing." Kate's eyes darted to Wesley, who had come up behind Harriet. "Where's John?" she asked bluntly.

"Well, I . . . I wouldn't know," Harriet faltered. "He was late, so . . . " She chanced a glance at Wesley, who did not look amused. "This is Wesley Elton. From the bank. This is my friend, Kate."

"Charmed," Wesley said with a false smile.

Kate did not respond besides giving him a dismissive once-over. "Well, I guess this explains why I saw John wandering around before like a lost sheep."

Harriet pulled her gaze away from Kate's accusing stare, disturbed by the thought of John as a lost sheep and angry at her friend for using an image she knew would be upsetting. It wasn't fair! *She* was the one who had been abandoned! Still, she couldn't help glancing guiltily around the park.

"We should probably get going," Wesley said stiffly, reaching for Harriet's arm. "The music is going to start soon, and you look busy here with your . . . " Wesley looked dismissively at the baskets lined up haphazardly. " . . . artifacts."

"Want us to save you a seat?" Harriet asked weakly.

Kate raised an eyebrow. "No, you two go on. I'm sure you have a *lot* in common and, therefore, endless things to talk about. And I need to stay here." She pulled the woven Indian blanket draped around her shoulders a little tighter.

"You a real Indian?" a little boy interrupted before Wesley and Harriet moved away. He had pushed his way in front of them, a sticky lollipop in hand.

A man hurried up behind him.

"Willie! Mind your manners!"

"Well, are you?" the boy asked, ignoring the man, whom Harriet guessed to be his father.

"As a matter of fact, I am," Kate said majestically.

"Are you really?" the man asked. "What tribe?"

"The Sauk."

"Up near Prairie Du Chien way?"

Kate gave a stiff nod.

"You don't say! What's all this?" He surveyed the goods. "Baskets? Did you make them?"

"Do you have any scalps for sale?" the boy asked, looking under the board.

"William! That's quite enough, young man."

"Aw! But I want to know, Father!"

"How much are they? The baskets, I mean?"

"Three dollars."

"Three, eh?" The man rubbed his chin. "That's a bit steep."

Kate remained unmoved.

"Think Mama would like one?" he asked the little boy.

The boy shrugged, clearly uninterested at this point.

"Alright then." He pulled a black leather wallet from his inner pocket. Opening it, he extracted three one-dollar bills and handed them to Kate, who shoved them into her dress pocket.

"Which one should we choose?" the man asked the boy, but the little boy merely shrugged again and ran off.

"I'll take this one," the man said, picking up a sage-and-gold one before hurrying off through the crowd after the boy.

"Three dollars!" Harriet exclaimed. "Is that what you're charging for each of these?"

"It depends on how much they can afford."

"Well, how do you know what they can afford?"

"I can tell by their clothes. Also, by the fact that the boy had a lollipop *and* a bag of popcorn, and the father had a gold watch fob."

"She's good!" Wesley said, as if Kate were some sort of carnival act.

"Yes, but I'm not the only one who's good at fooling people." She stared at Harriet. "Especially themselves."

Harriet looked away and gripped Wesley's arm tighter. "I think we should go, Wesley, or we'll never get a seat."

Wesley tipped his hat to Kate. "Miss . . ."

"It's just Kate. Or Indian Kate if you prefer."

"Kate, then," he said dismissively and led Harriet away. "Friend of yours, did you say?"

"Yes, she is." Harriet looked over her shoulder at Kate, who was still staring at her. "You mustn't mind her, though." She turned back to Wesley. "She's just a bit rough around the edges. She doesn't mean anything by it."

"Oh, I don't mind. I've met her type before."

Her type?

"Anyway, she seems quite protective of you," he said appreciatively. "As is Melody, which suggests that you are indeed something quite special."

Harriet felt her face flush. "I'm not sure about that."

He brushed her cheek with his knuckle. Something about Wesley had changed. Was it the mention of John Schneider? "You're quite pretty you know, Harriet," he said seriously and then broke into a grin, as if he were teasing. *Was* he teasing?

The only two vacant seats were in the very middle of a row toward the back. Wesley squeezed them along, Harriet apologizing to each person they disrupted as they went. Finally, they were able to plop down on two wobbly chairs. Wesley slung his arm across the back of Harriet's and helped himself to some of her caramel corn, popping it into his mouth.

"What time does the Merc close?" he asked.

"Well, normally, it closes at five." She picked up a few pieces of popcorn herself. "But it stays open until seven tonight. You know, for the Fest. We always get people coming in after the music on their way home."

"Shame Melody has to stay, isn't it?"

"Yes, I wish she would have let me stay and help. Not that I'm not enjoying myself!" she added hurriedly. "I really am. I just feel bad for her is all."

"Yes, she seems very dedicated."

"Oh, she is! She's marvelous!"

"Yes, isn't she? I'm surprised she isn't attached. Engaged, I mean. A girl like her."

"Yes, I suppose you're right," Harriet mused. "Though I do think she's mentioned someone back in Chicago."

Wesley's face tightened. "Chicago, eh?" He looked away briefly and then back at her, a grin creeping across his face. "Well, Chicago's a long way off, isn't it?" The hand of the arm draped across the back of her chair patted her shoulder. "He's there, and we're here, aren't we?"

Harriet blushed again. "Yes, and she's so busy with the Merc. I guess she doesn't have time to think of herself. With her father being ill and all that. She's very selfless. I wish there was more I could do."

The music started then, and Harriet turned to watch the band, who were beginning with a thrilling march. Strings of electric lights had been strung up all over Fountain Park, zigzagging over the tops of the booths and across the gazebo as well, and they glowed brighter now as the sun began to set. It was glorious to be here! She wished her mother could see it all; it was like the fairy villages she was always describing. Harriet had tried to persuade her to come, but Rosemary had insisted on staying behind, saying that fests weren't for her. But it was all so lovely and delicious—so romantic!

A stray thought of John came unexpectedly to mind then, and she instinctively looked around the crowd for him one more time. But he was nowhere in sight. Maybe he hadn't actually been late but had instead changed his mind about going with her and hadn't been man enough to tell her, she mused. Kate's irritating description of him looking like a lost sheep resurrected, but she quickly quelled it. Surely, Kate had been exaggerating.

Harriet glanced at Wesley, sitting solidly beside her, and she did not pull away when she felt his arm go around her a little tighter. Maybe Melody was right; maybe John *wasn't* for her.

Wesley's face relaxed into a smile. A real smile. He leaned in close, so close that she could smell his delightful cologne, which, in truth, caused her pulse to speed up a little. "I wish there was more I could do, too," he whispered. "If there's any little thing I might do to be of service to Melody—or to you, of course—you'll let me know, won't you?"

"Shh!" said a woman in front of them, turning sharply around.

Horrified, Harriet returned her attention to the music and was quickly drawn back into it, her heart fluttering along with the flutes.

She clapped loudly when the first piece ended and was surprised when Wesley leaned close again and whispered, "Let's go."

Harriet's light heart suddenly deflated. She was enjoying the music and didn't want to leave, but neither did she wish to disappoint Wesley, so she obediently began to gingerly make her way down the row, whispering "Excuse me, excuse me" as each person either shifted their knees or stood up to let them pass.

"Sorry!" Wesley said once they had emerged from the packed rows of chairs. It was nearly dark now, and though the hog roast was long over, the smell of the woodsmoke still hung heavily in the mist that had rolled back in. "But I can only take so much Sousa. How about you?" He lit a cigarette.

"Oh, yes. Me too," she fibbed. She had no idea who Sousa was.

"Anyway, it's almost time for the bonfire." He looked at his watch. "Wanna go?" He pulled a silver flask from inside his jacket and wiggled it. "I think it will be fun."

Harriet hesitated. Her mother was expecting her home soon. And besides that, she rarely drank alcohol. She didn't want to admit that to him, though. "I should probably get back," she mumbled and looked around for Kate, who was nowhere to be seen. She must have sold everything or given up and left.

"Come on! Don't be such a spoilsport! Everyone will be there." His eyes narrowed. "Or are you waiting around for this John guy?" He swayed slightly. "Look, I've spent a lot on you today. Least you could do is come along to the bonfire with me." He inhaled deeply and blew out a large cloud of smoke from his nostrils.

Harriet wasn't sure she wanted to travel all the way out to Dalsing's farm, where she was sure to know no one. It wasn't that she didn't feel safe with Wesley, necessarily, though he *was* beginning to leer at her in an uncomfortable sort of way.

"Look, what are you worried about?" he asked, as if he could read her mind. "Melody's going to be there. And probably a lot of other people you'll know. I mean, you work in a damn shop; you must know almost everyone in town by now."

"Well," she murmured, surprised by his sudden aggressiveness and not wanting to upset him more, "maybe for just a little while. I suppose." She tried to smile.

"Hot dog!" Wesley said excitedly. "Now you're talking!" He clapped his hands, his cigarette dangling from the corner of his mouth. "Hey, you're shivering. Here," he said, quickly removing his jacket, "take this."

He carefully draped it around her shoulders. It smelled of him, and, Harriet had to admit, she liked it. Melody's comment about John's farm smell came to mind, but she pushed it away.

Wesley put his arm around her again, this time tighter. "I like you, Harriet. You're a good egg. I'd sure like to see more of you."

Again, she wasn't exactly clear on his meaning, but she couldn't help but feel a rush of giddy excitement as he guided her across the park. She leaned into him a little, wanting to savor this moment, and couldn't contain the smile that suddenly erupted. Perhaps Melody *had* been right, she thought again. Wesley really was a catch. *Harriet Elton*. It had a nice ring to it. She glanced over her shoulder, wanting to take one last look at the Fest to remember this night, their first night together . . . only for her heart to sink when she saw John Schneider, leaning against his battered Ford truck, watching her go.

CHAPTER
TEN

As they bounced along in Wesley's spiffy Oldsmobile sport coupe toward Dalsing's farm, Harriet tried her best to pay attention to Wesley's intricate regaling of what she assumed was supposed to be an impressive anecdote about an account he had recently handled at the bank. He had done so well, apparently, that Mr. Carson, the bank president, had congratulated Wesley on his work. Well, not formally, Wesley admitted—not, for example, in the form of an award, say—but, still, he had acknowledged it. "Good work, Elton," Mr. Carson had said as he passed Wesley's teller cage.

"That's nice," Harriet mumbled, though she was barely following the story, so preoccupied was she on John Schneider's sad eyes, reflected in her own now, as she stared out the glass window. She shook her head slightly and forced herself to focus on the rows of corn they were whipping past.

Thankfully, Wesley seemed not to notice her inattentiveness and launched into yet another story, this one about how he had detected that several bank employees were taking a few too many extra minutes on their noon hour and was even now drawing up a report to submit to Mr.

Carson. It was just the sort of thing, he predicted, that would get him promoted. "It's the details, you see," he said, glancing over at Harriet.

"Yes, I suppose you're right," Harriet murmured and was saved from having to comment further by their arrival at the farm.

For years, the Dalsing's lower field had been the site of the Harvest Fest bonfire, starting back when the Dalsing kids were just teenagers. That generation had since grown up and had their own kids now, some even a few grandkids, but the tradition had stuck. Occasionally, old Mel Dalsing still wandered down from the farmhouse at the top of the hill to make sure nothing was too amiss or just to say hello, but tonight he was absent, laid up as he was with "a bad ticker."

Wesley rolled the car across the rutted ground and haphazardly parked it near the others. He quickly jumped out, banging the door behind him. Harriet waited for him to come around and help her, but he did not. Instead, he cupped his hand around the cigarette he was now trying to light, so Harriet opened the heavy door herself and slid out. She still had his jacket draped around her shoulders and pulled it tighter, the air here in the valley being significantly cooler and damp.

"Come on! Hurry up," he called, twisting around and beckoning her with a wave of his hand. He was already several paces in front of her.

Harriet followed, but as they approached the crowd laughing and joking around the fire, she suddenly wished she hadn't come. She recognized a few people, but no one stopped to talk to her beyond a simple greeting or a nod. Wesley skillfully weaved them through to a big metal tub filled with bottles of beer floating in lukewarm water, grabbed two, and then guided her to a couple of empty stumps near the fire. Harriet eased herself onto one and let Wesley's jacket slip down, the heat emanating from the giant fire warming her. She took a drink of her beer, wincing it down, and glanced over at Wesley. He was not as talkative now, and he seemed on edge, upset. He lit another cigarette, inhaled it deeply, and then pulled out his flask. Dubiously, he held it out to her, as if he didn't expect her to take it, and when she shook her head, he frowned, jerked it back, and took a long swig.

Silence ensued, and Harriet shifted uncomfortably. She should probably ask him something that would prompt him to talk more about himself, but she was at a loss for topics. She knew so little about him!

"What's Madison like?" she finally managed, remembering that he had mentioned being there recently to learn more about banking, or something like that.

He turned to her, his brow furrowed, almost as if he didn't understand the question. "Madison?" He gave a quick shrug and looked back at the fire. "It's big. Bigger than here. Better by a long shot." His right leg began to bounce slightly, and he glanced irritably at his gold wristwatch.

"Where the hell is Melody?" he muttered, flicking his cigarette butt into the fire. "She should have been here by now!" He stood abruptly, nearly tripping over his legs. He took another long drink from his flask and then looked down at Harriet. "I'm goin' over an' talk ta the guys," he slurred, gesturing with his drink toward a group of young men who had gathered under the lone oak tree. Several of them had their jackets off and a few had loosened their ties, all of them appearing to be in some state of drunkenness. "I'm not waitin' anymore."

Harriet was not sure how to respond to this, so she remained silent, her face burning with embarrassment. *She knew it!* She knew that Wesley preferred Melody, that she was more to him than "Fred Merriweather's little sister." She took another sip of beer and then looked around cautiously, wondering if anyone had noticed that Wesley had abandoned her. It didn't seem like it. Everyone was engaged in lively conversation or had probably wandered off into the corn field to participate in acts that they would have to confess the next Saturday to Fr. Eggert if they were Catholic, or Pastor Wilson if they were Lutheran. No eyes were on her, she noted with relief, but she still tried to make herself as invisible as possible, wrapping her arms around her bent knees, wishing she had never come here.

Why hadn't John Schneider turned up at the Merc when he said he would? She set her beer bottle down on the dry dirt, trying to find a patch without a scraggly tuft of grass so that it wouldn't spill. If he had, she further contemplated, then she wouldn't be here right now, or maybe he and Melody would be here, too, and she wouldn't be this miserable. She should have insisted that they wait a little longer for John to turn up. But she could already guess what Melody would say: that if he were serious about her, then he would have been punctual. Maybe Melody was right, she thought, as she drew a line in the powdery dirt with her finger. But why had he looked at her so forlornly as she walked across the park on Wesley's arm?

She glanced over at Wesley and the guys again and saw that Marjorie Hodges had joined them. Marjorie was one of Doc Hodges middle girls. There were five Hodges girls in total, and it was generally thought that Marjorie was the wildest of the bunch. Wesley had his arm around her shoulder now and was whispering something in her ear. Marjorie laughed prettily at whatever he had said.

Harriet stood up. It was late. Much later than she had intended to stay, and she was suddenly in a panic about how badly her mother must be worrying. She slipped off Wesley's jacket, folded it over one arm, and then picked her way across the uneven ground to the oak tree. She stood on the periphery of the group, waiting for Wesley, or anyone, really, to notice her, but no one did. Wesley's arm was still around Marjorie as he tossed back another drink and then continued the story he was in the middle of telling.

"Never seen a tin can that foxy. Asked Callahan how much, and he said a hundred bucks. A hundred bucks! For a car? 'Pally, it had better run like eggs in coffee for that much,' I says, 'or you're getting squat!'"

The group around him laughed, and he again leaned and whispered something in Marjorie's ear. As he did so, he finally caught sight of Harriet, standing slightly behind him. "Yeah?" he slurred. His scowl took her aback.

"I'd like to go now, Wesley," she said, handing him his jacket. "If you don't mind. It's late. My mother will be worried."

Wesley grabbed the jacket and flicked a cigarette butt. "Yeah, in a minute," he said and turned his back on her, his arm still around Marjorie, who shot her a little look of disdain. A couple of the guys snickered.

Harriet's face burned. She wasn't sure what to do. She looked around for anyone who might take her home, but she saw no one she dared ask. Perhaps she could walk? It would be hard going over Christmas Tree Hill at night, though, and to go around it via Portzen's Woods would take forever. She bit her lip and tapped Wesley on the shoulder.

He turned quickly, his face eager, as if he were expecting someone else, but then he frowned. "You again?"

"Wesley, I really have to get home. Can you please take me?"

"I said in a minute. Now beat it. I'm busy here with my friends."

His harshness brought tears to Harriet's eyes, and, embarrassed, she retreated toward the bonfire. What was she to do?

"Harriet?" asked a voice suddenly beside her.

Cal! She had never been so happy to see him, so much so that she was tempted to hug him.

"I thought it was you. What are you doing here?" He looked out over the crowd, and when his eyes locked on Wesley and his friends, his jaw clenched. "You here with him?"

Harriet nodded. "Well, I was. Sort of." She looked at the ground.

"Want to sit down?" Cal nodded toward the stump she had abandoned. "Or can I get you something to drink?"

Harriet twisted her hands. "I really should be getting home, Cal. My mother will be worried, and Wesley . . . well, he's not quite ready to go. Could you . . . could you take me, maybe? Or are you here with someone?" She glanced around. She hadn't considered the possibility Cal might have a girl. He had never mentioned one, but then again, Cal rarely spoke about his life.

"Not just at the moment."

Harriet wasn't sure what that meant, and it was hard to read his expression in just the flickering light of the bonfire.

"Here." He held out his arm. "Let's go. I'm happy to see you home."

Harriet gave another look around the crowd as if trying to spot whom he might be with, but, on the other hand, she could not imagine he would abandon whoever it was. She wrapped her arm through his. "Well, if you don't mind."

"Course I don't."

Harriet hesitated. "I suppose I should tell Wesley I'm leaving. Otherwise, he might worry."

"I'll tell him," Cal offered stiffly, looking at the group again.

"Are you sure?" Harriet murmured, but Cal was already striding over. Harriet followed at a distance.

Cal approached the huddle and tapped Wesley on the shoulder. "Hey, bonehead."

Surprised, Wesley spun around, dropping his arm from around Marjorie in the process. "What do *you* want, butcher boy?"

Several guys laughed.

Harriet saw the muscles in Cal's neck tighten. "Seeing as you're sloshed, I'm taking Miss Mueller home."

Wesley's small black eyes darted suspiciously between Cal and Harriet, and then he broke into a sly grin. "Be my guest, Fraiser. Have at it." Laughing, he turned back to his little gang.

Cal's right hand formed a fist.

"Come on, Cal," Harriet urged, stepping closer. "Let's go."

Cal relaxed his shoulders, rolling his head from side to side. "You're right. He's not worth it. Come on." He held out his arm again. "My truck's over there," he said roughly, as if still trying to control his anger, and nodded toward the far patch of grass where the smattering of automobiles were parked.

Harriet took his arm, grateful all over again that he was here. "You're sure you don't want to stay?" she asked.

"Harriet, there's no other place I'd want to be right now than escorting you home," he said quietly and proceeded to lead her past the jovial group around the bonfire and through the shadows on the periphery.

CHAPTER
ELEVEN

Melody crept through the shadows flooding the third-floor hallway of Victory Memorial, the only light source being the glow of a lamp at the nurse's desk. She had never attempted to visit Pops this late, and she wasn't sure her cigarettes would work on the overnight staff.

When she had told Wesley that she might not attend the bonfire because she had to visit her father, she had never intended on actually doing so. After all, it had been almost nine o'clock by the time she finished tidying and locking up the shop—by herself, no thanks to Cal, who had had the audacity to march straight out the back door at exactly seven o'clock on the dot without even a hint of a goodbye! But standing alone in the darkened High Street, she had suddenly felt an overwhelming urge to speak to her father, to tell him how the Fest had gone, and to confess that she had failed on several counts.

Though the Merc had been busy all day, the sales of her luxury items had been abysmal, and the cider hadn't done much better. No one seemed interested in the thick brown jugs beside the counter, even when Melody remembered to suggest them to customers as she was ringing them up. She had kept the cider idea a secret from her father, hoping to be able to announce a windfall after the Harvest Fest, but now she wasn't sure it was even worth mentioning.

And the day hadn't exactly been a success in terms of the staff, either. It still rankled that Mrs. Haufbrau had simply walked out on her to sing in some stupid choir. She would ask her father whether he really did sanction this every year, or if Mrs. Haufbrau had made the whole thing up just to thwart her. Mrs. Haufbrau, singing in a choir? It seemed too absurd to be true, as Melody couldn't imagine anything even remotely melodious emanating from Mrs. Haufbrau's wizened throat.

But worse had been Cal's reaction to her plan regarding Harriet and Wesley. It was a shame, really, as before John Schneider had come in and ruined everything, she had actually been enjoying Cal's company. He had worked quickly and efficiently, his fingers light and nimble, and several times he had even laughed at something she said.

She groaned as she made her way down the darkened hallway towards her father's room—thankfully, no nurses in sight. It was obvious that Cal disapproved of her trying to help Harriet, but it wasn't her fault that things had turned out the way they had. If anything, it was Mrs. Haufbrau's for abandoning her, and John Schneider's for turning up almost a full hour late!

She paused outside her father's room and leaned her ear to the door, listening to make sure there were no staff inside. She loosened her coat and was just about to give a perfunctory knock when she froze at the sound of voices. Stern, hard voices.

"Four hundred bucks. That's what you owe us. Remember?" a man growled.

"But what can I do from here?" answered her father in an unfamiliar tone. He sounded afraid, something Melody had never once heard in her entire life! "You've got to give me more time. Please," her father begged.

"Spare us the waterworks, old man."

Waterworks? Was her father crying? Melody resisted the urge to burst into the room.

"Listen," Pops gurgled, "better to give me a couple more months than not get anything at all."

"A couple of months? You think we're stupid or somethin'?"

"I can get you the money. All of it! I just need a little more time."

Silence followed, during which Melody thought she might be sick. One hand went reactively to her mouth. *Why was it so quiet in there?*

She was again about to burst in when the man spoke.

"Tell you what, we got hearts, don't we, Mick? We'll give ya till the first of the year, won't we?"

"Oh, thank you!" Pops blurted.

"But then you gotta pay us five hundred."

"Five hundred? I only borrowed four. That's robbery!"

"Some might call it that. Others might call it business. Take it or leave it. Or do we have to get the boss involved?"

"No, no. I'll . . . it's fine. Yes, just give me the extra time, and I'll come up with the cash."

"You better. Or you might find something terrible might happen. Something like a fire, say. Or maybe something might happen to yer wife or yer girls. Wouldn't that be a shame?"

"Don't you dare," Pops rasped.

The man laughed. "Remember, first of the year."

Melody could hear them moving toward the door now and panicked. She looked up and down the hallway for a place to hide, and in desperation, ducked into the room next to her father's. It was completely dark, but she could tell it was occupied by the sound of heavy breathing and a terrible odor, like urine or perhaps decaying flesh. She put her hand over her mouth again.

"Nurse?" came a feeble voice from the bed.

"She'll be right here," Melody mumbled through her fingers and opened the door a crack. She had no desire to run into the thugs, but if she stayed in this room much longer, she was afraid she would well and truly vomit. She opened the door wider and chanced a glance down the hallway. It was clear. Whoever they were, they didn't mess about. She crept out of the room and leaned her head toward her father's door. There was no noise from inside.

Tentatively, Melody pushed open the door. "Pops?"

"Melody?" he said, his voice oddly hoarse. "What are you doing here?"

"Pops!" She rushed to his side. "Who were those two men? I heard them threatening you."

"Those two? Don't worry about them, Mel." He tried to laugh, but only a dry little cough came out. "Just jokesters. That's all. Nothin' to worry about."

"They didn't sound like jokesters. They sounded like criminals." She searched his eyes. "Why are they demanding money from you?" Several reasons raced through her mind, none of them good. "Please tell me, Pops," she urged gently. "I should know. Are you in danger?"

Louis Merriweather pulled his gaze from Melody's, turning it toward the wall.

"Pops, please." She took his hand. "Tell me."

After several long moments, he turned back, his eyes heavier than she had ever seen them. "I'm ashamed to say it, Mel."

"Don't be." The sorrow and regret on his face caused a wave of fear to erupt within her from a place deeper than she knew she had. "Let me help you," she whispered.

"Can't help me with this, Mel. Not unless you've got five hundred dollars."

She gripped his hand. "But why? Are they . . . are they blackmailing you?"

"No." He let out a low breath. "That's what I owe them. After we lost everything and Joe killed himself, I . . . well, I panicked and borrowed money from these sharks. Just enough to keep the Merc going until we could get ahead. Now the loan's due, and they want their money. Plus interest." He looked at her. "And you and I both know I don't have it, 'specially after I landed in here."

"Is this what you meant by having a few tricks up your sleeve?" She thought back to their previous conversation and wondered how long this had been going on.

"I'm sorry, Mel. I've let you all down," he muttered. "We're gonna have to sell the Merc or the house or the car. Something. I've tried to warn your mother, but I don't think she realizes the hot water we're in."

Melody felt a gut punch. *Sell the Merc? Sell the house?* Granted, she had wanted an escape from the Merc, but not like this. "But surely there's something we can do?" She tried to think. "We did a ton of business today. I . . . I haven't gone over the accounts yet, but I'm *sure* we made money." This didn't seem the time to tell him about the failed cider project.

"One day, even a big day like the Harvest Fest, ain't gonna do it, Mel. I think you know that." He sighed heavily. "I think we're done."

"You can't say that! Shouldn't we tell Fred?" Melody urged. "Maybe he could think of something? Or maybe he could quit—just for now—and finish later?"

"He's in his final year, Mel. Not gonna call him home for this."

"Well, what's going to happen when he comes home after graduation and finds us living in a badger hole?"

Pops let out a rusty little chuckle. "Fred's tuition is already paid, so there ain't no use calling him home. There's nothing he could do, anyway."

"Well, there has to be something! Maybe borrow from the bank?"

"Already borrowed to the hilt. Nah. Only thing you can do is pray for a miracle, Mel."

Melody could no longer hold back the tears, her throat aching with the effort, and she buried her face in his massive stomach and began to sob. It was bad enough when she thought that her biggest problem was finding a way to make the Merc some extra money and to get back to Chicago, but this was infinitely worse. Selling the Merc or The Willows? It was unthinkable!

"Hey, girl, don't cry," he said softly, stroking her hair. "We've had a good run, haven't we? Had it good for a long, long time. Not many people can say the same, can they?"

"But there has to be something we can do," she said, raising her head.

A nurse banged in through the door, then, startling Melody.

"What are you doing in here?" the nurse snipped. "Visiting hours are long over! Mr. Merriweather, we've warned you about this before."

"Can't I stay a little longer?" Melody asked, wiping her tears. She thought about offering her the cigarettes in her pocket, but the woman standing in front of her didn't seem the type to succumb to bribes.

"No, you best go on, Mel," her father interceded. "It's late."

"Are you sure, Pops?"

"Yeah, you go on. Don't say anything to your mom."

"I won't," she said, giving him an awkward sort of hug since it was impossible to get her arms around him completely. She kissed his cheek. "Don't you worry. I'll think of something."

Pops gave her a sad smile and then turned his attention to the nurse, who was standing beside the bed, needle at the ready.

Melody gave him one last look and slunk out of the room, trying to control her rising panic. There had to be *something* she could do. Frantically, her mind raced through the entire inventory of the Merc, wondering what they could capitalize on, and finally came to rest back on the cider. Yes, the cider. It was the best product she had, she decided, if only people knew what it was. She just needed a better way to sell it.

CHAPTER TWELVE

The delicious smell of bacon—and sausage, if she was not mistaken—hit Melody's nose as she trudged down the stairs the next morning. Despite the fact that her stomach had begun to growl, she resolved to have words with her mother and Helenka. They needed to stop having such elaborate meals. They needed to economize!

As she stepped into the foyer, she heard Brahms drifting in from the music room, which further annoyed her. Bunny would have to quit piano lessons; that's all there was to it!

She knew she was being irritable, but she couldn't help it. She had hardly slept at all, her father's dire words swirling around in her head all night.

Annoyed, she switched off the overhead Tiffany light, realizing that in so doing she had officially turned into her mother, which caused a fresh crush of despair to wash over her. She rifled hopelessly through the mail basket. She had neglected to check it last night after returning from the hospital. But there, behind what was probably the electrics bill, were two letters for her! One from Elsie and the usual from Douglas. She ripped open Elsie's, needing to escape her reality as soon as possible. She would read Douglas's later, as she could already predict what it would say.

Dearest, Melody, Elsie's letter began—

"Oh, there you are, Melody!" her mother interrupted, coming around the corner from the front room. "I can't believe you're just getting up now! Go in and sit down; Helenka's been holding the eggs. Bunny!" she called.

The Brahms stopped.

Melody let out a frustrated sigh and reluctantly folded up the letter and tucked it into her skirt pocket. "How did you make out at the Fest?" she asked, following her mother into the dining room. "Any new recruits?"

"Oh, yes, it was fine." Mums bustled into the room and took her seat at the head of the table. "But I have some other news," she chirped as Helenka hurried in with a silver carafe of coffee and a flask of juice. "Bunny!"

"What is it, Mums?" Bunny strode into the room. "I've already had breakfast, and I really need to practice!"

"This won't take but a moment," Mums said sternly. "Now. I've found two lodgers!" She looked from one to the other eagerly, as if expecting congratulations.

"But Mums!" Bunny whined. "How horrid! Not to mention embarrassing!" She slumped into the nearest chair. "What am I to tell my friends at school?"

"Now, Bunny . . . we must all make sacrifices. It's just until your father is better. And even then, it will be a long time before he's well enough to work again."

Melody had forgotten about the lodgers, and wondered how much they would bring in.

"Who are they?" she asked, reaching for a cinnamon bun.

"A Mr. Frank Churchill and a Mr. Julius Fairfax. Brothers. Or, half-brothers, I should say."

"Men?" Melody exclaimed. "We can't let out rooms to men, Mums!"

"Well, who do you think are in need of rooms, Melody? There aren't many young women coming from out of town to look for work in Merriweather, as you know. Quite the other way round."

She was right, of course, but somehow Melody had envisioned someone like Imogene Kaufmann and her mother, or Miss Elliot, Bunny's piano teacher, taking the rooms.

"Now we won't be able to walk around in our nightgowns," Bunny whined. "Oh, Mums! This is terrible."

"No, it isn't, Bunny. Lots of people don't have it as good as we do. You should be grateful." Mums nervously patted her hair, giving Melody the impression that she was also trying to convince herself.

Bunny's lower lip began to quiver. "Well, they're not having my room!" She folded her arms roughly across her chest and stared at Melody.

Melody was tempted to stick her tongue out at her, but she refrained. "Obviously, Bunny. Don't be so melodramatic. I'm sure they'll get Freddy's room."

"Yes, I thought Freddy's room and the guest room," Mums put in. "They can choose between them. But if we get more, you two will have to share."

"More?" Bunny exclaimed incredulously.

"Yes, more. That's all there is to it, Elizabeth!" Mums scolded, heading off Bunny's protest.

"Where did you find them?" Melody asked, taking a bite of her bun, butter and cinnamon oozing from it.

Mums's face relaxed a bit. "They came quite highly recommended. Mrs. Weston at the Elks mentioned to her cousin in Platteville that we had rooms available. And they're her father-in-law's nephews. By his sister. If that makes sense."

It actually didn't, and Melody was about to ask for clarification when she decided that it really didn't matter. What mattered is that someone, somewhere had vouched for them. "They're from Platteville?"

"No, Mrs. Weston's *cousin* is from Platteville. The gentlemen in question are from Milwaukee, I believe. Or maybe it's Chicago."

"Well, why are they here? I mean, why do they want to live in Merriweather?"

Mums let out a deep breath, as if she were suddenly exhausted. "I haven't the faintest idea, Melody. Something about real estate, I think. You can ask them all about it when they arrive, if you're so curious."

"Hopefully, they'll keep to their rooms, and we'll never have to speak to them!" Bunny exclaimed.

"Well, that would be very uncomfortable, seeing as they will be breakfasting and dining with us each day."

"What?" Bunny frowned. "We have to eat with them, too?"

"That is a standard arrangement, Bunny." Mums scowled. "They're paying extra for board."

"You should advise Helenka to stop making such elaborate meals, then," Melody added, glad of a chance to bring up the topic.

Mums flashed her an indignant look. "What do you mean?"

"We could be saving money if Helenka didn't make beef roulade, and Wiener schnitzel, and . . . and chicken paprikash every night, along with at least two side dishes and a dessert."

"It's hardly extravagant, Melody! Just simple cooking."

"Simple cooking? According to who? Most of the country is starving!"

"Really, Melody. Sometimes I wonder about you."

Melody wanted to say more, but she bit her tongue. "Well, when are they coming?" she asked instead.

"Who?"

"The lodgers!"

"Next week sometime, I believe."

"Are they paying up front?"

"Yes, your father was very insistent on that point."

"How much?"

"My, Melody! You're quite keen." She looked her over. "They're paying four dollars per week per room, and two extra dollars each per week for food."

"So that's twelve dollars a week?" Melody said hopefully, quickly calculating how long it would take to raise five hundred dollars. Almost a year. Too long. But better than nothing.

"Why are you always so horrid, Melody?" Bunny whined. "Is that all you ever think about, money? And now you want us to cut out dessert?"

"Don't be such a child, Bunny," Melody retorted and then quickly stuffed the rest of her bun in her mouth. She was tired of listening to Bunny's complaints, though she herself had been nearly of the same mind not but a few weeks ago. She stood up. "I'm going upstairs. I have some correspondence before church."

"But you've barely eaten anything," Mums entreated, taking a sip of her coffee.

"I'm not hungry." Melody trudged up the stairs, leaving Mums to deal with the still-complaining Bunny, and shut the bedroom door behind her, leaning against it briefly. She flopped onto her bed, then, and pulled her letters out of her pocket. She desperately needed an escape from her current woes, and Elsie's letter, at least, was sure to do the trick.

Elsie's letter was indeed wonderfully long and filled with news that read almost like a Cinderella story. Well, not exactly, but it at least seemed like a happily-ever-after. She was living in one of those big houses in Palmer Square that her horrible—well, previously horrible—grandfather had set the family up in, complete with a full staff, including a butler who doubled as a chauffeur. Granted, she had to care for her younger siblings and her ill mother, but she did have a nurse, a nanny, and several maids to help. And then there was little Anna, the girl she and Gunther had become the adoptive parents of. She still suffered from epilepsy, Elsie wrote, and that it was a condition the girl would live with forever, as there was no known cure. *Still, we pray for her every day, and she is speaking more and more.* The girl had stopped talking after being admitted to an insane asylum after a particularly bad epileptic fit, where she had undoubtedly seen horrors that would have frightened an adult, much less a child. And Gunther was enjoying his new professorship at Loyola, an appointment also arranged by Elsie's repentant grandfather. And, she announced happily, she was to be an aunt! Her sister Henrietta, who had married the heir to Castle Linley in England—and who was now, indeed, to be formally addressed as "Lady Linley"—was apparently expecting a baby!

Elsie's life read like a glorious adventure tale! Melody had always known she was a dark horse! And this was the proof. All this time, she had believed she was taking Elsie under her wing, when Elsie had not needed her in the slightest. Well, that wasn't exactly true. Elsie had been painfully shy and friendless when she had started at Mundelein.

Melody read the next bit with increased keenness:

As for myself, I do enjoy my classes at Mundelein still, though I sometimes feel a fraud, as if I don't really belong there. I feel guilty for leaving Ma and Anna and Doris and Donny while I go and attend class, but I do so love it. Also, Gunther is insistent that I continue my studies. He is so wonderfully patient, Melody, even with Ma, who is so very trying at times. But I am utterly in love with him.

Melody paused. *She* wanted to be utterly in love with someone, she realized suddenly. More than being a sister of the English aristocracy or even having a chauffeur. She loved Douglas in a certain way, but could she really say, "I am utterly in love with him" in the dreamy, tender way Elsie said it here? She wasn't sure.

I wish you could see him now. He is quite changed from when he was our custodian, fixing doorknobs and shoveling snow. He looks so elegant now when he leaves for his classes, dressed in a suit and tie. He has even taken up smoking a pipe! You'd hardly know him.

Melody turned to the second page.

From time to time, I still see Cynthia and Charlie and Douglas on campus. In fact, we all had tea together one afternoon, which was kind of them to include me. Cynthia also invited Vivian Anderson—you remember her, don't you? She and Cynthia seem to be great friends now. And, as you might remember, there is never a shortage of conversation when Vivian is around. In fact, we all struggled to get a word in edgewise. Poor Douglas attempted to ask if I had had any news of you, but I had barely a chance to answer before Vivian proposed that we all go to the Aragon the following Friday, a proposal which I, of course, declined. Cynthia and Charlie agreed readily enough, but Douglas seemed hesitant. Vivian then wrapped her arm through his and insisted that he come, saying that it would be deliciously fun. "You're not still pining for Melody, are you, Dougie?" is what she said. "You're too, too adorable! Isn't he, Cynthia? He simply has to come, doesn't he? We'll cheer you up." In the end, I do believe they did all go, and, according to Cynthia, Vivian danced with him the entire night. "Wouldn't let him alone!" is how she described it.

Well, dearest, I write all of this to you because I am not sure what your real feelings are toward Douglas. Though I see him infrequently, I would agree with Cynthia that he is not himself. And though I am not the matchmaker you are, I do wonder if Vivian might be vying for your place in his heart. But perhaps you no longer care about Douglas Novak? I would not be surprised, as you are never short of friends or potential lovers wherever you go. I so admire you for that, Melody. Making friends is very difficult for me; I wish I had your open grace and joyous personality.

I pray that you are doing well and that your father is much improved. I hope that you will return to us in the spring or even next fall. Would that I could repay you for all that you have done for me. If you are ever in need, you have only to ask.

Your loving friend,
Elsie

Melody read through the letter again before letting it fall onto the chenille bedspread. Vivian Anderson? What would she want with Douglas? Vivian favored tall, dark-haired men who were mysterious and swarthy. Perhaps a little dangerous. Douglas, with his plain brown hair, cropped close, was certainly not her type. What was she playing at? And was Douglas falling for it?

She quickly opened Douglas's letter and was initially glad that there was absolutely no mention of Vivian Anderson. In fact, it was almost a carbon copy of his old letters, except that this one, she noticed with surprising alarm, did not repeat his offer of marriage.

CHAPTER
THIRTEEN

"Just set them there," Melody repeated, pointing to the side counter.

Cal set down the old wire basket of empty glass bottles he'd brought up from the cellar with a bang, causing them to clink together dangerously.

"Careful! Those are all we have until I can order more."

"What do you want them for?" Cal asked, taking a step back and resting his hands on his hips.

"I'm thinking we should put the cider in these instead of the jugs."

"In bottles?" Cal's face looked dubious. "Why?"

In truth, Melody wasn't exactly sure why she thought the cider might sell better this way, but she felt it was worth a try. All morning, as the rain had poured, keeping customers away, she had stared at the brown jugs scattered about the store. The problem, as she had previously concluded, was that no one knew what they were. And even when she told customers during the Harvest Fest that they were jugs of cider, they seemed uninterested. Honestly, she could see why. They resembled jugs of common moonshine, nothing special at all. What they needed was some pizzazz. Something to make them stand out the way she had tried to make her luxury items stand out. But simply placing them in the front window and adding some kind of sign indicating what they were was not enough. They needed to *look* like something special.

"But they won't hold as much," Harriet commented from where she stood behind the main counter.

Mrs. Haufbrau was fortunately not present for this unveiling of Melody's impromptu plan, as, in lieu of any customers to wait upon, she had declared her intent to organize the storeroom. "Looks like a tornado's hit it," she had chided Melody.

"Yes, but the smaller size is a good thing," Melody said now to Harriet. "We put in less cider and reduce the price a little from what we were charging for a jug, but we make an even bigger profit."

"Why not just get smaller jugs?" Harriet asked.

"Because jugs are too plain, too ordinary." Melody picked up one of the bottles and tried brushing off the thick dust. "We need the cider to look like a luxury product without the luxury price."

Cal's brow furrowed. "Well, putting it in those won't exactly make it look like a luxury product. It's just brown liquid in a glass bottle."

"My, you're cheery, aren't you?" Ever since the Harvest Fest, Cal had returned to his frosty demeanor. He did not mention the debacle between Harriet and John, but it was obvious he was still upset by how things had turned out. What else could it be? Well, Melody decided with a little toss of her head, she couldn't worry about Cal's good opinion. She needed to find a way to make five hundred dollars by the end of the year, and bottling the cider seemed to be her best option.

If she closed her eyes, she could still see her dad's haunted face. She was determined to rescue him from the thugs, but there was one thing that niggled. "There ain't no use calling him home," Pops had said, referring to Freddy. "There's nothing he could do, anyway."

Nothing he could do? If this was true, was it the reason Pops had insisted *she* take over instead of Freddy? Because he knew the Merc was dying anyway? Was she simply meant to shepherd the Merc to its death? It filled her with added anxiety.

"We'll need a name," she announced, pushing her fears aside.

"A name?" Cal frowned.

"Yes, a name for the cider." She put the bottle back in the wire basket with a clang. "It will help it to sell."

Cal shrugged. "I suppose so."

"I think that's a good idea, Melody!" Harriet chimed in.

"What about Merriweather Cider?" Melody suggested, trying her hardest not to look at Cal.

"Ooo, yes!" Harriet said. "That sounds good."

"How original," Cal grunted. "As if you need anything else named after you."

"You can really be a pill sometimes, you know that?" she said, turning to face him. "Then *you* suggest something."

Cal scratched his cheek, thinking. "New Grimsby Cider? Or Christmas Tree Hill Cider? Since it's made out that way?"

"That's too long," Melody said. "And it also sounds too Christmasy. No one will want to buy it in July."

"If we're here that long."

"Are you *ever* optimistic?" Melody walked to the door and peered out at the soggy street. The rain had let up, but the sky was still dark, and puddles the size of small ponds had sprung up along the curbs. "What about something to do with mining?" she asked, turning back. "Lead Cider? Lead House Cider? Lead Tree Cider? Lead Works Cider?"

"Oh, I like that!" Harriet said. "Lead Works."

Cal nodded slowly, turning this over. "Yeah, me, too."

"Okay, then," Melody said. "Lead Works Cider it is. Now, we just need some labels." She walked back to the counter and picked up another bottle, twisting it this way and that.

"Labels?" Harriet asked. "You mean like a price tag?"

"No, I mean a fancy label that would cover the front of the bottle." She looked around the store until her eyes caught sight of a can of Franco-American mock turtle soup. She grabbed it. "See? Every can of Franco-American soup has this fancy label with the little chef. When it's priced the same as Campbell's, it sells more."

Holding up the can, she looked from one to the other. Neither seemed inspired.

She pinched the bridge of her nose and set the can back on the shelf. "We need to come up with a label so that people know what it is. Otherwise, as you so helpfully pointed out, Cal, it just looks like brown liquid in a bottle. Secondly, the label makes people feel like they're buying something special. And they'll look nice in the window, especially with the holidays coming up."

"At the risk of sounding pessimistic," Cal said, holding out his hands defensively, "where are you going to get these labels?"

"Well . . ." Melody paused. "One of us can draw them. To begin with, anyway."

"Draw them? Can you draw?"

In truth, art was not one of Melody's skills. She wondered if she could persuade Bunny, who was infinitely more creative than she was, but getting her to do it would be a battle and not a request that she could trust Bunny to be silent about around her mother. As of yet, Mums had no idea she was brewing and selling cider, and Melody wanted to keep it that way, considering her mother's involvement with the Temperance League.

"I . . . I think I know someone who could do it," Harriet interrupted timidly. "She's very artistic."

Melody's brow crinkled. "Who?"

"Kate Kerwyn?"

Melody searched her memory. She did not remember a Kate Kerwyn.

"Indian Kate? From school?"

Melody blinked. "Oh. Her?"

"Yes, she's a . . . well, a friend of mine. She might be persuaded to do it. But she'd want to be paid. She . . . she needs the money, you see."

"Yes, of course," Melody mused, trying to calculate how much all of this was going to cost. Right now, there were plenty of old brown jugs in the cellar, but few bottles. If she went ahead with her plan, she would need to buy more and also pay for the labels, not to mention the original cost of the apples and paying Mrs. Mueller to make it. Well, she would have to try. "How about . . . how about three cents a label?" She forced herself not to look at Cal. She was becoming awkwardly aware of her habit of looking to him with every decision, as if *he* were in charge and not *her*.

Harriet nodded slowly. "Yes, I think she might do it for that."

"Tell you what, have her draw something using Lead Works Cider, and I'll see."

"Alright! I'll talk to her tonight, if the rain lets up, that is."

"Why don't you go now?" Melody suggested. "There's hardly any customers and probably won't be for the rest of the afternoon."

"Well," Harriet hesitated. "If you don't mind, like."

"No, go on! I'm anxious to know what she says."

"Alright, then." Harriet eagerly reached for her coat and bundled herself up. "Say goodbye to Mrs. Haufbrau for me, would you?" she said and hurried out the door without looking back.

Melody ventured a glance at Cal. He smiled at her. An uneven sort of smile, but his eyes were bright. "I have to admit, it's a good idea," he said, tilting his head slightly in that attractive way of his.

Melody was about to ask him more, delighted by this sudden vote of confidence, when the shop bell tinkled, and Wesley Elton entered, carrying a big black umbrella and what looked like a ledger under his arm.

Finally! She had been hoping Wesley would show up one of these days to further converse with Harriet or to possibly ask her out. Melody had relentlessly probed Harriet about how the Harvest Fest had gone, but her young protégée had said little, merely reddened slightly, which Melody had decided to interpret as a good sign. *Yes, she had had a nice enough time,* she had told Melody. *Yes, Wesley had been kind—* though she had looked away when saying this. *Yes, they had gone to the bonfire.* But beyond that, Harriet said little. Melody was not sure if this was because the girl was shy, or if it was because it had not exactly been love at first sight between the two. Well, either way, it was a start. She was sure that over time, Harriet's feelings would deepen, and perhaps she might then share more of Wesley's efforts at romance. The fact that he had come by now, in a rainstorm, said much.

"Oh, Wesley! Harriet's just left! You might catch her if you hurry," Melody encouraged, thinking about how romantic it would be for the sweethearts to meet in the rain, clutching each other as they hurried along, maybe ducking into the Checkerboard for a cup of hot cocoa.

"It's not Harriet I came to see."

His eyes flicked toward Cal, who was of course scowling.

"Official business," Wesley said, awkwardly pulling the ledger from under his arm. "But I can come back a different time, if it's more convenient."

"What's this all about?" She eyed the ledger nervously.

"I think it best to speak in private. Maybe your father's office?"

There was no doubt it was more bad news, and for a few moments Melody tried to think of an excuse. But she was at a loss. "Okay." She exhaled deeply and moved from behind the counter. "Will you watch the front, Cal?"

Cal did not answer, just continued to shoot daggers at Wesley, who gave him a grin and a quick sideways nod before following Melody toward the office.

Melody perched herself behind her father's old makeshift desk and gestured at one of the chairs wedged in front of it. "What's this all about, Wesley? Is there something wrong with our account?" She pressed her lips together and raised her eyebrows, trying to act as if she had no idea they had money problems.

"Not really." He tossed the ledger onto the desk and grinned.

Melody felt a flicker of hope. "What do you mean?"

Wesley knitted his hands together and stretched them behind his head. "I'm not here in any official capacity. Look," he said. He leaned forward and flipped through the pages of the ledger, revealing that they were all blank. "It's not even a real account book."

Melody's eyes narrowed. "Just what are you playing at, Wesley?"

"Oh, come on. It was just a joke. I just wanted a moment alone with you, and this is the only thing I could think of."

Melody's previous hope evaporated, only to be replaced by a wisp of dread. "To talk about Harriet?" she suggested uneasily. "Good idea! What did you want to discuss?" Somehow, she knew this wasn't the case, but she decided to pretend anyway.

"No, for God sakes," Wesley muttered. "How much more obvious do I have to be? I want to talk to *you*."

Melody squirmed. "But what about Harriet?"

He seemed genuinely confused. "What about her?"

"You went to the Harvest Fest with her!"

"Only because you forced me to!"

"Wesley," she tried to say calmly, as if talking to a child. "You haven't given her enough of a chance. Harriet's a lovely girl. You'll see."

"*Harriet Mueller*? Have you lost your mind?"

"What's wrong with Harriet?"

"She's a scummy little Mueller from New Grimsby, and her mom is half-baked." He gave an irritated shrug. "And she has nothing to offer."

Melody's temper flared. "Oh, and I do, do I?" She gestured around the office. "A bankrupt shop from another century?"

"No! That's not what I meant!" Wesley leaned forward, throwing his arms on the desk. "Look, can't you see I'm crazy about you? I always have been. Why do you think I befriended Fred in high school? I . . . I could help you with this, with the Merc, I mean." He lowered his voice. "I could arrange another loan from the bank. You'd be free of it, then.

The bank would bring in a managing director, and you wouldn't have to worry about any of this anymore. You could have time to . . . to peruse other things."

"Like keep house for you?"

Wesley's expression was one of surprise, but he eased himself into a smile. "Well, yes. If you'd have me."

Melody felt as though she wanted to retch. "I don't think so."

"Yes," he said hurriedly. "We're rushing things. You don't have to say anything just now."

"I'm afraid it's impossible, Wesley."

"Impossible? Which part?"

"All of it." *Oh, why couldn't he just like Harriet?*

"You've someone else, don't you?" he demanded. "Harriet told me. Someone in Chicago."

Melody smiled, suddenly absurdly grateful for Douglas. "Yes. That's it. I do! His name is Douglas Novak. He's . . . he's asked me to marry him."

"Did you agree?"

"Wesley, I really don't think this is any of your business."

"Melody, let me prove myself to you," he whined.

"No! I'm not interested. I'm not the least bit attracted to you. There, I've said it." Standing, she came around from behind the desk. "I don't mean to be cruel, but how else can I convince you? I think you should go now." She opened the office door.

"I could make things very difficult for you, you know," he said, his pleading voice turning into a snarl. "At the bank."

Melody's face flushed. "Are you seriously trying to blackmail me into liking you? Don't you see how ridiculous that is?"

"I'm not trying to blackmail you." He stood up. "But I'm . . . I'm serious about us."

"Us? There is no us."

Wesley stared at her, his nostrils flaring. "You know, you Merriweathers think you're so high and mighty. Fred off at law school and you in Chicago, big house, new cars. But what did you just say about the shop being from another century? You're right. And things change. What's that old saying? *This too shall pass away*. Eventually the mighty fall."

"How dare you! Get out!"

"Fine," he barked as he moved toward the door. "But think about what I've said, Mel."

"It's Melody to you!"

"Think about what I said, *Mel*. I'm not too proud to scrape up the fallen." He grabbed her waist and pulled her so that her chest was pressed up against his. She balled her fists and tried to push away, but before she could, he pressed his thin lips against hers. "We could have a good life, Mel, you and me," he rasped, breathing heavily. "You want your old man's shop to keep going, then I think you know what to do." He pulled back so he could look into her eyes. "And don't think it's running off to Chicago to marry some Polack. We'll close your account before you even make it to Beloit." He ran his hand across her behind.

"How dare you!" She yanked herself away, trembling. "You can't close our account!"

Wesley pulled his jacket back into place and smoothed his ruffled hair with one hand. "Really? We'll just see about that; I'll speak to Mr. Car–"

"Everything okay in here?" Cal said from the doorway. His arms were crossed tightly against his chest. Wesley took a step back from Melody and returned Cal's glare, looking as if he were considering taking a swing at him. His chest heaved. "Yeah, just fine, Fraiser. You always seem to turn up where you're not wanted, don't you? Think you're so perfect? Well, I saw who you were with at the bonfire, and I don't mean Harriet, the wallflower. You're not as innocent as you make out," he snarled.

"Get out, Elton." Cal's face was dark. "And stay away from the Merc."

Wesley slunk past him and slammed out the front door, causing the shop bell to ring wildly.

Shaken, Melody stared at Cal.

He uncrossed his arms and put his hands on his hips. "You okay?" he asked, his voice oddly soft, though his face was still dark.

She nodded slowly.

He stared at her for a moment as if he was going to say something more, but he instead silently turned and went back to the meat counter, leaving Melody standing in her father's dusty office, trying to make sense of what had just happened.

CHAPTER
FOURTEEN

"Kate?" Harriet rapped on the door of the badger hole.

"Come in!"

Harriet pushed open the heavy door and found Kate seated at her little table, weaving reeds together to form what looked like another basket.

"You shouldn't just say 'come in,' you know. I could have been anybody!"

"Probably not. The only two people—okay, three if you count Ma—who know I'm here are you and Edmund, and he's just been here, so I assumed it was you." She returned her attention to the basket, this one large enough to possibly hold something like laundry.

Harriet perused the table and, seeing no open space amongst the various pieces of grass and weeds, thread, and rope, set her basket on the floor. "Mom sent some soup. And some bread."

"I do know how to fish, you know. And hunt."

"Yes, but usually that only works if you have a gun."

"As a matter of fact, Edmund said he'd bring me one"

"They have one to spare?"

"Probably just an old shotgun."

Harriet looked Kate over. She was dreadfully thin. "Well, until you catch something, there it is."

Kate glanced down at the basket hungrily, but she continued to weave.

"Hard at work, then?" Harriet pulled out the chair opposite and sat down. "How'd you do at the Fest?"

"Sold most of them."

"That's wonderful, Kate!"

"Yeah, but I spent most of what I made on new supplies. I need stronger material than just reeds. I'm experimenting with rope and also trying to figure out how to dye them." She held up her hands, the fingertips of which were stained a bluish purple. "Speaking of the Fest, did you ever find John?"

"No. Well, I did see him at one point." Harriet shifted. "But we didn't talk."

"So, you stayed with what's-his-name?"

"Wesley?"

"Yeah, him."

Harriet propped her chin in one hand. "Yes, I did, actually. Well, mostly. We went to the bonfire out at Dalsing's."

Kate bit the piece of thread she was handling in two, peering across the table at Harriet.

"It's not what you're thinking! Nothing happened." Harriet straightened, surprised that Kate seemed to know about the carousing that usually occurred at the Harvest Fest bonfire. "He went off drinking with his friends, if you must know. Luckily, Cal was there."

"Who's Cal?"

"Cal Fraiser? He works at the Merc."

Kate shrugged. "Never heard of him."

"Well, you probably wouldn't have. He's from Dodgeville."

"So, you just sat with him all night? Wasn't *he* there with someone?"

Harriet pursed her lips. "I'm not sure. I think he felt sorry for me."

"Who took you home?" As usual, Kate got right to the heart of the matter.

"Cal did. Wesley was a bit too tipsy." She didn't add that Wesley had also not wanted to leave, nor that his arm was around Marjorie Hodges most of the night.

"Hmm." Kate picked up a reed off the table. "Are you serious about him?"

Harriet's eyebrows rose. "Who? Cal?"

"No, Wesley."

"Well, I'm not sure. I . . . I don't think he likes me in that way." It still made her face burn when she thought of how it had all turned out. More than once when Melody had jovially asked her about how the Harvest Fest had gone, she had been tempted to tell her the truth, but she had not wanted to disappoint her. And, maybe, Harriet worried, it was something *she* had done wrong. Or perhaps it had merely been the effects of the whiskey. Her mother had often enough said that men sometimes acted differently after a few pints and weren't to be held responsible for their behavior. Harriet wasn't exactly sure she agreed with this line of thinking, but remained silent, nonetheless.

"Well, if you ask me, which you're not, I realize, you'd be stupid to give up John Schneider." Kate did not look up from trying to thread the reed through the one running around the rim of the basket.

"Give him up?" Harriet's stomach clenched a little. "He isn't mine to give. He stood me up the night of the Fest! Anyway, he's just a farmer." She tried to say it the way Melody would have said it, but it came off sounding horribly petty and shallow, even to her ears.

Kate looked up slowly. "Just a *farmer*? My, you've come up in the world. Melody Merriweather must be rubbing off on you." She bit another thread. "Well, it's a shade that doesn't suit you, Harriet. It doesn't suit you at all."

"Well, if John did fancy me," she retorted, Kate's reprimand stinging like a slap, "he'd have come round the Merc to explain, but he hasn't. Today, it was one of his brothers who delivered the eggs." She gave her hair a little toss, another Melody mannerism she had recently adopted, though her curls did not flip as dramatically as Melody's long brown tresses.

Kate, however, was relentless. "And you don't think that means something?"

"Yes, it means he doesn't care."

"Or that he's angry. Or hurt. You never know with men. It's usually the same thing."

Harriet mulled this over. Perhaps Kate was right. But she was tired of thinking about it all. She rubbed her forehead. Kate was in a foul mood this afternoon, and she regretted coming at all. She rose from her chair. "Well, I should go. Mom will be worried." She walked to the door, but then remembered why she had come in the first place. The labels! She turned back with a sigh. "I forgot to ask. Would you be interested in creating a label for bottles of cider?"

"A label? What kind of label?" Kate looked up curiously, seemingly unaware that she had hurt Harriet in any way.

"You know. A bottle label. Melody has come up with the idea of selling bottles of cider at the Merc. My mom is making it. We sold some in jugs at the Harvest Fest, but not all that many. Melody thinks that if we put it in a bottle with a fancy label, it might sell more." She tried to read Kate's blank face. "She's willing to pay you."

"How much?"

"Three cents a label. For now. It's going to be called Lead Works Cider."

For once Kate didn't have a sarcastic retort. It was clear that she was interested. "I don't have good paper or even any ink." She set down the basket and stood up. "Why don't I sketch it in pencil on some scraps of paper, and you can show it to her. See if she likes it. Or maybe I could do a couple of different designs and then she can choose."

"Oh, that's a good idea!" Harriet said, relieved not only that Kate's attention was finally diverted away from Harriet's romantic troubles, but more so that she was actually interested in the proposal.

"But there's one condition," Kate added, and Harriet's heart slumped a little. Of course, Kate's complete cooperation, even paid cooperation, was too good to be true.

"What is it?"

"I want Melody to agree to sell my baskets at the Merc."

"Sell your baskets?"

"Yeah. Why not? They sell every other kind of thing in that dump. Why not my baskets?"

Harriet ignored the quick irritation that rose in her chest at the Merc being called a "dump" and concentrated instead on Kate's condition. "Well, I'll ask her," she said tentatively. "But I can't guarantee that she'll say yes." Nor could she imagine what Mrs. Haufbrau would say. Or Cal.

She tended to agree with Melody that the two of them were at times, well . . . difficult to win over. "I'll try, though."

"Well, that's my condition," Kate said aloofly, picking up the basket again.

Harriet waited for Kate to continue, but she didn't, and there seemed nothing more to do but to leave. Her mother would be worrying by this point, anyway. Harriet marveled that her friend could be so resolute when she was basically starving. She had been sure that Kate would jump at the chance to make some extra money. Maybe she was simply bluffing?

"Well, goodbye, then," she said, pausing at the door.

"Goodbye," Kate said simply. "I'll get started on the drawings tonight. And you'll talk to Melody?"

Harriet let out a little groan. "Yes, I'll see what I can do."

* * *

Despite Kate's promise to work on the labels right away, Harriet was nevertheless surprised to find a small stack of sketches shoved under the doorway the next morning. Quickly flipping through them while she waited for the coffee to boil, Harriet was impressed. Each one was better than the last, and she marveled at how quickly Kate had been able to produce them. She must have stayed up all night! But that was typical Kate. Once she got an idea in her head, she became obsessed with it.

She was sure that Melody would like them, and she prayed she would not only choose one but agree to Kate's condition. It wasn't a bad idea, selling the baskets at the Merc, but she wasn't sure where they would put them, given the fireworks that had already gone on between Melody and Mrs. Haufbrau regarding the front window display. Harriet didn't see what the issue had been. If it had been up to her, she would have simply shoved everything in the display window and left it at that, but, as it was, she was not in charge, which, in truth, she was quite glad of.

Harriet quickly ate the bowl of oatmeal her mother set before her and hurried out the door, the sketches tucked neatly in her handbag. For once she wanted to be early. She raced up Magnolia, cut through the abandoned lot, crossed Elm, and picked up High Street. When she passed Ben's Bakery, she took special care to avert her eyes; she had no desire to see the lovely display of pastries in the window. She had eaten every drop of the oatmeal—and had even run her finger around the inside of the bowl to scoop up every bit—but she was still hungry, as usual, and she didn't want to be tempted by the wares inside the bakery.

Unfortunately, though, just as she was passing, the shop door opened, and not only did it release the smell of freshly baked sugary confections, which made her stomach growl, but it also released a person—one who made her stomach twist in a very different sort of way.

John Schneider.

Suddenly face-to-face, the two of them stared at each other. Harriet's heart betrayed her by beating just a little faster than it should. She tried commanding it to slow, but it seemed to have a mind of its own. John, too, seemed to be struggling with something internal, if the rippling of his cheek muscles was anything to go by.

"Hello, Harriet," he finally said. He sounded hoarse, as if he were possibly coming down with something. Or upset.

"Are you alright?" she asked before she could stop herself, hoping he wasn't ill.

John's brow creased in confusion. "Why wouldn't I be?" His tone was harsh, but his expression was sad.

"You didn't deliver the eggs yesterday."

John did not respond to this comment and instead cleared his throat. "I saw you at the Fest."

Harriet bit her lip. "Yes. I . . . I saw you, too." *Why were his eyes this blue?* She closed her own for a second, trying to remember that it was him who had essentially stood her up. In truth, she did feel a little guilty that she had gone with Wesley (the fink!), but it hadn't been her fault. She did *not* owe John Schneider an explanation; he owed her one! She turned her attention to the bakery window, the result of which was nearly as bad, since her gaze settled on a large chocolate éclair. She squinted one eye, as if this might help, and looked back at John. If he had simply been running late that day, wouldn't now be the time to tell her? The fact that he hadn't offered any explanation at all, however, told her much and in fact deflated her entirely, despite the way she had so dismissively spoken about him last night with Kate.

"Did you . . . did you enjoy it? The Fest, that is?" she asked finally, not able to think of anything else.

"Let's just say, it wasn't what I was expecting." His tone was stiff.

"No, it wasn't." She clutched her handbag more tightly, waiting for him to go on, but he did not.

There seemed nothing left to say.

"Well, good day, then, John," she murmured. "I guess I'll see you around." She stepped past him, quickly brushing the corner of her eye with the back of her hand.

"Harriet, wait," he called, tugging the sleeve of her coat.

"Yes?" She spun around.

He stared at her for several long moments, her coat sleeve still clutched in his hand, before he finally dropped it and pulled his gaze away. "Tell Melody we'll have more eggs ready tomorrow."

Harriet let out the breath she was holding and blinked rapidly, the truth settling over her like thick honey, though this was anything but sweet. Melody had been right about him after all.

"I have to go," Harriet grunted and forced her feet to propel her forward. One step after another, she moved further and further from him and did not allow herself to look back even once. Her heart hammering, she picked up speed until she was practically running, and she continued to run until she reached the Merc.

Once there, she banged inside, the shop bell ringing furiously, and leaned against the door, panting, as if she had just outrun a thief. She put her hand on her chest, breathing hard, and was surprised to see Mrs. Haufbrau already at her usual post behind the back counter, cool as a cucumber and peering at her as if she were some sort of lunatic. Harriet stood up straight and pulled off her hat. She had to concentrate on the task at hand.

"Is Melody here yet?" she asked, trying to keep her voice even as she slipped out of her coat.

Mrs. Haufbrau tilted her chin, indicating that Melody was in the office, and resumed dusting the already-dustless shelves with a large blue feather duster. Harriet proceeded to the office and gave the open door a quick needless knock.

Melody was sitting at her father's desk, her fists propping up her temples as she stared at a ledger book. "Oh, hello, Harriet. What is it?"

Still flustered, Harriet was tempted to tell Melody all about her encounter with John, but the somber look on Melody's face gave her pause. It was obviously not the time to talk about personal matters. Melody looked all business, so Harriet saw no choice but to get straight to the point.

"I've got the labels," she mumbled, digging around in her handbag for the sketches.

Melody's face brightened a little, and she closed the book. "Already?"

Harriet pulled out the small stack of papers and laid them on the desk.

"That was fast!" Melody picked up each one and examined them carefully. Each had a different lettering for LEAD WORKS CIDER and different images. One was of what looked like a badger hole, one was of Christmas Tree Hill, one was a mining shack, and one was a giant oak tree, with LEAD WORKS CIDER woven into the branches.

"Oh, I quite like this one." Melody held up the last one. "Which one do you like?"

"That's my favorite, too." Harriet twisted her hands, wondering how she should bring up Kate's condition. "She . . . she just has one request. Kate, I mean."

"To be paid? Yes, I know."

"Well, yes, but there's something else."

Melody looked at her quizzically.

"She wants you to sell her baskets. In the Merc, that is."

Melody rubbed the back of her neck. "What baskets?"

"She . . . she makes baskets out of reeds. And other stuff. They're really good."

Melody did not look convinced.

"She had about six of them at the Harvest Fest, and she sold them all!"

"How big are they?"

"All different sizes."

"How much did she sell them for?"

Harriet shifted. "Well, she sells them for whatever she thinks the person interested can afford."

Melody raised an eyebrow.

"I saw her sell one for three dollars."

"Three dollars!" Melody absently picked up a pencil and began to rapidly tap it on the desktop. "Well, I suppose we could try. But obviously, she'll have to put a set price on them. And the Merc gets thirty percent. Think she'd agree to that?"

Harriet thought this through and quickly decided that all things considered, Kate could not exactly be choosy. "I think so."

"Good. And how soon can she make more of these?" Melody pointed her pencil at the drawing.

"Well, she needs the labels and some ink."

"Ink? Doesn't she have any?"

"Well . . . not at the moment. She's just moved, you could say, and she doesn't have a lot of stuff."

Melody looked at her disbelievingly. "Who doesn't own a pen and ink?"

Harriet wrung her hands. "Well, she's actually living in a badger hole right now, so . . ."

"A badger hole! Like this?" Melody pulled out one of the drawings, which, upon closer inspection, did sort of resemble Kate's current abode.

Harriet nodded.

"But why? Doesn't she live with the Kerwyns?"

"Not just at the moment."

"Is she really an Indian?"

Harriet shrugged. "She thinks she is."

"Well, why is she living in a hole in Christmas Tree Hill?"

"It's not as bad as it sounds, actually. It's really quite cozy. But it's kind of a longer story." Harriet glanced over her shoulder. Customers were beginning to enter, and Mrs. Haufbrau would be irritated for the whole day if she had to wait on everyone alone, even if it was for only ten minutes. Mrs. Haufbrau was fierce in her grudges.

"Alright." Melody opened various drawers of her father's desk until she found a stack of yellowing labels. They were the old-fashioned type with tie strings. "I guess these will have to do." She handed them to Harriet and opened more drawers until she found a bottle of ink and several old fountain pens. "How about these?"

"Yes, that should do it." Harriet placed the items into her handbag. "And this design?" She held up the drawing of the oak tree. "Or . . . or do you need to ask Cal?"

"No, just go with that one. I don't need to ask Cal Fraiser every little thing," she said irritably.

Harriet paused. Melody was certainly not her bubbly self today. Perhaps it was the cares of the Merc weighing her down? She knew she should get out onto the floor, but maybe now was the time to tell her she had been right about John Schneider. Surely this would raise her spirits.

"Oh, and I forgot to tell you," Harriet said, hovering near the door. "I saw John in the street just now, and . . . well, you were right about him. He's not for me." She tried to say it nonchalantly and with a smile, but she was pretty sure she failed, if Melody's expression was anything to go by. Melody had closed her eyes and had put a hand to her head.

"What is it? Are you ill?" Harriet stepped closer.

Melody opened her eyes and let out a deep breath. "No, I'm not ill. But you shouldn't be so quick to applaud me. Never mind John Schneider; it seems I've made a big mistake about Wesley."

"Wesley?" Harriet bit her lip. Had Melody found out what had really happened at the bonfire?

Melody covered her face, her elbows leaning on the desk. "Perhaps you should sit down."

Harriet instinctively shut the office door and eased back into the chair opposite, suddenly quite worried. "What is it?"

Melody's lips twisted. "Wesley stopped by the Merc yesterday afternoon. It was after you left and just as Cal was leaving. He said he wanted to discuss the Merc's finances, but when we were alone, he . . . well, he stated that he . . . that he isn't attracted to you and that he has feelings for *me*! She let out a little chortle. "I had no idea, though I suppose certain things make sense now." Her brow was knitted as she looked across the desk at Harriet. "I'm sorry."

So. Wesley *did* prefer Melody to her. Harriet examined her hands in her lap. In truth, she felt an odd sense of relief to be rid of him—or the idea of him, at least as far as Melody was concerned—but it still stung to be so openly rejected.

"Did I . . . did I do something wrong?"

"No, of course not, dearest!" Melody said quickly. "You're perfectly marvelous! You mustn't waste one more thought on the likes of Wesley Elton. You're well rid of him. The right man will come along anytime now, someone infinitely more deserving. I'm sure of it!"

A fleeting image of John Schneider came into Harriet's head, then, but she didn't dare mention him as a restored potential suitor, as she feared Melody would still not approve. And besides, she realized suddenly with renewed agony, he had just snubbed her in the street.

CHAPTER
FIFTEEN

All night long, Melody tossed and turned, thinking about how Wesley had grabbed her in the office and tried to force–*force!*–her to marry him. The thought was abhorrent, and even his suggestion that the Merc's money problems would be over if she succumbed to him did not make his offer remotely tempting. She'd rather the Merc fail than marry Wesley Elton.

For just a moment, though, she allowed herself to imagine what *would* happen if she married him. What would Fred say? Or, she realized with a sickening sort of dread, had that been Wesley's real motive? To finally have one over on "ole Fred"–to have him return and find that the Merc, not to mention his little sister, had slipped through his fingers? But would Fred even care with his big law career ahead of him?

Melody flung off the covers, suddenly very hot. Surely not. And surely Wesley wasn't that smart. Or was he? He *did* seem awfully cunning . . . *Oh, what did it matter?* She wasn't going to marry him anyway. She rolled onto her side. And how on earth had she thought he would have been a good match for poor Harriet? She groaned aloud at the memory of the girl's flushed face when she had related what had happened. How could she have so badly led her astray?

The first birds were beginning to chirp now, so she decided to give up any further attempts at sleep and climbed out of bed. It was still dark, but she slipped on her pink silk robe and sat down at her desk. She would write a letter to Douglas. Though the decision to do so had *nothing* to do with Wesley's preposterous proposal and everything to do with how much she missed poor Dougie. She was very lucky to have him, she told herself, but, as she sat now with pen in hand and a blank sheet in front of her, she couldn't think of anything to say.

Dearest Douglas, she began. *How are you?*

She tapped her pen against her lips. She had nothing to report that would be remotely interesting to Douglas or any of the gang. Mrs. Ehlers's youngest broke his arm last week? Old Russ Thomas sold his lower thirty to the Portzens? Miss Yates from the library was the latest to come down with the flu? Melody rubbed her forehead and then wrote, *Things here are . . .* horrible? desperate? ridiculous? She crumpled the paper and tossed it in the can beside her desk.

She took a new sheet and bit the end of the pen, thinking. *Dearest Douglas,* she began again.

> *How are you? I must apologize for not writing sooner, but we've just had our Harvest Fest, and I was quite busy. I wish you could have been here to see it; Merriweather is quite lit up during the Fest, eager to show its best side, and this year was no exception. Even the Green Bay Acrobatics team came down and participated in the parade!*
>
> *My father, of course, is still in the hospital, and remains quite weak. I thought he might have been recovered by now, but,*

alas, no, though Mums hopes he might be home by Christmas. We are managing as best we can without him, and we are to take in two lodgers. Two bachelor men, half-brothers apparently, who are to arrive tomorrow. Mums, as you can imagine, is in quite a tizzy to get all ready.

But before you go and get yourself jealous, dearest Dougie, I wouldn't worry. I'm sure they are very old and probably very dull, and given that most of my time is spent at the Merc, I'll probably hardly ever see them.

She bit the end of the pen again and reached for a second page.

But speaking of being jealous, I've had a rather delightful letter from Elsie. She mentioned that she had tea with you and Charlie and Cynthia and the gang and also that you all went to the Aragon together, where you danced the night away with Vivian Anderson. How very kind you were to take pity on poor Viv, though I'm surprised she needed your escort, as she's never short of a partner, is she? No, indeed; she's the type that likes to flit from man to man, always teasing in that coy way of hers. I hope you won't fall under her spell, as I don't think the two of you would at all be right for each other. Not that you're in the slightest bit interested. I know you don't go for tall, curvaceous blondes.

Melody stopped to reread. With a sigh, she crumpled it into a ball and tossed it onto the floor. She picked up a new page and tried again.

I've had a rather delightful letter from Elsie in which she mentions all of you. How nice that you were all able to meet up together, and now I'm the jealous one! It was torturous to miss the fall ball, but I'm sure you all had fun. Thank you for your many suggestions to return to Chicago for a visit, but, sadly, I don't think I can spare any time away, especially with the holidays coming up. We are producing a new product—bottles of cider, which I'm most excited about. Of course, I miss you all, especially you, dearest Douglas. I love you to bits, as you know, and I think I have come to a decision about the question you put to me not so very long ago—

"Melody!" It was Mums. "I'm leaving now. I'm going to Dodgeville."

Dodgeville? Melody hurried out into the hallway.

"Wait!" she called, leaning over the banister to peer at her mother below, dressed in her good wool coat and sporting her best hat.

"Well, what is it, Melody? I'm in a hurry." Mums began pulling on her gloves.

"Why are you going to Dodgeville?"

"If you had come down to breakfast," Mums answered crisply, gesturing toward the dining room with one gloved hand, "you would know that I need to go to Wolski's. Helenka is making her famous pickle soup for the lodgers tomorrow, and she needs a special type of pickle. Apparently, you can only get it at Wolski's in Dodgeville. No one in Merriweather carries it."

Melody groaned. Her mother, and now apparently Helenka, were acting as if the lodgers were revered guests, not paying customers. Already, Mums had insisted that the whole house be cleaned from top to bottom, including washing all of the curtains and beating all of the rugs. Likewise, she had forced Melody and Bunny to rake up all the leaves and deadhead all the perennials, a task Melody resented considering how much she was already working at the Merc.

"And don't forget to finish trimming the hydrangeas," Mums said now, picking up her handbag. "Now, where are is the key? Maybe Helenka has it," she muttered and began to rummage through her handbag.

"Mums, I hardly think two bachelor men are going to notice if the hydrangeas are trimmed. Or if their curtains are washed and ironed, for that matter, or if the soup has the right kind of pickle. At this rate, they'll be *costing* us money!"

"Don't be fresh with *me*, Melody! You're like an old mother hen these days. What's gotten into you?" Mums opened the tiny drawer in the Chinese cabinet, still looking for the key to the Daimler. "And pick some flowers to put in their rooms!" she called as she bustled down the hallway out of sight.

"Flowers?" Melody leaned further over the banister. "It's October, Mums! Everything is dead!"

"You know very well there are plenty of asters. Pick some of those." She came back into view. "Ah! Here it is!" She pulled a key out of her coat pocket.

"But, Mums, *I* need the car today. I told Harriet I'd pick her up." Mrs. Mueller had the first batch of cider ready in the new bottles, and rather than have Harriet carry them all on her own, Melody had offered to pick her up in the Daimler.

"Well, I didn't know that, Melody, did I? I daresay Harriet will just have to make other arrangements." She opened the door. "I hope you don't think you're going to start driving to work now. You'd be wasting good gasoline."

Melody briefly closed her eyes at the irony, given that her mother was about to drive all the way to Dodgeville for some pickles.

Without another word, Melody retreated to her room. She would have to hurry. Maybe if she got to the Merc early, she could send Cal out to help Harriet. As she strode to her closet, peeling off her robe, her eye caught sight of her unfinished letter to Douglas. Well, she thought, it would have to wait.

She dressed quickly and ran down the stairs, grabbing her coat from the coat stand. But before she banged out the door, she had the sudden idea to telephone Harriet to let her know that the plans had changed and that she would send Cal. Unfortunately, though, it was Mrs. Mueller who answered.

"Why, Harriet's already left, Melody. Walking awfully slow carryin' all those bottles. You might just catch her if you hurry. How's your dad doing?"

* * *

Melody eventually managed to extract herself from further conversation and dashed out the door without any breakfast at all. She half hoped to see Harriet on the way, but she did not. As soon as she reached the shop, she called to Cal and suggested that he go pick her up. For once, Melody noted gratefully, he did not argue and seemed almost eager to go look for Harriet.

Melody tied on a shop skirt and tried to concentrate on the day ahead. This was an important day—the unveiling of the new product— well, the new packaging, anyway—and already it had started out badly. She hoped it wasn't a bad omen. She strode over to the display window to make sure all was in order. It was still the "Get Ready for Winter!" arrangement, but, as promised, she had added some of Kate's baskets, filling one with colorful Indian corn and another with apples. She had also placed a few of the smaller ones on the counter near the register. She picked one up now. She had to admit that they were good quality, but she wasn't sure they would sell any better than her luxury items, which she had now sadly relinquished to the back of the shop with the rest of ladies' wear. It grated on Melody that this had annoyingly been Mrs. Haufbrau's original suggestion, but she tried to ignore it.

Melody glanced at Mrs. Haufbrau now, busily going through one of the receipt books at the back counter. "Third time this month that girl's been late," she muttered.

Melody checked her wristwatch yet again. *Where on earth were they?* Just then, the shop bell rang, and Melody spun around hopefully. It was indeed Harriet, followed by a tall young man.

"I'm here!" Harriet called. "I'm sorry I'm late."

With a grunt, Harriet set a wire basket filled with eight bottles on the counter. Her companion did the same, minus the grunt.

Melody did not think she had ever seen this man before, but that was not entirely unusual. Given that Merriweather had a population of 2,800, Melody didn't know *everyone* in town. Plus, not everyone was partial to shopping at the Merc.

He was extremely attractive, with wavy brown hair and soft brown eyes, which held both intelligence and what could only be described as merriment. He was well-dressed in a tweed jacket and an argyle vest, complete with a striped yellow tie and good-quality shoes. He was immaculate, and when he smiled, it was an easy sort of grin that made Melody want to smile back.

Without even taking off her coat, Harriet held up two bottles. "Shall I put these in the window?"

Melody gave her a nod and moved to help. They needed to display the new product as soon as possible!

"May I assist?" the young man asked, removing his leather driving gloves. "I came upon this fair maiden on the road and offered to assist her. Like a fairy godfather," he said, rolling his hand in the air and then gesturing at himself. He had a dramatic, almost flamboyant, air. He picked up two bottles and carried them to Harriet, who had already climbed up into the window. "Along the way," he went on, as if telling a story, "this maiden enlightened me as to your wonderful project. You, of course, must be Melody Merriweather." He held out his hand, which she seemed to have no choice but to take. "Charmed, I'm sure."

"And you are?" As much as Melody was eager to get the bottles of cider into the window for the customers that were beginning to shuffle in, she was intrigued.

"Frank Churchill, at your service." He made a slight bow.

Frank Churchill? This was one of their lodgers! "You're not supposed to be here until tomorrow!"

Frank laughed. "Yes, I do apologize. There was a change in our itinerary, and we arrived early." He looked around the Merc appreciatively. "And this must be the famous Merc."

A trickle of unexplained embarrassment rippled through Melody. This elegant stranger did not remotely resemble what she had envisioned the lodgers would be like, and she suddenly wished, more than she normally did, to be anywhere but here.

"Exquisite." He continued gazing at the Merc's interior. He was obviously joking—who would describe the Merc as exquisite?—and yet he *seemed* sincere. "And what are these?" He picked up one of Kate's baskets.

"Oh, those are just some baskets that . . . that someone made."

"They are extraordinary," he said. "Do you have more?" His eyes darted around the shop again.

"Well, a few."

"I'd like this one," he said, picking up the biggest one and setting it on the counter. "And a bottle of cider."

"Oh, no! I wouldn't think of charging you for the cider. After you helped Harriet and all."

"No, I insist! All artists must be paid for their crafts, do you not agree? What else do you have that has been made by local artisans?"

Artisans? Melody vaguely knew what the word meant, but there were certainly not any artists around here, not by a long shot. "Artisans?" she asked feebly.

"Yes, you know, people who make things to sell. Local products." He gestured at the cider and the basket.

"Well, there's the Schneider honey," Melody offered hesitantly. "And their cheese. But that's in the back." Melody thought for a moment. "There's also the sausages. Cal makes those—a few different types. I don't know if that counts?"

Frank tilted his head in appreciation. "I'll take a sampling of the cheese and one of each flavor of sausage."

"Oh, Cal's out at the moment."

"Out?" Harriet asked from where she was still working in the display window.

"I sent him out to pick you up." Melody glanced out the front windows, wondering now where Cal had gotten himself off to.

"I'll go back and wrap them," Mrs. Haufbrau said grimly, placing the receipt book under the back counter.

Melody looked around at the various shelves but could not think of anything else. "I guess that's it."

"Don't forget the soaps Imogene makes!" Harriet called.

"Soaps?" Frank's eyebrows rose in curiosity, as if she had just mentioned that they had treasure hidden around the shop.

"Well, yes, there's those." Melody scratched her cheek. "But I'd hardly call them *artisanal*." Melody was tempted to call them dust-collectors, as they had yet to sell even one.

"I'm most intrigued. Perhaps you might point me in their direction?"

Melody led him to the back where the cleaning supplies were. "They're there." Melody pointed to the bottom shelf.

Frank bent down and picked one up. "But why do you have them all the way down here? These are lovely." He picked up several and then sniffed one, closing his eyes appreciatively. "Different scents," he observed and read off the different types. "Lavender, Rose, Peppermint, Bergamot, and Rosemary. I'll have one of each," he said, trying to balance them all in his hands.

"Mr. Churchill, please. I appreciate what you're trying to do, but it's really not necessary. Thank you, though."

"But I *do* want to purchase these things. It is why I am here, in a manner of speaking. And what are these delightful creatures?" He stopped in front of Melody's luxury collection and, awkwardly shifting the soaps, stroked a scarf. It was the one with swirls of paisley in greens and blues, Melody's personal favorite.

"Those aren't homemade."

"No, I can see that." He winked at her. "But I simply must have one." He selected the blue-and-green paisley, draped it over the soaps, then proceeded with his stash to the front counter. Mrs. Haufbrau joined them, setting down the requested packages of sausages and cheese wrapped in white butcher paper and labeled with her spidery handwriting, before hurrying to the back counter, where Mrs. Tierney was now waiting.

Melody picked up the first item to begin ringing, but her attention was pulled away when Cal suddenly blustered in the front door. "I couldn't find—" he stopped abruptly. "Oh, Harriet," he said, catching sight of her in the window. "You're back." His eyes traveled to Melody and then to the mysterious stranger.

"You must be Cal Fraiser," Frank said with his easy grin and held out a hand.

Cal shook it hesitantly. "Do I know you?"

"No, my good sir, you do not. I have the advantage, for which I apologize. Your young assistant, Miss Mueller—"

"Oh, call me Harriet!" the girl called from the window.

"Harriet," Frank corrected himself, "told me all about everyone on our short drive over. I'm very pleased to meet you."

Cal was obviously trying to size the man up, which, Melody conceded, was a difficult task. Frank Churchill seemed to be teasing them in some way, and yet he also seemed entirely sincere. "You're not from around here, are you?" Cal asked.

"No, you have me there. I am not. I'm from Libertyville, Illinois. Ever hear of it? It's between Chicago and Milwaukee. Probably closer to Milwaukee. But my grandparents are from Merriweather."

"They are?" Melody asked, intrigued. "Who are they?"

"The Herrigs? Alfred and Odelia?"

"The Herrigs were related by marriage to the Warehams," Mrs. Haufbrau called from the back counter, obviously eavesdropping as she wrapped up a bottle of cough syrup for Mrs. Tierney. Mrs. Haufbrau was a living encyclopedia on the inhabitants of Merriweather, her own family being one of the oldest in town, not unlike the Merriweathers themselves.

"Yes, that's it!" Frank said delightedly.

"Just visiting, then?" Cal's tone was wary.

"In a manner of speaking," he said. "If you count the cemetery. They are long since passed on."

"I was just going to say that," Mrs. Haufbrau called.

Cal tossed back his lock of hair. "That's a long way to come to lay flowers on a grave."

"Honestly, Cal!" Melody exclaimed. "It's none of your business what Mr. Churchill is doing in town!"

"Call me Frank, please." He shot Melody a smile. "I appreciate your concern, my good man," he said, looking back at Cal, "but I–"

"I'm *not* your good man." Cal crossed his arms.

"Cal! Don't you have something to do?" Melody looked toward the meat counter. "I think there's customers back there." Cal remained firmly in place, however. *Why was he acting this way?*

"Undoubtedly, you are all suspicious. And well you should be. Strangers in town, and all of that. But I mean you no harm, I promise. My purpose, and that of my brother, will be revealed all in good time." His eyes darted around the Merc again.

"If you must know, Cal," Melody added, "Mr. Churchill–"

"Frank."

"Frank," she continued, "and his brother are renting rooms from us. They are to be our lodgers."

"Lodgers?" Cal looked at her skeptically. "Since when do you have lodgers?"

"Since tomorrow," she said stiffly, emphasizing each word. "And before anyone asks, yes, my father does know, and so does my mother. This was her idea. Not that we mind," she said, giving Frank an uneasy smile.

"What do I owe you?"

"Oh, yes! I forgot to finish ringing you." She moved past the rigid Cal again and quickly began to push the worn buttons on the cash register. "I'm afraid it comes to $10.65," she said tentatively. "You sure you don't want to put something back?"

Frank laughed. "Not at all. Here you are." He gave her two ten-dollar bills, and she counted out his change while Harriet, who had finally left the window and taken up her spot behind the counter, bagged up his purchases.

"Thank you, Miss Merriweather, Harriet. I'll be off now."

"I think you should call me Melody, don't you?" Melody handed him his packages.

He smiled. "Melody."

"Oh, but wait! Where are you off to? We weren't expecting you until tomorrow! I . . . I suppose I could take you over to the house now, but no one's home at the moment." Well, except Helenka, who would *not*, Melody knew, be pleased to see the guests a full day early.

"Heavens, no! Julius and I are quite happy to spend the night at the hotel." He nodded in the direction of the Baker Street Inn, which was an odd name for the establishment since there wasn't a Baker Street in Merriweather. "We wouldn't dream of arriving early. No, no, no."

"Oh! But what a waste of money! I can take you over a little later. There's a very good diner just down the street, the Checkerboard, if you'd like to wait."

Frank laughed again. "I wouldn't hear of it! No, I insist. We will spend the night at the Baker. We've already checked in. We'd like to explore and get a feel for the town. We will arrive at your home tomorrow at four o'clock, as expected. Until then, I bid you adieu. Harriet, Melody, Cal—it was a pleasure meeting you." His packages tucked under his arm, he gave a formal sort of bow and exited the shop, the bell tinkling.

Upon his exit, all three of them stood looking at the door for several moments.

"What an odd man," Harriet finally said. "But in a nice way, don't you think?"

"I'll say he's odd," Cal said, turning toward the back. "You can do what you want, but I wouldn't trust him."

Melody rolled her eyes. "Well, I think he's quite pleasant. Charming, even. And that's exactly what this town needs more of," she said, loud enough for Cal to hear, "some charm!"

CHAPTER
SIXTEEN

"What a charming room, Mrs. Merriweather," Frank Churchill commented as he took a seat at The Willows's dinner table the following evening. "This shade of green is perfect, do you not think, Julius?" he asked the young man who was squeezing himself into the seat across from him.

Indeed, while Frank Churchill was thin and trim, his half-brother was somewhat plump. In fact, the two looked nothing like each other, save their noses perhaps, though Melody wasn't sure. She was trying not to stare.

Julius smiled briefly in agreement and pushed his spectacles closer to his eyes with one finger.

"Thank you, Mr. Churchill," Mums said regally, taking her seat as well. She was wearing her best peach Lanvin gown and had demanded that Melody and Bunny dress accordingly. Melody had put on her scarlet Vionnet, and was glad, truth be told, that Mums had insisted, as their two guests had both descended in black tie! Oh, how she wished Cal were here to see what men of culture wore at dinner. Or Harriet, for that matter. One look at Mr. Churchill and Mr. Fairfax would put the last nail in the coffin on any romantic ideas Harriet might still be harboring for John Schneider, despite her protests to the contrary. Melody had not failed to see a telltale sparkle in her eyes, albeit faint, as the girl had reported her recent denouncement of John. Harriet had simply not been exposed to men of a better caliber. Wesley did not count, as he was obviously *not* of a better caliber. But she didn't want to think of that right now.

Frank rose to hold her chair for her, and she slipped into it. While she did enjoy dressing in the lovely things from her Chicago days, she wondered if her mother intended to keep up this dress code every night. She wasn't sure she could sustain it. After all, she was bone-tired after working at the Merc all day, and just the thought of donning an evening gown each night exhausted her.

"Do sit down, Mr. Churchill," Mums twittered from the far end of the table.

Frank gave her a slight bow and sat down with only a quick glance at his brother. "But you must call us Frank and Julius. We insist, don't we, Julius?"

"Y . . . yes, of course," he stuttered.

Melody had noticed the stutter as soon as the two men had arrived. Frank, with his classic good looks and easy manner, was the natural spokesman for the pair, while his older brother—at least he *seemed* older, as some of his hair was already thinning—was quiet and shy. It was unfortunate, Melody reflected, that one brother had been given such a handsome physique and winsome ways, while the other, who was not ugly, per se, was certainly not what one would call attractive, nor did his personality seem to lend itself to pleasant conversation. Melody wondered if they shared a father or a mother.

"I must thank you for the asters," Frank continued. "They are lovely."

"That was me!" Bunny chirped from where she sat on Julius's left.

Melody resisted the urge to sigh. It *had* been Bunny who had put the flowers in the guests' rooms, but only after she had been forced to. Melody gave her sister a quick glance and observed that her previous sulking attitude regarding the lodgers had already been miraculously transformed into one of genuine interest and consideration. Melody was pretty sure it was due to Frank's high praise of her skill at the piano during Mums's tour earlier in the afternoon, which Bunny had apparently refused to participate in. Instead, she had stubbornly perched herself on the piano bench and had begun playing Mozart's "Allegro in D Minor" as loudly as she could. She was just finishing this piece when Mums and the two brothers happened to pass through the music room, and Frank, apparently, had applauded and asked her to play more. He and Julius had even taken up chairs and waited with what seemed sincere anticipation until Bunny had obliged with a short étude from Chopin. This was the probable cause of the random smiles that continued to erupt on her sister's face. Even now, Bunny was looking at Frank in a shamefully adoring sort of way.

"Thank you, then, Bunny. And might I say, what an intriguing nickname. It is a nickname, is it not?"

Bunny blushed again. "Yes, it's short for Elizabeth."

"How ever did you become Bunny?" He flashed his gorgeous dimples.

"I really don't remember, except that I had a pair of pet rabbits as a little girl. And soon we had too many." She laughed. "I think it was Freddy who started calling me Bunny. Isn't that right, Mums?"

"Yes, something like that," Mums said dismissively. "Mr. Churchill—Frank—would you mind pouring the wine?"

Wine? Melody had somehow not noticed the bottle near her mother's right elbow. While they certainly had a respectable stockpile in the wine cellar, thanks to Pops, Melody knew it was a finite supply and one they could not afford to squander. Mums's apparent desire to impress the lodgers was admittedly rubbing off on her a bit, but having wine every night at dinner was, like the evening gowns, not something they could manage for long.

"But, of course, Mrs. Merriweather." Frank stood and moved around the table, pouring a French burgundy into each glass.

"We're ready, Helenka!" Mums shouted.

Helenka immediately came through the swinging door—as if she had been hovering on the other side, say—and placed a bowl of what looked like potato soup in front of each of them as well as a basket of hot, fresh rolls in the center of the table.

Frank, upon elegantly returning to his seat, was the first to take a tentative sip of the soup. "Why, this is delicious! It reminds me of the one we had in Kraków. Remember, Julius?"

Julius nodded briefly as he shoveled the soup into his mouth.

"Quite astute," Mums said approvingly. "Helenka is Polish. She's a wonderful cook."

"You've been to Europe, then, Mr. Churchill?" Bunny asked.

"Frank," he corrected. "But, yes. Julius and I have traveled extensively."

"Oh! Tell us where!" Bunny exclaimed. "Have you been to Paris?"

Frank smiled. "Yes, several times."

"Is it as lovely as they say it is?"

He winked at her. "Better."

Frank launched into a tale of a palace they had toured on the outskirts of Paris, which lasted until Helenka returned to clear the soup bowls and began serving the main course, beef Wellington in a bed of rich gravy. When the last plate was set down, she stood waiting for Mums's nightly invitation to join them—but tonight, Mums simply said, "Thank you, Helenka. That will be all."

Despite the absurdity of their nightly ritual, Melody felt sorry for poor Helenka, who seemed not to know what to do. Melody tried to give her an encouraging smile, but Helenka's eyes remained on Mums, who finally looked at her and gave a quick tilt of her head toward the kitchen. Helenka slunk away.

Melody took a deep breath and turned her attention back to their guests. "So, what brings you to Merriweather, then?" she asked. "Work?" She took a bite of her entrée. The beef was perfectly tender and the pastry light and flaky. It was certainly delicious, though Mums and Helenka had obviously ignored her plea to economize.

"You could say that." Frank took a bite. "This is delicious!"

"What work do you do?" Bunny asked.

"Julius and I are in what you might call the restoration business; isn't that right, Julius?"

Julius nodded and delicately dabbed the corner of his mouth with his napkin.

Restoration? Melody perked up. "Well, you've certainly come to the right place. The whole town needs restoring!"

"Julius and I feel as though the world is changing too rapidly," Frank continued. "That there is not enough emphasis on the things of the past. Modernity is taking us over. The old ways are passing by the wayside, and we wish to do our bit to stop such things."

Melody blinked. This was not what she had expected him to say. "What are you talking about? We need to go forward, not backward. Look at the mess we're in with the mines closed and the Depression. Plus, the war and everything."

"It is exactly because we have abandoned a simpler way of life that we are in the mess we're in."

Melody blinked several times.

"Have you not heard of William Morris?" He looked around the table.

Melody could tell by the way her mother's chin pivoted toward the kitchen that she was about to ask Helenka through the door, but she caught herself and took a sip of wine instead.

"Who?" Bunny asked.

"William Morris? He was an English textile artist of sorts, also a painter and a writer. He was part of the Birmingham set in Oxford and shared ideas with the likes of Edward Burne-Jones. They greatly admired Carlyle and Ruskin and even Malory. They espoused a deep love for craftsmanship as a way of life, almost a religion. And being unable to separate their ideals of beauty with societal reform, they founded the Arts and Crafts Society."

"My!" Mums exclaimed. "I haven't the slightest idea what you're talking about, Mr. Churchill."

Frank chuckled. "Forgive me, Mrs. Merriweather. All I'm saying is that the Arts and Crafts movement valued craftsmanship and beauty, and they reviled the modern factories springing up across Victorian England. Where craftsmen once enjoyed their work, conceiving of a design and then shaping it into an object—a spoon, a chair, a rug—such as in medieval times—factory workers began to file into a dark cavern and mechanically produce *parts* of an object, which only later came together to form a whole, and into which they had no input regarding its design or purpose. The workers themselves became parts of a machine and were made to produce something not of their mind, and certainly not of their heart. Thus it is that a great sadness has come over the world. People think it is because of the war, and while that is true in a certain way, the brutalness of this last war was itself a result of this deviation from the natural way of things."

"So you feel that factories and machines are bad?" Bunny asked. "But what about cars and . . . and all of the other new things being produced these days? Aren't they good?"

"Not when it rips our very souls apart, dear child. This is why there is so much unhappiness in the world. And, in turn, this is why the medieval age was one of the great periods of history—because the craftsman took pleasure in his work. Look at the great cathedrals of Europe. They are beautiful masterpieces created by hand by unsophisticated peasants."

"My!" Mrs. Merriweather exclaimed again and caught Melody's eye. It was the first indication that she was perhaps having second thoughts regarding the choice of lodgers.

Melody, however, found them fascinating and was grateful to be back in the presence of someone who wanted to discuss something besides the weather or the price of corn. She was reminded of the lectures she and Elsie had sometimes attended on Sunday afternoons at the Newberry Library. She wished Elsie were here right now! She would love this! "Where did you say you're from? Chicago?"

"I grew up near Chicago, yes, but I studied for several years in London, which is where I met . . . which is where Julius joined me. From home, that is." He gave Julius a quick glance. "He is a great scholar of medieval literature, are you not, Julius?"

Julius nodded. "N-n-not great," he stuttered. "But y-y-yes, it is my area of ex-expertise."

"Julius is much too modest!" Frank exclaimed, looking around the table. "He took a first from Oxford, and it was Julius, bless him, who introduced me to the concepts behind the aesthetic invention and social imagination of central Europe and also to the theories of the Birmingham set, as I mentioned before. Brilliant thinkers. Fascinating stuff. So much so that we have decided to devote our lives to it."

"To what exactly?" Melody asked. "I thought you said you were in the business of restoration."

Frank laughed again. "Yes, we are hoping in a small way to restore society. We are traveling around the Midwest, looking for a place to form a community of artisans and craftsmen. To found our own artists' colony, our own arts and crafts society, as it were."

"Are you artists?" she asked, looking from one to the other.

"Sadly, no. But we *appreciate* art, do we not, Julius? We are ever in search of it. Even the most lowly amongst us can be an artisan. This is what is so thrilling—the discovery!"

Melody took a large drink of her wine. Might as well not waste it. "Now I see why you were so interested in the local products at the Merc yesterday."

"Exactly! And very good they were."

"But why Merriweather? Why not some other town?"

"In truth, it *could* be any town, but I decided to begin with my own roots, to return to the town my grandparents immigrated to, though we are considering Dodgeville and Prairie du Chien as well.

"Were your grandparents Cornish? Or German?"

"They were Cornish, I believe. I do have a few vague memories of visiting them, but I'd like to explore more. It's quite a charming town from what we've seen so far, is it not, Julius?"

Melody blinked. *Merriweather? Charming?* It was not the word she would have selected, though she supposed one *could* call it charming if one looked at it in a certain way.

"Plus, there's the fact that it was a mining town," Frank went on, "now defunct, which belies a certain romanticism. It is perfect. A phoenix rising from the ashes, as it were."

"Have you ever been down in a mine?" Mums asked skeptically.

"No, I have not, and I understand your sentiment, Mrs. Merriweather. I do not mock the brutality of the miners' toil, plunging into the dark bowels of the earth like their brethren, the factory workers, descending into the caverns of a factory. No, Julius and I wish to honor their hard work through preservation and education and the sale of the products of their handiwork. Too much of our history is being torn down. We wish to protect and save it. To encourage a simpler, more noble way of life."

"That all sounds well and good, Mr. Churchill, but I don't think that sort of thing is going to fly in a place like Merriweather. It's not at all sophisticated." Mums wiped her mouth.

"We're not looking for sophisticated. Quite the opposite, in fact." He glanced at Melody. "Take your young butcher, for example. This

Cal Fraiser. A perfect specimen of an artisan, his honest hands grinding meat and forming them into sausages, one by one. What if he were given more latitude for creating other things, other products? Would that not be freeing? More pleasurable to him? And the community as a whole would benefit from his handiwork."

Melody almost spit out her wine at this fanciful description of Cal, who was anything but an artisan longing for avenues of creativity. But Kate Kerwyn was, she thought as she set her glass down, slowly swirling the remains. Kate's drawing for the cider labels, not to mention her baskets, really were quite good. She was about to say so, but Frank spoke first.

"Julius and I would very much like to tour the old zinc mines and maybe the original village. What was it called?"

"New Grimsby?" Mums asked.

"Yes, that's it. I'm almost sure that's where my grandparents lived."

"Well, you'll be disappointed with the zinc mines. All dilapidated now."

"Still, we'd like to see it, would we not, Julius?"

"Mmm," Julius mumbled agreeably.

"Do you think you could find time to accompany us?" Frank asked Melody.

"I could go!" Bunny offered.

"You'll do no such thing!" Mums replied. "You have school tomorrow."

Frank maintained his gaze on Melody. She averted her eyes and tried to think. Although it was tempting to have a day away from the Merc, she felt it would be unwise to leave the shop's helm just as they were rolling out the new bottles of cider, especially since Mrs. Haufbrau had thus far refused to touch it. Plus, there was the embarrassing fact that Melody knew very little about New Grimsby.

But, she realized with a smile, Harriet did.

CHAPTER
SEVENTEEN

Harriet carefully climbed out of the shiny Buick Roadster with the help of Frank Churchill's hand. She had been reluctant to accompany the brothers to the mines and to New Grimsby, but Melody had been quite insistent. And when Melody was insistent, Harriet found it hard to deny her.

The three of them had first driven out to the old zinc works north of town, which Frank was quite disappointed by, but that didn't surprise Harriet. There wasn't much to see. The mines were abandoned, with big weeds growing everywhere, nature reclaiming the space. Doors were hanging off the buildings, and the windows had nearly all been broken by gangs of kids throwing rocks.

Frank and Julius had walked around as much of it as they dared but had eventually given up. They had hoped, Frank had confided to Harriet on the drive to New Grimsby, to make something of the ruins, but it was obvious now that it would cost a small fortune to do so. Harriet could have told them that, but of course, they hadn't asked.

"Well, this is it," she said now, gesturing awkwardly down Magnolia Street. New Grimsby was basically just a row of limestone cottages.

Frank stood, his hands on his hips, surveying the street while Julius climbed out of the back. "Yes," Frank murmured. "I'm sure this is it. I'm sure I remember this."

Julius joined him and tented his eyes with one hand.

"It's beautiful, is it not, Julius?"

Julius did not answer beyond a slight nod. Harriet looked down the street again. Even with the hollyhocks and the morning glories growing at the base of many of the cottages, she wouldn't call them beautiful, per se. They were just, well, cottages. Nothing like the stately homes on Ridge. Though she herself didn't see the appeal, it was kind of nice that someone else thought they were nice.

"And what is that there?" Frank pointed to the hill beyond the cottages. "I seem to remember it had a name."

"Christmas Tree Hill? That's where the first mines were."

"Yes, that's it!" Frank gazed up at it and then back at her, as if waiting for her to go on.

"Well," Harriet faltered, not knowing exactly what to say, "when the first miners got here from Cornwall, they began digging holes, like badgers, on Christmas Tree Hill, looking for lead. That's why they were called badger holes. They lived in them, too, until they built the cottages. They found a little bit of lead, but they eventually started mining further north where the vein was stronger."

"And are these badger holes still there?" Frank shot Julius a hopeful glance.

"Well, yes." Harriet hesitated, wondering if she should tell them about Kate. "My friend lives in one of them, actually," she offered, making a spur-of-the-moment decision. "She's the one who makes the baskets."

"Baskets?"

"At the Merc? You bought one of them. You said they were 'exceptional,' I think is how you put it."

"Indeed?" Frank beamed. "The artist lives *here*? In a hole in the ground? Why, this is marvelous, is it not, Julius! May we meet her?"

"I . . . I suppose so. If you want." Harriet wondered if Kate would be angry. Probably. Certainly annoyed.

"Yes, yes. We can go now if you like. Lead on," Frank said eagerly.

"The fastest way is to cut through the field behind our cottage. But we should probably stop and say hello to my mother first, or she'll wonder who's traipsing through the back. We get a lot of hobos wandering through, you see," she tried to explain. "They get off the trains down by the depot."

"Hobos, you say? But this is perfect! And your mother is the one who makes the cider, is she not? It's quite good. Julius and I finished off a bottle between us. Lead on, lead on, we must meet her, too."

Harriet proceeded up the flagstone path, wondering what her mother would make of the two strangers.

"Mom?" she called upon opening the door. As usual, her mother was standing at the stove. Rosemary jumped and turned around sharply.

"Oh! It's you, Harriet! What are you doing home? Something happen?"

Harriet stepped inside the dim interior. The thick limestone walls kept most of the cottages in New Grimsby cool no matter what the weather, but the Mueller cottage was always warm due to Rosemary's nearly constant baking. Today was no exception, as the delicious smell of baking pasties hung in the air.

"No, nothing's wrong, Mom."

Frank and Julius followed her in, looking around curiously. "Utterly charming," Frank muttered. "Perfectly delightful, is it not, Julius?"

"Who's this then?" Rosemary asked, peering at them.

"Mom, this is Mr. Frank Churchill and his brother, Julius . . . ?"

"Fairfax," Frank answered for Julius.

"They're visiting Merriweather," Harriet explained. "Melody sent me to show them around."

"Did she now?" Rosemary wiped her hands on a dish towel. "Well, why would you bring them to Grimsby? Should show them the opera house. Or maybe Fountain Park. Or the Falls out near Summer Valley. That's usually what people come to see. Here, sit down. Have you had your lunch? I've just made a batch of pasties. Gone on, sit down!"

"Mom, we can't stay. We're just on our way to see the badger holes," Harriet insisted, glancing nervously at the brothers.

"Badger holes? Well, there's plenty of those to see. They'll wait. Sure you don't want a pasty?"

Frank looked at Julius. "I suppose we could sit a while. I haven't had a pasty since I was a little boy," he said with a smile. "Are you sure you have enough?"

"Oh, plenty," Rosemary said, opening the oven door to inspect them. "Harriet, you set the table. Quick, like. These are done."

Slightly mortified, Harriet saw no other choice but to hurriedly set the table. She hoped the brothers weren't just being polite. She put the brown sauce on the table just as Rosemary brought over their old stoneware platter, piled with pasties. Frank and Julius took a seat at the worn, circular oak table, and Rosemary unceremoniously plopped a pasty onto each of their plates with her hands. Harriet, her face pink, studied the embroidery on her napkin.

"There you are! Now, you get stuck in while I make some fresh tea. Don't forget the sauce," she called over her shoulder on her way back to the stove.

Frank and Julius peered at the half-moon-shaped pastries with curiosity. Frank leaned over his to absorb the aroma. "It's just what I remember!" Julius, meanwhile, picked up his knife and fork and carefully punctured his.

"Dear Julius," Frank implored, "while you of course may consume this delicacy with the aid of cutlery, you may, according to local custom"—he glanced at Harriet as if for approval—"simply pick it up with your hands and eat it. Like so." He lifted the pasty and took a tentative bite and immediately rolled his eyes in pleasure. "Delicious!" He took another bite.

Julius, a bit perplexed, set down his knife and fork and followed suit, taking a small bite, after which he nodded in agreement with Frank's previous exclamation.

"Here, try it with sauce," Harriet said, pushing the jar toward Frank.

"What is it?" Frank asked as he spooned some onto the pasty's gooey center, which was filled with soft potatoes and carrots and thyme.

"It's kind of like ketchup," Harriet explained. "It's an old Cornish recipe. Mom makes it herself."

Frank applied another spoonful. "Mmm, delicious," he mumbled through another bite. "Do try it, dear Julius," he said, handing him the jar.

"Where'd you have pasties as a boy?" Rosemary called from the kitchen as she poured a kettle of hot water into a teapot. "That's what you said, right?"

Frank swallowed what was in his mouth. "Here, actually. I used to visit my grandparents in Merriweather as a boy."

"Did you now?" Rosemary carried the teapot to the table. "Don't recall any Churchills . . . That's what you said your name was, right?"

"Yes, but they were my mother's parents. The Herrigs?"

Rosemary's face lit up. "Odelia and Al? Yes, I knew them. Quiet old couple. Lived down at the end, till they passed. Didn't even know they had grandchildren. Not that I can recall, anyway. They had a daughter . . . Pearl, I think her name was. That would have been your mother, wouldn't it? She went off somewhere. I forget where." She looked at Harriet as if she might supply the answer. "My memory isn't what it used to be, is it, Harriet? Didn't realize she had children."

"Well, it was just me. I was an only child."

Rosemary looked at Julius. "Thought you were brothers."

"Stepbrothers. I should have said. We share a father, you see." He shifted slightly.

"Ah! That explains why you look nothing like each other. Well, I'll be. Odelia and Al's grandson, sitting right here."

"Is there anyone living in their old cottage?" he asked hopefully, taking another large bite. "If I'm remembering correctly, it's the one at the end?"

"No, no one's there now. The Murphys had it for a spell after your old Al died, but they lost it in the crash. Bank foreclosed. Surprised your ma didn't come back and claim it."

"Well, she died." He said it plainly, briefly. "They both died."

"Sorry to hear that," Rosemary mused. "What of?"

"Mom!"

Frank smiled politely. "Diphtheria. But that's a story for another time perhaps." He took a sip of the tea Rosemary had poured out. "So there's no one there now? In the cottage, that is?"

"Nah, it's abandoned. All boarded up."

"Well, we'll have to inquire, won't we, Julius? See if we can have a look at some point." He pushed back his empty plate. "That was utterly delicious, Mrs. Mueller," he said, his pleasant manner returning. "I haven't had something that good in a long time, and that's the truth."

Harriet was surprised by this, considering he had eaten at the Merriweathers' last night, and they had a *real* cook.

"Mom's Cornish, too, aren't you, Mom?" Harriet pushed back her empty plate, too, but not before surreptitiously licking her thumb and pressing it against the few crumbs left. She quickly deposited them into her mouth.

"I am, yes." Rosemary grinned. "Came here as a babe in arms."

"What's your maiden name, may I ask?" Frank inquired.

"Pengelly."

"Ah, yes! An entirely Cornish name."

"That's why her cider is so good," Harriet added. "She uses a secret ingredient."

"Don't you go tellin' now, girl," Rosemary chided, though the corners of her mouth turned up into a smile.

"We've had your cider, haven't we, Julius? And I can say I haven't tasted any finer."

"My, Mr. Churchill. You must stop or my head won't fit through the door!" Rosemary smiled fully now.

"Speaking of doors, shouldn't we get going?" Harriet asked. As much as she was enjoying this time away from the Merc, she was beginning to feel guilty.

"Yes, quite right." Frank stood, as did Julius.

"Here, I'll wrap a few of these up for Kate since you're going up that way." Rosemary shuffled over to the sink and pulled out the old basket. "It'll be just like the old days when miners took these down to the pit for their dinner. A whole meal in one, you see." She held one up as if to illustrate her point and then wrapped it in a cloth and set it in the basket.

"Yes, my grandmother told me."

Rosemary looked around for anything else she might include and settled on a jar of newly canned wax beans and what was left of the zucchini bread they had enjoyed yesterday.

"Here ya are, Harriet." She handed her the basket. "Told her a hundred times to stay here with us, haven't we? She isn't half stubborn, though. Got a will of iron, that one, doesn't she, Harriet?"

Harriet did not respond but merely took the basket and moved toward the door.

"Oh, wait! Take this!" Rosemary called, grabbing a small bouquet of rosemary from several hanging nearby. She nestled it into the basket. "I just made these. Tell her to hang it by the door so that the f—"

"Yes, Mom! I know," Harriet interrupted, suddenly mortified that her mother was about to lapse into fairy talk. *Honestly!* Talking about fairy folk and brownies and giants was fine around the fire at home, but it would never do for her mother to mention such things in front of other people. It was embarrassing. Harriet already suspected that her mother was considered odd by the rest of the townsfolk, and she had no desire that these newcomers should think so, too. "Ready?" she called to Frank and Julius. Without waiting for an answer, she hurried outside, where the cool October air was welcome against her overly warm face.

"It was a pleasure, Mrs. Mueller!" Frank said enthusiastically, as he bent slightly to duck through the doorway. "I do hope we meet again."

"Stop on your way back, if you want!" Rosemary called, waving a dish towel as they followed Harriet around to the back.

Harriet, still flustered, led them quickly through the rows of vegetables, past the small chicken coop and the outhouse, and then through the sun-bleached cedar gate attached to a stone fence, which was so crumbling and sunken that they could have easily just stepped over it. Harriet, however, chose to go through the gate as a point of pride.

The field beyond had been recently shorn, and the stiff stubbles underfoot pressed uncomfortably into the soles of Harriet's thin shoes. No doubt her guests, with what looked like expensive shoes, did not notice. She tried to keep ahead of them, as she had no desire to engage in any more conversation, which wasn't hard to do. In fact, she was nearly three-quarters up Christmas Tree Hill when she thought to turn and check on her companions' progress, only to find that they were barely halfway up. They had stopped climbing and were turned now toward the town, pointing at various structures on Magnolia Street below them.

Harriet felt a rare burst of irritation. She did not relish introducing these strangers to Kate, who would undoubtedly be annoyed, nor did she enjoy the fact that it was taking time away from the Merc. At this rate, she would miss the evening rush, which was when Melody most needed her.

"It's this way!" Harriet called. The two men looked up and then resumed their climb up the old cow path. Satisfied that they were now following in earnest, Harriet continued as well, quickly stepping toward the right and narrowly avoiding a cow pie.

"This friend of yours," Frank puffed, finally catching up. "What's she like?"

Harriet looked over her shoulder briefly and then back at the path, which was steeper now and needed her attention. "There's not much to tell. She . . . she's very independent. She wants to make her own way."

"Has she always lived up here?"

"No, this is recent. She grew up with the Kerwyns. Then she tried going away to Stoughton to be a maid, or something like that, but it didn't suit her. So now she's living out here. She . . . she likes to be alone."

"But you bring her things," he said, nodding at the basket.

"Yes, but it's not charity. It's just Mom's way. Kate doesn't ask for it; in fact, she doesn't like it!" Harriet said, suddenly feeling the need to defend her friend.

"No, but this is real community. This is what Julius and I are striving for, a sense of belonging. A fraternity, a collective of craftsmen—and women!—who are devoted to the joy of their art and who help each other. This is our dream!"

Harriet wasn't so sure Kate was weaving baskets for the joy of it, and she certainly wasn't doing it to be part of a collective. She was doing it to survive. Still, Harriet didn't say this aloud. Instead, she tried to think of a different subject but was interrupted by the sound of a cry coming from further down the hill. Julius seemed to have tumbled over.

Frank gave a little gasp of alarm and slid back down the path to help the oldish young man. "Dear Julius!" Frank exclaimed, tenderly taking him by the arm. "You must be more careful," he chastised gently, giving him a look of concerned affection. Harriet began to wonder if there was perhaps something wrong with Julius. He had yet to utter one word. Perhaps he was a mute? Or maybe a half-wit?

"Are you okay, Mr. Fairfax?" she called.

"Yes, he's fine, aren't you, Julius? Carry on, Harriet! We'll follow." Harriet tried to slow her pace for the last little bit out of compassion for the newcomers. She was relieved when Kate's dwelling came into view. "There it is," Harriet said over her shoulder as she pointed. "It's just ahead."

"This is utterly fascinating, is it not, Julius?" Frank said breathlessly when they finally reached the little plateau. The two of them gazed at the magnificent view of Merriweather below.

Harriet, meanwhile, approached the door and gave it a knock, suddenly praying that Kate was out somewhere cutting weeds or gathering sticks or pebbles or fish or whatever else she collected. Perhaps if no one answered, she could persuade the brothers to turn back. But her hopes were dashed by the sudden opening of the door, which revealed Kate herself, dressed oddly in trousers and what looked like a boy's shirt, though her black hair was still woven into two tight braids.

"Kate?"

"I told you not to knock."

Harriet's eyes narrowed. "Where did you get those clothes?"

"Edmund brought me some things. I can't live up here in a dress. It's ridiculous. This is much more freeing." She turned to the left and the right and then let out a rare laugh.

In truth, Harriet was intrigued by women wearing trousers, but she had no desire to don a pair and draw unnecessary attention to herself. Melody had sported a pair one day, which had utterly shocked Mrs.

Haufbrau and probably all of their customers. Cal, too, had taken notice, Harriet observed, going by the number of times she had caught him staring at Melody that day.

"Who's this?" Kate demanded, peering past her now as Frank and Julius approached. Julius was puffing slightly and wiping his forehead with a handkerchief.

"Kate, this is Frank Churchill and Julius Fairfax. They're lodging with Melody's family for a while. They like crafts and . . . things." Harriet didn't know how else to describe them.

"It's a pleasure to meet you, Miss . . .?"

"You can just call me Kate." She looked them up and down. "Or Indian Kate."

Harriet let out a quiet little moan.

"Indian?" Frank's eyes widened. "Are you an Indian?"

"Yes, I am." Kate folded her arms across her chest now, almost as if imitating . . . who? An Indian chief?

"Well . . . you don't know that for sure, Kate," Harriet tried to say.

Kate ignored her and continued her hard stare at the men.

"We saw your handiwork—your baskets—at the Mercantile in town, and we were quite impressed, were we not, Julius?"

Julius gave a slight nod and continued to mop his forehead.

Kate did not say anything in reply but continued to stare at them disapprovingly.

"We are . . . my brother and I . . . searching for a place to start an artists' colony, if you will." He gazed around the hill.

Kate dropped her arms. "Here?"

"Well, not exactly here on this spot, but somewhere near here. Someplace where artisans and craftsmen can work and ply their wares.

A community, you see," Frank said eagerly. "New Grimsby, with its proximity to the mines, would be perfect. The cottages themselves, hewn from the earth by the miners, would be ideal. I can think of no better spot, can you, Julius?"

Julius did not answer.

"Might we impose upon you and see inside?" Frank asked.

Kate's brow furrowed. "Why?"

"We wish to see the unpretentious dwelling of a local artisan, without affectation and presumption, in its purest form. This, you see, is what inspires creativity and is that which Julius and I seek to replicate."

Kate raised one eyebrow at Harriet.

"It's just for a minute," Harriet promised.

"I suppose you can come in, but there's not much to see. Also, I'm not an artisan." Kate stood aside, waving them in.

Frank and Julius tentatively entered, followed by Harriet, who mouthed "I'm sorry" to Kate as she passed.

"Ah, this is exquisite, is it not, Julius? This is what we have been searching for. Are there any more like it?"

"There's probably hundreds of these, though not all this nice," Harriet commented.

"Before you get any fancy ideas, it's dangerous up here," Kate added. "Hobos jump off the trains coming through and crawl up into these and sleep. Lot of wild animals, too. I wouldn't advise it–" She broke off in a cough.

"And yet *you* are here." Frank's eyes were merry. Everything seemed amusing to him.

"Well, I know what I'm doing. Plus, I've got a gun," she said through another cough and nodded toward the shotgun propped behind the door.

Frank turned to look, then grinned. "So you do." He pointed to the reeds on the table. "And this is where you work?" He stepped closer, observing her current project. "You see," he gestured widely, "the craftswoman and her craft and her home are one. It is the perfect union, the perfect path to a better society—a better world—if all would simply embrace it."

Kate shot Harriet a confused look.

"Sorry," she whispered. "Here, these are from Mom." She set the basket on one of the chairs.

Kate let out a sigh, but eagerly dug through the basket. "Oh! I like her pasties. And her beans." For once, she seemed grateful. Maybe she was getting hungry. "And what's this?" she held up the small bundle of herbs with one hand and coughed into her other.

"Oh, nothing." Harriet shot a worried glance at the brothers, but it was only Julius who was watching. Frank's eyes were roaming the rest of the hut. "Mom says you should hang it by the door," Harriet said under her breath. "And how long have you had that cough? It sounds bad."

"What's it for?" Kate asked, ignoring her question.

"It's to ward off evil spirits. Or f-fairy folk, is it not?" Julius asked softly.

Startled, Harriet turned to him. She wasn't sure what surprised her more—the fact that he had spoken at all or that he had referenced fairies.

Frank looked at Julius in appreciation. "Julius is a scholar of medieval literature, are you not, dear . . . brother," he added.

Julius cleared his throat. "Well, y-yes," he said softly, "in a manner of sp-speaking." He looked nervously at both Harriet and Kate.

"Julius's expertise is the folklore of the medieval peasant." He looked proudly at the flushed man. "Myself, I am more interested in textiles, patterns. They repeat constantly throughout history, you see, and during the medieval age, the natural world formed much of their inspiration. Take this pattern you are working on here. In my opinion, this is not Native American, but rather Slavic. Hungarian maybe. Which would make perfect sense, the Hungarian language being Finnish and Estonian in origin. Are you Hungarian by chance?"

"Hungarian?" Kate spat. "No! I'm an Indian. Everyone knows that." She held up a braid.

"Well, no one *really* knows," Harriet put in. "She was found as a toddler. An orphan."

Julius let out a strangled little cry. "An orphan? Dear F-Frank," he said, his tone one of excitement. "Do you n-not recognize Yeh-hsien?" He gestured around the hut.

"My dear Julius," Frank cooed. "You are a perfect genius. "But of course!"

"What's Yeh-hsien?" Kate demanded.

"Yeh-hsien is not a wh-what, but . . . but a who," Julius explained tentatively. "She is the heroine of the m-medieval Cinderella story. It is an ancient t-tale from China about a mistreated orphan who d-dwells in a c-cave, finds a magical f-fish, loses a shoe, and m-marries a powerful m-man. The similarity is extraordinary!"

Kate frowned. "Well, I wouldn't exactly say that." She tossed the rosemary bundle she had been fingering. "Look, if you don't mind, I need to get back to work and you two obviously have much to discuss."

She ushered them to the door. "Goodbye. I wouldn't advise setting up camp anywhere near here, if I were you. Lots of scary fairies about." She wiggled her fingers. "Also, witches and creatures and all sorts of terrible things." She partially shut the door but paused to give Harriet a look. "Thanks a lot," she hissed before it slammed shut.

"I say, what an extraordinary young woman!" Frank exclaimed, gripping his lapels. "Don't you agree, Julius?"

"Oh, yes. Indeed," his brother said, stuffing his handkerchief back in his pocket.

"You must tell us her whole story," Frank urged as Harriet began to descend the path. "And then show us the empty cottage." He drummed his fingers against his hat before placing it carefully on his head. "The one where my grandparents used to live."

CHAPTER
EIGHTEEN

Melody nervously drummed her fingers on the counter. It was Friday morning, normally a busy time, but there were fewer customers than usual.

She and Harriet had worked late the past week creating a Thanksgiving-themed window, which the Merc had never sported before. They had lugged in bales of hay and placed real pumpkins and other gourds next to wooden crates, upon which they had artfully displayed, or *tried* to artfully display, bottles of cider. Melody had even commissioned Kate to make a new sign that read "A Grateful Thanksgiving!" Finally, she had cut out some turkeys from construction paper, which she and Harriet had painstakingly hung from the ceiling with fishing line.

She had hoped that customers would see the window display and flood the shop, but they hadn't. And even more disappointing was the fact that they had only sold sixteen of the new bottles of cider, which had resulted in a mere twelve dollars. How on earth was she going to raise five hundred dollars at this rate? Time was racing past, hurtling them toward the end of the year and the due date of her father's debt.

Harriet moved from behind the counter and began straightening cans of vegetables. "Where's everyone at?" she asked, as if she could read Melody's mind.

"People are moving over to Heitman's," Mrs. Haufbrau snipped from her perch.

Melody turned. "Why?"

"Because they think the prices are too high here."

"Too high? We haven't changed any prices at all!"

"Doesn't matter if you have or haven't. It's those fancy hats and scarves and gloves. Hasn't taken long for people to start believing that *all* our prices are high. And knowing Dick Heitman, he's lowered some of his prices by even two cents. Serves to reinforce the fallacy." She patted her hair. "I told you those were a mistake." She nodded toward the back where the luxury items now sat.

Melody fumed. Was Mrs. Haufbrau ever going to stop harping on about the hats and gloves? They were the least of her problems right now.

"It's not the fancy hats," Cal chimed in, his voice getting louder as he walked slowly up from the back.

Melody's shoulders momentarily relaxed. Could Cal Fraiser actually be agreeing with her?

"It's Wesley," he said. Melody looked up and gasped when she saw that his left eye was bruised and purple.

"What happened to your eye!"

"I got socked." He gave a brief shrug. "Wesley. He got one right back, though."

"Oh, Cal!" Harriet exclaimed, hurrying over. "What happened?"

"It looks worse than it is."

"Did he attack you?" Melody asked, still alarmed.

"Not exactly. I was drinking in the Miner last night, and I heard Wesley spouting his mouth off about our cider being sour and acidic. I took exception, and, well, it turned into a bit of a scuffle."

Sour and acidic? Was Wesley really stooping to slander? He was even worse than she had thought. "But . . . but why would Wesley Elton even be somewhere like the Miner in the first place?" The Miner was a drinking man's bar, frequented by rough types.

Cal stared at her. "But it's okay for someone like me?"

"No! That's not what I meant! It's just that . . ." Melody placed a hand on her forehead. She didn't know what she was trying to say. "Why didn't you tell me?"

"That Elton's spreading rumors about the cider or that I got punched in the eye?"

"Well, both, of course," she said, feeling guilty that she hadn't noticed his eye until now.

"I didn't think it was important," Cal grunted.

"I told you the cider wasn't a good idea." Mrs. Haufbrau flipped a page of the receipt book without looking up at any of them.

"Not important?" Melody said to Cal, deciding to ignore Mrs. Haufbrau. "Of course it's important."

"Why would he make up lies like that?" Harriet asked.

Melody tapped her foot, thinking. "Probably to sabotage us."

"Sabotage us? Why?"

"Because he wants the Merc to fail." Melody considered relating what had happened between her and Wesley in the office, as she was sure it had something to do with his current nastiness, but she didn't want to do it in front of Mrs. Haufbrau, who needed no extra fuel to fan her fire of disapproval. Plus, it was humiliating.

"Well, what are we going to do?" Harriet finally asked, breaking the silence that had settled over the little group.

Cal scratched his forehead. "Why don't we give out samples? Give a sample to every single person that comes in. That'll prove the cider's worth."

"A sample to everyone?" Melody tried to quickly calculate how much they would need. "We'll deplete our whole stock."

"Yes, but it would be worth it." There was a trace of actual enthusiasm in his voice, like there had been that day in the cellar. "Just a tiny amount. And then we have Mrs. Mueller make more. Your mom's already started more batches, hasn't she, Harriet? With all of those apples we dropped off?" Melody had sent Cal and Harriet on a trip to Gays Mills last week to purchase as many bushels as Cal's old DeSoto could hold.

Harriet nodded. "Yes . . . but those won't be ready for another week or so."

"I think we have enough to hold us until then. Have your mom keep making batches though, just in case."

Melody considered the plan. "I suppose it's worth a try," she said. "We can use the shot glasses in Pops's office and wipe them out between customers."

"Yes, that's the perfect size," Cal agreed. He shot her a rare smile, and Melody couldn't help but bask in his approval.

"Would you get them, Mrs. Haufbrau?" Melody asked, since she was the closest to the office.

"I certainly will not!"

Melody turned in surprise, shocked by the woman's sharp reply.

"I've told you," Mrs. Haufbrau retorted, "I'm not going to do anything illegal. Nor immoral. I warned you before that I'll quit, and I will if I must."

"Immoral? What do you mean *immoral*?"

"Drink is the cause of all evil. I'll not be a part of the selling of the devil's own creation."

"Since when do you think alcohol is evil?" Melody's eyes narrowed. *First, illegal, and now evil?* "If I didn't know better, I'd think you'd joined the Temperance League."

Mrs. Haufbrau drew herself up. "That's exactly what I *did* do. Saw the light, I did."

Melody was stunned. "Since when? Two weeks ago?" She pinched the bridge of her nose. Was *everyone* out to thwart her?

"Yes, as a matter of fact. I'm a changed woman."

"A changed woman? You're choosing *now* to be a changed woman? Don't flatter yourself, Mrs. Haufbrau!"

"Don't you dare speak to me that way! After all your father and I have been through. We—" She stopped abruptly. "Never mind. But I'll tell you one thing—I quit! I've been longing to say those words ever since the day you took over, and now that you're trying to force me to do something against my conscience, I can in all honesty do it. So let me repeat—I quit."

Melody's face drained. "Quit? You can't just quit!"

"Yes, I can. I quit. And it's not just Wesley Elton you'll have to worry about. I'll bring the whole Temperance League against you."

Melody's stomach twisted in fear. Would she really bring the Temperance League against them? Would her mother find out? And worse, they could not afford to lose a staff member just now, not with the holidays coming.

"What will you do for money?" Melody asked crisply.

"The good Lord will provide." Mrs. Haufbrau bent to unearth her handbag from beneath the counter. "You know, there was a time I was proud to work in this shop," she said, straightening and looking slowly around the Merc, as if giving everything a final goodbye. She slung her coat over her arm. "But not anymore. You've effectively ruined it, Melody Merriweather. I hope you're happy." She lifted her chin and made her way from behind the counter to the front door, which she passed through without another word and slammed behind her.

Melody stood in a state of shock, her frantic heartbeat matching the pace of the shop bell still ringing furiously. Despite the fact that she had wished for this day for months, she suddenly felt oddly cheated, as she had always envisioned *herself* as being the one to dismiss Mrs. Haufbrau, not the other way around. *And what would Pops say?*

"Do you think she means it?" Harriet finally squeaked.

Melody pushed down her panic. "Well, I certainly hope so!" she said, avoiding looking at Cal. "Good riddance!" She tried and failed at a little laugh. "She's been a pain in my side this whole time. Longer than that. I've never liked that woman, even when I was a little girl!"

Melody tried to control the pounding of her heart. *Maybe she should run after her. Try to convince her to come back—*

The shop bell rang again, and for a brief moment, Melody thought it might be Mrs. Haufbrau coming back . . . but no. It was only Imogene Kaufmann. Melody let out a little groan. Not Imogene. Not now.

"Yes, Imogene?" Melody's tone was sharper than she meant it to be, but she had little time for her spinster neighbor right now! She was still trying to decide if she should go after Mrs. Haufbrau.

"Oh, hello, Melody. My, aren't you looking nice. But, then, you always look nice, don't you? And mother always thinks you look nice. I noticed the window." She gestured weakly at the display behind her but kept her eyes on Melody. "It's marvelous, isn't it? Thanksgiving. I never thought to do a whole window with Thanksgiving! But then, you are clever, aren't you? Oh, yes. Very clever. That's what mother always says. Why just the other day—"

"Can I help you with something, Imogene?" Melody glanced anxiously at the door. "This really isn't a good time."

"Oh! Yes, but of course! Yes." She looked nervously at Harriet and then Cal and then held up yet another old box. "I . . . I wondered if you might like these. To sell, like. I was quite encouraged by the sale of even just one of my soaps—I think it was to Mr. Churchill you told me last time I was in. Yes, quite encouraged. And so I . . . I've taken to working on these. Of course, I have to wait until Mother's asleep, as she does like to meddle. Not that I mind, mind you, it's just that she can quite interfere with the hot wax, and that can be dangerous, you see. Already, she's burned herself once. Nothing serious, but it did blister something terrible. I said to her—"

"What *are* they?" Melody interrupted, taking the box. She opened it to find what looked like candles of various sizes and colors, most of them misshapen. "Candles?"

"Yes. Well, yes. They're candles. I . . . I thought they might sell, you know, better than tapers. And they're quite easy to make, once you get the hang of it, you see."

Melody picked up an orange one and examined it. It was basically a lump of wax with a wick. Who on earth would buy such a thing? She closed her eyes at the sheer frustration of it all! She could barely sell hats and scarves and bottles of cider for a profit, much less these little pieces of junk. It would be useless, and, worse, they would take up valuable shelf space.

She handed her back the box. "I don't think so, Imogene."

The woman's face fell. "But are you sure? Perhaps you could try? I . . . I wouldn't dream of bothering you, but we . . . well, we don't really get much money from the soaps."

"I can't help that," Melody snapped, trying to ignore the niggle of guilt that irritatingly washed over her. Despite Frank Churchill's inquiry as to why the handmade soaps were displayed on a bottom shelf, she hadn't moved them. To be honest, she had forgotten.

"Oh, no! Of course not. Oh, no, I would never blame you. It's just that, well, things are a little bit tight at the moment. Mother's been a bit chesty these last few weeks. It started as a cold in her back, you see, and traveled to her chest. I had the doctor out, but she's a bit laid up, and it seems we've run up a rather large bill at Heitman's and at Slater's. And, well, I thought maybe if I made something new, then maybe—"

Melody was at the breaking point. There was no use going after Mrs. Haufbrau now; she was surely halfway home at this point! "Look, Imogene. I can't sell these. I—"

"Well, maybe you could just set them on the shelf, like. Next to the soaps? Or a little bit higher?"

"Imogene, please!" Melody suddenly felt as if she might cry. "I'm busy. Believe me, no one is going to buy *anything* you make. Do you understand that? It's all just rubbish. You're wasting your time. Not to mention mine." She grabbed the box, marched over to the soaps, and tossed them all in.

"Here." She thrust the box back into Imogene's hands. "Just take them. They're only taking up space. No one wants these. If people wanted fancy soaps they'd buy Kirk's or Lux, not this rubbish. Please, just go."

Imogene stood silent for once, opening and closing her mouth in surprise. Melody thought she saw her bottom lip quiver, but she did her best to ignore it. She *did* feel sorry for the poor woman, but now was not the time! The Merc, and possibly her father, were dying; all of her business ideas seemed to be failing; and now her father's oldest, and according to him, best employee had just quit and was threatening to report them to the Temperance League! She didn't have time to soothe Imogene Kaufmann's hurt feelings. If she herself was having to learn reality the hard way, it was only fair that everyone else did, too.

"Oh." Imogene was barely audible. "Yes, I see. Yes, I suppose they are rubbish, aren't they?" She looked sheepishly at Harriet and Cal and then back at Melody. "I . . . I'm sorry I bothered you. Really I am. I had no idea. I must tell Mother. She was never fond of my soaps, either. I thought it was just her being contrary, but now I know. Yes, indeed. Thank you for telling me. They *are* just rubbish, aren't they?" Her eyes glistened with tears.

"Imogene, I . . . that's not really what I meant—"

"No, I see. I—"

She didn't finish, and instead turned and hurried out the door.

Melody braced her hands on the counter and closed her eyes. *What else could possibly go wrong?* She let out a deep breath and opened her eyes to find Cal glaring at her. Gone was his easy smile from just a few moments ago. She should have known his good mood was too good to be true.

"What?" She wasn't sure she had the strength to battle with Cal right now. "Don't look at me that way." She straightened. "It's just Imogene."

"*Just* Imogene?" He stared at her, and she suddenly felt very small. "The Kaufmanns are very poor, Melody. You, who have everything, would you deny her a chance to make a few extra pennies? You know what?" He paused, his brow furrowed and his eyes staring at her in his most condemning way yet. "You're a snob! Yes, that's what you are—a snob. And you deserve everything you get!"

Melody was utterly stung. A snob? She was anything but a snob! Had he any idea how close they were to losing everything?

Cal took off his apron and tossed it on the counter. "I was waiting for the right time to tell you; seems this is it. I have to go back to Dodgeville. Some family stuff. I'll be back when I can."

Melody's racing heart suddenly sank. Two tears formed in the corners of her eyes, but she blinked them away. "What do you mean you have to leave? Is it . . . is it your uncle?"

"Would it matter?" He nodded toward the Kaufmanns' apartment. "Would it matter if someone in my family was ill?"

"Cal, please." She wiped a stray tear. She wasn't sure which was worse—him deserting her or him leaving with such a low opinion of her. "How . . . how long will you be gone?"

"I don't know. A week? Two weeks?"

"A week! What will we do without you?"

Cal looked at her bitterly and shrugged. "Seems you're doing just fine on your own," he muttered and walked out.

CHAPTER NINETEEN

Melody managed to hide her shock and embarrassment at being chastised by Cal until Harriet had also gone—reluctantly, or so it had seemed. The girl kept asking if she was okay, which only made it worse. Finally, Melody had insisted, after which the dutiful Harriet slunk out, leaving Melody the opportunity to finally throw herself into her father's swivel chair in despair.

Oh, God! What was she to do? She couldn't possibly hope to make an extra five hundred dollars by the end of the year with just herself and Harriet! She had hoped that with the holidays coming they would somehow be able to sell loads of cider, but now it all seemed hopeless. But perhaps it had been hopeless from the beginning. She groaned aloud and braced her face in her hands. She would have to tell Pops. Or maybe she should tell Mums and force her and Bunny to help. Yes, that's what she should do, she decided, though when she tried to imagine Mums and Bunny behind the counter, it seemed ludicrous. Neither of them would be of any real help. Mums may have worked at the Merc in the early days, but she had definitely risen above that role since then, not to mention the fact that she now had varicose veins. Standing all day would only irritate them further. And Bunny would just complain the whole time about getting her precious fingers dirty.

Perhaps she should hire someone new? But how? She would have to place an advertisement or put a sign in the window. Granted, there were plenty of people out of work, but how would she have time to weed through them all when she was already so pressed for time? And would Mrs. Haufbrau really bring the Temperance League against her? Or inform the authorities? It was one thing for the police to turn a blind eye to the selling of illegal alcohol, but quite another if someone were to turn them in. And even if it were an idle threat, there was still the problem of the cider not selling, which may or may not be the result of Wesley's cruel rumors.

She closed her eyes and tried to think. Perhaps she should write to Freddy and explain the situation. He would have to come home; that's all there was to it. And yet, as comforting as it would be to have Freddy come in and help, she did not relish admitting defeat. Freddy would be horribly put out and take it out on her—nothing new there—and she dreaded to think how disappointed her father would be. Not only would she have to own up to running the Merc into the ground, she would be responsible for ruining Freddy's future law career. *Oh!*

She braced her cheek on her fist and stared at the big black clock on the opposite wall. It was nearly six. She would have to get home quickly, or she would miss dinner. Her eyes dropped to a photograph hanging beneath the clock in a plain black frame. It was of her grandfather as a young man. He was standing in front of the Merc with a little boy beside him, the boy being, of course, her father. The sepia image was grainy, and yet their eyes were vivid. It was as if they were staring right at her, imploring her. Or were they blaming her?

Melody covered her face with her hands. She had to see Pops. He was the only one who could possibly help her, though she dreaded telling him the Merc's current state of affairs. But it had to be done. She would own up to all her mistakes. Wearily, she stood, and with one last look around the office, switched off the light.

* * *

"Pops?" she called, rapping lightly and poking her head into his room.

"Mel?" His eyes fluttered open. "That you?"

Melody crept closer, suddenly *seeing* him for the first time in a long time, as he really was. He looked so small and weary, nothing like the strong, robust man in her memory. He had lost quite a bit of weight— how had she not noticed?—and his thinning hair was greasy. The nurses hadn't shaved him today, so his chin was stubbled with black and gray whiskers. She slipped her hand in his, just as she had so many times as a little girl.

"What's wrong?" he rasped and patted a space on the bed beside him. Something about this gesture or the sadness in his eyes caused tears to well up in Melody. She had come here to tell him all of her problems, but, looking at him now, the thought of them quickly evaporated. A feeling of dread crept over her then, and she realized in the space of a moment that he wasn't ever going to get better, not really. She burst into tears.

"Hey, now, girl. Come on. Sit with your old man. Can't be all that bad."

Melody blindly sat down on the little sliver of the bed next to him. She laid her head on his chest. She should be comforting *him,* and yet she so desperately needed him right now. She continued to cry while he stroked her hair until she was all cried out. She lay there, limp and hiccupping.

"Better?" he finally asked.

She wanted to remain where she was and go to sleep just as she would have as a little girl, but she forced herself to sit up. "I'm sorry," she said, pulling her sleeve across her eyes.

"For what?" He gave her a small smile.

She looked at him, trying to memorize his face . . . just in case . . . but this was not the image of him she wanted to remember.

"You want to tell me?" he asked hoarsely.

"Oh, Pops," she moaned. "I've ruined everything."

"Can't be all that bad. Just seems like it sometimes."

"No, I've really ruined it this time."

"Can't be any worse than the mistakes I've made over the years."

She paused, wondering what mistakes he might have made at the Merc. In her memory, she could think of none, but, then again, as a child, she had thought her father perfect.

"Well," she began unsteadily, "in the first place, I bought fifty luxury scarves and hats and gloves, thinking that they'd sell for a big profit, but all they seemed to have done is drive customers away."

Pops surprised her by letting out a little rattle of a chuckle. "That all? I did the very same thing when I took over from Dad. Bought a whole bunch of Cuban cigars, thinking I would make a fortune. Turns out no one wanted to pay for an expensive cigar. They just wanted plain ole cheap ones."

"What did you do?"

"I sold some of 'em, but mostly smoked 'em myself." He laughed again, but it quickly turned into a coughing fit. "I wouldn't worry about your fancy hats too much."

"But, Pops, that's not half of it. I . . . well, *we*–Cal and I, that is–decided to try to sell cider."

"Cider, eh?" Pops's weary face looked as intrigued as a sickly man's could. "Not a bad idea. Not bad at all. Who's brewing it? You? Or did you get Helenka to do it?" His eyes crinkled in amusement.

Melody gave a wry little smile. "No, Rosemary Mueller's making it. We tried selling it in jugs, but it didn't go over so well. So, we put it in bottles with a fancy label, but it's still not selling as much as I'd hoped . . ." She considered telling him about Wesley's sour rumors but quickly decided not to open that can of worms, seeing as there was a marriage proposal involved. "And now Cal's gone back to Dodgeville, and Mrs. Haufbrau's quit!"

Pops's face was now finally one of concern. "Marcella quit? Why?"

"She's joined the Temperance League and thinks that alcohol is both immoral and evil."

Pops scratched his chin. "Doesn't sound like Marcella." He lowered his hand and looked at Melody. "Why'd Cal leave?"

Melody's stomach roiled with guilt. "Family problems, he said." She did not add that he was upset by how she had treated Imogene and winced *again* at the memory of him calling her a snob. "Oh, Pops! How am I going to run the Merc with just one person?"

"I did. Back in the early days."

"Yeah, but the Merc was smaller then. And, anyway, I'm not you."

"Thank God for that." He smiled at her.

"I'm so sorry," she whispered, tears welling up again. "I've been so stupid!"

"Don't say that, Mel. That ain't true, and you know it. Just growing pains is all."

Melody sniffed. "I know I was kind of . . . kind of disagreeable in not wanting to take on the Merc for you, but now I . . . well, I wish I could have been a success. Although . . ."

"Although what?" Pops said weakly.

Melody hesitated. "Did you ask me to come back and run the Merc because you knew there was no hope anyway?" she asked quietly. "Is that why you didn't ask Freddy? Because it was alright for me to fail, but you wanted to spare him that?"

Pops eyes widened as if he had been struck, and she immediately regretted what she had said.

"Oh, my sweet girl. Is that what you think?" He took her hand and feebly squeezed it. "Never think that, Mel. I asked you because you were my only hope. You're the smartest one of the bunch. Yes!" he urged when she started to protest. "You are. Freddy's at law school, I know, but you could have easily done the same, Mel, if circumstances were different. You think fast on your feet, and you're good with people. That's the main thing. That's what you need most to succeed in life, and you've got that in spades."

Melody wanted to weep again. She didn't know how her father could possibly think she was "good with people" after the mess she had made of everything. She used to be good with people during her carefree days at Mundelein, but that era was definitely over.

"I know I didn't give you much of a chance," Pops went on, "but I figured if there was anyone that could maybe pull this off, it was you. But it's not your fault. It's mine. I'm the one who lost the Merc. You were up against the wall, and you gave it your goddamned best. I'm proud of you, Mel. And your grandpa would have been, too." He squeezed her hand again.

"It's not your fault, either, Pops. It was Uncle Joe's!"

"That might be," Pops said wearily, "but it's no good playing the blame game. Doesn't matter whose fault it is. The important thing is we went down swinging."

"Well, we're not down yet," Melody sniffed, suddenly feeling a new resolve after her father's praise, whether it was deserved or not. "We've still got until New Year's to come up with the money, right?"

Pops sighed. "Don't you worry about that anymore. Let those two sharks do their worst. Take the Merc, if they must."

"No, Pops! There . . . there has to be something we can do! Maybe sell something?" she suggested desperately. "What about the car? Or maybe some of Mums's jewelry?"

Pops gave his head a tiny shake. "No, Mel, I can't ask her for that. Can't ask her to give me back something I gave to her in love. Besides, I don't want her to know."

"Well, she's going to find out pretty darn soon if we don't do something!"

"Well, let her spend the holidays thinking everything's okay. My gift to her," he wheezed.

Privately, Melody did not think this a very good gift, and, anyway, Mums, she knew, already suspected money troubles, or she wouldn't have brought in lodgers.

"Anyway, we still got a couple of weeks," Pops said, a false smile on his lips now. "A miracle could still happen."

Melody had never known her father to be overly religious, and yet this was the second reference to a miracle he had made. She was all for miracles, of course, but somehow this didn't seem like something God would care all that much about. This seemed like something they had to get themselves out of. She tried to think of anything of her own that *she* could sell. But what did she have of any real value?

"You're a lot like my dad, you know. Got the same drive, the same determination." He looked at her appreciatively.

"Same as you!"

"Nah. I think I was always a disappointment to him. Coulda gone farther. But I was happy to work at the Merc. I liked it. Now, you. You've got a head on your shoulders. You remember that."

"I will, Pops, but . . ." She had a terrible feeling of foreboding. "But why are you saying all this now?"

"I don't know," he said with a smile. "The cider is a good idea. Give it time."

"But time is exactly what we don't have," she added morosely. "And how am I going to manage with only one clerk?"

"Get Imogene down. She can fill in. Have her work the butcher counter. She has in the past, you know."

"Oh, Pops, no!" She had no desire to tell him about how she had hurt Imogene's feelings. She had already decided on the walk to the hospital, Cal's scolding having its usual effect, that she would go up to the apartment in the morning and tell Imogene that she would sell her stupid soaps and candles. What did it matter at this point? But she balked at her father's suggestion to hire the woman. "She'll talk the heads off any customers we still have!"

Pops wheezed out a chuckle. "She does like to talk, but she's okay once she's busy. And the customers like her. It's just your mother who didn't."

"I thought she was a kleptomaniac."

Pops laughed again. "Is that what your mother said?" He paused to cough, a long, rattling one. "Nah, she wasn't really," he said. "She did take a few boxes of Hershey bars, but it wasn't her fault."

Not her fault? This made no sense, but Melody didn't feel like delving deeper into Imogene's disordered mind. Regardless of her father's suggestion, she had no intention of hiring her. "What about Mrs. Haufbrau and the Temperance League? What should I do about that? I can't openly sell the cider anymore."

"You can get around it by saying it's medicinal. But don't you worry. Marcella ain't gonna do that."

"I don't know. She says she's reformed or repentant, or something like that. That she's a changed woman."

Pops twisted his mouth, thinking. "Hmm. That may well be, but she'll come round. She always does. We've been through a lot together."

"That's what she said. What does that mean?"

Pops smiled sadly. "It's a long story for another day. As for the Temperance League, leave that to me. I'll make a couple of calls. I've got a few buddies on the board and a few favors to call in."

"Make a call? From your sickbed?"

"The nurses'll help me."

"Pops! You need to rest."

"I've been resting for weeks, Mel. I've had all the rest I need." As if on cue, Pops closed his eyes. He kept them closed for several moments before they fluttered open again, but now his look was one of utter love.

It cut her to the quick—so much so that she was suddenly afraid she might begin to cry again, but she bravely held it in, her throat aching from the effort.

"You're going to be home for Christmas, aren't you, Pops?" Melody urged, her voice hovering close to begging.

"Course I am, Mel. Course I am." He closed his eyes again, and Melody waited for him to go on, but his breathing eventually became deeper until she realized he was asleep. She didn't want to leave him, and yet, she had a lot to do.

CHAPTER
TWENTY

By the time Melody arrived back at the house on Ridge, dinner was well over, and she silently ate her plate of meatloaf, kept warm for her in the oven by Helenka, while she listened, despairingly, to Mums and Bunny and Frank and Julius enjoying themselves in the front room. They were playing records on the Victrola, and every once in a while, a burst of laughter emerged. She finished her meal and set the empty plate in the sink. She was dead tired, and she didn't think she could bear joviality right now. Instead, she decided she would simply go up to her room to read her latest letter from Cynthia.

She was halfway up the stairs, however, when she changed her mind. Maybe joining in would improve her mood. Or maybe she just needed someone to talk to.

Silently, she crept back down and wandered into the parlor, which was now deserted, the party having apparently, from the sound of it, retired to the music room. Melody made her way back and leaned against the door frame of the open pocket doors, her arms crossed languidly.

Bunny was at the piano, playing show tunes. Julius stood beside her, singing along loudly. Mums sat in an armchair nearby, singing, too, and Frank sat further off, watching with a big smile. He was the first to notice her and patted the sofa next to him.

Melody meandered over and threw herself down beside him with an unladylike "umph."

"Long day?" he asked in a low voice, though his eyes had returned to Bunny and Julius.

"You might say that." Melody let out a deep sigh. "Horrible, in fact. Two of my staff quit."

"Dear me." He looked at her. "In this climate? It must have been something serious. Care to talk about it?"

"Not really." Melody picked up one of the embroidered sofa pillows and hugged it. "It's too long of a story. But with Christmas coming, I need to find someone to fill in right away."

"Well, I'm sure you'll find someone," he said encouragingly. "You're quite industrious."

Melody wasn't sure that was quite the right word to use in this situation. She studied him. "Say, why don't *you* work in the shop?" She hadn't thought of this possibility until this moment, but it suddenly seemed like a very good idea indeed.

"*Me?* Dear, girl, no." He let out a little chuckle. "No, my job is to discover the artist in the rough, not *be* the artist."

Melody bit the inside of her cheek. "But I'm not asking you to be an artist, just to work in a shop. It's surprisingly easy. And think of all the townspeople you'd get to talk to," she suggested eagerly. "Isn't that what you want? Find out who is harboring secret hidden talent? *And* you'd get to be around Harriet," she said teasingly.

With everything that had occurred these past few days, she had almost forgotten this one bright spot in her life. Harriet had recently shared that she had, in fact, formed a new attachment. Granted, this revelation had been forthcoming only after Melody had probed, asking poor Harriet how she was holding up in light of her disappointment regarding Wesley, but she had been pleasantly surprised when Harriet had responded that it was of no consequence, that her heart now belonged to another.

"It's . . . it's not John, is it?" Melody had asked tentatively.

Harriet had given a little laugh. "No, it's not John. I am quite over him, as I've told you. No, I took your advice and have set my sights on someone better. Someone more deserving, as you suggested." She had blushed prettily, then, and given a furtive smile. "I wonder if you can guess."

Harriet had not met anyone new, not that Melody was aware of . . . except, of course, Frank. *Could Harriet have fallen for Frank?* she had mused, instantly intrigued. Yes, she must have! Who else could it be? *But Frank and Harriet?* Melody had turned it over several times, thinking it through carefully. Yes, she had decided, growing more excited by the moment, they would make a charming couple!

"Bravo!" Frank called out from beside her now, causing Melody to jump a little. Bunny and Julius's impromptu duet had ended, and any encouraging reaction the mention of Harriet might have elicited from Frank was unfortunately drowned out by his enthusiastic clapping.

All eyes turned to him.

"Oh, Melody!" Mums twittered. "I didn't even hear you come in! When did you get home?"

"A little while ago."

"Well, I hope this isn't going to become a habit. Do sit up, dear! Stop slouching. What will our guests think?"

"I haven't the faintest idea, Mums," Melody said, sitting up and tossing the pillow to the side. "I was visiting Pops, if you must know."

"You were? Well, why didn't you say? How is he?"

"Tired." She let out her own tired breath. "But until I find someone to hire at the Merc, I'll probably be late every night."

"What do you mean 'until you hire someone'?"

"Mrs. Haufbrau has quit, and Cal had to go back to Dodgeville for something. A family thing, he said."

"Well! I never. Marcella quit? Why? What did you say to her?"

Melody fought the urge to scream. "Nothing, Mums."

"Well, I've never known Marcella to be like that. You must have said *something*, Melody."

Melody pressed her lips into a thin, hard line. "Regardless of Mrs. Haufbrau's reasons for quitting," Melody said tightly, "I can't go into the Christmas season with just one clerk." She glared at Bunny, who had twisted around on the piano bench to follow the conversation.

"Don't look at me, Melody!"

"Mums, it's ridiculous! Bunny needs to help! She can come after school."

Mums sighed. "Well, perhaps you should, Bunny. Seeing as how Melody has gotten herself in such a pickle."

"But, Mums! I can't! The recital is next week, and Miss Elliot says I have to spend every spare minute practicing!"

"Who cares about your dumb recital?" Melody snapped. "There are more important things in life!"

"I beg to differ, if I may," Frank put in. "All artists must be nurtured and supported. This is the very essence of life, is it not? Young Elizabeth shows much talent, indeed, and all must be sacrificed to bring it to its proper manifestation."

"Well, being able to play Mozart and Beethoven will be of little consequence if we lose the house!" Melody said, her voice raised.

"Why do you have to be so horrid!" Bunny shouted, gathering up her sheet music for what was sure to be one of her grand exits.

"Bunny, sit down!" Mums commanded. "The evening isn't over. You mustn't let Melody's overdramatics affect you so. Go on, get another piece ready. Melody," she scolded, "you've gotten yourself into this mess, and you'll have to get yourself out. I can't imagine what you said to Mrs. Haufbrau to cause her to quit. She's been with the store from practically day one. You'll just have to try to get her back. And I hope you didn't worry your father with all of this."

"Fine," she said bitterly and stood up.

"Don't go," Frank requested, though it sounded half-hearted at best.

Her chest heaving, she practically ran up the stairs and flung herself into her room, shutting the door with a slight bang. She leaned against it, breathing heavily, but she refused to cry. She was tired of crying, and it was obvious that she was on her own. If Bunny or Mums or Frank wouldn't help, she would figure it out herself. She would go down swinging, as Pops had put it. She would find some money somewhere!

Her eyes darted around the room, looking for something she might sell, but there was nothing. Nothing that was entirely hers anyway. She began opening the desk drawers and rifling through the contents. A glass paperweight from the world's fair? No. A gold crucifix necklace she had received upon her high school graduation? No, she couldn't possibly sell that; it would be sacrilegious. Finally, she opened her bottom drawer, and her eyes fell on a small box covered in blue velvet. Douglas's engagement ring. She hadn't opened it since he had driven away that day in August, which seemed like a million years ago now.

She stared at the box for a few moments and then drew it out, carefully prying it open. The ring consisted of a diamond, not overly large, but rather unique in its cut. It was a very beautiful ring, but one, Melody decided as she examined it carefully, that could not possibly be worth all that much. After all, where would he have gotten the money? His family had wealth, but Douglas, she knew, did not. At least not yet. So where had he gotten it? He had admitted he hadn't been planning on proposing to her that day, that it had been a spur-of-the-moment decision. Which meant he had probably not packed a ring before his hurried drive to Dubuque to rescue her from the convent. No, Melody decided, fingering the ring, he must have purchased it somewhere along the way or even here in town after he had driven her all the way home from Dubuque. Maybe at Woolworth's? But if this was true, was it even worth selling? She wondered how much she would get for it . . .

But how could she possibly sell an engagement ring?

Melody stood up and looked out the window. The street below was dark, and she could see nothing. Douglas had told her the ring was hers to do with as she wished, but she was sure he hadn't meant that she could sell it. She fingered the lace curtain, which oddly made her think of a bridal veil. She stared at it for several minutes, observing its intricacies, until the truth settled over her like a shroud. If she was even remotely considering selling this ring, she realized sadly, she clearly did not want to marry Douglas Novak.

She had finally arrived at the truth.

And though she was relieved by this in some small way, it still made her feel inexplicably sad. She let out a slow, weary breath as she dropped the curtain. She simply didn't love Douglas in that way, not enough to marry, anyway. No one, she reasoned, hides an engagement ring in a drawer under the guise of wanting to think about it. If thought was needed at all, the answer was probably obvious.

A small tear ran down Melody's cheek despite her earlier resolve. She *did* love Douglas, and a tiny part of her mourned the life she was giving up, but she couldn't force it any more than she could force a life with Wesley, though a marriage to either of them would surely help her financial situation. Well, Wesley's might. A marriage to Douglas would not save the Merc, but it would be her escape from it. She could go off and live a life of comfort and maybe even luxury somewhere as the wife of a young doctor or engineer or whatever he decided to be, but how could she ever be happy, leaving her family in the lurch?

She watched a lone car rumble down Ridge. She could not desert them, or the Merc. After seeing her father today, she was convinced he was not going to get better, no matter what Mums said, and Fred was never going to come back and help. Nor could she count on Bunny. It was all down to her, she realized heavily as she sat down at her desk. It was the hand she had been dealt, and there was no getting out of it.

She looked down at the ring box in her hand again. It was wrong to sell it, she knew, but she was desperate. Any amount it brought in would be better than nothing in her fight to save the Merc. And she would make it up to Douglas, she convinced herself. She would pay him back, *and* she would write a letter to him as soon as she could to let him know of her decision. In fact, she would do it now, she decided, reaching for a sheet of stationery. If he knew he was free of his proposal to her, perhaps he would turn to Vivian. Maybe the two of them *would* be good together. What did she know?

Obviously, nothing, she thought as she picked up her pen, except that she was done with matchmaking. She had made a terrible mess of things, though she did hope that perhaps Harriet and Frank might work out. She would dearly like to claim at least one success story before throwing in the towel. There was Cynthina and Charlie, of course, but could she really take credit for their relationship? More than likely, they would have ended up together anyway out of sheer proximity. She paused, thinking about how Cynthia would take the news. Undoubtedly, she would be crushed, as they had always planned on having a double wedding, but Cynthia would get over it. And, truth be told, those silly college antics were beginning to seem . . . well, silly.

* * *

The next morning, Melody left the house before anyone else was up, except Helenka, of course. She paused only for a cup of coffee and then hurried into town, her letter to Douglas and his ring tucked safely in her handbag. She hoped he would not be too upset by her refusal. Perhaps he was having second thoughts anyway, if his last letter and its lack of a repeated proposal was anything to go by.

She walked quickly down Cross Street toward Van Dyke's, the only real jeweler in town. She had debated taking it to the Peddler, the consignment shop, thinking that if she did, she might be able to someday get it back, but she had decided against it, as she was sure she wouldn't get anything close to what the ring was worth. Besides, the Peddler always made her feel sad. Not only was the air thick with rot and mildew, but the sea of items left there by her fellow townsfolk always felt like items washed up on the shore after a horrible shipwreck, which, after all, was exactly what the big stock market crash had been.

Melody pushed open the door of Van Dyke's and was relieved, upon a quick perusal, that there was no one else behind the counter except old Mr. Van Dyke himself. She had no desire for her sale to be gossiped about by Margaret Cole or Bessie Owens, both of whom worked here. It was one of the reasons she had come so early.

"Ah, Melody! I should say Miss Merriweather. All grown up. How are you? Good to have you back."

"Thanks, Mr. Van Dyke. I'm fine."

"How's your dad? Getting better, I hear."

"Yes, he's . . . he's getting better."

"How's it going down at the Merc?"

"Oh, the same. You know the Merc. Never changes."

"That's good, isn't it?" He gave her a wan smile. "So, what can I do you for?"

Melody swallowed hard, doubt suddenly overcoming her. "Well, I was wondering if you might want to buy a ring." She cleared her throat, hating that her voice had faltered at the end of her sentence. She set her handbag on the glass counter, under which was a dazzling array of rings and necklaces, even some watches. She pulled Douglas's ring out of a little velvet box. "Here it is." She held it out, painfully aware now of how small it looked compared to the gems beneath her handbag, glittering under tiny spotlights.

Mr. Van Dyke took it carefully and held it up to one eye, the other squeezed shut. "Hmm," he said in a tone Melody could not identify as positive or negative. He carried it to a small table and sat down, placing a loupe over one eye.

"It's quite fine. Where did you get it?" he asked, looking up at her as he let the loupe fall.

"I . . . it was a gift."

"Hmm. It appears to be quite old. Maybe an heirloom?"

Melody bit her lip. "I . . . I don't think so." She prayed it wasn't.

"Well, I can give you two hundred for it," he said, standing up again.

Two hundred?

"Doubtless, it's worth more, but that's all I can give." He put it back in her hand. "I understand if you want to take it somewhere else."

Melody stared at the ring, shocked. Had Douglas really given her such a valuable ring? She had convinced herself it was a rash purchase. But maybe it really *was* an heirloom. What if it had been in his family for generations, and she was just recklessly selling it to try to shore up a dying dry-goods store?

"Are you alright, Miss Merriweather? You don't need to make a decision right now. Obviously, you need time to think. Or maybe take it to Madison or Milwaukee. I wouldn't blame you if you did. It's a fine piece."

"No," she said hurriedly. "No, I'll take it. The two hundred."

"Are you sure?"

"Yes," she said, trying to force a smile. "Yes, I'm sure."

"Very well." He took it out of her hand again. "I'll polish it, and then display it for more than I'm paying you. You understand, right?"

"Yes . . . yes of course. That's business."

He smiled kindly. "But, if you change your mind before someone else buys it, you can always come back and get it for the price I'm giving you. Is that fair?"

"Yes, of course. That's very generous, Mr. Van Dyke. Thank you."

Mr. Van Dyke set the ring on a blue silk cloth on the back table and proceeded to the cash register, which he opened with a loud clang. He counted out exactly two hundred dollars, which he then handed to her. "Nice to see you again, Melody," he said pleasantly. "Come back anytime. And say hello to your dad for me."

Melody exited the shop and stood outside a moment, trying to push down her guilt. *I'm sorry, Douglas! I'll make it up to you. Promise.* She tightened her grip on the money and then stuffed it in her handbag. Only two hundred eighty-three more to go, based on her current sales as of yesterday. It seemed an impossible number, but she was determined to do it somehow. Now, she just had to mail the letter, and with a heavy heart, she snapped her handbag shut and marched in the direction of the post office.

CHAPTER
TWENTY-ONE

"You call those chops?" Mr. Dixon demanded. Melody was struggling to wrap the pork chops she had just sliced. Admittedly, they were horribly uneven. "How's Esther s'posed to cook those?"

Melody gritted her teeth and wiped her hands on a towel. She hadn't the faintest idea how Esther Dixon was supposed to cook these pork chops. Or anything else, for that matter.

"Where's that kid that's usually back here?" Mr. Dixon strained his neck to look beyond her, as if Cal was somehow hiding. "He cuts nice ones."

The question was a good one. Where *was* Cal?

Thanksgiving, which had been a quiet affair for the Merriweathers without Pops and Freddy, had come and gone, and there was still no sign of either Cal or Mrs. Haufbrau. Melody knew that Cal lived in Dodgeville, but she didn't know where exactly. In a moment of weakness, she had tried to telephone him, but the operator had not been able to place the call. She considered trying to contact Lyle, but he lived way out in Summer Valley, and she was pretty sure the telephone lines didn't stretch that far. She rubbed her brow and tried not to think about Cal's previous reprimand that she knew so little about her staff. Even without being here, he was still scolding her!

"He's gone for a couple of weeks," she said pertly. "He'll be back, though."

"Well, I ain't takin' those," Mr. Dixon said, nodding at the chops she was still attempting to wrap.

Melody stopped what she was doing and leaned on the counter with both hands. "How about I give them to you for half off?" she asked, trying not to sound too desperate. If Mr. Dixon didn't take them, she'd be forced to take them home to Helenka, who would undoubtedly complain to her mother about the very same thing Mr. Dixon was complaining about, and then the whole topic of the staff problem, including the missing Mrs. Haufbrau, would be resurrected.

Mr. Dixon tipped his hat back. "Well, alright, Melody, but I can't keep taking these sloppy seconds." His voice lowered. "Look, we've always shopped at the Merc. Me and your dad go way back, like, but I can't keep paying good money for this. I'm already in hot water with Esther. When that kid comes back, I'll come back, but until then, I'm gonna have to get my meat from Heitman's. You understand, right?"

Melody nodded. She handed him the meat, minus Cal's neat packaging. By contrast, hers looked like a fluffy pillow. "Would you like a sample of cider?" she asked weakly.

"Nah, I gotta go."

Melody leaned against the chopping block and rubbed her forehead. It was obvious, and had been all week, that something had to be done. It was easy enough to wrap sausages and scoop hamburger, but handling the rest of the inventory, which was beginning to pile up in the cooler, was a different thing altogether. Not only were she and Harriet running ragged each day, but as her exchange with Mr. Dixon proved, they were losing customers. And she had no time to try to push the cider. She considered simply shutting down the meat counter until Cal came back, but she was worried that if her customers started getting their meat from Heitman's or even Slater's, the Merc would never get them back.

No, she needed to hire someone quickly. As in today.

Melody wiped her hands. She had meant to go before now to see Imogene and offer to sell her soaps and candles, but with everything being as busy as it was, she had not found the time. And now she would have to go and not only apologize, but also beg her to come work for them. Melody did not relish eating such a large slice of humble pie, but she didn't see any other solution. It was pointless to try to hire someone off the street at this juncture, and, anyway, it was better to take the devil she knew. Though, she conceded, as she slipped off her blood-streaked apron, Imogene could hardly be called a devil, just annoying.

"Harriet! I'm going out for a minute," she called toward the front.

"Now?"

"Yes, while we're slow."

"What if we get busy?" Harriet called nervously.

"I'm just going upstairs to see Imogene. I'll be back in minute."

* * *

Melody quickly climbed the wooden steps that hugged the back of the building. She couldn't remember the last time she had been up to the apartment, although she had a vague memory of visiting her grandparents up there. She had been given a cup of cocoa, and she thought she could remember the wallpaper—faint blue stripes with tiny birds every so often.

Halfway up, she gripped the worn railing. She didn't remember the stairs being so steep. She paused for a moment at the top to catch her breath and, before she could change her mind, rapped on the door.

She could hear movement inside, but no one answered. She knocked again, and this time she saw the slight rustle of the curtain in the window further down. Someone was indeed home, and given the rapidity of the curtain's swish, she assumed it was Imogene, as Mrs. Kaufmann was quite elderly.

"Imogene!" Melody called.

Nothing.

She knocked again. "Imogene! It's me, Melody. I need to talk to you. Please!"

There seemed to be some argument occurring on the other side of the door, and Melody leaned her ear closer, trying to hear. Before she could make anything out, however, the door opened a crack to reveal Imogene herself. "Yes? Oh, Melody! It's you!"

"Um. Yes, hello, Imogene. May I come in?"

"Is something wrong?" Still keeping the door partially closed, Imogene stuck her head out and peered at the street below, as if expecting to see some sort of disaster occurring.

"No, I just . . . just want to ask you something. It won't take long."

Imogene looked over her shoulder and then back again. "Well, now's not such a good time. Though we would be ever so glad of a visit any other time, I'm sure. You've never called on us before, and Mother would be delighted to see you. I'm sure she would. But as it is, I'm just getting Mother's stockings on for the day, and it's . . . well, it's quite a chore. And"—she looked over her shoulder again—"we're not quite set up for company."

"Imogene, I don't have a lot of time. I have to get back down to the Merc." Melody was already beginning to regret her decision.

Imogene stared at her for a moment or two, as if trying to make up her mind. A frown appeared, then, but she nonetheless opened the door wide for her to pass through. "Well, alright. If you must, but just a few minutes, like."

Melody stepped inside only to stop short, utterly dismayed. Nothing could have prepared her for the complete disarray in front of her. This was a hundred times worse than the Peddler, and it certainly didn't match the warm childhood memory she had of her grandparents' first home. Everywhere were stacks of newspaper, balls of string, and boxes and boxes and boxes of every size, stuffed and overflowing with clothing and other items. In one corner, a small herd of old milk bottles huddled. Indeed, only a narrow strip of the floor could be seen leading from the front room to the back of the apartment, so packed was the place.

And in the midst of this collection of trash sat Old Mrs. Kaufman in the front room, or what was once the front room. She was entrenched in a torn armchair with one crumpled, arthritic foot bare and the other with a stocking pulled only halfway up her leg. The old woman stared at Melody with cloudy eyes but did not address her. Melody wondered if she was blind.

"Who's there, Immy?" Mrs. Kaufmann suddenly barked.

"It's Melody, Mother!" Imogene shouted back, one hand cupped around her mouth.

"Who?" Mrs. Kaufmann blinked slowly, like a great horned owl, which she oddly resembled with her big bushy white eyebrows.

Imogene stepped closer and spoke into the woman's ear. "It's Melody! From downstairs. You know, Mother, don't you? Mr. Merriweather's daughter."

"Hello, Mrs. Kaufmann!" Melody shouted.

Mrs. Kaufmann did not respond beyond a small shrug. "Stockings!" She jabbed a crooked finger at her crooked foot.

"In a minute, Mother!" Imogene turned back to Melody and wrung her hands slightly. "I . . . I'm sorry I can't offer you much, Melody. We just had the last of the bread. And the tea is gone, I'm afraid. We each get only one cup, you see, which is quite enough for us. Yes, quite enough. Well, sometimes Mother wants more, so I give her mine. But that's okay, because I'm quite happy with water. Can I offer you some water, perhaps?"

Melody's eyes darted to the sink, where a giant pile of dirty dishes loomed.

"I . . . I was just going to do those," Imogene faltered, her eyes following Melody's. "Right after I get Mother's stockings on. They're horribly tight, you see, and it takes all my strength to get them on. But I don't mind. It strengthens my fingers, which is quite a good thing. Never hurts to have strong fingers, does it? Some say women should have delicate hands, don't they? But that doesn't make sense because women have to do so much work. That would be a disadvantage, I'm thinking, wouldn't it, Melody?"

"Immy!" Mrs. Kaufmann shouted, weakly banging a fist on the arm of the chair.

"Oh! Yes, Mother!" Imogene hurried over and knelt before her. "What is it you wanted, Melody?" she asked, entirely fixated now on tugging the stocking the rest of the way up her mother's leg. "Is it about the other night?" she grunted. "I'm terribly sorry. I . . . I don't know what came into my mind. I . . . I shouldn't have bothered you like that. How stupid of me! But then, I'm always doing stupid stuff, aren't I, Mother?"

Mrs. Kaufmann did not answer but merely stared straight ahead with her ghostly, cloudy eyes. She made no move to help Imogene with the donning of the stockings, not even holding out her leg. She simply sat there, a large lump, like a dog or a doll, waiting to be dressed.

"Don't say that, Imogene," Melody said gently, suddenly even more remorseful for all she had said to this poor woman. "I'm the one who should be apologizing. I've . . . I've changed my mind, in fact. That's why I'm here."

"About the soaps and the candles?" Imogene paused momentarily to look over her shoulder. "But you said they were rubbish. I threw them in the trash, though Mother made me dig them back out. She doesn't like to throw anything away, as you can see. But I suppose she was right. We can use the soaps ourselves and burn the candles at night." She gestured at several candle stumps positioned around the room. Melody hadn't noticed them against the backdrop of all the other garbage. "Save us paying the electrics, you see." She went back to tugging on the stocking.

"No, they're not rubbish at all. I . . . I *do* want to sell them," Melody faltered. "But there's . . . there's something else, too." She paused, thinking her decision through one last time. "As it turns out, I'm . . . well, I'm down a couple of staff members just at the moment. And I was wondering if you might consider coming back. To the Merc, that is. To work. Temporarily. Maybe the butcher counter?"

Imogene stopped and sat back on her heels. "*Me?* Come back to the Merc?" Her face was one of such incredulousness and gratitude that Melody suddenly felt ashamed.

"Well, yes. If you . . . if you think your mother can spare you." In truth, Melody had had no idea Mrs. Kaufmann had gotten so infirm. This was unfortunate, of course, but on the positive side, it probably meant there was little chance she would be able to escape the apartment as she had done during Imogene's previous stint of employment.

Imogene got awkwardly to her feet. "Oh, yes! Oh, yes, of course, I'll do it. The meat counter? But what about Cal? Is he not there?"

"He had to go back to Dodgeville, and I'm not sure when he's coming back. And Mrs. Haufbrau has . . . has also left, so I . . . I really need you. I'm sorry I was harsh before. I wasn't myself."

"Oh, you don't have to apologize! Not at all! It was my fault for bothering you. I should have thought. I told Mother that when I came home. Didn't I, Mother?" she shouted, one hand cupping her mouth again. When Mrs. Kaufmann did not respond, she turned back to Melody. "When should I start?"

"Whenever you want. As soon as possible." Melody looked around the dismal apartment. "If you think you can leave your mother, that is. Do you think she'll be okay here on her own?"

"Mother? Oh, yes, she'll be fine. How about tomorrow?" She glanced at her mother. "You'll be okay, won't you, Mother?" she shouted and then turned back to Melody. "No, don't you worry. I'll get everything arranged up here."

Melody doubted that Imogene could even remotely arrange anything at all in this mess. "Well, if you're sure," she said apprehensively. "But I must get back now. I'll see you tomorrow." Having not really moved from the spot where she had entered, as there was no other space to move to, Melody simply turned around. She paused, though, before exiting and opened her purse, pulling out a ten-dollar bill. "Here," she said, holding it out to Imogene. "Why don't you get some fresh bread and milk, and maybe some . . . something for your mother." Hadn't Imogene mentioned the other night that her mother was ill? Maybe she needed medicine.

"Oh, no!" Imogene tried to push the money back into Melody's hand. "No, we don't need this. We don't need charity."

"It's not charity," Melody said gently. "Consider it an advance on your wages. How about that?"

Imogene wavered. "Well, are you sure?"

"Yes." Melody patted her hand. "Perfectly. Now, I really must go. Harriet is all alone down there."

CHAPTER
TWENTY-TWO

The image of the Kaufmanns' apartment haunted Melody the rest of the day and even into the evening. She was unusually quiet at dinner, and when Mums asked what was wrong, she made the mistake of telling her she had hired Imogene Kaufmann to help at the Merc. That, of course, had led to a barrage of disparaging stories about Imogene and Esmerelda Kaufmann, mainly for the benefit of the lodgers, Melody was sure. But now started, there was nothing she could do to stop it, though she was oddly tempted more than once to defend the poor woman.

She contemplated telling her mother about the sad condition she had found the apartment in, but she did not, calculating that rather than aid her cause, her mother might be so upset about it she might even urge Pops to kick them out.

Frank, however, seemed intrigued by Imogene and promised to stop by to meet the soap artist, a title Melody thought generous in the extreme. Mums seemed to be in agreement, as she let out a laugh, or more of a chortle, saying that Imogene Kaufmann could hardly be called an artist. Someone to perhaps be pitied, but an artist? No. Frank persisted in his desire to stop by, however, so much so that Melody wondered if it was really just a thinly veiled excuse to see Harriet.

"And, anyway," Mums said disapprovingly, "whatever happened with Marcella? Didn't you get her back?"

"Not yet, Mums," Melody said with a heavy sigh as she pushed her peas around her plate, praying that she would not have to go begging to Mrs. Haufbrau as well.

* * *

With this thought still in her head, Melody was determined, as she opened the shop the next morning, to make it work with just the three of them. Likewise, she was determined to have a clean slate in regards to Imogene, to give her the benefit of the doubt, and even to try to be kind.

Sadly, however, all of her good intentions nearly went out the window when Imogene walked in wearing the most hideous dress Melody had ever seen and carrying her small shoe box of rubbish under her arm.

"Oh, hello, Melody. Don't you look nice? But, then, you always look nice. Isn't it nice out today? I was just telling Mother that she should sit by the window and collect some sun before it turns cold. Supposed to have a cold winter, the Almanac says. Did you hear that, Melody? I *did* hear that. I heard it somewhere else, too. Might have been Mr. Slater. But, then again, it could have been Mrs. Owens. Or maybe it was Mrs. Borman. Saw both of them in Slater's just yesterday. I went out when Mother was asleep, you see. She does sleep an awful lot, which is good, isn't it? Prevents illness, so they say. Which is a good thing, as the flu is supposed to be bad this year. I hope we don't get it. I hope none of us get it. Here you are." She thrust the box into Melody's hands. "Here's the candles and the soaps, just like you asked. My, it's good to be back.

Hello, there," she said to Harriet, who for once had arrived on time and was already at her station.

Melody had of course apprised Harriet of her decision to hire Imogene, but even the kindly Harriet seemed a bit taken aback by Imogene's early-morning verbosity and threadbare dress, which was actually ripped in some places. Imogene looked little better than a hobo.

"Hello," Harriet said tentatively before peering questioningly at Melody.

Melody set the dusty box on the counter. "Imogene . . ." Melody faltered. "I . . . I assumed you had a shop skirt and a blouse from working here before."

"Oh! I . . . I forgot." Imogene wrung her hands. "I must look upstairs. I'm sure I can find them somewhere."

Considering the shambles upstairs, Melody doubted this. "Well, until . . . until you find them," Melody said haltingly, trying to phrase her words carefully, "do you not have a nicer dress to wear? What you had on yesterday, for instance, would be fine."

"Oh!" Imogene looked back down at her dress again, awkwardly gripping the sides, the fabric bunching in her fists. "Well, I didn't want to wear anything too good. Mother said I should wear this one so that people won't think the shop is making too much money. It irritates Mother in the extreme when shopgirls are decked out fancier than the customers. That's logical, isn't it?"

It was not logical at all, but Melody decided not to counter her, though it was horribly tempting. "Well, perhaps," she said instead. "But when you're waiting on customers, your dress should be clean and fresh, and preferably have no rips."

Imogene turned a deep red. "Oh, yes. I see that now. I'm sorry, Melody. Oh, dear. I've already made a mistake, and I haven't even started." She twisted her hands back into a tight ball. "I'll go change now, should I? It won't take but a minute."

"No, it's alright. Your apron will cover most of it." She handed her Cal's. "Here, put this on. There, that's better. It will do for today."

*　*　*

Melody spent the next hour reorienting Imogene to the meat counter, the workings of which she seemed to remember well, but, then again, nothing had changed back here in eons. They waited on customers together, during which time Imogene had, as Melody feared, a propensity to engage excessively in conversation with each and every person who stopped by, despite Melody's attempts to hurry them along. Finally, after Imogene had spent a full twelve minutes—Melody timed it—discussing Mrs. Gartner's aching tooth and the best remedies for such a malady, Melody felt the need to intervene.

"Imogene," she said, once Mrs. Gartner had finally departed for the front register with a pound of bologna, "I appreciate that you are so friendly with the customers, but you really can't go on and on, especially if we get busy. You understand, don't you? We can't hold people up. Just fill the order and hand them their package. A smile and 'have a nice day' is all you need to say."

Imogene's face fell. "Oh, I'm sorry, Melody! I do go on, I know. Mother is always telling me that I talk too much. I'll be better, I promise."

"Okay. I'm going to leave you on your own now. I have to go back up front for a while. But remember. Keep it short."

Imogene nodded vigorously.

Melody considered whether she should really leave the woman on her own, but she had to keep pushing the cider samples. Harriet, she feared, was too shy.

"Harriet, have you not given any out?" she asked, sliding in beside her at the counter. The glasses were still neatly stacked near the register.

"Well, it's not even noon yet, so I thought I should wait. Being that it's alcohol," Harriet responded tentatively.

Melody rubbed her brow, knowing that didn't matter in a town like Merriweather.

"I sold two bottles, though," she said proudly.

"Oh! Well, that's good, Harriet! Hello, Mrs. Koenig," she said to the woman who had just come in. "Something I can help you with?"

"Just need some bacon," Mrs. Koenig said. "Cal back yet?"

"No, but Imogene Kaufmann is back there. She'll be glad to help."

"Imogene Kaufmann! Well! Haven't seen her in an age. Thought she didn't get on here."

Melody let out an irritated sigh. "Well, that was a long time ago, Mrs. Koenig."

"Does your father know she's back?"

Melody felt weary to the bone. She wasn't sure how much longer she could take any of this. "Yes, as a matter of fact, it was his idea," she replied, forcing her voice to be sickeningly sweet. "Would you like me to assist you instead?"

"No, no." The woman hobbled toward the back. "I was just wondering is all."

Melody folded her arms and turned to Harriet, trying to recenter her mind on the cider. "Does your mom have another batch ready?"

"Yes, almost. But I wish Cal were here with his truck. They're so heavy."

"Hmm. Yes, it's too much for one person to carry all that way," Melody agreed and wondered if she could wrangle the Daimler from Mums. "I'll see if I can get the car. But we'll need more labels," she mused. "Do you think Kate could make more? I'll have to see about getting some printed. She can't keep hand-drawing these."

Harriet nodded. "Yes, I'll go tonight. I haven't been out to see her in a while."

Melody tilted her head, then, trying to listen to Imogene and Mrs. Koenig. Imogene was going on about how the flu was going around and who exactly in town had already succumbed. Melody pinched the bridge of her nose. How did Imogene even know all of these things, considering that she spent her entire life locked in an apartment with her deaf and demented mother? She would have to go back and rescue poor Mrs. Koenig. But before she could, the shop bell tinkled again and in walked Frank Churchill. She had forgotten that he had said he would stop by. She should have warned Harriet! Melody quickly looked her over and determined that she looked well enough, her hair tied up in a pretty green ribbon.

"Ah! Here is the proprietress, standing amidst her wares!" Frank announced, gesturing widely. "And her charming assistant!" Frank smiled broadly at Harriet, who returned it, a faint blush on her cheeks. Melody smiled, too. Despite the fact that she really wasn't in the mood for Frank's moralizing and philosophic speeches, she did relish the opportunity to witness the development of his and Harriet's budding relationship. She was suddenly quite proud of her young protégée, who was proving to be a much more amenable pupil than Elsie.

"You'll excuse me for a moment, won't you, Frank? I need to rescue poor Mrs. Koenig," Melody said, thinking that it would be good to give the potential sweethearts some time alone. She would have to encourage Frank to ask Harriet out. Or maybe she should invite Harriet to dinner some night . . .

"Rescue?" Frank said, grabbing hold of his lapels. "Do you need my help?"

"Oh, no, I just meant that I need to . . . redirect Imogene. I won't be a moment!"

"Oh, let me come, too!" Frank said eagerly, spoiling her plan. "I must meet the mysterious soap lady. But first, let me take some in hand." He darted toward the row of cleaning supplies before Melody could stop him. He returned just as quickly, his face holding a rare frown. "Where are they? Did you sell them all? Or did you move them?"

Melody bit the inside of her cheek. She was tired to death of Imogene's stupid soaps! And she was irritated that Frank was missing an obvious chance to be alone with Harriet. "No." Melody crossed her arms. "I removed them temporarily. Where did you put them, Harriet?"

Harriet reached under the counter and retrieved the shoe box.

"But why?" Frank seemed genuinely confused.

"It's kind of a long story." Melody uncrossed her arms.

"Well, let me help you find a place for them," he said eagerly. "What you should do is fill the front of the shop with *local* items." His eyes roamed around the shop as if looking for some. "People need flour and thread and cloth and boots, so put those in the back. Make people walk through the store to get to them. At the front, you should display your local products, such as the honey, the soaps, the baskets, the cider, and whatever else we can uncover. We must look backward to go forward, you see." He gave her a dashing little wink. "Think of it, Melody. You could be a pioneer in transforming Merriweather into a place where artists can thrive, displaying their wares and selling them!"

A pioneer? An image of her grandfather suddenly came to mind, but she brushed it away. "But why?" Melody, in truth, was already growing a little tired of the "artist colony" speech. "And why do you care about Merriweather? It can't just be that you came here as a kid to visit your grandparents."

Frank gave a little shrug. "Call it a feeling. Intuition, if you will. Let's face it. The mines have closed. Many people have already left for the cities. Merriweather must reinvent itself if it is to survive." He gestured widely. "If we transform the town into a beacon of the arts, people will begin to flock here, even from Chicago. It will become a tourist mecca, and business, *all* business, will increase. People will of course need staples—" he gestured toward the shelf of canned goods—"but what they will come for is the artists' wares, and you'll be a forerunner in selling them."

Melody thought about this. There might be some truth to what he was saying, but it didn't help her situation in the immediate future. She needed money *now*, not years from now. And if it did eventually become a destination for tourists, the Merc would probably be gone by then, seeing as it was nearly dead already.

"It wouldn't take much," Frank said, sensing her doubt. "Allow me." He gave a quick look around. "Here." He grabbed one of Kate's woven baskets and set it on the counter near the register. "You should place this here. Like so. And then put some honey next to it, like this. Then the cider. See?" His hands moved quickly, arranging the items, and then he took a step back, tilting his head as he examined his tableau.

"It makes it look like someone is about to go on a picnic." He picked up the metal Wrigleys gum display at the far end of the counter and set it on the floor. "And the soaps would go here." After rummaging through Imogene's box and selecting several, he grabbed another basket of Kate's from the shelf, this time a small one. "We can use this to display the soaps, but we need something else. Maybe one of those pretty silk scarves," he murmured. He walked toward the back and returned with a lavender one. He draped it over the basket and then attractively arranged the soaps inside. "See?" He glanced at Melody and Harriet with a big smile. "Utterly charming!"

Melody was surprised by how well he was able to create such an enticing display with such little effort. He did indeed seem to have an artistic eye and an almost feminine touch. It was uncanny.

"Yes, I see what you mean. What do you think, Harriet?"

"Yes, I think . . . I think Frank is right. It's better this way." Harriet gave him a shy smile, which caused a delicious idea to pop into Melody's mind.

"Say, Frank, might I ask you for another favor?" Melody twirled a lock of her hair.

"Certainly."

"Would you be able to help Harriet to bring in another load of cider? It's awfully heavy, and we need a car, you see."

"Ah! But of course. I'd be delighted. Just tell me when, and I'll be there!"

Melody looked at Harriet.

"Um, well, I think the new batch should probably be ready by Thursday?" Harriet faltered.

"Very well, I'll be there bright and early."

Mrs. Koenig appeared then, having apparently broken free of Imogene all on her own. "I'll ring you up, Mrs. Koenig," Melody called. "Anything else I can get you? How about a little sample of our cider? Homemade." Melody held up a bottle. "It's quite good."

"Well, if you're pouring some," she said sheepishly. "Why not?"

Melody quickly poured her a small glass full.

"Oh, my!" she said after taking a sip. "That's real good. Reminds me of the cider my grandma used to make."

"Yes, it's an old recipe. And perfect for the holidays coming up. Might want to get some before we sell out."

Mrs. Koenig's face furrowed, but Melody could tell she was close to a sale.

"How much are they?"

"Seventy-five cents a bottle."

"Seventy-five cents, eh? That's not bad." Mrs. Koenig thought for a moment. "I'll take two bottles then."

"Alright," Melody chirped. She rang up the total while Harriet bagged everything.

"Good day, Mrs. Koenig," Melody said. "You might want to tell Mrs. Owens to stop in and get some of this cider before it goes."

"I will, Melody! Tell your father we're praying for him," she called over her shoulder as she left.

Frank, who had taken to leaning against the shelves during the transaction, straightened. "You're a born saleswoman!" he said appreciatively. "I daresay you're going to be alright. A trio of ladies, manning the ship. It is perfect! And speaking of, I really must meet your third. This Imogene."

"I'll follow you back in a minute," Melody said. "You're more than capable of introducing yourself, I'm sure."

"That is true. Until Thursday, Harriet?" He lifted his hat and then sauntered off toward the back.

Melody bent to pick up the Wrigley gum display. "You've chosen a winner there, Harriet. He's utterly enamored of you, I can tell. Here, move those papers, would you?" She nodded to the stack of newspapers to the left of the cash register. Harriet hurriedly lifted them, and Melody set the gum down and brushed her hands. "I must say, I'm quite impressed by how contained the both of you are around each other."

Harriet looked at her, puzzled. "What do you mean?"

"You and Frank, of course. I thought he might be one of those . . . well, never mind. But then when you told me you set your sights on him, I realized I must be wrong. Not if you both have feelings for each other, that is."

Harriet's cheeks were very pink. "Frank? I . . . I never said I like Frank!"

Melody gave her a quizzical look. "You distinctly told me that you had set your sights on someone else. Someone 'more deserving,' I think you said. And this was right after you took him on a tour of New Grimsby."

Harriet's face remained a blank.

"Who else could you mean?" Melody asked.

Harriet shook her head, but then a shy smile erupted as if she finally understood. "No, I wasn't referring to *Frank*," she said incredulously, her voice low. "I barely know him! I mean, he's nice and all, but he's . . . well, he's a bit too flamboyant for me. And too old, I think."

"Then who *were* you referring to?"

Harriet's face went from pink to red. "I was referring to Cal."

All the breath seemed to go out of Melody's lungs. Cal? *Cal?* She scurried for something to say. "You can't possibly be serious," she murmured.

Harriet's eyes flashed in a rare moment of anger. "Yes, I *am* serious."

"But that's . . . that's ridiculous!" The image of Harriet and Cal together was almost laughable.

"Why is it ridiculous, Melody?" Harriet's voice held an icy tone. "You yourself said that I should set my sights on someone better. That's Cal all over." She grimaced. "Or is it me you don't think is good enough?"

"No, that's . . . that's not what I meant."

"What *did* you mean, then?"

"Just that . . . does . . . does he feel the same?" she dodged.

Harriet bit her lip, her previous defiance melting into what seemed like self-defeat. "I don't know." She shrugged. "But he *did* take me home from the bonfire. And he always . . . well, he always has a smile and a kind word."

Melody felt a brief reprieve, wondering if the situation was salvageable, though she wasn't sure exactly why she thought it *needed* salvaging. She rubbed her arm. "Well, I would just caution you to . . . to guard your feelings until you know for sure."

"I was hoping to speak to him when he comes back." Harriet tightened her apron. "*If* he comes back."

"Yes, who knows if he'll come back?" Melody added quickly. "If I were you, I wouldn't put too much stock into Cal Fraiser, Harriet. He's

. . . well, he's temperamental and unpredictable. And moody. He's really not for you."

Harriet's eyes flickered again. "Not really for me? How would you know? And you're the one that seems awfully moody and temperamental, Melody. Maybe what's really bothering you is that you want Cal for yourself."

CHAPTER
TWENTY-THREE

Harriet wiped her eyes again as she stumbled along to Kate's. It was already dark, and the weather had shifted the last few days. It was considerably colder, and winter was not far away. In fact, if Melody hadn't asked her to get more labels, Harriet would have preferred to sit in the cottage with her mother and drown her sorrows in a cup of cocoa. As it was, however, she had to go. She had hoped that the walk up Christmas Tree Hill would clear her mind, but it did not. She simply could not stop thinking about the look of dismay on Melody's face when she admitted to liking Cal. It was humiliating! Though Melody had tried to deny it, it was clear that she thought her enormously inferior to Cal Fraiser.

Thinking it all through again, Harriet supposed it made sense. Why *would* someone like Cal like a girl like her? She wasn't sure which she was more hurt by—the fact that Cal probably did not return her feelings or that Melody had such a low opinion of her. Either one made tears well up. Perhaps she really *had* misread Cal's feelings. She had thought his actions at the Harvest Fest and his pleasant demeanor on their trip to Gays Mills, not to mention the fact that he sold her cheap cuts of meat, meant something. But maybe she had been wrong. Oh, dear! *Had she been?* She stepped carefully over a fallen tree branch.

And why had she accused Melody of wanting Cal for herself? Melody and Cal didn't even *like* each other. They were always bickering, and, anyway, didn't Melody have someone back in Chicago? Douglas, she remembered his name being, though it *was* odd that she never really spoke about him. Perhaps Melody was not as serious about him as Harriet had been led to believe.

She let out a low moan as she tromped along. This was really all Melody's fault! She hadn't even been thinking about love until Melody had filled her head with romance and courting and wedding bells. True, she had already agreed to go to the Harvest Fest with John Schneider before Melody had even gotten involved, but that had been just an innocent sort of thing, nothing like the mess she currently found herself in. As it stood now, John had rejected her, Cal was apparently out of reach, and Melody had thought that Frank Churchill—*Frank Churchill?*—was an appropriate suiter. *Oh! What was she to do?*

She could see Kate's dwelling in the distance, and she contemplated telling her friend the whole thing, though she was pretty sure she knew what Kate would say—that she was foolish for having let John Schneider go in the first place. Also, that she shouldn't be taking advice from the likes of Melody Merriweather, "who doesn't know her behind from a hole in the ground." Personally, Harriet felt this a bit unfair and had said so, but Kate had merely to remind her of the Wesley Elton debacle to squash any arguments. "Anyone could have seen he's an idiot. Why did she try to set you up with him in the first place? I wouldn't trust her."

While Harriet had to admit that Melody *was* somewhat out of touch with "normal people"—Kate's words, not hers—she usually found herself defending Melody, but today, she couldn't help but be disappointed in her friend, not to mention annoyed.

Puffing slightly, Harriet stepped into the little clearing and noticed now that there was no smoke coming from Kate's chimney. There had been frost overnight, and it was currently so cold she could see her own breath. Why did Kate not have a fire burning? Harriet's eyes darted to the woodpile, wondering if she had already burned through it, but, no, it was still piled relatively high. In fact, it looked almost untouched.

Harriet knocked at the door.

"Kate?" she called, but there was no answer. "Kate?"

She knocked again and put her ear to the door. She turned and peered into the darkness, wondering if Kate was still outside somewhere. Maybe cutting reeds down by the creek?

"Kate?" she called a third time. When there was again no answer, Harriet pushed open the door and poked in her head. All was quiet and dark. It was hard to see anything in the blackness, though the moonlight coming through the still-open door illuminated at least a bit of the dwelling. Kate's bed was unmade, and her basket materials were splayed out on the little table near the stove. She stepped closer and saw a plate of food, crusted over, as if it had been sitting there for at least a day.

Fear suddenly gripped Harriet's heart. Where could Kate be? Had she gone somewhere to visit, maybe? But where? And wouldn't she have tidied up first? Harriet stepped back outside and looked around again. "Kate?" she shouted, though she was pretty sure even Kate wouldn't be so foolish to be out at this time of night. Something, Harriet realized with mounting fear, must have happened to her . . .

Harriet pulled the door shut and scrambled back down the hill, picking her way as fast as she dared, conscious of the fact that if she inadvertently stepped into a cow rut, she was likely to twist her ankle. As soon as she was on more level ground, however, she picked up her pace and practically ran across the back field. She should telephone someone . . . but who? Perhaps the Kerwyns? Yes, she decided as she breathlessly banged through the cottage door, she would start there.

"You back already?" Rosemary asked, looking up from her sewing and peering at Harriet over her wire-rimmed spectacles.

Harriet did not answer but ran toward the telephone.

"What's wrong?" Rosemary set her sewing aside and rose unsteadily, gripping the arm of the rocking chair. "Something out there?" She glanced nervously at the front window.

"No, I . . . I can't find Kate," Harriet panted as she picked up the receiver.

"Can't find her? Well, maybe she's out foraging. You know her."

"At this time of night?" Harriet rapidly clicked the holder.

Ethyl Moore's nasally voice came on the line. "Operator. May I help you?"

"Ethyl, can you get me through to the Kerwyns? This is Harriet."

"Gus or Jim or Lee?"

"Gus."

"One moment. You okay?"

"Yes, I just need to . . . to check something."

"You got it." The line was silent for a moment, and then Ethyl came back on. "There doesn't seem to be any answer. Want me to try again in a few moments and call you back?"

"Oh, yes! Thanks, Ethyl!"

Harriet hung up and bit her fingernail. She wished she had a car! But where would she go? The Kerwyns? She wondered if she should telephone the police. But, no . . . that was silly. She tried to calm herself down. There must be a perfectly rational explanation, she told herself. Kate had obviously gone to see someone. But then why was her place in such a state? Harriet did not think Kate overly neat, but this was unlike her . . .

The telephone rang then, and Harriet jumped. Thank God!

She picked up the receiver eagerly. "Hello? Mr. Kerwyn?"

"Uh, no," said a man. Harriet thought she recognized the voice, and her heart picked up a little. He sounded awfully like—

"Harriet, this is John Schneider."

Harriet's stomach clenched, and she suddenly didn't know what to say.

"Hello? Are you there?" His voice, though deep and resonant, seemed unsteady.

"I . . ." She cleared her throat. Why was John Schneider telephoning her? "Yes, I'm here. What do you want?" she asked bluntly and then realized how rude it had sounded. "I mean, I was just trying to get ahold of the Kerwyns. I thought you were them."

"Oh. Well, that's odd. That's why I was calling, actually. I have some news about your friend, Kate."

Harriet's clenched stomach tightened further. "What do you mean? Where is she? I've been looking everywhere." This wasn't *exactly* true, but true enough.

"She's here. At our house. She's very ill."

"At your house? What happened?"

"Doc Hodges just left. Says she has pneumonia."

"Pneumonia?" Harriet looked worriedly at her mother, who had crept closer, listening.

"Excuse me," Ethyl interrupted. "But there's another call on this line."

"Yes, okay," John said hurriedly. "Harriet, Kate is asking for you. Can you come?"

"Now?" Harriet looked at her mother.

"I . . . I could pick you up." She heard him swallow. "If you want."

Harriet put her hand over the phone and whispered to her mother. "Kate is ill. She's at the Schneiders and wants me to come. John's offering to drive me."

Rosemary nodded and moved to the kitchen where she began packing a basket.

"Yes, okay," Harriet said into the receiver. "But, John, is . . . is she really that bad?"

There was silence on the line for a telling few seconds. "Ma thinks she'll pull through," he said finally, "but I'm not so sure. I'll explain it all on the way, okay? We should get off."

* * *

John arrived not twenty minutes later, which meant that he must have really been speeding. In that space of time, however, Harriet had managed to convince her mother that it would be insulting to the Schneiders to bring a basket of food for a girl already in their care. Surely, the Schneiders were providing anything Kate needed at the moment. In the end, Rosemary finally acquiesced, but she insisted that Harriet at least take along a special blend of tea that was said to be good for the lungs.

The tea pouch in her pocket, Harriet opened the door to John's rapid knock and was surprised by the way her heart—*again!*—betrayed her at the sight of his blond curls and deep blue eyes. With his height and broad shoulders, he filled the tiny cottage with his presence. He looked, for lack of a better description, like a gentle giant. He wrenched his cap in his hands and gave Rosemary a deep nod of deference. "Hello, Mrs. Mueller." He glanced at Harriet then, his Adam's apple giving a nervous bob. "Should we go?"

"Yes, alright," Harriet said, pulling on her coat. She gave Rosemary a quick kiss on the cheek. "Goodbye, Mom."

"I'll drive her home, Mrs. Mueller."

"It'll be late, though. Perhaps you should stay, Harriet."

"Mom!" Harriet was utterly mortified by this suggestion.

"We . . . we'd be glad to have you," John said, his face a strange shade of pink. "But I don't mind driving you back, either." He twisted his cap more. "It's whatever you want."

"Well, let's just see, should we?" she said, giving her mother a stern look.

John helped Harriet into his truck and shifted it into first and then high gear, rumbling up Magnolia Street. The interior was cold and smelled of oil and grease and metal tools. She kept her eyes on the dark road and only occasionally looked over at him. He had begun to grow a beard, which was also blond, and she felt a bizarre urge to run her finger along it. *What on earth was the matter with her?*

She balled her hands in her lap and looked out the side window. She must be stronger! And she was determined to be her old happy-go-lucky self, not the love-crazed romantic that Melody wanted her to be. She glanced back at John and caught him looking at her. He quickly pulled his eyes away.

"So, what happened?" she asked.

"What do you mean?" He kept his eyes on the road.

"With Kate? What happened?"

"Oh." He shifted gears again. "I don't know all the details. Just that Ed Bertram was walking down through the hollow on his way to visit her and found her lying in the field. Picked her up and carried her to ours."

"Oh, my!" Harriet tried to imagine her friend lying, unconscious and alone in a field. It was horrible! "But why your place?"

"Well, we're the closest, I reckon. Ed could have cut through Portzen's Woods and gotten over to the Gartners', but he went south toward us. Six of one, half a dozen of the other. Mom saw him a ways off and sent Jimmy out to help him. Kate was unconscious and burning up. Mom called Doc Hodges. She also called the Kerwyns."

"Did they come?"

"They wanted to. Wanted to bring her to theirs, but the Doc said she shouldn't be moved just yet. Her mom came for a little while, but she had to leave. Her littlest one apparently has the flu."

"Oh, my God," Harriet whispered. Poor Kate!! She should have insisted that she go to the doctor when she had noticed her cough. "Is she going to be okay?"

John turned onto a dirt road and shifted into a lower gear. "Doctor said it's touch and go. She's strong, but she's a bit malnourished. That won't help things."

Harriet was silent for a few moments, trying to make sense of it all. "But why did you call *me*?"

"She asked for you." He glanced at her and then back at the road. "She was upset and insistent. Probably delirious with the fever, but we thought we should try to find you. Just in case," he added quietly.

Harriet decided to ignore the implication hidden in his last comment. Oh, poor Kate! Why was she always so stubborn! Why hadn't she gotten her cough seen to when Harriet had suggested it?

John parked the truck under a huge oak tree near a big white farmhouse, then came around to help Harriet step down from the running board. Once she was safely on the ground, he strode quickly toward the house, as if eager to deliver his quarry. Harriet followed, trying to take in her surroundings as she hurried after him, but besides the hulking red barn in the distance, it was too dark to really see anything. They climbed the few wooden steps of the wraparound porch and entered a big bright kitchen, the screen door banging softly behind them. The aroma of baked chicken hung in the air, and Harriet felt her stomach rumble, despite having had an egg sandwich earlier. Several kids sat around the kitchen table, some of them writing out sums on their slates.

"Ma," John said to the plump woman standing near the stove. "This here's Harriet." He looked at her sheepishly and then at the ground.

"So I see," Mrs. Schneider said pleasantly. "Haven't seen you in years, Harriet. You've sure filled out. How's your mom?"

"She's fine." Harriet shifted uncomfortably. "But how's Kate?"

"Maybe a dash better. You go on up. John'll show you. I'll make you some cocoa. Or do you want some soup?"

Harriet hesitated. "Maybe both? If it's not too much trouble?"

Mrs. Schneider laughed. "Course it's not. I like a girl who knows what she wants."

"This way," John said with an awkward gesture.

Harriet tentatively climbed the narrow stairs after him, impressed by how neat and tidy the house was. He led her down a hallway to a room at the end. After rapping lightly, he poked his head in and then opened the door wide.

The room was small, the iron bed and oversized wardrobe taking up most of it. A braided rug partially covered the thick wooden floorboards, and near the bed stood a worn chair. Kate lay on the bed, dressed in what was obviously a borrowed nightgown, a quilt covering her lower half. Her eyes were closed and her breathing shallow. Harriet looked to John for instruction, but he gave none, so Harriet crept closer and gingerly sat on the edge of the bed.

"Kate?" she said softly. Tears pooled in her eyes, making it difficult to see her friend. "Kate!" she said, taking her hand. "I'm here." She could hear the deep wheeze and rattle in her chest. Harriet looked back at John again, who was still standing in the doorway, his cap in his hands. He did not look hopeful.

"Why don't you sit there?" he suggested, nodding at the chair. "You'll be more comfortable."

Harriet decided he might be right. She stood up gently, so as to not disturb Kate, and realized that she hadn't even removed her coat. She shrugged out of it and looked around for a place to set it. John lumbered forward.

"I'll hang this," he said, taking it from her. "I'll be right back."

Harriet sat down in the chair, which was surprisingly comfortable, and took Kate's hand again. "Kate," she said softly. "It's Harriet. I'm here. What did you want to tell me?"

Kate remained lifeless. Harriet racked her brain, trying to guess what Kate could have possibly wanted to tell her. Something about the baskets or the labels? No, it couldn't be something that trivial. Something about Edmund maybe? Or some deep, dark secret? But as far as she knew, Kate had already shared all of her secrets, even the ones about the things Ray had done. Had something else happened, maybe? Something in Stoughton? Is that why she had left so quickly? Or perhaps what Kate had wanted to tell her wasn't a deep dark secret at all. Perhaps she had something of value hidden, the location of which she wanted to reveal in case she . . . in case she . . . Harriet stopped herself.

There was a light rap on the door, then, and Harriet jumped a little. It was John, holding a steaming mug of cocoa. "Ma sent this up. Says your soup is ready whenever you want it. It's on the stove." He handed her the mug. "Careful. It's hot."

As soon as she gingerly took it, he shoved his hands in his overall pockets. He seemed to have rid himself finally of his cap.

"Thank you, John." She blew on the mug. "You've been so kind. Thank you—and your family—for taking care of Kate."

"Don't worry about that. You'd do the same, I'm sure." He lingered awkwardly in the doorway. "I . . . I could sit with you for a while if you want," he hesitated. "Or do you want to be alone?"

"No, I'd like some company. If you . . . if you don't mind. If you don't have anything else to do. I don't want to keep you." *A farmer's work is never done*, she knew, but she had no idea what chores were done in the evening.

John grinned. "You're not keeping me from anything. Nothing that can't wait, anyway." He hurried out of the room and returned with a cane-backed chair and set it beside her.

She took a sip of the cocoa. "What do you normally do in the evenings?"

"Sometimes I repair tack." He sat down carefully beside her. "Or sharpen blades. Grease the equipment. That sort of stuff. But that's mostly winter work." He looked at her sideways. "I—" He broke off and looked down at his hands.

"What?"

"I like to read." He gave her a furtive look and then a longer one.

A little part of her heart fluttered. This was certainly unexpected.

Seemingly encouraged, he went on. "I like to read on the porch swing at night in the summertime or at the kitchen table in winter after everyone's gone to bed. Dad don't like me readin', though. Says it's a waste of time." He gave a little shrug. "But I still do anyway."

She took another sip and studied him. She was more than intrigued. "What do you like to read?"

"Novels mostly. I'm reading *Great Expectations* right now."

"Is it good?"

"It is," he said enthusiastically. "I like all of Dickens's stuff. I'm at a real good part." He looked down at his thick, calloused hands, as if trying to think of something to say. "What about you? You like to read?"

Harriet hesitated. She *did* like to read, but nothing so lofty as Dickens. Her taste ran more along the lines of comedic periodicals. Also, she didn't have a lot of free time, but then again, neither did he, she supposed. "Well, sometimes. I . . . I like the stories in the *Saturday Evening Post*." Now it was her turn to shoot him a furtive glance. "Sometimes in the evening I read them out to Mom while she sews. We like the funny ones."

He smiled. "What else do you do? In the evenings?"

Harriet thought for a moment. "Well, after dinner, I have to feed the chickens. Then I help Mom with the gardening and the canning if there's any to be done."

"I meant for fun."

"Oh. Well, we play cards sometimes."

"You do? What do you play?"

"Rummy mostly. You?"

"Rummy or Euchre."

"My dad used to play Euchre. Before he died, obviously."

He studied his hands again. "How old were you? When he died?"

"Five."

"Five? That's young. Do you remember him?"

"A little." She gave him another sideways glance, wondering how much to share. "My mom talks about him, *to* him, I should say, if I'm being honest, all the time, so I feel like I know him, though I'm not really sure which are my memories and which are hers." She took a sip of cocoa. "That probably doesn't make any sense."

"Sure it does. It's kind of like that with my grandma. I only remember bits and pieces."

They were both silent then and turned their attention to Kate's chest, rising and falling.

"Harriet, I'm sorry about what happened at the Harvest Fest," he said finally, his voice barely above a whisper.

Harriet's heart began to beat a little bit faster, but she kept her eyes on Kate.

"I was late because one of the cows was calving, and it was breech. I couldn't leave. As soon as it was over, I washed up and drove to the Merc, hoping to still catch you, but Melody told me you had already left. So, I went over myself, and that's when I saw you with Elton."

Harriet blinked rapidly, trying to make sense of this. "But why didn't you tell me this?"

"Well, I wanted to. That day I saw you in the street. God knows I did, but I held back."

"Why?" she murmured.

"I didn't want to interfere if you really had feelings for Elton," he said, leaning his arms on his knees and folding his hands together. "I thought that would be the right thing to do." He kept his eyes on his hands. "Stand aside. If that's what you wanted. Didn't half hurt, though."

"Oh, John! Is this why you've stayed away from the Merc?"

John gave the briefest of nods. He gazed at her through those long eyelashes. She observed the smattering of freckles across his nose and cheeks and bit her lip.

"But I . . . I *don't* have feelings for him!" she blurted. "He . . . he turned out to be a bit of a snake."

"Yeah." John said quietly. "I kinda thought he might be." He sat up, straightening his shoulders. "Harriet." He took one of her hands, swallowing deeply. "I—"

The door opened then, revealing Mrs. Schneider. John immediately dropped Harriet's hand, but by the look on his mother's face, Harriet was pretty sure she had seen it.

"Harriet, it's getting late," she said slowly, looking from one to the other. "You're welcome to stay if you wish, or John can run you home. But he's got to be up to milk in the morning."

"Oh, I'm sorry!" She wasn't sure what she was more mortified by—the fact that she had been caught with her hand in John's or that she had overstayed her welcome. "I . . . I don't want to be a nuisance."

Mrs. Schneider came around the bed, felt Kate's forehead, and tsked. "John, go tell Janie to fetch some fresh cold water." She bent and wrung out the rag floating in a basin of water on the bedside table and placed it on Kate's forehead. John dutifully took the basin and left the room.

"Do you think she's going to be okay, Mrs. Schneider?"

"It's hard to say." The woman frowned, the wrinkles above her pursed lips deeply furrowed now. "But she's going to need nursing through the night," she said, her hands on her hips. "The girls and I can take turns."

"Is Mrs. Kerwyn coming back?"

"In the morning. Don't forget, she lost two in the last epidemic, and now Minnie's down with it, poor little thing."

Harriet stared at Kate's flushed face. "I'd like to stay, if I might." She glanced back up at Mrs. Schneider. "I want to take a turn."

"You sure?" She gave Harriet a tired smile.

Harriet returned it with an eager nod. John came in then, carrying the fresh basin of water.

"You go on, then, and telephone your mother. John'll show you. And have your soup. I'll sit with her till you come back up."

"Thanks, Mrs. Schneider." She gave Kate a last look and then followed John back down the stairs.

Everyone was gone from the kitchen, presumably off to bed. John went to the telephone on the wall and cranked the handle for the operator. "Rosemary Mueller, please," he said and then handed Harriet the receiver. He remained standing near her, however, so near that she could practically feel his breath. As it was, she could see the blond curls of his chest hair peeking up over his undershirt and, as on the drive over, felt the urge to reach out and touch them . . .

"Hello?" came her mother's voice, crackling over the line. "That you, Harriet?"

"Yes, Mom," she said, abruptly turning away from John's chest. "I'm going to stay here the night."

"I thought so. How's Kate?"

"Not too good, Mom." Harriet's voice caught.

"She'll be okay," Rosemary said gently. "Did you give her the tea?"

"Not yet. But I will."

"What about work?"

"I'll try to telephone Melody tomorrow. She'll understand if I'm a little late." Harriet hoped this was true. She had a bad habit of being late, and Melody seemed quite out of sorts these days. Well, it was a risk she would have to take. Besides, she was still a little irritated with Melody after the whole Cal-and-Frank misunderstanding.

"Well, good night, then."

"Good night, Mom. I love you." She handed the phone back to John and realized that this would be the first night she had ever spent away from home. She was suddenly filled with misgiving. Maybe she really should have John take her home . . .

"Here, sit down," John said, pulling out a chair for her. "Your soup's still a little bit warm."

Harriet looked at the soup and at John eagerly holding the chair. It was no use now. She had made her decision to stay, and so she would. She sat down heavily, and John slid into the chair beside her. She lifted a spoonful of the broth to her mouth but then paused when she realized he was watching her. "Want some?"

John smiled and shook his head. "I had some earlier."

The soup was surprisingly good and warmed her right through, not that she was necessarily cold. She ate quickly, ravenous. John watched her, his eyebrows raised. "Want more?"

"No," she said sheepishly.

"Didn't you eat dinner?"

"I did, but it was right when I came home, and it was just an egg sandwich."

"Yes, there's always eggs. 'Specially around here."

Harriet looked around the pretty kitchen, twice the size of theirs. "This is a nice farm. You're lucky."

"We *are* lucky. Not always, though. Almost lost it in '30. Couldn't pay the mortgage one month, and the bank had already given us an extension."

"What'd you do?" Harriet set her spoon in the empty bowl.

"My mom paid the mortgage that month with her egg money," he said in a low voice. "The few cents we get a week for them." He studied his thumb. "She saves that, you see. For a rainy day, she always said." He nodded toward a big Folger's can perched on a shelf above the sink. "Well, our rainy day came, and all those pennies saved the farm."

"Oh." Harriet was unexpectedly moved by this story. "I . . . I didn't know."

John simply looked at her, in that strong and steady way of his, each second ticking into the next, and then reached out his hand and wrapped her tiny one in his. "Harriet, if I don't say this now, I might never get another chance."

Harriet's first impulse, after being caught in the act not even thirty minutes ago by his mother, was to pull her hand away, but she found it hard. His touch had sent a thrill through her, especially now that his thumb was rubbing small circles on her palm. She felt a surge of something in her lower regions, and her breath caught in her throat. "Don't, John," she whispered.

"Is there someone else?" His voice was so low and gentle, she thought she might burst into tears.

An image of Cal floated briefly into her mind, but it floated out just as quickly. *Cal? Why on earth had she ever thought she cared for Cal?*

Granted, he was kind and handsome in his own way, but she had never felt her heart beat as hard as it did now.

She shook her head slightly and gave John a small smile.

"Then I'm free to speak." He let out a long breath. "Harriet, I'm in love with you." He said it almost mournfully, like a man in pain. "I have been forever, I think. Can't remember a time when I wasn't." He swallowed hard and addressed their grasped hands now. "I know this might seem sudden, but . . ." His gaze shifted to her eyes. "Harriet Mueller, will you marry me? Be my wife?"

Harriet inhaled sharply. Was John Schneider really *proposing*? Her mind scrambled. What could she possibly say to that? What did she *want* to say to that? She knew what Melody would tell her to say, but she also knew what Kate would say.

"I know I don't have much to offer," he added hurriedly. "But we'll get our own place eventually. Your ma can live with us if she wants. But I love you, Harriet. These last few months when I thought I'd lost you have been the worst of my life. I don't want to lose you again." His voice was hoarse, and as he gazed at her now, it was not as a nervous farm boy, but as a man, a serious stillness in his eyes.

Harriet's blood, on the other hand, was anything but still. She stared at him, his blue eyes full of . . . well, of love, and she felt the same rise up within her. She had always loved him, she suddenly realized with a rush of knowing, no matter how many others she (or Melody) had tried to replace him with. She didn't want to replace him, not even for a second. She knew that now. With her free hand, she finally allowed herself to rub the back of her finger along his bearded jaw and was surprised to feel him tremble beneath her touch. He covered her hand with his and, turning it, kissed her palm, causing her to melt entirely.

"Oh, John," she whispered, "of course I'll marry you."

Without waiting another second, he leaned forward and kissed her. Their lips moved awkwardly against each other's until they found a rhythm, and when they did, Harriet felt a jolt of electricity pulse through her whole body. It must have created a similar reaction inside of John because the kiss then intensified into one of deep passion before he eased it into something long and tender. Finally, John pulled away, his breath ragged, but his lips still hovering near. He gave her another quick kiss and then leaned his forehead against hers.

"I love you, Harriet," he said softly, and all poor Harriet could do, her heart beating wildly, was simply nod.

CHAPTER
TWENTY-FOUR

Melody, her heart beating wildly, stood at the door of the small white house on Pendarvis Street that belonged to Marcella Haufbrau.

Despite Pops's reassurance that his oldest employee would return to the Merc like some sort of loyal homing pigeon, she had, in fact, not, and Melody wasn't sure how much longer they could go on without a fourth person. With the sale of Douglas's ring, thirty-nine bottles of cider, one hat, one scarf, three of Kate's baskets, and two more of Imogene's soaps, she had managed to amass $249.00 above and beyond what the Merc normally took in, which she had stashed in a worn leather bank pouch from her father's desk. She was halfway there, but to make it, she knew, the Merc needed to have its biggest December ever.

To that end, Mrs. Mueller was brewing cider almost daily now, and Melody had even put a Christmas tree in the Merc's display window, carefully placing under it various shiny toys she had ordered from Barnum's. It was a risk, she knew, but one she hoped would pay off. In a moment of doubt, she had consulted Frank, who also thought it worth a shot, though it would be better, he opined, to have homemade toys, made by a local woodworker, say.

He had a point, Melody knew, but there was no time for that sort of thing, and, anyway, they would be too expensive. Instead, she had chosen the cheapest dolls and firetrucks and puzzles she could find in the supply catalog and hoped that between them and the cider, it would be enough to make up the missing half of the money needed to pay her father's debt. But to really achieve this, she had come to realize, she needed her original staff.

Imogene was doing well enough, despite her tendency to talk too long to the customers, but without Mrs. Haufbrau, she and Harriet were running ragged and consequently did not have time to give shoppers individual attention nor to encourage them to make purchases they were not already inclined to make. Likewise, they were forced to stay late each night to restock and tidy the shelves, though Harriet, to give her friend credit, had not once complained and seemed to have endless energy. In fact, she was the happiest Melody had ever seen her.

At first, Melody assumed it was because her friend Kate was improving from her illness, but somehow it seemed more than that . . . and more than just holiday cheer. If Melody didn't know better, Harriet's effusive bubbliness had almost the flavor of . . . well, of love . . . and she wondered, with not a little concern, if there really *was* something between her and Cal. But wouldn't Harriet have said so?

Maybe not, Melody mused, considering how she had chastised Harriet the last time the subject had come up. Melody still felt enormously guilty, as she had obviously hurt Harriet's feelings, which hadn't been Melody's intention at all. She had half expected Harriet to be moody and distant after their conversation, but instead, she had returned to the Merc the very next day, happier than Melody had ever seen her. It was a mystery. Had Harriet somehow met up with Cal and told him of her feelings? If she had, he must have reciprocated, Melody reasoned, otherwise, why would she be this . . . this *joyous*—for lack of a better word?

Regardless of Harriet's newfound zeal, however, and Imogene's at least adequate butchering, they couldn't go on as they were if they wanted to maximize their sales and their profit for the month. She was running out of time, and she couldn't wait another minute for Mrs. Haufbrau to see sense and come begging for her job back. It was obvious that the old crone had no such intention. No, Melody had realized with a sickening sort of dread, her fear had come true, and it was she who was going to have to beg.

Melody took another deep breath and rapped at the door. A little dog within immediately began yapping, which was quickly followed by the sound of Mrs. Haufbrau snapping at it to be quiet. Even the *muffled* sound of Mrs. Haufbrau's sharp voice made Melody's stomach clench, and for a brief moment, she considered fleeing. But before she could, the door was quickly opened to reveal Mrs. Haufbrau herself, tightly holding a tiny dog.

Mrs. Haufbrau's eyes narrowed. "What are you doing here?" She dropped the dog to the ground, where it immediately began yapping again, running in a little circle near her feet.

"Hello, Mrs. Haufbrau. May I . . . may I come in?"

Mrs. Haufbrau hesitated. "Why?"

Melody forced herself to smile, though she was sure it probably resembled more of a grimace. "I was hoping to . . . to talk to you. About the Merc."

Mrs. Haufbrau continued to study her through her beady, pinched eyes until she finally let out a sigh and opened the door wider. "Fine, but I'm busy. I just have a few minutes."

"It won't take long," Melody offered, hoping this was true. As she carefully wiped her feet on the mat, she could not help but at least take a couple of surreptitious glances around her archenemy's lair.

In stark contrast to the Kaufmanns' apartment, Mrs. Haufbrau's abode was one of exceeding neatness, even minimalism. In the front room was a plain sage-green sofa and two matching chairs, each adorned with lace doilies and arranged symmetrically around a fireplace. On the mantel stood a brown Bakelite clock, but no other ornaments were in sight, nor was there a speck of dust. Only a side bureau along the far wall held various photographs. Three of the frames held images of young men in uniforms from the Great War. Her sons? Melody groaned internally, hearing Cal's voice again accusing her of knowing nothing about her staff.

"Well?" Mrs. Haufbrau stood in front of her, her arms crossed tightly.

Melody hesitated. "Shall we sit down maybe?"

"Fine," Mrs. Haufbrau grumbled. "S'pose I should take your coat, then."

Melody slipped it off and handed it to the older woman before taking a seat at one end of the sofa, careful not to sit too far back, not wanting to ruffle the stiff doilies. No fire blazed in the fireplace, and the room was exceedingly cold—much like Marcella Haufbrau's heart, Melody couldn't help but think. She shivered and wished that she had kept her coat.

Mrs. Haufbrau reentered the room, the little dog, who had yet to stop barking, following at her heels.

"Twinkles!" Mrs. Haufbrau scolded, turning swiftly around to confront the dog.

Twinkles? Melody bit back a naughty smile.

Twinkles ignored her mistress, however, and continued to yap.

"I don't know what's wrong with her," Mrs. Haufbrau huffed, scooping her up. "She normally likes people." Mrs. Haufbrau carried the dog to the kitchen, tossed her in, and shut the door on her, which seemed to stop the barking at least for now.

Melody's eyes darted back to the photographs. She could see another one in the back, behind the three soldiers, that looked like a wedding photo. Perhaps Mrs. Haufbrau and her husband? He had died long ago; Melody at least knew that much.

When Mrs. Haufbrau returned, Melody hurriedly pulled her gaze from the photos, as if she had been caught breaching some sort of private sanctum. By the look on Mrs. Haufbrau's face, she seemed to be of the same opinion.

"Are those your sons?" Melody tried to say with a pleasant smile.

Mrs. Haufbrau gave a curt nod. "Were. They died in the war. All three."

"Oh, I'm sorry," Melody uttered. *How awful!* She tried to remember if she had ever heard this story before from Pops, but she couldn't recall. "I—"

"What is it you wanted, Melody?" Mrs. Haufbrau asked stiffly from where she had positioned herself behind one of the armchairs.

Melody felt awkward being the only one sitting. Perhaps she should stand, too? "Well," she began, deciding to remain seated. "I . . . well, I've come to ask how you are, first of all," she fibbed.

"You can see I'm fine."

"Yes, and . . . well, the truth is, I've come to ask you if you'd consider coming back to the Merc." She thought she saw a wave of something cross the woman's face, but she couldn't be sure. When Mrs. Haufbrau did not respond, she went on. "We really need you, Mrs. Haufbrau. The Merc isn't the same without you."

"Are you still selling alcohol?" she said stiffly.

"Well, yes. But . . . but you wouldn't have to sell it."

"I don't see how that's possible."

"You . . . you could work the back counter exclusively," Melody suggested. "You wouldn't have to ring up the cider at all."

"It's the root of all evil, you know." Her eyes bored into Melody's.

Melody desperately wanted to spew out a retort, but she bit the inside of her cheek instead. "Perhaps for some," she said, "but, well . . . look, Mrs. Haufbrau, we . . . *I* need your expertise. I can't do it alone."

Mrs. Haufbrau remained unmoved.

"I . . . I went to see my father," she faltered. "And he told me not to give up on you. He said that you're the best clerk the Merc has ever had and that you would be faithful to it."

Still, Mrs. Haufbrau's face remained immobile except for the slight lift of one eyebrow.

"He's very fond of you," she quickly added. Melody still did not understand why, but she couldn't dwell on that now. "He said you two had been through a lot together."

Mrs. Haufbrau's eyes darted to the photos. "Didn't stop him from putting a call into Bert at the League, though."

So, Mrs. Haufbrau *had* reported them! How dare she! Thank God for Pops. It explained why no one from the League had shown up to harass them. "Mrs. Haufbrau, please. I'm . . ." She hesitated. "I'm begging you. It's Christmas after all."

Mrs. Haufbrau let out a deep breath and studied the back of the armchair. "Alright," she said finally. "I'll do it. But not for you." She gave Melody a look of utter disgust. "You're an insufferable, spoiled brat. You always were, Melody Merriweather."

Melody recoiled as if from a blow, her cheeks beginning to burn.

"I'll do it for your father . . . and your grandfather, God rest his soul. And I'm not touching a drop of that stuff."

"Thank you, Mrs. Haufbrau," Melody said stiffly. "I appreciate it."

"It's no wonder you're floundering," the old woman went on, a little too pleased with herself for Melody's liking. She knew she had won; Melody could see it in her face. "What with the likes of Imogene Kaufmann at the meat counter. She's a dimwit if I ever saw one. Why you got her in is a mystery to me."

"It was my father's idea, actually," Melody answered. "And, anyway, she's just helping out until Cal comes back."

Mrs. Haufbrau let out a gurgle, which Melody was pretty sure was supposed to be a laugh.

"Cal Fraiser ain't coming back."

"What do you mean?" Melody frowned. "He . . . he said it was only temporary." She gripped her hands, it suddenly occurring to her that he hadn't *exactly* said that.

"Well, with him getting engaged last week, I assumed he'd be staying up there."

Melody felt she had been punched in the gut. "Engaged?" she croaked.

"That's what I heard, anyway," Mrs. Haufbrau said, another crooked smile erupting. "'Bout time, too. He's been courting Jessie Lange for years. Time to make an honest woman of her."

CHAPTER
TWENTY-FIVE

"Good heavens, is that the time?" Mums exclaimed, glancing at the old grandfather clock in the front room as she bustled in from an evening visit to the hospital. "Oh, Melody, I'm glad you're home," she said, carefully unpinning her hat. "Where's Bunny?"

Melody shrugged. "Upstairs, I think."

"Well, I have some good news. Bunny!" Mums called up the stairs.

"What is it?" Melody asked unenthusiastically. Ever since Mrs. Haufbrau had mentioned Cal and this Jessie Lange, whoever she was, Melody could not shake her malaise.

"Can't you guess?" Her mother seemed in a particularly good mood, but it was not enough to raise Melody's spirits. And she didn't have the energy to guess what was probably something trivial.

Her mother stared at her for a few expectant moments and then with a disappointed sigh announced, "Your father is coming home for Christmas."

"Christmas? But that's only a couple of weeks away! Are you sure he's strong enough?"

The last few times Melody had gone to visit Pops, he had seemed quite weak. In fact, he looked worse now than when he had been admitted, at least in her opinion. He could barely walk—only up and down the hospital hallway with the aid of a cane and a nurse on each side—and he grew tired easily. How were they to care for him at home this way?

"Of course he's strong enough. Honestly, Melody, why are you such a grump lately? The doctor obviously knows what he's doing."

Melody supposed this was true, but she was still concerned. She had tried asking Mums at various points during Pops's recuperation what his exact prognosis was, but Mums never seemed to know. In an attempt to take matters into her own hands, Melody herself had managed to corner various nurses and doctors, but they, too, were vague, saying that it was impossible to tell how many years her father had left, but that he would never be the man he had been before. He would need constant rest, the doctor had told her. "No exertion of any kind."

"Bunny!" Mums called upstairs again, and after waiting for a moment, she rolled her eyes in defeat and marched toward the kitchen. "Helenka!" she shouted merrily. "I have news!"

As predicted, Mums's announcement threw everyone in the house into a tizzy of excitement, even more than what normally existed at Christmas. Only Melody seemed worried. Everyone else went about their preparations for Christmas with excessive zeal. It was as if Pops and their finances had somehow been restored to perfect health, as if they lived in some sort of fairy tale, especially Bunny, whose idea of getting ready for Christmas was to endlessly bang out carols on the piano.

Frank and Julius, who had yet to even meet Pops, were likewise quite merry, and were proving to be surprisingly useful. For instance, it was Frank's idea to convert the study to a bedroom for Pops instead of taking up the front room. Mums had wholeheartedly agreed, and Frank and Julius had thus carried a bed frame down the stairs and lugged in one of the mattresses. And it was Julius who had offered to decorate the house with ropes of evergreen and sprigs of holly.

Mums's—and therefore by default, Helenka's—focus was, of course, the food. Mums was spending way too much on special treats and candies, despite Melody's attempts to dissuade her. "What's wrong with you, Melody?" Mums chided when Melody protested the purchase of a one-pound box of chocolates from the Sweet Chalet on Hill Street. "You're becoming a regular Ebenezer Scrooge! When are you going to get into the Christmas spirit?"

Melody rubbed her brow. "It's not that I don't have Christmas spirit, Mums," she fibbed, as in actuality she didn't, "but we don't have the money for fancy things this year."

"Tsk, tsk," Mums responded. "Of course, we do. And bring home a ham tonight, will you? Helenka wants to make your father's favorite for his first night home."

"I'll try," Melody sighed, "if they're not already all gone. You should have told me before now."

"Honestly, Melody, must you always be difficult? You have a whole counter of meat!"

Melody decided not to respond and, shrugging into her coat, hurried off to the Merc for another long day.

With only two weeks until Christmas to go, the Merc was busier than ever. Mrs. Haufbrau had returned, as she had said she would, but if she could be described as merely cordial before, now she was positively frosty. She had a few pleasantries for Harriet each day, but she out-and-out ignored Imogene, even when the poor woman directly addressed her.

As for Melody, she said nothing beyond what was absolutely necessary. After only two days of this, Melody was already beginning to have doubts.

Upon arriving at the Merc now, Melody gave the display window a quick glance and then went in. Harriet and Mrs. Haufbrau were already positioned behind the counters. Melody gave them each a brief hello before heading back to the meat counter to make sure Imogene had everything ready to start the day and to see if there were, indeed, any hams left.

"Oh, hello, Melody!" Imogene called brightly from behind the butcher's block, where she was carving out roasts. "Don't you look a picture? I have said to Mother on any number of occasions how pretty and smart you always appear. It's a marvel, really, and Mother agrees, though she did comment just last week that you were beginning to fill out nicely. Maybe a few pounds too many, but I said no, the extra weight suits you. Don't you think, Melody? I think so. And so does Mother. She's quite fond of you, you know."

Melody pressed her lips together, trying, as she always did now, to simply ignore whatever nervous prattle came out of Imogene's mouth. Despite Melody's constant reminders, Imogene still tended to ramble on too long with the customers. Several times, Melody had had to dash back and help her when the line at the meat counter got too long. Likewise, there had been a few occasions when Melody had had to man the meat counter entirely after Imogene had abandoned her post to run out and help her mother, who, growing ever more confused, had tried to come down the rickety outside stairs, asking for her dead husband and to announce that the Confederates were almost upon them. And just three days ago, the poor woman had fallen down the last few steps. Thankfully, she wasn't hurt beyond a twisted knee, but the doctor had to be called, and Melody had given Imogene the rest of the day off to tend to her. It was a terrible situation for poor Imogene, and one which Melody felt more than a little guilty about. After all, if Melody wasn't in such desperate need for her help, Imogene would still be upstairs, giving Mrs. Kaufmann the care she so obviously required.

Which forced Melody to think about Cal all over again. She had tried to harden her heart regarding his romantic affairs and to consider only how his . . . his marriage might affect the Merc. If it was true that he wasn't coming back, she would have to find a new butcher. She would have to ask Pops . . . But she didn't want to think about that at the moment. Instead, she observed the contents inside the counter.

"Imogene, do we have any hams in the back?"

"Hams? Why, no, we sold the last one yesterday." Her eyes widened with anxiety, as if she had just killed Melody instead of telling her they were out of something she requested. Imogene put one hand to her mouth. "Oh, dear. Did we? Yes, I'm pretty sure we did. Oh, Melody, I'm sorry! I can go in the back and look. Maybe I overlooked something. It won't take a minute, I—"

"No, Imogene, it doesn't matter. I'll think of something else." Melody waved her hand, trying to stave off further despair on the part of Imogene, never mind her own, or, rather, what would be Mums's. She would worry about it later. "You wash those knives there, and I'll start slicing cheese." She had already figured out that giving Imogene a task was the best way to distract her. "I expect that today will be busy, and I—" She paused, an odd smell hitting her nose. She set down the block of Schneider cheese she was holding. "Do you smell that?" A tendril of alarm rippled through her.

Imogene lifted her nose to the air. "No." She anxiously looked around for the source of the offending smell. "What is it?"

"It smells like something's burning." Melody eased herself from behind the counter.

"Probably Slater's, burning boxes."

"No, it doesn't smell like that."

Melody opened the back door and took a step outside, instantly wrapping her arms around herself against the cold, and looked up and down the alley. No one was burning boxes. She stepped back inside and sniffed the air again. Yes, there was definitely something burning!

"I think it's coming from somewhere in here . . ." She hurried back behind the meat counter and into the cooler, but there was nothing. It didn't smell electrical, but rather of burning wood. Melody ran to the office and threw open the door, but there was nothing. She ran to the front. Both Harriet and Mrs. Haufbrau were casually waiting on people, not alarmed in any way. Melody opened her mouth to ask if they smelled smoke, but quickly thought better of it, not wanting to alarm the customers if there was no need. She jogged back to the meat counter, where Imogene was now poking around behind various barrels and crates, as if looking for a lost button or a coin instead of a fire!

Melody ran back out into the alley, looking up and down the street again. Again, she saw nothing, but the burning smell was definitely stronger out here. She ran across the alley to their burn barrel, but it was empty and cold and even still held a light dusting of the snow they had gotten a few days ago. Frustrated, she turned back toward the Merc and then saw, with immediate alarm, a black wisp of smoke coming from the upstairs apartment!

"Imogene!" she called, "It's coming from upstairs!"

Without waiting to see if Imogene had heard, Melody pounded up the stairs, fear gripping her heart. She didn't bother to knock and instead threw open the door to the Kaufmanns' apartment. A cloud of smoke immediately engulfed her, filling her lungs. She bent over, coughing, until she caught her breath. Leaning an arm on the thin railing that ran along the tiny landing, she straightened. Imogene was behind her now.

"Mother!" Imogene shouted, dashing into the apartment before Melody could stop her. "Imogene, wait!" she called, but to no avail.

Panicking, Melody covered her nose and mouth with the crook of her elbow and followed. She could not see Imogene anywhere due to the thick smoke that was already stinging her eyes.

"Imogene!" she shouted, removing the crook of her arm from her mouth for a moment and then quickly replacing it. "Imogene!" she shouted again, but the woman did not respond. Melody tried peering through the smoke, and only then did she see what she assumed was the source of the fire. The kitchen cabinets and the wall behind the stove were burning! *Oh, God!*

Melody hesitated, not knowing what to do first. Her first instinct was to put out the fire, but maybe she should instead plunge into the billowing smoke to try to find the Kaufmanns? She decided to try to put out the flames. But how? She looked around her. To her left, in the front room, she spotted an afghan draped on a nearby chair, so she grabbed it.

Approaching the fire until she could no longer stand the heat, she threw the afghan in the direction of the flames, hoping to smother them. Much to her horror, however, the afghan's airy material fueled them all the more. Frantic, Melody looked around for something else, but it was hard to see in the smoke.

"Imogene!" she shouted between coughs, but there was still no response. "Help!" she shouted now, though her throat was raw and her voice hoarse. "Help!" She considered running back downstairs to alarm someone to call the fire department, but she couldn't just abandon Imogene and her mother, nor could she leave the fire unattended. What if it spread? The stacks of garbage everywhere made this whole place a perfect tinderbox!

Desperate, she looked around again and saw a thick blanket on the side of the sofa. She made her way through the garbage and yanked it off. Using it as a sort of shield, she inched back to the kitchen. When she could go no further, she threw the blanket, hoping this one would land appropriately and, unlike the afghan, at least diminish the fire a little bit. As luck would have it, it landed on the stove itself, which did serve to smother the flames there, though only momentarily before they erupted again. The wall behind the stove continued to blaze.

"Step back!" someone shouted, and Melody turned to see . . . Cal! Without even giving her the slightest glance, he threw a bucket of water on the flames. "Here, go in the bathroom and fill this!" he shouted, handing her the empty bucket while he threw another one.

Still coughing and holding her arm in front of herself, Melody picked her way to the bathroom as quickly as she could. She thrust the pail into the sink and turned on the tap. It seemed to take forever to fill! Finally, she lifted it and ran back to the kitchen, trying not to slosh any of its precious contents over the side.

Cal immediately tossed it onto the flames. She picked up the empty one and ran to fill it. When she returned not a few minutes later, Cal again grabbed it and tossed it onto the flames, which continued licking the wall behind the stove. It was certainly dying, but was not out yet. She ran to get more water.

"Here!" someone new shouted from the kitchen. It was Mr. Martin from next door, who also had a bucket of water.

She heard a siren wail below.

Cal ran into the living room and found another blanket, which he threw onto the rest of the flames, so that when the first fireman entered, the flames themselves were pretty much out, though the wall continued to smoke. The fireman proceeded to spray it with a wave of water from the thick hose he had dragged up the stairs.

"Precaution!" he shouted over the noise of the water hitting the singed back wall. Smoke still emanated from the burnt patch.

Imogene appeared then, leading her mother by the hand, and another fireman moved to assist, putting an arm protectively around her.

"No!" Mrs. Kaufmann cried, trying to pull away. "Get off, you Confederate beast! I ain't going."

"Mother!" Imogene shouted. "Mother, come on. You've got to get out now."

"Jack!" the fireman called out the window. "Help me! We got two victims."

"No!" Mrs. Kaufmann shouted again, but between Imogene and the two firemen, she was eventually half carried down the stairs, barefoot and kicking with surprising strength. Melody blindly followed, trying to make sense of what was happening. Her first thought was to telephone her father, but as much as she wanted him to rush in and fix the situation, there was nothing he could do from a hospital bed except worry, and besides, she was supposed to be the one in charge. *Yes, and look what had happened! The Merc had almost burnt down on her watch!*

Mrs. Kaufmann started screaming obscenities as the firemen attempted to help her into an ambulance. She was convinced that she was about to be ravaged by Confederate soldiers, which was an odd delusion considering that not one Confederate had ever stepped foot in the whole of Wisconsin, except as prisoners . . .

Imogene was crying profusely now. "I'm sorry, Melody," she kept wailing.

"Don't worry," Melody said, though she wasn't sure if Imogene actually heard her due to her mother's continued shouting. Melody took Imogene's hands. "It'll be okay, Imogene. Don't worry."

Eventually, the firemen were able to secure Mrs. Kaufmann in the ambulance, and then one of them guided Imogene inside as well. Imogene dutifully took a seat on a side bench beside her mother, who had finally been successfully strapped to the stretcher.

"I'm sorry, Melody!" Imogene cried again through the still-open doors. "I'll be back as soon as I can." Tear tracks ran down her sooty face.

"Don't be silly, Imogene. I can manage. You take care of your mother. And yourself."

An ambulance man brushed past her then and shut the door. "We've got to go, Miss," he called apologetically and hopped into the front seat. Even with the door closed, Melody could hear Mrs. Kaufmann's screams, which were soon surpassed by the wail of the ambulance siren. Watching it go, Melody began to shiver. *What had just happened?* Numb, she stood staring at the empty street, the ambulance having already disappeared around the corner. Her shivering increased. *What had just happened?*

She could feel tears welling up, but she fought to push them down. She jumped when she felt an arm go around her shoulder. She was stunned to see that her comforter was none other than Mrs. Haufbrau.

"Come on. Come inside now," she said with gentle authority.

The woman's normally pinched face was one of compassion. A small crowd had gathered, and a few women came forward, one of them draping a coat around Melody's shoulders. "Oh, you poor thing," several of them chirped. "She needs hot tea with honey, Marcella. Maybe a little rum."

"We've got her now," Mrs. Haufbrau said, looking to where Harriet stood holding the door. "She'll be okay." Her arm went fully around Melody, then, holding her up, as she steered her back toward the Merc. "Thanks, everyone, but we've got her now."

Mrs. Haufbrau skillfully led Melody to the back office. "Harriet, put on the kettle," Mrs. Haufbrau shouted to the girl hovering behind them. "And bring me a bottle of cider."

Harriet promptly returned, bottle in hand. "Here you are, Mrs. Haufbrau. The water will be ready in a minute."

Mrs. Haufbrau pulled out the cork, poured a glassful, and handed it to Melody. Melody drank it eagerly, and Mrs. Haufbrau immediately poured another.

"I thought—" Harriet began.

"Never mind what I thought," Mrs. Haufbrau snapped. "This is an emergency."

Melody took the glass and stared at it, feeling something begin to unravel inside of her. Mrs. Haufbrau's sudden kindness was too much. Feebly she set the glass on the edge of the desk and began to sob. Deep, gut-wrenching sobs. She covered her face with her hands and curled forward, her head in her lap.

"There, there," Mrs. Haufbrau said, stiffly patting her back. Melody sobbed all the harder.

"This is all my fault!" she cried through her hands. "I should never have asked Imogene to help out. Now look what's happened! The Merc has nearly burnt down. And on my watch! What will Pops say?" She cried for nearly a minute and then sat up wearily. "And I'm not even sure he's ever going to be strong enough to come back to the Merc!" she moaned, addressing just Harriet. "And I can't keep doing it for him! The Merc needs someone better than me." She wiped her eyes with the back of her hands. Her sobs had abated for the moment, and she turned to Mrs. Haufbrau. "You do it. You be in charge. It should have been you from the beginning, Mrs. Haufbrau."

"Nonsense." The older woman thrust a handkerchief at her. "You're doing fine just as you are." She cleared her throat. "And I know what it feels like to make a mistake and . . . and nearly lose something . . . or someone. You'll get over it." She handed her the glass back. "You drink this now. It'll help."

Melody stared blankly at her. "Thanks, Mrs. Haufbrau." Her voice was ragged, either from her tears or the smoke, or both.

"Call me Marcella." She patted Melody's shoulder.

Melody downed the cider and suddenly became aware as she did so that the shop bell was ringing furiously. She peered around the corner of the office and saw that the front of the Merc was full of people now. People who either did not want the show to be over, or who wanted to offer genuine support, or who had simply come in because they actually needed something.

"Harriet, you go tend the counter. I'll be out in a minute," Mrs. Haufbrau commanded.

"Yes, Mrs. Haufbrau!" the girl answered and hurried out of the office.

"You've had a shock," Mrs. Haufbrau said to Melody now. "You sit here for a bit and collect yourself."

Melody wiped her face with the sleeve of her blouse, which was soot-stained and wet in places from the water. She stood up wearily. "No, I should go up and get Imogene some things. Take them to the hospital."

"I'll go get them."

"No . . . I . . . thank you, Mrs. . . . . Marcella," she pleaded, "but I . . . I need to see it for myself. Please."

Mrs. Haufbrau studied Melody's face and then nodded, seeming to understand her request to face the scene. "You take your time, then. Harriet and I can handle the shop. But then you're going to go home for the day. Agreed?"

Melody considered arguing, but she didn't have the strength. She nodded.

"Go on, then."

Wearily, Melody climbed the stairs. At the top, she hesitated for a few moments, suddenly remembering what one of the thugs had threatened Pops with—*You might find something terrible might happen. Something like a fire . . .*

Surely not, she reasoned, trying to control her renewed panic as she gingerly stepped through the open doorway into the charred mess. She looked around, bewildered, working to take in the extent of the damage. Were the thugs really responsible for this? But it wasn't fair; it was not yet the due date!

Cal suddenly appeared, then, from down the hallway, thoroughly startling her. She let out a little scream. In the confusion with Imogene and Mrs. Kaufmann and the ambulance, she had forgotten about him.

"It's just me," he said, tossing the towels he was carrying onto the counter.

Melody was embarrassed that she had screamed. "I guess I didn't realize you were still here." Her throat was still raw, and her voice hoarse.

"Yeah, I didn't want to leave it like this. Water everywhere." He replaced a sopping towel with a dry one from the counter.

"You don't have to do that," she said blankly, not sure what else to say.

"I know." He didn't look at her and instead continued to wipe up the water. "But I don't want it to leak down into the Merc's ceiling."

Melody groaned. She hadn't even thought of that. She knew she should try to help him, but she couldn't seem to get her legs to move. She shook her head, as if trying to wake herself up. "Why'd you come back?"

"I told you I was coming back." He glanced over his shoulder. "I wanted to surprise you." He threw the towel onto the stove. "Guess I picked the wrong day."

"I'll say you picked the *right* day. How did you know to come up here?"

"I saw the smoke from the street." He looked fully at her now, his dark eyes full of what looked to be pity. It was suddenly too much, and she burst into tears again. "Oh, Cal!" she sobbed.

"Hey!" Cal darted forward and put his arm around her. "Hey, it's alright. It's not all that much damage. It looks worse than it is. Don't worry. I'm here now. Hey, I'm here now," he repeated gently. "Believe me; it's going to be alright."

Melody allowed herself to lean her head on his shoulder for a few moments, relishing in the comfort his strong arm afforded, but in truth she found it hard to believe everything was *really* going to be okay. Not only was the building now damaged by fire and water, possibly at the hands of the thugs, but the Merc was still losing money, her father was very probably permanently incapacitated, his debt was coming due, and Cal, she realized with a sinking heart, would soon be leaving them. To get married.

She pulled away and wiped her tears with the back of her hand. She had somehow lost Mrs. Haufbrau's handkerchief. "We should get going," she rasped. "There's a lot to do."

CHAPTER TWENTY-SIX

"And you wouldn't believe it," Harriet exclaimed to a prostrate Kate, propped up on a mound of pillows. "The fire department had to come and everything! You should see that kitchen. Burnt to soot, really. The chief came out the next day and said it was due to a pan left burning on the stove. Terrible! Poor Imogene. I feel awful for her."

Kate did not appear to be overly interested in this story, as she said nothing, just listlessly petted the black cat nestled beside her, but Harriet was determined to tell the whole of it, so excited was she to have her friend back. After a few days of touch and go, Kate had finally been deemed well enough to be transferred back home to the Kerwyns, though she was still quite weak. Harriet had dutifully come to see her every day, but today was the first that Kate was really awake and cognizant.

"Turns out Mrs. Kaufmann was fine," Harriet continued, still hoping to elicit some interest, "besides a bit of smoke in the lungs, but they can't go back to the apartment, so they're staying with the Merriweathers! Can you believe it? And just when Mr. Merriweather arrived back home. Melody keeps saying the fire is all her fault, but I don't see how it could be. It was obviously Mrs. Kaufmann who left the pan on the stove."

"Maybe she feels guilty that she hired Imogene in the first place," Kate croaked, her voice rough from underuse, "instead of a real replacement for Cal."

Harriet considered. "Well, maybe . . ." she said reluctantly. Leave it to Kate to come up with this. She was always one step ahead in the brains department. "I guess I never thought of it that way."

Unsettled, Harriet looked around the room again. Granted, it was just a tiny attic room with a dormered ceiling, but the walls had been papered with a print of pink rosebuds. It was cozy, if nothing else. Perhaps that's why Kate didn't mind the smallness of her badger hole, which she was insisting on returning to as soon as she was well enough.

"Why don't you want to stay here? Now that . . . now that Ray's moved out," Harriet said tentatively, drawing her eyes back to her friend.

Kate shook her head wearily. "You wouldn't understand."

"I think I *do* understand. Not everyone is the enemy, you know," Harriet murmured. "You can trust some people some of the time."

"I know," Kate uttered unevenly. "I'd just rather be on my own is all."

Harriet took her friend's hand in hers. "Well, I'm just glad you're getting better." She squeezed it. "What did you want to tell me, anyway? I've been waiting all this time to ask you."

Kate looked at her, her brow furrowed.

"The night you were brought to the Schneiders? Remember? Apparently, you asked for me, said you had something to tell me. That was why John telephoned me. So. What was it?"

Kate blinked, as if trying to recall. "I don't remember."

"Yes, you do! What was it?"

Kate shook her head. "I honestly don't." Her lips twisted into a wry smile. "Maybe it was just my way of trying to get the two of you together."

A happy blush covered Harriet's cheeks. She wasn't sure it was the right moment to share the news of her other big event, but after thinking it over for all of two seconds, she decided it was and held up her left hand. "I guess it worked." She let out a little laugh.

Kate's eyes grew large at the sight of the tiny ring on Harriet's fourth finger. "You're engaged?" The cat opened its eyes as well and stretched itself out.

Harriet nodded rapidly, her dimples showing.

"To who? Please don't say it's Wesley Elton."

Harriet's blush deepened. "Of course, it's not Wesley! It's John Schneider."

"Well, thank God for small mercies. But are you sure? I mean, I'm all for John Schneider, but the last time we spoke about it, you were determined to throw him over because he was a farmer."

Harriet lowered her hand. "Yes. I'm *very* sure," she said with a shy smile. "I don't know what I was thinking. I guess . . . I guess I just got turned around by Melody lately."

"I tried to tell you that."

"I know. I should have listened. But I got there in the end. Or, I should say, we did." She laughed again. A deep, happy laugh.

"That's a nice ring."

Harriet held out her hand again. The ring John had given her the day after he proposed was gold with the tiniest pearl in the middle. She had put it on to come over to see Kate, but she dared not yet wear it to work, lest Melody see it. "*I* think so! It's small, but, well . . . it's beautiful. Don't you think?"

Kate smiled weakly. "Very beautiful." She took Harriet's hand and squeezed it. "Do his parents know?"

"Course they do! They're ever so nice, as I guess you know from staying there, though I suppose you don't remember all that much. We announced the engagement to them on the third . . . or maybe it was the fourth? . . . night you were there."

"Glad I was useful even on my deathbed."

"You weren't on your deathbed," Harriet said, pulling her hands away and folding them tightly in her lap. "Not really. And, anyway," she said, smiling now, "they were overjoyed. It was after supper, and we were sitting in their front room."

"I thought you were there to visit *me*. Why were you downstairs with them?"

"Well, I couldn't spend hours up by your bedside, could I?"

"Well, that's generally what it means to attend at a sickbed."

"We all took turns," Harriet said defensively. "And besides, you were out of the woods by then."

Kate smiled. "I'm just teasing. Go on. Enthrall me with what came next."

"Well," Harriet shifted, settling in to tell the happy tale, "as I was saying, we were all sitting in the front room, and John looks across at me and gives me a little wink and then he stands up and says, 'I've got something I want to say.' His mom looked up from the socks she was darning, and his dad looked up from his paper, and then John says, 'I've asked Harriet to be my wife.' Then he held out his hand to me, and I took it and, oh, God, Kate, I was so nervous. 'And she's honored me with a yes,' he says. Then he gave me a quick kiss on the cheek, and I couldn't help but laugh a little. They were staring at us with a look a shock that would have stopped your heart. I was starting to feel squeamish when Mr. Schneider got to his feet and took both of my hands in his and says, 'Well, welcome to the family, Harriet!' Then he turns to John and says, 'Well done, son. Well done.' And then his mom stands up—and, oh, Kate, I was still so nervous—but she gave me a big hug, too, and then she says she hopes I'll be happy joining their family."

Harriet was beaming now. "Honestly, Kate, I thought I was going to cry right then and there. John was all smiles, and he kissed me on the cheek again, and then everything just seemed to erupt. His little brothers and sisters were all running around whooping and shouting and saying, 'John's gettin' married, John's gettin' married!' I . . ." she broke off. "It's so different than what I'm used to, just me and Mom. Our place is so quiet, and theirs is like a circus. I like it, though."

Kate stared at her for a few moments and then gave her a smile—a real one, though she seemed a little pensive. "I'm happy for you, Harriet," she said, her voice gravelly. "Truly."

"Thanks, Kate." Harriet let out a deep breath. There seemed nothing more to say.

"How did your mom react?"

"She's happy for me, too. A little sad, though, I think. John said that when we get our own place—he's got an eye on a little farm, though his dad said he'd sell him a parcel of his—that Mom should live with us, but she says she won't. Wants to stay in her own little place."

"Well, I can understand that."

"But I don't know if I can leave her, Kate."

"Sure you can. You'll soon have babies running around, and you'll forget everything else."

"Well, I don't know about babies." She gave a shy smile. "But either way, I'm not going to forget everything and everyone else. Certainly not Mom. And not you."

Kate looked at her tiredly. "What did Melody say?"

"I haven't told her yet," Harriet murmured. In truth, she was afraid to. She wasn't sure what she would say, nor did she want anything to change. Not yet.

"Why?"

"Well, I was going to, but then there was the fire and everything. I'll tell her soon."

"You should stop caring what Melody Merriweather thinks." Kate began petting the cat again.

"Well, it's not exactly that . . ."

Kate cocked an eyebrow.

"It's just that she's had so much trouble with the staff lately, though now that Cal's back, maybe everything will go back to normal. I'm going to miss it, though."

"What do you mean you're going to miss it? Are you quitting?"

"Not right away, of course." Harriet fidgeted. "But once we're married, there will be so much to do!" In truth, Harriet relished the idea of being a farmer's wife and hoped the garden she would plant would be every bit as good as her mother's.

Kate looked as if she were about to say something, but she instead turned her attention to the cat.

No doubt she didn't approve, Harriet guessed, just as she suspected Melody would not, but she didn't care anymore. She loved John, and she wanted to be his wife. Wanted to keep house for him, help him with his work, give herself to him completely, start a family with him. It filled her with so much joy, she could barely contain it. She wished everyone could feel what she was feeling right now, especially her friend, who seemed so alone in the world despite the loving family who had taken her in.

"You sure you want to go back to the badger hole?" she asked wistfully.

"Yeah, I think so. I really want to keep working on my baskets. Laying here day after day, I have some more ideas."

"Don't *you* ever think about getting married?"

"Me?" Kate chortled. "No."

"What about Edmund?"

"Edmund?" Her pale cheeks suddenly flushed.

"I think he really cares for you."

"Well, it doesn't matter if he does. We're practically siblings."

"Except you're not. Not even remotely."

"We grew up together," Kate retorted, as if that explained everything.

"Which still doesn't make you siblings."

"Look, it doesn't matter. He's just friendly. Besides, he says he's going to join the army soon."

Harriet's eyes widened. This was news to her. "The army? Why?"

Kate gave a little shrug. "I don't know. His dad was killed in the war, and he thinks he has something to prove, I suppose."

There was silence, then, and Harriet looked around the room again, wondering what to say next. It was Kate, however, who broke it.

"What do you think about that Julius guy that came 'round a few weeks ago saying I'm not Indian but Hungarian or Slavic or whatever?"

Harriet tried to recall, but all she could remember was his story about the Chinese Cinderella. "Does it matter?"

"It does to me. Things like this don't bother you because you know where you came from. Who your family is. But I don't." She broke her gaze with Harriet and looked instead at the tiny circular window near the eaves, blinking rapidly, as if to fend off tears. "But I'll tell you one thing," she said, her voice hard now, "as soon as I'm better, I mean to find out."

"How are you going to do that?"

"I don't know yet, but I'll figure it out."

Harriet wasn't sure what to say. "I've no doubt you will." She stood up. "Well, I should go. Are you sure you don't want to go to Melody's Christmas party? You might be well enough by then. John could come by and get you."

Kate shook her head. "No, I don't think so. Even if I *was* strong enough, I wouldn't want to."

"You're a strange one, Indian Kate, who's probably not an Indian."

"Why do you say that?"

"Because Indians live in a tribe. In a community. And you're a loner."

"I'm not a loner. I've got you. And Edmund, so you say. And Fanny, here," she said, rubbing the cat's head as it purred.

"Two people and a cat hardly make a tribe."

"That depends on your definition of tribe."

Harriet leaned against the door frame. "Do you think you'll be this difficult forever?"

Kate did not look at her but only at the cat. "Probably. I certainly hope so, anyway."

CHAPTER
TWENTY-SEVEN

Melody sat alone in her father's office, counting the pile of money in front of her. She had already done so twice, and she hoped that this third time, it would come out differently. Sadly, it did not. $362.00. That's all she had managed to accumulate beyond what the Merc normally produced, and the first of the year was just over a week away. And she didn't even want to think about what fixing the fire damage to the upstairs apartment was going to cost. She had asked Ralph Borman, the local handyman, to look it over, but he hadn't given her a price yet.

With heavy resignation, she stuffed the money back into the old leather pouch and tucked it into the top drawer of her father's desk. She should be happy, she supposed, that she had even made this much. In the week since the fire had happened, there had been an intense outpouring of sympathy from the townspeople, who had come into the Merc in droves, the result of which was that nearly all of their stock— well, maybe not *all* of their stock, but certainly all of the toys, cider, and even a decent amount of the "luxury" items—had gone. Likewise, a fair number of Kate's baskets and Imogene's soaps and candles had been purchased as well. They had made an extra one hundred and thirteen dollars in just one week's time, but sadly it wasn't enough. Perhaps if she had had more time.

But she didn't, and she worried what would happen now. Would the thugs really resort to violence, as they had threatened? The fire chief had been insistent that the upstairs fire had been caused by a pan on the stove, but she still worried. Her father couldn't possibly deal with these brutes; he was too weak. But could she? She hesitated to involve Cal after everything that had happened. Maybe Frank? But despite Frank's sturdy build, he did not seem to be overly masculine, and she was pretty sure if asked, he would spout some sort of philosophy about nonviolence. Maybe Fred when he arrived home for the holidays? . . .

The shop bell rang then, which broke her out of her reverie. It was past closing time, and she was alone. Had Mrs. Haufbrau forgotten to switch the sign on her way out?

Melody stood up uneasily. "Hello?" she called, her heart beating a little faster. She nervously peered around the corner and saw, of all people, Wesley, a smug smile on his face and his hands in his pockets.

"Hello," he drawled. "Saw the light on. Figured you were still here."

"What do *you* want, Wesley?" In truth, she felt a little nervous to be here with him alone after he had tried to force himself on her, but she was determined not to let him know it. She slipped behind the counter and crossed her arms tightly.

"That's not a very nice way to greet Santa Claus."

Melody's eyes narrowed. "What's that supposed to mean?"

Wesley pulled a fat envelope out of his jacket's inner breast pocket and tossed it onto the counter with a thump. "Just what I said. I'm here to deliver a Christmas miracle."

"Whatever you're playing at, it isn't funny. I'm busy."

"Too busy to open a Christmas present?" he asked wryly. The two stared at each other for several moments, and when she failed to respond, he let out a sigh. "It's an actual gift from the other shops," he said. "Turns out most of them have a heart. It was Mr. Van Dyke who got the ball rolling, apparently, and they all chipped in."

Melody's brow creased. *A gift from the other shops?* She suspected a prank. But when she tentatively reached for the envelope and peeked inside, it was filled with cash! "Oh!" she cried, tossing it. "I can't take this!"

"Why not?"

"I can't accept charity."

"There you go again. All high and mighty. It's a *gift*, Melody. You'd do the same if it had happened to any of the others, wouldn't you? And anyway, Christmas is the time for c-h-a-r-i-t-y. They both have almost all the same letters."

Melody ignored his dumb attempt at a joke and considered. While it was true that she would have donated to a fund had another of the shops suffered a fire, it still didn't sit well. "No, I can't take it."

"Well, suit yourself. You can take it and pay off your dad's secret side loans, or you can let it lie there. I can't take it back. I have no idea who gave what, and I'm not about to ask, nor do I have time."

Melody let her arms slip. "How do you know about my father's side loans?"

"Oh, me and Mr. Carson know a great many things. You'd be surprised." He looked around the Merc again in a self-satisfied way. "As the president of the bank, *he* was supposed to deliver this to you." He nodded at the envelope. "But I begged to be the one. Wanted to show you something else, you see. And to thank you."

"Thank me?"

"Turns out you did me a favor. It was after you rejected my proposal that I realized you were right. I don't love you. Even a little. And it showed me how much I'm actually in love with Marjorie Hodges. In fact—" he grinned again—"I'll let you in on a little secret." He rifled through his front jacket pocket and unearthed a small box. A box that looked surprisingly like . . .

"Whatdya think of this, then?" He yanked open the lid unceremoniously.

Melody's stomach lurched. It was Douglas's ring!

"Pretty, ain't it?" he asked, looking at her in such a way that made Melody suspect he somehow knew. "Got it at Van Dyke's, if you can believe it. They usually don't carry something this nice. Old Van Dyke said someone down on their luck sold it to him. I paid three hundred for it, but I had it appraised in Milwaukee. Seems it's actually worth five. So, I got a bargain. Feel sorry for the poor sap who sold it for . . . I think for two hundred is what Van Dyke said? Course he shouldn't have told me what he paid for it, but, well, I have a way of getting things out of people." He looked pointedly at her, a smile curling. "Well, aren't you going to say anything? Don't you like it?"

Melody stared at him, fury and regret and loathing welling up within her. In fact, she ached to hit him over the head with something. She glanced at the Wrigley gum display as a possible option, but quickly dismissed it. It would make too much of a mess, and she didn't have time to clean it up.

"Yes, it's lovely," Melody managed to force out. "Marjorie is a lucky girl." Though Melody had never particularly liked Marjorie, she did now feel sorry for her, and hoped that she would appreciate the ring, as it was a poor exchange for a life tied to one such as Wesley Elton. "I wish you every happiness, Wesley." She smiled falsely.

"Well, we all have to fall sometime, don't we? Myself, I'm ready for the ole ball and chain. Sad that you don't have anyone, though, isn't it?" He twirled his hat. "Still, lots of spinsters lead full, happy lives. Just look at Imogene. There's a great example for you." He raised both eyebrows mockingly. "Well, a Merry Christmas," he said, nodding at the envelope. "Be seeing you."

Melody was tempted to follow him out of the shop and pommel him with a *Saturday Evening Post*, but of course she did not. She waited for him to saunter down the street before looking back at the envelope lying forlornly on the counter. She stared at it for several moments before finally picking it up again. Pulling out the stack of cash, she began to count. Fifty, one hundred, two hundred, three hundred, four hundred, five hundred . . . In all, it was $535! *$535?* A small fortune! Her father would easily be able to pay off the thugs now on New Year's Day. It would be her Christmas gift to him!

Melody counted it again and this time noticed a folded piece of paper still inside the envelope. She eagerly read the message written in fine, neat handwriting:

Dear Melody and family,

Please accept this small Christmas gift from all your local friends on High Street. We've all been through tough times, and Louis Merriweather has always stood by us, so now it is our chance to stand by him—and you. Wishing you all a very merry Christmas and a prosperous New Year.

Very best,
Alan Van Dyke

Below this brief note were the signatures of at least twenty other shop owners, and below that was a postscript.

I wanted you to know that I sold your ring for more than you paid me, as I told you I would, but I have enclosed all of it back to you. Your father once did me a very great service, and I have long since waited for a chance to repay him. I am overjoyed that that moment has arrived.

Merry Christmas,
AVD

Melody put down the note, tears in her eyes. The people of Merriweather had thoroughly come through for her . . . well, not really for *her* specifically, she knew, but for the Mercantile, and more so, for her father. She glanced blearily around the shop, trying to take in what he and his father before him had built, and for once she wanted her mother's words to be true—that she was just like her father.

CHAPTER
TWENTY-EIGHT

Christmas Eve was finally upon them, and Melody, according to her father's custom, had shut the Merc promptly at three and sent her little staff home, but not before reminding them for the umpteenth time about the Christmas party that night at The Willows. Normally Christmas Eve for the Merriweathers was reserved for Mass and carols, followed by an exquisite buffet prepared by Helenka, and then what was inevitably a laughter-filled round of charades or twenty-one questions before gifts were finally handed out.

This year, however, Melody had persuaded Mums to have a party for the staff instead, insisting that it was the least they could do after they had worked so hard these past few months while Pops was recuperating. Mums was hesitant to break with tradition, especially given the fact that Pops had just gotten home from the hospital, but, in the end, she capitulated, noting that with the lodgers and now the Kaufmanns living with them, it wouldn't be the same, anyway.

Mums had been predictably opposed to the prospect of Esmerelda and Imogene Kaufmann living under her roof, even temporarily, but Pops had insisted. "It's the least we can do, Leola," Pops had pleaded breathlessly from where he was propped up with pillows and blankets in one of the overstuffed armchairs in the front room, as if he were in danger of frostbite, not a damaged heart.

He had arrived two days ago, amidst a flurry of activity, and even though he was weak and pale, he was not too weak to spread his own brand of goodwill and cheer. Indeed, a spirit of excitement now rippled through the house. Even Bunny seemed in a better mood and actually left her piano long enough to help the nurse who came in each day to check on him. It was as if everything had been made right again, except for the fact that they were all squeezed in like sardines. Melody could not remember a time when the house was this full, except maybe when her cousins on Mums's side had come down from Green Bay for Thanksgiving one year.

To add to the crowded conditions, Freddy was due home this evening, and Frank was insisting that he give the son of the house his room back and gallantly offered to bunk with Julius, who did not seem to mind this idea at all and, in fact, seemed rather pleased by it. Thus, a cot had been dragged down from the attic and set up next to Julius's. The Kaufmanns, in turn, were given Bunny's room after a fierce private debate between the sisters as to who should give up their room. Mums ultimately made the decision.

"Well, where am I to sleep?" Bunny whined.

"You can sleep with me, since your father is sleeping in the study."

"Why can't Melody sleep with you? Why me?"

"Because Melody is a terribly restless sleeper. She'll kick and fidget all night. No, Elizabeth!" Mums raised her hand to stop any more protests. "I've decided and that's that."

Melody was tempted to stick out her tongue at Bunny behind Mums's back, as she might have done even a few months ago, but she was not that person anymore. Her concerns were far greater than looking for opportunities to lord it over Bunny. And anyway, it made sense for Bunny to sleep with Mums. They were two peas in a pod.

As it was, Melody was extremely grateful for the private space she was allowed to keep, as it was proving to be a much-needed retreat from the likes of Imogene, who had developed a tendency to follow her everywhere. And if Imogene had been a nonstop talker before, now she was positively maniacal, obsessively apologizing for the fire almost every other hour. At first, everyone went out of their way to reassure the poor woman that the fire had not been her fault, but after two days of their remonstrances falling on deaf ears, they now tended to ignore her. Even Helenka had become irritated with Imogene, who was constantly offering to help in the kitchen or to tidy the house, which Helenka did not seem to appreciate, probably because Imogene's help came with a steady torrent of words. Or perhaps it was out of loyalty to Mums, who was still put out by Pops's insistence that they take them in in the first place.

Mums, for her part, was not unkind to her guests, but she was not overly nice, either, and dealt with the extra burden by simply pretending that they weren't there. She was willing to put up with them while repairs were being done on the apartment, but not a day more. Little did she know, though, that Ralph Borman was predicting it would be well into the new year before the apartment was deemed habitable. Apparently, there were several repairs besides those from the fire damage that had long been needing to be done that Imogene had failed to bring to Pops's attention.

Which raised an uncomfortable point, not just in Melody's mind, but in Pops's too. Given Mrs. Kaufmann's increasing confusion and growing immobility, not to mention the hoarding tendencies of both mother and daughter, the question surfaced as to whether or not the upstairs apartment was really the best place for them. It was clear that Mrs. Kaufmann could not be left alone for more than a few minutes, which meant that poor Imogene would have to return to a life of sitting by Mrs. Kaufmann's side every minute of every day, which was a horrible existence for anyone. It also meant that Imogene would not be able to earn money, which was a problem, as the pair had not a cent left to their name. They had apparently exhausted the small savings Imogene had managed to amass during her working years, and now they had nothing. They had not, Pops confessed, paid any rent at all for the last six months, which further explained why the Merc was so behind. But where would they go?

It was Frank, as it happened, who came up with an idea, suggesting that they take up residence in the old Murphy cottage, which he and Julius were in the process of purchasing with the intention of converting it into a working model of what a miner's cottage might have been like. And it would be the headquarters of the artist community they hoped to found. His idea was that Imogene and her mother would be allowed to stay in the house for free, provided they did not hoard anything. In addition, they would be given a small stipend in exchange for dressing in period costume (which wouldn't be difficult for Esmerelda, as she was practically dressed that way anyway) and being tour guides. Meanwhile, he and Julius would rent the apartment above the Merc until they could purchase their next building.

"Are you sure this is what you want to do?" Pops had asked when he and Melody and Frank were alone in Pops's study. Like Melody, Pops seemed to immediately trust Frank and liked him very much. "It's very generous."

"Yes, I'm sure," Frank answered as he leaned against Pops's desk, which had been pushed against the far wall to make room for a bed. "Imogene, when trained, will make a very good guide, I think, and Esmerelda, sitting by a butter churn or some such implement, will only add to the interpretation." He removed the pipe he was smoking and gave a little shrug. "It might not work forever, but it's worth a try."

"It's very kind of you, Frank," Melody put in, "but why are you helping us so much? How can we repay you?" Indeed, as he had once suggested, Frank seemed like a fairy godfather in so many ways.

Frank let out one of his booming laughs. "Repay me? You've done so several times over. Opening your house to us." He took a deep puff of his pipe.

"But it's not as if you're guests; you're paying lodgers."

"Yes, but we were never treated as lodgers. You welcomed us into your family, allowed us to dine with you, took the time to show us the town. Julius and I should be thanking *you*." He looked from Melody to Pops. "And let's not forget that it's not all charity. We hope to eventually make money from this venture."

Pops shifted—as much as he *could* shift considering the many pillows that walled him in. "I still don't understand how this miners' cottage and a colony of artists is going to make you money, though."

Frank chuckled. "I suppose it is a bit of a gamble. But it's one I feel confident about. All business is a bit of a gamble, is it not?"

"Yes, I suppose you're right." Pops nodded slowly, deep in thought.

"But let's wait to tell the Kaufmanns until Christmas, eh?" Frank went on. "It's only a couple of days away, and it will be a surprise. One that I hope they will like."

"I don't know who will be more excited—the Kaufmanns or Mums." Melody grinned. "Though she'll miss you and Julius. She's grown rather fond of you two."

"Well, we'll be around for a while yet." He gave her a friendly wink. "And besides, your brother will soon be home, will he not? That will distract her, I'm sure. There's no limit to a mother's love for her son."

Didn't Melody know *that*. Despite the fact that Mums spoiled Bunny terribly, Freddy was by far her favorite. Indeed, Mums had been running around like a chicken with its head cut off these last few days making sure everything in the house was perfect.

Melody, too, was anxious for everything to be perfect—not for Freddy, but for the party they were hosting tonight! Helenka had prepared a buffet, and while it was not as elaborate as they normally might have enjoyed on Christmas Eve, Melody thought it quite nice. Mums had declared that turkey-and-dressing sandwiches and baked beans would be more than enough, but Melody had managed to persuade Helenka to produce some of her specialties, namely pickled herring, braised chicken livers, German potato salad, and a lovely pistachio aspic. Not to mention a pleasant variety of Christmas shortbread and Vienna crescents with walnuts and raisins. And she herself had produced cucumber sandwiches with dill and even little wieners on toothpicks, drenched in a rich, tangy sauce.

Finally, though, Helenka had shooed her out of the kitchen, and Melody had hurriedly gone up to her room to finish wrapping her gifts. There was the money, of course, for Pops, which she was positively bursting to give him right now, but which she had forced herself to hold back until Christmas Day, placing it in a small box, which she then wrapped with thin red paper. For Mums she had purchased a brooch from the Peddler. She felt guilty buying someone else's forfeited treasure, but it couldn't be helped; she couldn't afford anything at Van Dyke's, and there was nothing at the Merc that would suit. For Bunny, she had taken one of the silk scarves; for Frank and Julius, a cigar each; and for Freddy, a tortoiseshell comb. She had likewise gotten a small box of chocolates for Imogene (resisting the wicked urge to give her a box of Hershey bars), and for Mrs. Kaufmann, a pair of woolen socks. And for Harriet, Cal, and Mrs. Haufbrau, she had an envelope each with a ten-dollar bill inside. The party was supposed to be their gift, but she couldn't help spreading some of the wealth she had received from the other shop owners. She wanted them to have a good Christmas, too.

Melody was arranging the gifts nicely under the tree when the doorbell rang. She looked at the clock, noting that it was exactly seven, and guessed that it must be Mrs. Haufbrau.

"I'll get it!" she shouted and hurried to open the door. But it was *not* Mrs. Haufbrau, it was Harriet and her mother, whom Melody had urged her to bring, seeing as so much of the Merc's recent success had been down to Rosemary's cider production. Melody had also asked Harriet to bring Kate, who, between her baskets and the labels, had likewise been a part of the Merc's resurrection. But Kate was not on the doorstep with them. Instead, it was John Schneider who hovered there awkwardly.

"Oh!" Melody chirped in surprise.

"I . . . I hope you don't mind, Melody," Harriet hesitated. "But I thought that since Kate couldn't make it, it might be alright to bring John. Since he supplied a lot of the apples. You know, for the cider . . ."

"Of course I don't mind," Melody exclaimed, opening the door wide so that they could shuffle in. She didn't think anything, even the unexpected appearance of John Schneider, could dampen her current Christmas cheer. "I meant to ask you, John, but I just forgot," she fibbed. "Here, let me take your things."

Melody took the opportunity to surreptitiously study her guests before her as they removed their coats and hats. Something about the way John looked at Harriet as they did so, and the fact that his hand briefly grazed hers, made Melody wonder if . . . if it was *John Schneider*, not Cal, who was the source of Harriet's newfound joy . . . *Oh!*

Eagerly gathering their coats in her arms, she actually prayed that this was the case, all of her previous opinions regarding John suddenly evaporating. She had been worried about how she was going to break the news of Cal's engagement to Harriet, dreading her being so cruelly disappointed in love yet again, but now, she needn't worry! She wondered if Harriet already knew about Cal . . .

"My, this is a big house, isn't it?" Rosemary Mueller commented as she unwrapped her unusually long scarf. Finally free of it, she blatantly studied the high ceilings and the painted border as Melody tried to find a place on the already-stuffed coatrack for their things.

"This is for you," John said when she had finally succeeded in wedging their coats into place. He thrust a small package wrapped in cheesecloth. "It's from my mom. For Christmas, that is." He shifted awkwardly. "It's her best fruitcake."

"Oh, thank you! You didn't have to do that! But tell her thank you." Melody was not overly fond of fruitcake, but Pops would certainly enjoy it.

"And this is from me and Harriet." Mrs. Mueller handed her a small box. "That's butterscotch toffee. Make it every Christmas, don't I, Harriet?"

"Why, thank you! Goodness, this is so nice of you all. Why don't you go on in? I'll set these in the kitchen."

The three of them shuffled toward the front room, peering at everything as if they were in a museum, while Melody hurried to the kitchen and set the gifts on the counter. Helenka was busy rearranging Melody's tray of cucumber sandwiches. "Almost done," she said, sweat running down her brow.

"Helenka, please let me help you," Melody said, grabbing an already-opened bottle of wine. "Why don't you go in and enjoy yourself for a bit. I'll do this."

Helenka's head jerked up as if she had been slapped. "No! Of course, I will not."

"But it's supposed to be Christmas for everyone."

"It is *not* Christmas. I will celebrate on Christmas Day. Not today."

Melody sighed. "Okay, but you really are having a rest then."

"Yes, yes." She shooed Melody out. "Go on. I am busy."

"I'll fill the glasses for you. Should I?"

"Yes, if you must. But I was just going to do that."

Melody left her, the bottle in hand, and had barely crossed the front hall when the doorbell rang again. She paused in front of the door, wondering if it was Cal, and hoped that he, too, had not decided to bring someone. She wasn't sure she was up to meeting Cal's fiancée just now. The bell rang again.

"Melody! Get that, would you? You're standing right there!" Mums shouted from the front room.

Melody took a deep breath and opened the door. Thankfully, it was not Cal, but Mrs. Haufbrau, whose eyes unfortunately went immediately to the bottle of wine in Melody's hand. Melody's first thought was to hide it behind her back, but she managed to fight the urge and instead forced out a smile. "Hello, Mrs. Haufbrau," she tried to say as merrily as she could. "Won't you come in?"

"Marcella," the woman said, stepping through the door. "Brought you this." She handed her a small box wrapped with Christmas paper.

Melody set the bottle on the Chinese table and took the gift. "For me?" Her brow crinkled as she looked up at Mrs. Haufbrau, who gave a slight nod as she shut the door quietly behind her. "Thank you, Mrs . . . Marcella." Why were the staff giving her gifts? She was trying to treat *them* by giving this party. "You didn't have to get me a gift. Should I open it now?"

Mrs. Haufbrau, still in her coat, crossed her arms. "Go on then."

Melody carefully ripped open the paper to find a box of pretty notecards.

"I know you like writing to your friends back at school."

Melody was utterly stunned. It was a beautiful personal gift, which must have cost a bit of money. And how did Mrs. Haufbrau know she wrote to her friends? Or used to anyway. She had sent everyone a Christmas card, including Douglas, though she had not received one back, nor had she received a response to her letter in which she had confessed she could not marry him. *It's not you, dearest Douglas. You've ever been a chum to me—more than a chum. But I find I cannot in all honesty marry you. Despite all of the happy times we've had together, I am convinced that I do not love you in the way a wife should love her husband. I pray we can always be friends, and I sincerely hope that I might someday have the pleasure of attending your wedding to someone who deserves you more than I do.*

"Thank you, Mrs. . . . Marcella. It's a . . . it's a lovely gift."

Mrs. Haufbrau's face cracked a brief smile, and, the formalities now completed, began removing her coat. Ever since the fire, there had been a different sort of rapport between the two of them. No words were spoken regarding this shift, but Melody sensed a sort of softening, a relinquishment of their former animosity. Mrs. Haufbrau was still the stiff, angular curmudgeon she had always been, but now she sometimes attempted a smile and had even once or twice mentioned her sons.

"Is your father home?" she asked, patting her hair.

"Yes, come on." Melody picked up the bottle and led her into the crowded front room, where everyone was chattering loudly beneath a haze of pipe and cigarette smoke. Carols churned out from the Victrola to add to the festivities. Bunny had been assigned the task of changing the records, a job she had originally protested, saying that she should play carols at the piano instead, but, as Mums pointed out, they could hardly all traipse back to the music room. They would sing carols on Christmas Day instead this year.

Julius sat near the youngest Merriweather and was particularly engrossed in looking through the record collection, the stub of a cigarette between his fingers, as Frank was chatted away to him, his loud voice booming out even over the music. Rosemary Mueller had found a place on the sofa near Mrs. Kaufmann and Imogene, and Harriet stood shyly beside John, next to the massive Christmas tree. Pops, dressed in his best suit, was seated in his armchair near the fire, sans pillows and blankets for the evening, beaming with delight at his guests, though there were dark circles under his eyes. Mums stood by his side, her hand resting lightly on his shoulder as she bent forward to chat with Rosemary.

"Mrs. Haufbrau is here," Melody called out.

Mums looked up, surprised, and hurried over. "Hello, Marcella! Oh, it's been so long!" She put her hand on Mrs. Haufbrau's arm. "Come on, come see Lou," she said, cheerfully leading her over to Pops.

"Marcella!" he exclaimed. "Merry Christmas!"

Pleased that her father was so happy, Melody took the opportunity to approach Harriet and John. She took two upside-down glasses from a silver tray on the sideboard and handed them one each. Melody held up the wine bottle she was still carrying, and when Harriet cautiously raised her glass to meet it, Melody caught the glint of a ring on Harriet's left fourth finger. She lowered the bottle.

"Harriet, are you . . . ?"

Harriet blushed. "Yes. I . . . I hope you don't mind, Melody."

"Mind? Well . . . well, of course, I don't mind!" Though she had suspected that the two of them were now a couple, Melody was stunned that they were actually engaged!

They were gazing at each other so sweetly that Melody could not help but be happy for them. Truly happy. She kissed her former, never-again protégée on the cheek. "You'll make a beautiful bride," she said and meant it. "I'm sorry, Harriet, that I doubted you," she whispered. "I won't again, and that's a promise."

Harriet did not answer, but merely smiled, her charming dimples lighting up the space around them.

"And you, John," Melody said, turning to him now. "You have my sincerest congratulations."

"Congratulations?" Mums called out. "Who are you congratulating, Melody?"

"It's our Harriet," Rosemary said proudly, her eyes bright as she looked across the room at her daughter. "Her and John. Gonna be married."

"Oh, Harriet!" Mums exclaimed, hurrying over to look at the ring. "How wonderful! Congratulations! When is the wedding?"

Harriet looked shyly up at John. "Spring, we think," she said.

"Melody, pour them some wine!" Pops called. "We need a toast!"

"But, Lou, maybe we should wait for Freddy. He should be here anytime now," Mums urged, looking at the old grandfather clock.

"No! We need to toast the happy couple right when the announcement has been made," Pops insisted. "We'll have another when Fred gets here. Pour out that wine, Mel!" Pops urged. Obediently, Melody turned back toward the happy couple and poured some wine into their glasses.

"Everyone have a glass?" Pops called out.

Melody surveyed the room and startled a little when she observed Cal standing by himself in a corner, watching her. *When had he arrived?*

"Mrs. Haufbrau doesn't!" Frank observed, removing his pipe momentarily. "No, allow me!" he said over the beginnings of the older woman's protest and wove his way skillfully across the room. Within moments he returned with a champagne glass full of orange juice, which he presented to Mrs. Haufbrau, who took the glass gratefully and returned a genuine smile.

"Okay. All set, I think," Frank said, giving Pops a nod.

"Someone help me up," Pops requested, his hands gripping the armrests as he attempted to stand. Frank immediately tucked his arm through Pops's and then heaved him up. Pops swayed unsteadily, so Frank remained at his side.

Pops cleared his throat and then raised his glass. "Here's to Harriet and John," he croaked as loudly as he could manage. "May you have a long and happy life and be as happy as Leola and I have been!"

"Here, here!" everyone shouted.

"And!" Pops called. "And!" he said again, weakly gesturing with one hand for everyone to quiet down. When they finally did, he raised his glass again. "And here's to each of you. It's been a long, difficult year, not the one any one of us might have expected, but I'm truly grateful to all of you. Merry Christmas!" He took a drink.

"Merry Christmas!" everyone repeated and likewise took sips.

"But! But!" Pops called, swaying dangerously. Melody was about to step forward and help him, but he gripped Frank's arm instead and managed to steady himself. "The evening wouldn't be complete without a special toast to my brilliant daughter, Melody."

Melody looked up, surprised. She had been so intent on her father's attempt to stand for this long of a time that she was totally thrown by his address. Her eyes traveled quickly around the room, and she winced a little to see that all eyes were on her now.

"Melody," Pops went on, looking directly at her, his glass raised, "it might not have been fair to put such a big responsibility on your shoulders." His voice dropped lower now, as if he were speaking just to her. "But I just want you to know, whatever happens to the Merc, I'm proud of you. Proud of what you've accomplished. You're a Merriweather through and through."

"Here, here!" everyone shouted in unison. "Here's to Melody!"

Utterly stunned by her father's public praise, Melody wasn't sure what to say or do. Mechanically, she held up her glass to all and tried to take a sip of her wine, but she found she couldn't for the big lump in her throat. She looked at her father, slumped back in his chair now, and whispered, "Thanks, Pops." He winked at her.

Melody suddenly felt in very grave danger of bursting into tears, a feeling which intensified when the strains of "Auld Lang Syne" now came rattling out of the Victrola. Frank had migrated over to Julius, and their arms were around each other now in apparent brotherly love. Both of them were singing loudly.

Should old acquaintance be forgot, and never brought to mind . . .

Melody took another sip of her wine, her heart beating hard, as she looked out over the crowded room. She didn't think she could be an ounce happier than she was at this moment, even if she were at the Edgewater Beach Hotel dancing the night away with Douglas and Charlie and Cynthia at the annual Winter Ball. No, she was coming to realize, this was where she needed to be, *wanted* to be. She was a part of Merriweather now in a way she had never been as a child. She was part of something bigger, carrying on her father and grandfather's legacy, so that what had previously felt like a burden, now felt like a privilege. A small part of her was ashamed that she had ever perceived it otherwise. She wiped an errant tear as "Auld Lang Syne" ended. She was indeed proud of the fact that she had saved the Merc, at least for 1937. What happened next year was another story, and while the prospect of being a shopkeeper didn't necessarily fill her with girlish thrills, it contented her, made her feel needed and wanted in a more important way than her days of arranging silly romances had done.

"Are you going to ignore me all night?" Cal asked, suddenly appearing at her elbow.

Melody jumped. "For goodness sake! You startled me!"

Cal Fraiser was certainly not the person she wanted to talk to after her father's touching address. He was sure to spoil it. "And I'm not ignoring you." She glanced at him briefly, as if to prove her point, and then looked away.

They had spoken little since the fire. He had simply returned to the meat counter and carried on as if he had never been gone. He offered no explanation as to why he had left in the first place, and though she was dying to ask about his engagement to Jessie Lange, Melody had never seemed to find the right moment.

Whenever images of the fire inopportunely flooded her mind, she recalled him putting his arms around her and telling her in an oddly tender voice that everything was going to be okay. But she always pushed this memory from her mind just as quickly. For all she knew, it might not have been real anyway. After all, she had probably been in shock and more than likely imagined it.

"I suppose I should congratulate you, too," she said, finally turning to him fully.

"About being right about John and Harriet?" He looked at her over the rim of his glass, a surprisingly devious smile on his lips.

Melody raised an eyebrow. "Yes, you were right about them, and I was wrong." She took a drink. A rather long drink. It was now or never. "But I was actually congratulating you on your engagement to Jessie Lange."

"Jessie Lange?" He looked genuinely confused. "What are you talking about?"

"Your engagement to Jessie?" Melody kept her voice cool. "Are you, or are you not getting married?"

"Where did you hear that?"

"From Mrs. Haufbrau." Melody folded her arms in triumph at being able to cite such a reliable source, though the victory was less sweet given the fact that he had not actually denied the engagement.

"Well, she's mistaken," he said slowly. "Jessie Lange was to be my brother's bride."

"Your brother?"

"Yes, my *brother,* Colyn. People often confuse us. He's ten months younger, but people always think we're twins—Cal and Col."

"Oh." Melody's mind was racing. "What do you mean she *was* to be his bride?" Had the poor girl died?

Cal looked at the ground. "She broke it off. It's a long story. I don't really want to talk about it."

"Oh." Melody desperately wanted to know more, but she could think of nothing to say that wouldn't potentially irritate him. Had Jessie found someone else? Or was it because Colyn had been cruel? If this were true, did it run in the family? Somehow this wouldn't surprise her, she thought grimly.

"Did you really think I would engage myself to be married and not tell you?" Cal asked now and then ran a hand through his hair. "Do you think so little of our friendship?"

His eyes held a surprising amount of hurt. She *did* in fact think he would keep things from her; didn't he already? Nor did she think they were friends exactly . . .

"That's why I had to go home. I . . . I always liked Jessie. Not in that way," he added hurriedly. "But she's turned to me these last weeks to comfort her. It's true that I've been out with her a bit," Cal confessed. "She came with me for a while to the bonfire, but that was only to get her mind off of things. I love my brother, but she's well rid of him. He's not right for her."

Melody took another drink. This didn't sound like a man who didn't have feelings for Jessie Lange, no matter what he might think. An awkward silence ensued. Desperately, Melody tried to think of something to say or a way to escape him. "Well, I should check on the guests," she finally muttered. "See if they need a top-up." She gave him a false smile and turned to leave.

"Hey, Melody."

Reluctantly, she turned back.

"I just wanted to tell you that–" He shifted uncomfortably. "That I was wrong, too."

Melody's brow furrowed. "About?"

"About you." His eyes held hers now, not in his usual accusatory or critical way, but tenderly, like just after the fire, and her breath unexpectedly caught in her throat. "I misspoke the other day. You're not a snob. I . . . I misjudged you." His voice was low. "What you've done for the Merc and your dad and, well, everyone, is really admirable. You were up against a lot, and not many would have risen to the occasion. I'm sorry I judged you otherwise."

Melody could only stare at him, completely caught off guard.

He seemed off as well and looked distractedly around the room before turning his attention back to her. He took a drink of his wine. "Now that your dad's back, what are you going to do? Go back to school?" He took a longer drink now, nearly draining his glass. "I heard you had someone in Chicago that you probably want to get back to."

Melody blinked rapidly. If she wasn't mistaken . . .

She cleared her throat. "I did. But that's all over now." She flashed him a small smile. "Turns out I kind of like it here."

His face contorted slightly. "Melody, I—"

Unfortunately, whatever Cal was or wasn't going to say next was interrupted by the ringing of the doorbell.

"Oh!" Mums called out cheerily, "That must be Freddy!"

"I'll get it," Melody said hoarsely, still staring at Cal, her heart racing for some ridiculous reason.

"Well, why would he ring the bell?" Pops asked.

"You know Freddy. Always wants to make an entrance," Bunny chirped from her stool by the Victrola.

Melody forced herself to turn from Cal and walk mechanically toward the door, trying to calm her now frantic thoughts. Did Cal actually have feelings for her? *And did she return them?* It seemed outrageous!

Suddenly, she felt especially desirous to see her older brother just now. Though they didn't always get along, it would be a relief to see his big dopey face and to joke with him. Eagerly, almost giddily, she threw open the door, ready to throw her arms around him, but she stopped mid-step, as it was indeed not Freddy standing on the doorstep.

It was Douglas Novak.

CHAPTER ONE

"But you must remember *something*," Kate called from where she was propped up on a sofa in the front room of the Kerwyn farmhouse.

"Honestly, Kate, I don't," replied a frazzled Mrs. Kerwyn, who was busy churning wet shirts through the kitchen laundry press. "Louisa, go out and bring in some more wood. If we don't get that stove hotter, these'll never dry." She pulled her gaze from the tub of dirty suds and inspected the clothes hanging from temporary, crisscrossing lines.

Louisa dropped the socks she was folding and let out a disgruntled harrumph. "Why can't Kate? It's not as if it's taxing to walk outside and grab a couple of logs."

"In this weather? She'd catch her death again. Go on."

Despite the fact that her sister was all of twenty, Louisa stuck her tongue out at Kate before moving toward the back door and pulling on a pair of black rubber farm boots. She didn't bother to buckle them.

"Mom, I can help," Kate insisted and set aside the afghan that Mrs. Kerwyn herself had tucked tightly around her legs. Kate had no real desire to ease the burden of her older, lazy sister, but she was sick to death of lying around.

She stood up, and in truth felt a little weak. Leaning one hand on the arm of the sofa to steady herself, she glanced quickly at her mother, hoping she hadn't noticed.

"Oh no you don't!" Mrs. Kerwyn exclaimed over her shoulder. "You lie back down. You know what Doc Hodges said."

"I know, Mom, but I've been lying in bed for nearly two months. If I don't walk around a little, I'm going to forget how." She concentrated on not wobbling as she made her way to the kitchen.

"Pneumonia is tricky, Kate." Mrs. Kerwyn kept her weak gray eyes on the rollers, careful not to get her fingers caught. "Takes a long time." Mrs. Kerwyn might have been considered pretty at one time, but her frizzled strawberry blonde hair had thinned, as had her frail body, and her eyes now had permanent dark circles under them.

Kate pulled out a chair and eased herself down. "Well, I'll just sit here, then. How about that?" She picked up the socks Louisa had dropped, folded them, then rummaged through the rest of the clothes on the table to look for more. She knew she couldn't push her mother too hard, as Caroline Kerwyn was overly protective when it came to sickness, having had two children die from the flu during the epidemic eight years ago.

It had been hard on all of them to lose Eula and Fern, but it had been hardest, of course, on poor Mrs. Kerwyn, who, in Kate's opinion anyway, had never been quite the same after. That same year, May had also left to marry her sweetheart, Will Dresden, which had further added to the family's sense of loss.

"Well, do you?" Kate asked, pulling a few small towels out of the pile.

Mrs. Kerwyn eased a wet shirt out of the rollers and shook it. "Do I what?"

"Don't you remember anything else from when you found me? What was I wearing?" Kate asked, hoping the answer might provide a clue as to her origins.

"Lord, Kate. How should I know?" Mrs. Kerwyn reached into the bag of clothespins and began pinning the wet shirt to the line. "That was fifteen years ago."

"You're not talking about all this again, are you?" Louisa banged through the back door and dropped an armload of logs onto the empty wrought-iron rack. She then pounded the snow from her boots on the braided rug, a few strands of her long blonde hair coming loose from the bun she normally styled.

Kate gritted her teeth. "Yes, we *are*, Louisa. No one asked you to be a part of it, so you can mind your own business."

"Why does it matter so much to you?" Louisa shrugged out of her coat and hung it on the peg by the back door.

It was a good question. Why *did* it matter? She supposed she just wanted to know, definitively, to whom she had once belonged. She had grown up thinking that she was a Sauk Indian, but, according to nearly every book on the subject in the Merriweather Library, the native Americans were very family-oriented, loyal, and honorable, despite their reputation for being blood-thirsty, vicious savages. It seemed impossible that they had simply abandoned her. Had they *meant* to leave her behind like some sort of cursed creature? Or had she wandered away and gotten lost? But if that were the case, why had they not searched for her? And how had she come to be wandering by the Wareham farm?

As a child . . .

Scan the QR code or
click the link to continue reading!

https://bit.ly/4ddCpGe

AUTHOR'S NOTE

It might seem to the careful Midwest reader that the town of Merriweather bears an uncommon resemblance to Mineral Point, Wisconsin. This is because it does. The fictional Merriweather is indeed a thinly veiled version of Mineral Point.

Had I known that I was going to someday spin Melody off into her own series, I might have titled her hometown as Mineral Point from the very beginning, but, alas, I did *not* know, and thus we are stuck with it. I could have gone back and changed the books in the Henrietta and Inspector Howard series, in which Melody Merriweather first makes her appearance, but I ultimately decided against this, as not only would this be time-consuming and laborious, but there is likewise something charming about the town being named after the Merriweather family.

Now that the cat is out of the bag, so to speak, I am free to point out the various similarities between the real and the fictious town as well as other inspirations in writing *Matched in Merriweather.*

To begin, Mineral Point is part of what is called the "driftless" area of the Midwest, designated as such because the last Ice Age glacier missed this region, meaning it did not flatten the area as it passed through. The result, besides the fact that the landscape—which includes parts of Wisconsin, Minnesota, Iowa, and the extreme northwestern corner of Illinois—remained hilly, was that rich deposits of lead and zinc remained behind as well.

The earliest "miners" were Native Americans who collected bits of lead near the surface to be used for jewelry or other decorative objects. Eventually, they began trading the lead with French fur traders in the 1600s. Later, in the 1820s, miners from Illinois, Kentucky, and Missouri arrived and began mining in earnest, the lead unearthed being primarily used to make lead shot. These miners dug shallow shafts, or "badger holes," into the hillsides in order to discover deeper veins. The men actually lived in the holes as well, putting logs, brush, or sod over them to create crude shelters. Thus, these early miners became known as "badgers," and Wisconsin, when it later became a state, was nicknamed the "Badger State."

An interesting side note is that the hill upon which Kate lives in her abandoned badger hole is in actuality called Merry Christmas Hill due to the fact that zinc was discovered there one year at Christmastime. "Merry Christmas Hill" seemed too awkward to continually write, so I changed it to "Christmas Tree Hill."

Following the "badgers," the next influx of miners came from Cornwall in the 1830s, bringing with them their own unique customs, including the building of thick limestone cottages from stone they quarried from the area around Mineral Point. In all, they built over thirty cottages, most of them located along Shakerag Street, which in the novel is called Magnolia Street. Harriet and her mother dwell in one of these. I took the liberty of calling this area of town "New Grimsby," which is completely fictious.

With the discovery of zinc, Mineral Point grew quickly. By 1870, the population had reached 3,275, and the town had a variety of churches, parks, shops, and even an opera house, as mentioned in the novel. I changed the original shop names and many of the streets, though I did elect to keep Ridge Street, which is where, all of the town's elite, including the fictional Merriweathers, built their beautiful homes and mansions.

Besides providing a setting for the novel, Mineral Point also unwittingly provided two characters—Frank Churchill and Julius Fairfax. Their real-life counterpoints were Robert Neal and Edgar Hellum—Bob and Edgar, as they were locally known—two men who were responsible for not only the preservation and restoration of several Cornish cottages, but the reinvention of Mineral Point as a center for the arts when the town fell into decay after the last mine closed in 1928.

Beginning in the 1930s all the way through the 1960s, Bob and Edgar worked to restore various Cornish cottages, including Pendarvis, which eventually became a Wisconsin Historical Site. They also founded a mail-order preserves business and started a nationally recognized restaurant, among many other things. They had a deep appreciation of the arts and antiques, and through their efforts, Mineral Point became a mecca for artists and craftsmen.

Though it was not a secret that Bob and Edgar were a gay couple, neither was it discussed or flaunted. The townsfolk seemed to turn a blind eye to that which was not socially accepted at the time in rural America, proving how beloved Bob and Edgar were to the people (and the economy) of Mineral Point.

But Frank and Julius are more than just representations of Bob and Edgar. They are also representations of Frank Churchill and Jane Fairfax from Jane Austen's *Emma*, of which *Matched in Merriweather* is a retelling. Frank and Jane enter the Austen story at the midway point, creating romantic and dramatic tension, especially after it is discovered that they have been secretly engaged to each other all along. Similarly, Frank and Julius pose as half-brothers, though in actuality they are lovers, just as Bob and Edgar were.

I honestly don't know which came into my mind first—the concept of Frank and Julius as Frank and Jane or as Bob and Edgar. Either way, these two characters perfectly tie the two worlds together in a way not even I, the author, originally envisioned.

And since we have now mentioned *Emma*, I am free to further elaborate on the retelling aspect of the novel. Jane Austen enthusiasts will surely recognize more of her beloved characters:

Melody Merriweather: Emma Woodhouse

Harriet Mueller: Harriet Smith

Cal Fraiser: Mr. Knightley (or is he Mr. Darcy?)

John Schneider: Robert Martin

Esmerelda and Imogene Kaufmann: The Misses Bates

Wesley Elton: Mr. Elton

Kate Kerwyn: Fanny Price

Edmund Bertram: Edmund Bertram

I must reiterate, however, before any of you rush to begin a closer study of Jane Austen or the history of Mineral Point, that this *is* a work of fiction and is meant to be read in that spirit. All deviations from the truth or Miss Austen's originals should therefore be accepted as just that—imagined deviations!

Having stated the disclaimer, I can now add that it was great fun to allow Melody to star in her very own series. Melody and her costars will continue to recreate four more of Jane Austen's works, the next in the series being *Mansfield Park*, which will feature Kate Kerwyn as Fanny Price.

I hope you have enjoyed reading this little tale as much as I've enjoyed writing it!

SOURCES

A Field Guide to Mineral Point by Nancy Pfotenhauer, Little Creek Press, 2012

Mineral Point, Wisconsin by Herbert Beall and Barbara Apelian Beall, Arcadia Publishing, 2000

Mineral Point, a History by George Fiedler, The State Historical Society of Wisconsin, 1973

On the Shake Rag: Mineral Point's Pendarvis House, 1935–1970, the State Historical Society of Wisconsin and the Memorial Pendarvis Trust, 1990

THE HENRIETTA AND INSPECTOR HOWARD SERIES

If you're curious about Melody's origin, you might try The Henrietta and Inspector Howard series, which is set in Chicago and abroad in the 1930s, and where you, gentle reader, `will be first introduced to Melody, though she does not appear (full disclosure) until the fourth book, *A Veil Removed*. But I can promise that it is a very enjoyable read getting to that point.

"Henrietta and Inspector Howard make a charming odd couple, mixing mystery and romance in a fizzy 1930s cocktail."

–Hallie Ephron, *New York Times* bestselling author

"Brimming with a dark plot on every page, this unpredictable literary thrill ride will transport you to the heart of 1930s Chicago and the love story of a lifetime."

–PopSugar

"Henrietta and Clive are a sexy, endearing, and downright fun pair of sleuths. Readers will not see the final twist coming."

–*Library Journal* (starred review)

Start the series for free!!

Download A GIRL LIKE YOU now!

https://qrco.de/bfUXQA

BUY DIRECT from me and SAVE!

By purchasing print books, ebooks, and audiobooks directly from me, I receive 100% of the profits from the sale of my books rather than having to splint a large majority of my royalties with the big box platforms. This helps me to keep writing more books, and **I'm passing on the savings to YOU!** Thank you!

FIND ALL MY BOOKS HERE:

https://qrco.de/bfyIVm

Sign up for my newsletter for alerts about new releases, free stuff, events, and fabulous giveaways! Be the first to know!

https://michellecoxauthor.com/newsletter-signup/

ACKNOWLEDGEMENTS

This is hands down the hardest page of the book to write, as there are so many people to acknowledge that I'm always afraid I'm going to forget someone. But, I'll try my best!

The strength of any book, I've come to realize, is in the editing, and I am so very grateful to have found Andrea Robinson, whom I grow to trust and respect more and more with each book produced between us. I have often suggested she share the byline, but she has thus far politely refused. Thank you, Andrea, for shaping this book into the very best version of itself. Any errors that remain are mine alone.

I'd also like to again thank the indie publishing community for helping me launch not only another book, but a whole new series, which is really rather daunting. I'd especially like to thank fellow author Tanya E. Williams for providing hours of help on the advertising and technical side of things. Your advice has been invaluable, Tanya!

Also in need of thanks are all of the people who helped produce the actual product: Kari Brownlie for her beautiful cover design and graphics, Ashley Santoro for layout, and Kaitlin Schmidt for proofing. Also, Lisa Dailey of Sidekick Press for website management and Yolanda Facio for newsletter formatting. And another round of thanks to my beta crew—Marcy, Amy, and Otto—for speed-reading an early version. Thank you for your unique insights and for cheering me on.

Lastly, of course, but certainly not least, I'd like to thank my family for putting up with my messy attempt at a career and for encouraging me to keep going. Writing is not for the faint of heart, and I don't think

I could do it without you guys at my side to pry me out of the 1930s and back into the real world. Thanks especially to you, Phil, for your unceasing support, and for believing in me even when the tax returns prove there is absolutely no reason to. That's called faith, though some also call it love. You remain my sweetest song.

Michelle Cox is the author of the Henrietta and Inspector Howard series, a mystery/romance saga set in 1930s Chicago often described as "Downton Abbey meets Miss Fisher's Murder Mysteries." To date, the series has won over sixty international awards and has received positive reviews from *Library Journal* (starred), *Booklist* (starred), *Publishers Weekly*, *Kirkus*, and various media outlets, such as *PopSugar*, *BuzzFeed*, *Redbook*, *Elle*, *Brit+Co*, *Bustle*, *Culturalist*, *Working Mother*, and many others.

Cox also pens the wildly popular "Novel Notes of Local Lore," a weekly blog chronicling the lives of Chicago's forgotten residents. She lives in the northern suburbs of Chicago with her husband and three children and is hard at work on her next novel.